FEB   2020

D1521664

MONTY
A St. Claire Novel

TINA MARTIN

CMPL
WITHDRAWN

CLINTON-MACOMB PUBLIC LIBRARY

Copyright © 2019 Tina Martin

MONTY

ISBN: 9781075158797

All rights reserved. This book may not be reproduced or distributed in any format including photography, recording information storage and retrieval systems without the prior written permission of the author. With the exception of small blurbs for book reviews, no part of this book may be uploaded without written permission from the author.

This book is a work of fiction. Any similarities to real people, names, places, things or events are a product of the author's imagination and strictly coincidental and are used fictitiously.

Visit **Tina Martin Publications** at:
www.tinamartin.net

MONTY
A St. Claire Novel

Chapter One

Cherish

I've never been the type of woman to completely lose my mind over a man but Montgomery St. Claire has always had that effect on me. I try to hide it but it's always there. He makes my head go blank. Makes me lose words, thoughts and involuntary bodily functions such as breathing and blinking. It's been that way since I first started working at The Hawthorne Estates two years ago and it's that way now. I think it's the beard – the way it frames his lips and adds a contrast to his caramel skin – the color of Milk Maid candy made by Brach's. Then again, it's not only the beard. It's the whole tower-of-a-man himself. He's just...

Just...

Strikingly stunning. The kind of *fine* that slaps you in the face like a sweltering summer heat wave. A man so fine it does crazy things to your eyes if you stare too long. Not that he'd ever catch me staring.

He doesn't know I exist. I'm just his measly personal assistant – well let's just say *assistant* – because there's nothing *personal* about it. He doesn't make meaningless small-talk with me. Doesn't speak, ask me how my day is

1

going or crack any jokes. I'm willing to bet every dollar I have he couldn't tell you the color of my eyes. He never looks at me. Doesn't talk to me. When he wants my attention (and that would be *only* because he needs something), he says, *excuse me.*

I guess that's my name.

Excuse-Me Stevens instead of Cherish.

I know why he does it. Why he avoids me. Men with money do it all the time. It's his way of refusing a connection with me and keeping to his no-nonsense business model of being strictly business – professional at all times.

I can't say I blame him. Montgomery is a very wealthy man. He's not just rich. He's *rich*, rich – worth $50 million dollars – but his company, Hawthorne Innovations, Incorporated is worth $5 billion. He comes from a family of inventors. Before his death, his father, Caspian Hawthorne, patented ten, profitable inventions. Montgomery must have his father's business savvy because to date, he has five inventions under his belt and is working on a sixth that he and his team are keeping top secret.

Honestly, that's what attracts me to him the most – his brilliance. Most women look at Montgomery and see the green-eyed, biracial man with S-curls (AKA *good hair*) who lives in a mansion and drives expensive cars, including a Porsche Panamera Turbo and a Mercedes AMG SL65.

What do I see when I look at him?

I see his drive. His work ethic. I see his brain working even when he's just walking around the house or standing at the window in one of his fancy suits, admiring all the acres of land he owns. But, I'm not blind. I see how fine he is, too! The man is so fine it wreaks havoc on my entire nervous system. It's like torture to be near him. That's how I feel on a daily basis.

Tortured.

Like that military-style *torture* that happens to POWs.

Stuff that plays with your mind and changes you in ways you can't explain.

Sometimes, I'm so caught up in the magnificence of him, I forget entire trains of thought. One minute I'm walking around the house with a dust rag in my hand, the next, I have no clue what I'm supposed to be dusting. He does that to me.

Even still, I have to be honest about something – most days I absolutely despise him. Why? Because he's a jerk. There. I said it. He's a world-class, Grade-A, top-shelf jerk! He's a guy who demands respect but chooses not to give it. The kind of boss who doesn't give a crap about his employees as long as, at the end of the day, the company is still posting million-dollar profits. With him, it's all about the *money*. The *company*. The *status*. Nothing or no one matters.

These are my thoughts as I'm sitting in my car, gathering my braids into a ponytail at three-thirty in the morning before driving to the estate. I get up super early since I need to be at work by four since Montgomery works from 5:00 a.m. to 5:00 p.m. Long hours for him means long hours for me.

I'm especially dreading work today because he's working from his home office this week. Yesterday he was yelling and tossing papers, hot under the collar about some patent that was filed incorrectly. Had the lawyers ready to quit. No one wants to be near Montgomery when he's angry. He's like a grenade. Once you pull the pin, he's guaranteed to go off. But he pays me fifty-thousand dollars a year to *assist* him so I'm hoping as long as I do my job and steer clear of him, I won't get blown up.

My official work hours are 4:00 a.m. to 6:00 p.m. I devote fourteen hours of my day to everything Montgomery St. Claire. As his assistant, I do practically everything for him and have access to his residence and every room in his wing of the house – his office, the libraries, the bedrooms, the kitchen, the gym, the indoor pool room and the conference room where he has a lot of his company meetings. Nothing is off limits to me because he – well his *team* – never know where I'll be needed.

As I'm driving north on Interstate 85, heading to Concord where he lives – a city right outside of Charlotte known for its forever-crowded Concord Mills Mall and the Charlotte Motor Speedway – all I'm thinking about is what suit Montgomery will want to wear today. I pick out his clothes every morning. And then there's the matter of food. I always stress myself over his menu, wondering if I made the correct choices in what I *think* he may want to eat for breakfast, lunch and dinner. I'm not his cook, but I curate the menus for her and I *think* I have it down to a science, but you never know when you work for a *grenade*. Grenades are sensitive. Sometimes they blast off for no reason.

In the mornings, he usually likes something healthy to eat like a protein shake with a side of mixed fruit, granola and yogurt. Or sometimes he likes peanut butter and banana toasts. He's not a bacon and eggs kind of guy, but he guzzles coffee like water. Drinks it black, too, like the bitter, awful taste of black coffee is second nature to him. As malicious as he is, he probably can't taste the bitterness. Bitter goes well with evil.

For his lunch menu, I chose a club sandwich on wheat with a side of pickles. He loves pickles with his sandwiches, but not the flimsy ones you can buy out of a jar at the grocery store. He likes the ones that have a crunch to them like those fancy deli pickles. And then there's the matter of dinner…

When he's had a hard day, which is *every* day, he likes a heavier, more filling meal, especially since he'll quickly burn off the calories with a gym workout or laps in the indoor pool. Today, it's mozzarella chicken breasts, rolls and a salad.

I pull up at Hawthorne Estates, park my Mazda Protégé in the designated parking for guests and yawn. I take more breaths before I get out of the car. I'm tired, but duty calls.

I let myself inside the mansion and deactivate the alarm while standing in the foyer beneath an elegant, crystal chandelier that, if it were to ever fall, it would totally kill somebody just by its weight alone. There are three staircases in the foyer. The one to the left leads to Montgomery's residence. The one in the middle leads to his brother's quarters and his mother, Sylvia Hawthorne, lives up the right set of stairs. They're together, but separate – three huge separate living quarters tied up in one enormous mansion. The bottom level has a conference room for the family business, a kitchen, a private indoor pool that's only accessible through Montgomery's residence, a dining room, laundry room and a living room, but no one is usually down there, and why would they be when they have all those things in their private residences? It's one, great-big, twisted, *strange* family setup.

I huff. I'm too tired to puff. I really don't feel like working today. I have to give myself a pep talk. "A'ight, pull it together, Cherish. You know the routine. Do your job and get out of the way."

I secure my purse in the coat closet and proceed up the west wing set of stairs to Montgomery's residence. I unlock the door, let myself in and head straight for the master bedroom. He doesn't like the maids in his bedroom so I'm in charge of organizing it as well. At this time of the morning, he's in the shower. I can hear the shower jets spraying while I'm working. I clear the empty water bottle from the nightstand. I put away his slippers, the Rolex and platinum cufflinks he wore the day before.

I go to the linen closet to get new sheets and pillowcases and start making the bed. He sleeps on the right side. The left side is always undisturbed. When I'm done with the bed, I find myself distracted. I'm usually super-focused with a get-in-get-out mentality but this morning, I'm lollygagging. I take a minute to look around his bedroom. It's massive – about the same square-feet as my two-bedroom house. Yeah, that's right. His bedroom is larger than the floor-plan of my house. And it's laid out – there's a wall of floor-to-ceiling windows draped in cream-colored, sheer curtains. He never closes the blinds in his bedroom. Through them, I can see the darkness that hangs before dawn.

A massive TV is mounted on the wall above his dresser – one that gets no play. The batteries in the remote are surely dead by now. His room is always neat and clean. Everything is organized and in its proper place. He's not a messy person and doesn't carelessly toss things to the side even though he knows he has workers to clean up after him. I find it truly amazing. I never knew men were so orderly and tidy. It's probably just *him*. I get a completely opposite vibe from his brother, Major. I've been to Major's residence a few times. He's definitely more laid back.

I snap out of my trance to busy myself with the next task on my daily chore list – picking out his clothes for the day. I open the double doors to his walk-in closet, flick on the lights and look around at the wide array of suits arranged by color. So are his shoes and neckties. He prefers dark colors over lighter ones, although he still orders light-colored suits for a reason that's beyond me. Seems like such a waste, but when you're a billionaire, what does that matter?

Fanning through the suits, I go with a navy blue Kiton suit and a pair of black Ferragamo leather shoes. I lay the suit out on a bench that's about the size of a twin bed. It sits in the center of his closet. Studying the suit, I decide I don't like the way it looks with the shoes, so I hang it back up and try again. I'm fanning through the black suits now – the Armani's, Tom Ford's and Brioni's. He has all types of high end, name brand clothing. Gucci *this*, Valentino *that*. I end up going with a black Givenchy suit. That seems to be his favorite brand of late and this suit is everything. It's so nice, I don't even want to touch it. I look at it and imagine how it would look on his lengthy body. I begin to think about which necktie would go good with it and which pair of cufflinks he should wear.

Then there's the matter of socks, the watch, and—

"What are you doing in my closet?"

Crap! I've been caught.

The sound of his husky, deep voice electrocutes me. That's the only way I can explain the awkward jerking motion my body makes at the deepness of his words. He's never found me in his closet before, but he's here now and I'm afraid to turn around.

What is he doing here so early? Or am I late? Am I late??

Crap! What now, Cherish?

He doesn't know I lay out his clothes for him hence his question *what are you doing in my closet?* Leave it up to him, he'd think I was trying to steal something and fire me on the spot.

I turn around to face the heat – to see if he's a grenade *with* or *without* a pin this morning – and I nearly faint.

Oh…my…goodness…freakin'…gracious! He's naked. Tall and naked.

Well, not *completely* naked, but partially. He just got out of the shower (how did I not hear the shower go off?!) and now he's standing here with his full, hairy, beefy chest on display. His nipples are looking at me, peeping out from beneath all that silky, black hair.

Mercy…

My eyes feast on muscles, nips, abs and hair. Lots of hair. Hair for days. More hair than I would've imagined on a well-kempt man like Montgomery, but something about it turns me on. Gives him that *real* man vibe. And then there were those carved-to-perfection arms and green eyes of his that are locked on me like the laser of a military-grade sniper rifle. I suddenly have a fever. I'm as good as dead.

Like a wimp or a person who's been busted, I halfway glance up at him. My body doesn't budge. Only my eyes are brave enough to move at this point.

He frowns.

I still don't move. I look, look away then look again.

His frown deepens.

His lower half is wrapped in one of the white Egyptian cotton towels I stocked his bathroom with yesterday before my shift was over. He only uses white towels. Only the Egyptian ones.

His curly, black hair is still wet – the hair on his head and chest. Even the thin strip of hair that travels down the center of his abs to the part of him that's hidden behind the towel is wet. I'm sure he can hear my heart pounding against my rib cage. It only beats more ferociously when he takes steps toward me. My body does that awkward jerk again, a motion I suddenly have no control over.

No, no, no. Stop. Don't come any closer. Stop. Stop!

He stops as if he's read my mind. Well, he probably thinks I've *lost* my mind. Yeah, that's it. He thinks I'm nuts.

"Excuse me," I hear him say.

He's standing on the opposite side of the twin bed – I mean – bench.

"Excuse me," he says again, louder this time. "Cherish."

I frown when I hear my name come forth from his mouth. It's too early for this. My heart can't take this kind of stress. What in the world is going on here? Did he just call my name or am I hearing things? He knows my *name*? Montgomery St. Claire knows my name?

I look up at him, try to swallow but my throat is dry like I just ate a pack of graham crackers. I instantly feel like I'm in trouble. Like the feeling of knowing you're speeding and you glance in the rearview and see a State Trooper on your bumper except *this* trooper is half naked, fine as all get-out and is staring at me like I'm a foreign object that has infiltrated his *precious* world.

I have.

I'm in his closet.

When I finally manage to swallow my anxiety and accept my fate, I look at him since he's still a safe distance away from me and say, "You—you know my name?"

His forehead creases. "Why does that surprise you?"

He's still frowning. Nipples still looking at me. Chest hair still beading with water. His eyes are lulling me into submission like those spinning red and white striped hypnosis wheels in cartoons.

Stop looking into his eyes if you know you can't handle it, girl. Just stop...

I'm not breathing. I'm going to die here today. I'm sure of it. A heart attack is coming in three...two...

"Cherish!"

"Ye—yes, Sir?"

He smirks. Shakes his head. He must know I'm distressed and somehow he finds humor in that. I've never seen the man smile but knowing I'm about to come to my end gives him a satisfying grin. Go figure...

"What are you doing in my closet?"

Just tell him what you're doing and get the freak out of here. Tell him. You can do it. He's just a man. No, he's not just a man. He's Montgomery-Freakin'-St. Claire. He's THE man. He's the boss. The HNIC. He has the authority to fire you, so tell him why you're here. Go on. Tell him!

"Okaaay. Gosh!" I say.

"What?" he asks, looking puzzled.

"Oh, nevermind." If he didn't think I was crazy before, I'm sure he does now.

"I'm going to ask you for the last time—what are you doing in my closet?"

I want to tell him, but my mouth isn't cooperating. It opens, but words don't come out. The pit of my stomach has bottomed out and hit the floor. Still, I make an attempt to answer him. I say, "Um—I—suit—water, hair—I mean shoes…"

"What?" His forehead creases. He crosses his arms. Muscles are bulging from every which way and the towel covering his male parts moves. And it wasn't his hand that made it move. He's standing still. The towel jerks forward again.

Oh my…

My fever increases. I feel like I'm going to spontaneously combust and burn down his whole house – well at least the west wing and all his luxury suits with it. I make another attempt at speech and say, "I—"

His dark brows raise. "You, what?"

"I was—um—I was picking out your suit for the day, Sir."

"Picking out my suit?" he says, he's eyes on me something fierce.

"Yes, Sir."

"I don't understand."

"I do this every morning," I explain. "I—I just don't— I don't usually get caught."

"*You* lay out my suits every morning?" he asks.

"Yes, and your necktie, shoes, socks and cufflinks, Sir," I respond, wondering why he added the extra emphasis on *you* like I'm incapable of doing this for him when I've been doing it for two years, ever since Sylvia Hawthorne hired me and told me this was one of my many duties that would make her son's life more *comfortable*.

"I thought Paige was in charge of this?"

Well, you thought wrong, wit'cho…wit'cho…good-looking self. Wait? What? How's that a diss, Cherish?

Paige – she's his mother's assistant – the privileged white girl who walks around here like she owns the place and calls herself *wifey* although she's not Montgomery's wife. Girlfriend, maybe – and I use that term loosely – but definitely not wife. Montgomery doesn't wear a ring and Paige never spends the night. Besides, he's too busy making money to be concerned with a wife and even if he had one, I doubt she'd be a little booty white girl who wears about ten layers of foundation on her face that's slathered on so thick, you could cut into it like a slice of pie and not draw blood.

"No, Sir. This duty falls under my umbrella."

"Well, go on. Do your job," he tells me. His arms are still crossed as he stares. Muscles bulging.

I take the Givenchy suit and lay it on the bench. Then I find the perfect tie, cufflinks, socks and shoes to match.

"There you are. I'll get out of your way now," I say, trying to make my great escape.

"Yeah, you do that," he taunts. "Oh, and by the way, if you're telling the truth and this *is* one of your duties—"

"It *is* one of my—"

"Do not interrupt me when I'm speaking," he says curtly. Then he starts again and says, "If you're telling the truth and this *is* one of your duties, I would suggest you have it done before I'm out of the shower. That way, we don't have to have this extremely awkward exchange. I don't have to see you. You don't have to see me. Understood?"

"Yes, Sir. It won't happen again. Sorry to have interrupted your morning."

I plaster a fake smile on my face and haul it out of there feeling small and stupid. That's what Montgomery does to people – make them feel insignificant. I've seen him do it to his mother, his brother and the rest of the staff. We're all insignificant compared to a man of his great wealth. That still doesn't give him the right to disrespect anyone. We're all here to serve him. To help him be comfortable so he can continue to amass his wealth. The least he could do was throw out a 'thank you' every now and then.

I hold on to the railing as I descend the spiral staircase. My heart is still racing. Palms, sweaty. Feet, unsteady. When I make it to the kitchen, I drink water and double check the breakfast menu I supplied to Naomi. I don't need any more run-ins with Montgomery today.

Chapter Two

Monty

After breakfast, I head straight to the conference room in the common area. I have a meeting with my mother and brother to discuss private business matters.

Mother walks in and I say, "Good morning, Mrs. Hawthorne."

She scoffs – hates it when I call her that, but I'm trying to keep things professional. If my father didn't teach me anything else before he died, he taught me how to be a businessman. How to remain professional at all times in the way I dress and carry myself. I know how to rock a poker face. No one ever knows what I'm feeling. I've mastered the art of hiding emotions on both ends of the spectrum – from anger and fear to happiness and sadness. No one can read me. I take great pride in that. Vulnerability is weakness. Keeping emotions in check is power.

"Good morning," she grumbles reluctantly.

My mother is beautiful. She has a full head of silver hair at sixty, but she takes good care of herself. Looks to be more in her fifties. She and my father were together for a long time – couldn't have kids – so they became foster parents to me and Major. I was seven. Major was five. They're the only parents we know. A few years ago, I found out my biological parents were deceased.

"How's life in the East wing?" I ask. We live in the same mansion and I hardly see her or Major. Our last meeting was two months ago. I can count on one hand how many times I've seen my mother since then.

"Good. What about the West?"

"Good," I reply. "Before Major arrives, let me ask you something. Paige Marion—isn't she responsible for laying out my clothes for the day?"

Mother shakes her head. "Absolutely not. For one thing, she's color blind. That girl will have you looking like a pure fool." She chuckles slightly. "You haven't seen what she wears up in here?"

"No. As far as I'm concerned, the staff is invisible. I make it a point not to look at or engage with them in any way."

"That's horrible."

"No, it's not. It's business." I lean back in my executive chair. Cross my arms. "Father used to say you can't be friends with people who will never reach your status."

"*Status* and money isn't everything," she tells me.

Sounds like the makings of a social media quote...

I grin. I'm sure she's making a joke. Has to be. Status, money, wealth and power is all this family has ever known. All I've known since adolescence.

She adds, "Plus, how do you think it's possible that you're able to accomplish all you do in a day? Everyone plays a pertinent role in making this company a success, Montgomery. It doesn't matter how big or small that role is."

"Yeah, well I have my way of doing things and you have yours. Now, back to my clothes—who did you put in charge of laying out my daily wardrobe?"

"Why does it matter?"

"I want to know. I never asked you to hire someone to do that for me, so I at least I would like to know who the assignment belongs to."

"Why...does...it...matter, Montgomery?" she asks testily.

I glare at her. For us to not have any biological connection, we have similar mannerisms no matter how much she gripes about me being *just like my father*. My personality encompasses both of them. She has the same stubborn streak I have.

This time, I offer the explanation she seeks by saying, "If you must know, I caught somebody snooping around in my closet this morning and I want to confirm she's not lying to me."

"You caught somebody snooping around in your closet?" Major asks amused as he steps into the conference room. He pulls out a chair. "I didn't know you were letting in thots on the west side."

"Letting in *who*?" Mother asks, looking confused.

"Thots," Major says.

Mother frowns. "Thots?"

"Yeah. Them ho—"

"Major, chill," I say interrupting.

"You *chill* and loosen up a bit. You're always so uptight. Jeez." He rolls his eyes and slouches in his chair.

Dismissing him as I always do, remembering he's younger than I am (and we have completely different personalities), I return my attention to Mother and ask, "Are you going to tell me, or do I have to find out on my own?"

"Tell you what?" she asks as if she'd forgotten what we were talking about that quickly.

"Who's in charge of my wardrobe?"

"You *should* be in charge of your own wardrobe," Major says under his breath. He speaks up when he adds, "Just because you fart hundred-dollar-bills doesn't mean you need someone to be at your beck and call."

He's one to talk. He's a millionaire although you'd never know it. He doesn't buy things. He lives life ordinary.

Mother finally answers, "Cherish Stevens—she's in charge of your wardrobe."

So the girl was telling the truth. Lucky for her. She was a breath away from getting fired.

"Poor Cherish," Major says. "It's funny how I knew that already but she works for *you* and you didn't know it.

Figures. Anyway, what do we need to talk about? I got a full schedule today and the quicker I can get to it, the better."

"I wanted to take a few minutes to give you the details of the patent I'll turn over to the lawyers soon. To be clear, no one knows about this and no one else will know until the first prototype is completed."

"We get it," Major says. "It's top secret. What is it?"

"It's a new, police-grade taser."

"A taser?" Mother asks. "Do you know how many different tasers are out there on the market. It's saturated with tasers."

"Mom's right," Major says. "I don't see the relevance in yet *another* one."

"You will if you keep your comments to yourself and give me time to explain."

Major gestures for me to have the floor. "All the time we hear on the news about how police are in pursuit of someone and they pull the *gun* instead of the *taser*. The results are usually fatal. They end up killing a suspect who they wanted to tase. Many in law enforcement claim the handles of both weapons feel the same. I've done the test myself and they *do* feel the same. In the heat of the moment when adrenaline is pumping and there are only seconds to make a decision, the wrong weapon gets pulled. This new taser is designed so that when its handle is grabbed, it emits a hard vibration that alerts the officer it's the taser their actually pulling. If it doesn't vibrate, it's the gun."

"Good idea, brother. I didn't know you could care so deeply about anyone's life besides your own."

"Enough with the sly comments, Major. Just let me know what you think about the idea since you'll be the one marketing it."

"I said it was a good idea, but it has to be perfect. I can see the lawsuits rolling in now from officers who claimed their taser didn't vibrate."

"Good point and that's already one of the guidelines I have the engineers working on. What do you think about the idea, Mrs. Hawthorne?"

"Will you stop calling our mother, *Mrs. Hawthorne*?" Major asks.

"Who runs this company? Me or you?"

Major glares. "You're ridiculous," he says, standing up. "I'm out."

"Look what you've done," Mother says to me. "You know what, Montgomery, I may not be your biological mother, but you can still show me a little respect."

"What makes you think I don't respect you?"

"Look at the way you speak to me. You're frowning right now and you call me *Mrs. Hawthorne* like I didn't spend my life raising you."

"Since father hired me on at the company, I've always called you Mrs. Hawthorne. It keeps things professional between us. You never had a problem with it before."

"That's because I'm always trying to keep the peace, but enough is enough. I deserve your respect and I shouldn't have to ask for it."

"I do respect you."

"Then you have a heck of a way of showing it!"

I glance over at her. She's a strong woman. Had to be strong to be with a man like my father, but she's not *like* him, nor is she like me. She's more in tune with her feelings. That's precisely why she can't run this company. Why father left me in charge.

I give her a minute to cool down, then jump right back into business mode and say, "A year ago today, you came to me with some paperwork I needed to complete to get my hands on the trust fund father left me and secure my role as CEO of Hawthorne Innovations. Has it been completed?"

"Yes, it's been completed. It still baffles me how quickly you signed it without even reading it over."

"Why wouldn't I sign it? It's five-billion dollars."

"So what? You're already rich."

"And now, I'm richer. Whatever those documents state wouldn't change my mind. Five billion is five billion. I can handle whatever comes along with it."

She shakes her head. "Your father sure did a number on you."

"You're right, mother. He did. He taught me how to be the man I am today."

"No, he taught you how to love money. Money ain't everything, Montgomery."

"You've said that already."

She blows an irritated breath. "My goodness—what happened to you?"

"Nothing's happened—"

"Where's the sweet, shy boy I raised? The one who handmade cards and picked wildflowers for me. The one who would give his last to help anyone. Where's *that* boy?"

"I'm not a boy anymore. I grew up."

"You grew into your father. That's what you've done."

"You act like that's a bad thing. He was *your* husband."

"Yeah, he was. A husband I was going to *divorce* when I saw the influence he had on you and Major, but—" Her lips tremble.

This is news to me. I had no idea she'd entertained the thought of divorcing my father. I take a hard look at her. She bites back her emotions and reconsiders what she wants to say. I'm not a cold-hearted person. I'm not so calloused that I don't feel anything for my mother. I do. I appreciate her in more ways than she knows, but what exactly does she and everyone else expects me to do when I have a billion-dollar empire to run? My father's legacy is at stake. I won't let him down under any circumstances.

"The money should be wired to your account in the next five business days."

"Good. I assumed you've already told Paige about this."

She frowns. "Paige? Why would I tell Paige anything?"

"Why wouldn't you?"

She throws her hands up then pushes away from the table. Leaves me there. Alone. Fine by me. It's how I spend most of my time.

* * *

After working in the office for a few hours straight, I get up and stretch like I don't have a care in the world (because I don't) and walk to the kitchen in the common area.

"Naomi, get me a bottle of Voss," I say, holding my phone, flipping through emails.

"Yes, Sir. Coming right up."

She screws off the cap and hands me the bottle. I take it to the patio and drink most of it before I can sit down. It's hot today. Early summer. The temperature is already eighty-five degrees. I glance at my watch. It's close to noon – too hot to be out here in a full suit. I step back inside, watching Naomi, the cook, make meal preparations. She's a short, heavy-set woman. Always sounds like she's running low on oxygen but she knows how to cook.

I usually wouldn't bother, but since mother called into question my interaction with the staff, I take a stab at communication.

"Naomi."

"Yes, Sir?"

"What's for lunch today?"

She looks surprised I asked, then says, "I am making you a club sandwich—fresh tomatoes, turkey, ham, bacon and lettuce on wheat bread. And, I got you some fresh deli-style pickles. I know you'd rather have those than fries."

"I would," I tell her. "I'm curious…how do you know what I like without consulting me first?"

"Oh, Sir, I'm just the cook." She chuckles. Her pot belly jumps. "I can't take credit for the menu."

"Menu? There's a menu?"

"There *showly* is a menu. Looka here. Lemme show you it."

She walks over to the refrigerator, hikes her weight up on her tiptoes to take a notepad from the top and hands it to me.

"She does a good job with this thing. I tell you, it's my cooking bible when it comes to making your meals, Sir. That girl spends so much time trying to get this right, she looks like she's doing calculus and all she doin' is figuring out what you want to eat. That's all. Making sure the same meal isn't prepared too close together. Checking nutrition content, protein, sodium, exaggerated fats—"

"You mean saturated fats."

"Yeah, yeah—all that stuff. She checks it all. Me, personally, I don't care nothing 'bout no calories. You can look at me and tell I don't know nothing 'bout no calories." She chuckles again. "But she does. Guess what, Mr. St. Claire. Guess what?"

"What's that?" I drawl out, but this woman reminds me of why I don't talk to the staff. Other than it not being necessary, they work my nerves with their ordinary speech, incorrect pronunciation and misuse of words. And who in their right mind brags about being overweight?

"I came in this world with high cholesterol and I'm leaving up out of here with high cholesterol. I'd rather be fat and happy than skinny and miserable."

I rub the back of my neck. I can feel my forehead tightening. I regret ever saying anything to the woman.

"Anyway, she must be doing a good job 'cause you never complain about the food."

"Who is this *she* you're referring to?"

"Cherry."

I frown. "Cherry?"

"Yes, Sir."

"I don't have anyone on my staff named Cherry."

She chuckles again. "Sorry. Her name is Cherish, Sir,

but I calls her Cherry. Takes too much effort to add the *ish* on the end. I gots waay too much stomach to be expending extra air like that."

I think about how *Cherry* and *Cherish* are both two-syllable words and her real name doesn't require an extra expenditure of air but I don't call Naomi out on it. I'm too busy thinking about the content of what she said. I ask, "Cherish Stevens makes this menu?"

"Every week, Sir."

Imagine my surprise to learn not only does Cherish handles my wardrobe – she also controls what I eat. All this from a girl I've hardly said a word to. "Would you happen to know where she is right now?"

"Probably somewhere messin' 'round in some flowers. That's usually what she does 'round lunchtime. A lil' gardening."

I leave out the back door, in search of *Cherry*.

Chapter Three

Cherish

Gardening doesn't fall under my job title, but I have an innate love of flowers that's borderline sickening. At home, my front yard looks like an outdoor florist shop. My neighbors come over all the time to prune, pluck and separate some of my plants so they can grow their own. I don't mind it. It's just that many.

Flowers remind me of life. Of love. Of *true* love. Flowers are innocent. Romantic. Flowers are beautiful and bountiful if they're well nurtured. I was once that way – well-nurtured – when my father was alive. He died when I was ten. Fatal car crash took him from us – from me and mama. Mama was never the same. Our relationship slowly lost its closeness when she fell into a deep depression. The smidgen of a relationship we had left completely died when she remarried.

"Hey, chica," Consuela says, walking over to me with gloved hands pushing a wheelbarrow full of mulch. She works for Chavez Landscaping & Irrigation – the company who does all of Mr. St. Claire's landscaping and with such a wide acreage of land, they're here at least four days a week. He's their biggest account.

"Hey, Consuela. What's up?"

"Just thought I'd give you a heads up—the boss is lurking, coming this way."

"Who?"

"Who do you think? The head honcho. The green-eyed bandit. Your secret crush." She waggles her brows.

"Montgomery?"

"Yes!" She laughs. "Mr. Montgomery St. Claire."

I dig another small hole to reset a flower. She knows Montgomery is my crush since she caught me staring at him one day. I was staring when I didn't even realize I was staring. That's how you know you got it bad – when you find yourself in a one-way trance with a person who's not aware of your existence.

"Whatever," I say, fanning her away. "I know you're lying. Montgomery's never on the grounds."

"Trust me, I know. That's why I thought it was strange to see him out here. Seems so odd to see his fancy leather shoes walking on actual grass. I thought he was too good for that. Anyway, gotta run. Don't say I didn't warn you."

"Wait...what makes you think he's looking for me?"

"He just asked my brother if he's seen you out here. Bye."

I giggle at the way she's haulin' it with that wheelbarrow. Nobody likes to run into Montgomery, not even the groundskeepers. No sooner than Consuela is out of sight and safely behind some bushes, I see Montgomery heading this way, wearing the ten-thousand-dollar suit I picked out for him this morning. His hair is shiny and curly beneath the midday sun. He's not wearing sunglasses, even though he has a wide selection to choose from. I'm low-key glad he doesn't have his eyes hidden. I like how the sunlight bounces off of them, making it appear different shades of green and brown. His caramel skin has me reliving the moment I saw him in all his hairy-chested glory this morning when he had me hostage in his closet.

What a beautiful man.

A beautiful man with a flawed personality and the body of an Adonis.

Oh my soul – somebody help me...

Actually, *he's* the one who needs help. All I want to do is save him, but there comes a point in time when you realize life is hard and you can't help everybody – especially those people who don't realize or *think* they need it.

My heart begins with the erratic beats again, same as this morning. Why? Because his mind-screwing pheromones greet me before he's able to. A stream of wind guided his smell straight to my nose. I glance up again and see him taking more steps with a walk so sensual, it should be outlawed. Is he really heading this way, or is it so hot out here I'm hallucinating? Seeing visions and mirages? Maybe it's time for a break. Some water. Some electrolytes. I must be dehydrated.

I continue minding my business, planting marigolds in front of the row of dark green hostiles I planted yesterday when he walks right up to me. I can literally look to my right and see his leather shoes beside my knee. I finish brushing the dirt around the plant and try my hardest to avoid him, but his feet are literally *right there.*

My eyes climb up his legs and torso until it reaches his face. He's so tall it seems like his head is in the clouds. In a figure-of-speech kind of way, it is. His intimidating presence has me questioning his sanity. Why is he here? And how does he go from not talking to me for two years – two *full* years – to having two interactions with me on the same day? Is there a lunar eclipse on the horizon? A blood moon? Wolf moon? Did the axis shift? Are the earth's plates breaking apart? Is the whole state of North Carolina about to physically break away from the country and become its own island in the Atlantic?

When I can't take the dark cloud of his presence looming over me as well as the one-sided chemistry *I* feel (because I know he doesn't feel *anything* for me with his mean, arrogant self,) I ask, "Is there something you need?"

"No. Not necessarily," he responds.

He continues standing there. He slides his hands in his pockets like he's micro-managing me. Studying me. Silently reviewing my work.

"Why are you not wearing any gloves?" he asks.

"I don't want to wear gloves."

"That's not a reason. Well, it is, but it's a little immature. How old are you?"

I roll my eyes, happy he didn't see me do it. I'm raking dirt around the flower I just planted, making sure it's stable and well-rooted when I ask, "What does my age have to do with anything?"

"It'll help me determine why you can't properly answer my question."

"I'm sorry—I'm not a *businessman* like you, Mr. St. Claire. I don't answer all of my questions like I'm sitting in front of the president of a company."

"I *am* the president, CEO or whatever you want to call it and as your boss, it is my requirement that my workers answer questions with a certain level of confidence and maturity like they know what they're doing."

"I *do* know what I'm doing."

"Good. Then tell me why you don't have on gloves."

I release an even sigh – one he can't hear. Maybe it was a good thing I was invisible to him for two years because if he's *this* obnoxious, I don't want the attention.

"I'm not wearing gloves because I'm a country girl at heart. I like to feel the soil on my hands. Is that a good enough answer for the boss?"

"Better than the first one you gave me. And, FYI, I don't want those dirty hands on my clothes. You better make sure those hands are squeaky clean when you find yourself in my closet again."

I better? Who does he think he's talking to?

"What do you think? I don't wash my hands?" I ask.

"I don't know *what* you do. I really don't know you."

"Well, I don't know you either, especially not enough for you to be invading my personal space while I'm trying to work."

"You mean like you invaded my personal space this morning while you were in my closet."

"Again, I was *working*."

He doesn't move. The heat of his eyes bearing down

on my back is more fierce than the blazing temperature of the sun. "I can see that you're working, but you're not a gardener. I have landscapers. This—playing around in dirt—isn't in your job description."

"So what? Half the stuff I do around here ain't in my job description. I just do what needs to be done and then me and my *dirty* hands go home."

He's quiet for a moment. I feel like it's an eerie calm before the storm. His presence bothers me to the point that the chemistry I *thought* I felt when I'm around him has completely withered. All I feel now is his bad energy and it's not something I want to be around. He's not a nice person. I knew that already, but in my mind, I *made* him a nice person. The mind has a way of making you believe things you know aren't true. Like a woman in an abusive relationship who's getting beat up by her husband – he says he won't do it again. Her mind wants to believe him – even convinces her that *this* time will be different – but deep down, she knows it's only a matter of time before the abuse starts happening again.

That's how my mind works with Montgomery. I look at him and see decency and that's probably only because he's so attractive. Society tells us that attractive people are naturally nice. False! My mind tells me he's a good person and he'll come around one day and actually be a nice human. But when he opens his mouth and starts spewing out all this garbage, snapping and yelling at people, calling his mother *Mrs. Hawthorne* instead of *Mother* and treating his brother like a second-class citizen – like Major is one of *us* – I know what I believe isn't true. He ain't coming around. At this point, I'm not sure if he's actually...human.

"I want you to come find me before you leave."

"Why?"

"Because you work for me and I asked you to. Have a good day, *Cherry*."

He walks away with a smirk on his face, satisfied, I'm

sure, that he has completely pissed me off and disrupted my day. All I can do is watch, smelling the fading, glorious scent of his cologne as he moves across the healthy lawn heading for the west entrance of the house.

Now, I have to work with a sour stomach for the remainder of the day, wondering why he wants to meet with me before I leave. Is he going to fire me?

Great, Cherish. Just great. You should've kept your big mouth closed.

* * *

It's four-thirty.

I'm sneaking all around the house in stealth mode trying to steer clear of everybody and by *everybody*, I mean Montgomery. When I'm sure he's in his office, I go up to his master bedroom, make sure everything is still tidy. It is. The room is clean. Bed still made. I go to his bathroom and switch out the bath towels. They smell like him. Smell so freakin' good I consider throwing them in a plastic bag and taking them home with me. Instead, I take them to the laundry room, a room about the size of his kitchen. It has two washers, two dryers, a washbasin, laundry sorter, two folding tables and two drying racks – a little overkill for me, but hey – people with money do things differently than us common folk.

My stomach growls. I usually don't eat lunch. I try to tame my hunger with water most days. Today, I couldn't eat or drink a thing, especially after the closet incident. Plus, I'm 'bout to be out on my tail soon. What am I going to do if he fires me? Why did I engage in a back-and-forth exchange with Montgomery? What was I thinking? No one wins against him. It's why he's the CEO.

I throw the manly-smelling towels in the wash, add some detergent and flick off the lights as I leave the room. I close the door and was about to walk to the bathroom down the hallway when I hear a voice behind me yell,

"Boo!"

"Eek!" I screech, convinced I've wet my jeans.

Meanwhile, Major, the current source of my anxiety, is cracking up laughing. "Did you really say, *eek?*" He folds over and laughs more.

"Major, I'm going to *kill* you. Why are you sneaking up on me like that?"

"Why are you yelling like somebody's after you? Oh, wait, somebody *is* after you. I heard Monty's been at you today. Said you were *lurking around* in his closet."

"I wasn't lurking around in nothing. I was picking out his suit like I do every morning."

"I know. I know. I'm just teasing, but for real, though—why don't you pick out *my* suits? I'm much nicer than he is."

I grin. Major is more down-to-earth than his brother. Don't get it twisted – he's about his business, too, but he's not as rigid. He actually smiles. I know what his teeth look like. He's handsome – has the same green eyes as Montgomery, but it's something about Montgomery that draws me in. Maybe it's the bad boy appeal and his blasé attitude like he doesn't need anybody. They say good girls always fall for the bad boys. For two years, I've been falling.

"I don't pick out your suits because I'm not your assistant, Major. Why don't you have an assistant, anyway?"

"Mother tried to hire one for me. I refused. I'm not ready for all that yet. When I get to the point where I feel like I can't handle any more additional tasks, then I'll hire an assistant. Right now, I'm straight."

"Wait—how did you know about the closet incident this morning?" I ask.

"Monty called a business meeting this morning and he brought it up."

"You're kidding."

"Wish I was. He wanted to know if you were supposed

to be there. He thought Paige had been picking out his clothes all along. Wanted to confirm it was supposed to be you. Mother confirmed it, but he was still pretty ticked off."

"Well, unfortunately for me, he requested I meet with him before I leave today. So, I gotta imagine today is my last day."

"Why would you think that?"

"Because he was bothering me today. He *never* talks to me, like *ever*. Today, he came outside and was asking me crazy stuff."

"Like what?"

"Like why I was working in the flowers…why I didn't have on gloves. Ugh…"

I sigh. Collect myself. "Look, it was nice knowing you, Major. Now, if you would excuse me, I have to go finish peeing."

He laughs. "I didn't scare you *that* bad, did I?"

"You did. You didn't hear me scream?"

"You call that a scream. You said, *eek*." He chuckles while following me to the bathroom. "I don't think I've ever heard anyone scream like that."

"Welp, now that I'm about to get canned, you'll never have to worry about hearing it again. Goodbye, Major."

"Whatever, girl. You're not about to get *canned*. Monty would never fire you."

"How can you be so sure?"

"Because he likes you."

I laugh and step into the bathroom. "Bye, Major," I say before closing the door.

"I'll see you later."

"Don't count on it."

Chapter Four

Monty

It's two minutes 'til six. Cherish has yet to come see me, so here I sit, at the dining room table alone, wondering if this girl is going to challenge me. She gets off work at six. I know this because I watch her leave every day. She doesn't know this. I doubt if anyone does.

I usually eat alone. The way my father had this place built was for every wing to be a separate residence. Therefore, I have a private kitchen and dining room. So does mother and Major. If or when we all eat together, we meet in the main dining room on the ground floor in the common area. That's where I am now – in the main dining room, my patience dwindling, waiting for Cherish. I can't recall the last time I had dinner with my mother in this room, just like I don't know the last time we saw eye-to-eye on anything. That's mostly my fault.

When my father died three years ago, a part of me died with him and I'm not saying that to emphasize how much he meant to me. I really mean it. A part of me *died*. I was close to him. I was his shadow. I studied him. Believed in him and his vision. I wanted to be just like him. So, I went to college. Studied business and didn't stop until I got my masters. I picked my father's brain, was with him all the time – then stomach cancer claimed his life.

During that time of the diagnosis, he grew bitter. He had all the money in the world, could afford every treatment there was to be had, but nothing could stop cancer from spreading. *Money* couldn't save his life.

That reality manifested itself in the form of anger and

bitterness. He lashed out a lot – at me, mother and Major. He pushed everyone away, especially my mother. She took offense – I just learned today she wanted to divorce him. I hope that wasn't during the time he was sick. He was a jerk, but I think it was his way of protecting her. He didn't want her to see him slowly waste away to nothing. He stopped taking medicine when he accepted his fate. He wouldn't accept the care of any nurses. He only wanted me by his side.

One of the last things I remember him saying to me while he was still well enough to speak was that money wasn't everything. Told me to take care of mother and Major. Told me to find myself. My purpose. Wanted me to fall in love and be happy. Said, in the end, love is all you have.

I watched my father cry that day. I'd never seen my old man shed a tear before then. That was the day he asked to see my mother. A few days later, he was gone. The life – the breath – went out of him as I held his hand.

His death rattled me to the core. It's one of those things you think about but can never really prepare for. I didn't cry. Didn't shed a single tear at his funeral. I was bitter. My heart, hardened. A year later, I'm the exact same way. It's like I'm holding my breath, swimming up toward the light, but I can never find the surface of the water. I know I'm going to drown. Drown in my own misery.

In this *hold-my-breath* stage, I don't know who I am, but I know I'm not fulfilling my father's last wishes for me. He told me to find myself and I haven't done that. I don't know who I am without this company attached to my name. I'm the CEO – the top boss that everyone hates.

He told me to take care of my mother and Major. I've failed. My mother despises me for being bitter like my father. I can't have a normal conversation with her without it turning into an argument.

Major turned out a lot better than I did, probably because he has a life outside of work. He doesn't have the same responsibilities I have. He doesn't have to make sure hundreds of people get their paychecks on time. Am I jealous of him because of that? No. Not at all. My problem with him is, he used to look up to me. Now, I can feel him looking *down* at me. He hates the man I've become, but he won't say it. His actions say it, but he won't verbalize it.

"You're eating in here today, Sir?" Naomi asks.

I automatically glare at her. "I'm sitting in here, aren't I?" I hate it when people ask obvious questions.

"Yes, Sir, you are. I'll start bringing your food."

"You do that."

I glance at my watch. It's 6:02 p.m. Naomi brings in a bowl of dinner rolls, a salad and another dish that she explains as being mozzarella chicken. It looks good – something I haven't tried before. She brings dressing in a stainless steel gravy boat and places it on the table.

"What kind of dressing is that?" I inquire.

"It's Catalina, Sir."

"I prefer blue cheese dressing with my salad. You should know that by now. How long have you been working here?"

"'Bout a year, Sir, and I know you like blue cheese *gressing* but Cherry said the tanginess of the Catalina *gressing* would go better with this particular meal. Said the blue cheese would overpower the taste of the mozzarella chicken."

"I see," I tell her, feeling my face tighten with frustration. "Would you like some wine with your meal, Sir?"

"Why don't you ask *Cherry*? You ask her everything else you want to know about me, don't you?"

"No, Sir, I just follow the menu—"

"Just go," I tell her, fanning her away. "And bring me some blue cheese dressing!"

Cherish steps into the room immediately after I send Naomi away. She's frowning. Has her purse on her left shoulder. Keys in her right hand.

"Why are you yelling at her like that?" she asks me, coming to Naomi's defense.

I look at her, trying to understand how she has the balls to ask me anything. "Don't concern yourself with something that has nothing to do with you."

She glares.

"Come in and sit down," I tell her.

Her glare ripens. Jaw clenches. She doesn't like my tone and I couldn't care less.

She goes for the seat on the opposite end of the twenty-seater table, trying to get as far away from me a possible until I say, "No. Here," and slap the table in front of the seat where I want her to sit – adjacent to me.

She sighs, mumbles something under her breath and walks over. Sits next to me. She places her purse on the floor. Her keys on the table.

"What is this about? I'm ready to go home."

I look at her. She has a flowery scarf tied on her head – over a full head of loose swinging braids that fall to her breasts.

I ask, "What have you eaten today?" I know for a fact she skips meals. I've seen her working during the time most people take their lunch breaks.

"Nothing."

"Nothing?"

"Correct," she says. "Nothing."

"Why not?"

"I'm too busy *working* to eat."

I shrug. "You could still eat."

"I could if I wanted to," she answers.

She doesn't look at me. Just answers my questions with attitude.

Naomi bounces back in the room with another fancy container and says, "Here you go, Sir. Blue cheese *gressing*." She places it on the table.

"Bring an extra plate and some silverware," I tell her.

"Why does she need to bring an extra plate and more

silverware?" Cherish asks.

"So you can eat," I tell her.

"I'm not eating."

"You *are* eating. I think it'll be nice if you had some of what you plan for me to eat, don't you think?"

"Is that what this is about? You're pissed because I plan your meals?"

"Who said anything about being upset?"

"I can hear it in your tone, or does being a jerk come naturally to you?"

I laugh, although I'm more shocked than amused. *Flower girl* has a chip on her shoulder and she doesn't hide her dislike of me like other people do. Gotta hand it to her for being real. Unfortunately, she doesn't know who she's messing with.

"Here you go, Ms. Cherry," Naomi says.

"Thank you, Naomi," Cherish tells her and when Naomi leaves the room, she tells me, "See, that's what you say when someone does something nice for you. You say *thank you*."

Ignoring her, I serve her food, adding some chicken, salad and a roll to her plate. Then I serve myself.

"Practice what you preach," I tell her. "I just served you food. You didn't say *thank you*."

"That's because I don't talk to demons."

I laugh again. "You're funny."

"Funny, but oh-so-serious."

"Eat," I tell her.

She sighs. She's irritated. She pecks at the salad first, then tries the chicken.

"Let me ask you something, *Cherish* Stevens. How long have you worked for me?"

"Two years."

"Two years?"

"Yes. *Two* years. Dos años."

"Two years and I've never had a conversation with you," I say looking at her lips but I quickly glance away.

"You sound surprised."

"I am."

"Why's that? You don't talk to the *help*. Actually, you don't *talk* to anymore. And before you try to refute it, barking orders and yelling at people doesn't qualify as conversation."

"That's what I do, huh?"

"On a daily basis. Yes. You just yelled at Naomi."

"I didn't yell at her."

"You did—over some dressing…"

I pour myself wine, offer her some but she declines. "You *do* know I have the power to fire you, don't you?"

"I'm aware of that, but you'd also have to hire ten people to replace me."

"You think you do *that* much work?"

"I do. I get up at 3:00 a.m. every morning to make sure I have enough time to get here by four. I make sure the menu is in order. I go down the list of everything that needs to be done for the day, all based around your schedule. You take a shower every morning around five on the dot so I try to be in and out of your room before your shower is done. I make the bed—change your sheets and pillowcases every morning. I put away your slippers, clean off your nightstand—I make sure everything is in place in your room. Then I go to your closet, pick out your suit, sock, shoes, necktie and cufflinks. Once I'm done with that, I tidy up your office, especially when I know you'll be working from home. I take your clothes to the cleaners, I do all the shopping, mostly for food. I schedule landscaping visits. Schedule the window washers. I call the plumbers if any repairs need to be made. I make sure your black coffee is ready in the morning. And when it's blooming season, I make sure to cut fresh flowers and put them in vases around the house because it's otherwise gloomy and dull around here. No one hardly ever smiles. Everybody's on edge. The only time I see you smile is when you know you've pissed somebody off. And yes, I make Naomi a menu every week because I don't like it when you yell at people who are trying to *serve* you and you've yelled at her one-too-many times. We're not robots, Mr. St. Claire. We're people who have feelings. You, on the other hand, have lost touch with that side of yourself."

She eats – eats more than she did before she went on her rant.

"Are you done?" I ask with a level of nonchalance that even I am surprised by.

"No, I'm not done. Fourteen hours a day. That's how much time I devote to this job. Not to you. The job. Fourteen hours. If you appreciated what I did, it would be for *you*, but it's not for you, Mr. St. Claire. I work for Hawthorne Innovations, Incorporated, hired by your mother."

She drops her fork on her plate.

"Now, are you done?"

She sighs heavily. "Yes. I'm *done*."

"Good. I could replace you in a heartbeat."

She stands and says, "Thank you for dinner."

"I didn't ask you to leave."

"You didn't have to," she says. "I'm not going to sit here while you insult me to my face. I go to bed every night at eight o'clock so I can get up at three o'clock in the morning to *serve* you, *Sir*, and you don't appreciate nothing."

She snatches her keys from the table, takes her purse from the floor and leaves the room.

And I thought I was a work-a-holic…

She wasn't exaggerating when she said she does the work of ten people. I'd be a fool to fire her. I know her value and what she brings to work every day. She gives her all and she could never be replaced. I can't show my hand and tell her that. As it stands, she has a mouth on her to match those pretty lips of hers.

I shake my head.

Something about her thrills me. It could be her pretty

face, her decadent chocolate skin or those exotic braids on her head. Most likely, it's the fact that she's not afraid to speak her mind around me. Most people wouldn't come at me the way she does.

I like it.

I know I have the power to shut her down whenever I want, but she doesn't look like the type to back down. At least I don't think she is.

I should probably keep with the same protocol I've followed for the two years she's worked here.

Ignore her.

Avoid her.

Pretend she doesn't exist.

She can't handle a man like me, and I have no interest in getting into arguments with a smart-mouthed woman. But why do I have a sudden craving for cherries?

Chapter Five

Cherish

My days are shorter than Montgomery's temper. Clarification: my workdays are long, but *my* days – my *personal* time – are short. Usually, I'd grab something to eat on the way home because getting off work at six and going to bed at eight doesn't give me a sufficient window of opportunity to cook a decent meal. So it's snacks, burgers and to-go stuff for me during the week. I drink plenty of water, spend a little time with my flowers and watch thirty minutes of TV. After that, I take a shower and then I'm in bed.

What a life, right?

In some twisted roundabout way, I think it keeps me sane. Staying busy is a way to occupy my mind with what's right in front of me instead of focusing on problems that try to catch up to me. Overworking helps me cope with the death of my father all those years ago and my aunt – both whom I loved dearly.

Today, something or shall I say, *someone*, disturbed my inner peace. For two years I dreamed of getting attention from Montgomery and today, I got it. Got it and didn't want it. They say be careful what you wish for. Whoever *they* are ain't never lied! I hope I never run into him again.

I take a bag of pretzels from my kitchen table that looks more like a pantry instead of an eating place. I pour myself a glass of lemonade and then sit on the porch and stare out into the yard. I'm stressed but I'm still able to smile. This old-fashioned, two-bedroom house is my sanctuary. My home. The place that saved me after I ran away from my real home – from my mother and stepfather

– at the tender age of sixteen.

My phone rings.

I take a glance at it to see that it's her calling. My mother. I haven't talked to her in a while. There's not much to say these days. Our relationship hasn't been the same since my biological father passed. Over the years, we talked sporadically. I may even run into her while she's out shopping at times, but the mother-daughter bond we used to have – yeah, that no longer exists and I doubt it ever will.

When the phone stops ringing, I toss a pretzel into my mouth. The ringing starts again but it's not my mother this time. It's Naomi. I wonder what Montgomery has done now?

Naomi usually leaves at seven after Montgomery is completely finished dinner. She discards the leftovers (because Montgomery is too good to eat leftover food) and then her day is done. If he wants late-night snacks, he's on his own.

"Hey, Naomi," I answer.

"Chile, have you done completely lost your mind?"

A slight sense of urgency elevates my heart rate. "What's wrong, Naomi?"

"I heard what you were telling Mr. St. Claire."

"At dinner?"

"Yes. At dinner."

"He was being disrespectful. He yelled at you—asked you to bring some salad dressing and when you brought it to him, he didn't say *thank you*. That's rude. Then he *demanded* you bring me a plate. Who does he think he is?"

"He's the man who signs our paychecks, honey."

I sigh. "I don't care. I don't like how he treats people, and I had enough. I had to call him out on it. I couldn't take it anymore."

"Chile, looka here…lemme tell you something, Cherry—I don't care what that man says as long as, at the end of the week, I get my paycheck."

"But there's a certain way you're supposed to talk to people," I tell her, angrily crunching on pretzels.

"Yes, honey, but you and I both know that man's a few peas short of a casserole." She chuckles, makes me laugh.

"Good one, Naomi."

"It's true. I've been doing some talking to his momma. From what I hear, he ain't been the same since his daddy passed."

That hits too close to home. It's a familiarity we both share. I lost my father, too. I know how it feels, even though I was a child at the time. He was an adult when his father died. I don't know which one is worse. I imagine the pain is the same in both instances, or maybe there is a difference.

As a child, I have a few memories of my dad that are pretty vivid. I have pictures. I've had time to get over his death.

Montgomery was in his early thirties when he lost his father. He had more years with his dad than I had with mine, and no doubt more pain is associated with the loss, I would imagine. But, if that's the case, why does Major seem so carefree and unbothered by everything while Montgomery is supposedly *going through it?*

Naomi continues, "Believe me when I say Sylvia Hawthorne knows that boy done lost his mind. Why do you think she stays good and tucked in on the east side of the house? She don't bother nobody and hardly talks to anybody. She keeps to herself and them boys keep to theyself. I ain't never seen anything like it."

"Me either. To be so wealthy, they're miserable."

"Mmm...hmm," Naomi says in a gossipy hum. "That goes to show they ain't wealthy where it matters the most. You catch my drift?"

"Yep," I say, then toss another pretzel into my mouth.

"Honey, what's that you crunching on in my ear? Cracklin's?"

"No," I say laughing. "I'm eating pretzels. Oh, and that

chicken was delicious, by the way. Montgomery *made* me eat some. I didn't want to, but once I started eating, I couldn't stop."

"Why did he request you eat with him? He usually eats all by his lonely…"

I shrug as if she can see me then answer, "I don't know. He was bothering me earlier, asking about the menu and stuff. I honestly thought he was going to fire me today."

"He ain't fixin' to fire nobody."

"He will, Naomi. I've seen him do it. He fired the cook that was here before you because she overcooked his steak. He fired the two maids that were here before Minnie and Isidora. I still, to this day, don't know why he did that. So, just make sure you watch your back."

"I will, babygirl, but you make sure you watch yours, too. He was pretty PO'd when you left."

"Yeah, probably because he couldn't *torture* me any longer."

"Don't know, but *something* interrupted his spirit. I tell you that much. After you left, he got up from the table in a rage. Next thing I know, I hear dishes hitting the floor. I run to see what's wrong, and you know me—I don't usually *run* for nothing. By the time I got to the dining room, I'm gasping for air 'cause I'm out of breath and all the food – his plate and your plate is on the floor, smashed. The salad, the chicken – sauce was everywhere. It was a mess."

"Wow," I say. That confirms it. He's mentally unstable.

"Needless to say I had to clean it all up. Minnie and Isidora were still there, so they helped me. So, I'ma say it again—be careful around that man. You never know when he's gonna snap."

"I'm sorry you had to go through that, Naomi, but thanks for the warning."

"You're welcome. I'll see you tomorrow."

"Okay. Bye," I answer, then hang up. Suddenly I'm not

looking forward to going to work tomorrow. I'm seriously considering calling in sick.

Chapter Six

Monty

When I was fifteen, my father had *the talk* with me and my brother. I think fifteen is a little too late to be having that kind of talk, but at least he tried. He was playing catch up. He was always busy working. Always behind on our school activities or anything else that involved us, but he knew the ins and outs of Hawthorne Innovations. Mother was more up to speed with us – our sports, our likes and dislikes – but I imagine she deemed it appropriate he have the birds and bees talk – something I really didn't need. I'd learned mostly everything I needed to know by then. Learned from my friends at school. From shows I wasn't supposed to be watching on cable. Learned where this and that goes. How to protect myself. How to kiss. I learned it all.

They had nothing to worry about with me and girls. Yeah, the chicks were at me. Why wouldn't they be? Mother always used to tell me and Major we would break hearts because of our eyes if for no other reason. Girls couldn't resist my green eyes. But I could resist them, and I did. I had no high school girlfriend. Girls had crushes on me, but I didn't sweat anyone. Didn't matter how pretty she was or if her body was bangin'. There was no woman in college that made me lose my mind and think about foolish things like rings and marriage. That was more of Major's speed. All my interests were wrapped up in Hawthorne Innovations.

I wanted to know everything my father knew about inventions and coming up with creative ways to do everyday things. Once he saw how serious I was about learning the trade, he taught me everything he knew. Showed me the ropes. Taught me how to come up with my own ideas from concept to product. I fell in love with it. With working and designing. I've *stayed* in love with it.

For years, nothing has come before my work. No woman. No other career aspirations or personal hobbies. Just work. It's like a drug that keeps me high and happy at the same time. There's no greater feeling than the euphoria I feel when I'm in my zone, doing what I love. When I feel like I'm coming off of my high, I scribble new plans to reignite my passion until my high returns.

But there's a downside to being this dedicated to working. It's becoming my demise. It's all I can think about. When making money happens so effortlessly, it becomes something I can never get enough of. I've made myself a prisoner. Given myself a life sentence. I'm a slave, but I'm set for life. I don't want for nothing. So, why am I lying on a twenty-thousand-dollar bed staring up at the ceiling because I can't sleep?

I know why. I don't want to admit this, but my life is going down the drain. My mother looks at me like she made a mistake. Like she should've fostered a different child instead of me. I'm carrying on father's legacy, but I'm a huge disappointment to her. She's not impressed by anything I do and perhaps that's why I treat her more like a business associate instead of the woman who raised me. I hate treating her that way, don't like calling her Ms. Sylvia Hawthorne, but since our personal relationship is non-existent, I don't feel comfortable calling her *mother* any longer.

Major says I'm selfish. I can argue with him all day long but he knows me better than anyone. I *am* selfish. I used to be proud of that. Now, I greatly dislike that about myself and I'm starting to envy him because he's everything I'm not. Major is the guy everybody likes. He talks to people. He's personable. Knows how to mingle and make people feel comfortable. I'm cold and distant.

My father sealed my fate when he told me this: *Son, if you want to take over this company after I'm gone, be prepared to devote every hour, every minute, every second to it. You have to be rigid. You can't let people walk over you. They have to know you're in charge when you step into a room. Any room. They should feel the power in your presence. You can take this company far. You have what it takes, son. I have faith in you.*

* * *

The next morning when I'm in the shower, all of this is heavy on my mind. It weighs on me. I think the load is heavier to carry today more-so than the days prior because of what Cherish said to me at dinner. *We're not robots, Mr. St. Claire. We're people who have feelings. You, on the other hand, have lost touch with that side of yourself.*

She's right. The woman who *works* for me, who's *beneath* me in so many ways is right.

Cherish Stevens.

Yesterday was the first time I've ever said a word to the girl, but it's not the first time I've noticed her. I see and hear things I don't speak on. I see how hard she works. I wasn't aware of her specific duties, but I know she's a hard worker. And she's pretty with her deep brown eyes that match her exotic, cocoa skin complexion – entices me on a daily basis. She intentionally hides her beauty almost as if she doesn't want to be noticed by anyone.

But I've noticed.

She wears her hair in braids that hangs at the center of her back and she always has on a scarf. Her fingernails are never painted. She doesn't wear color on her lips but I've watched her apply Chapstick on several occasions as she sits in her car and prepares to leave for the day. And back to her skin…it's smooth, deep brown and makes my mouth water for chocolate. Yesterday when she was in my closet, I could smell the scent of cocoa butter when she walked by. If I had to guess, I'd say she was about five-feet-six. I can't say much about her body because I've never seen her true figure. She always wears loose clothes and aprons.

I don't know her all that well, but she knows me better than I know myself, down to the detail of what food I like on specific days.

I get out the shower earlier than usual this morning hoping to catch her in my closet again. I wrap myself in a towel and walk there. She's already been here and gone. She's laid out a suit for me. A navy blue one. Brown leather shoes. Gold 'M' cufflinks. A dark purple tie that matches the argyle socks. I can feel her presence as I get dressed. Can smell the lingering scent of cocoa butter. She's fixed my bed, put away my slippers, cleaned off my nightstand. She does these things every day and I know nothing about her. That nags at me because I think I should know something. Then again, I don't want to know anything about her or anyone else.

I'm dressed, ready to start the day. I step into my office and to my dismay, Paige Marion is sitting in my chair. She's my mother's assistant and for some reason, she thinks she has a shot at getting my attention. Probably because I've taken her on a few important business dinners – my mother's suggestion – hoping her presence would help to complement important deals. It usually works, but it's completely destroying my mood this morning.

"Paige, get out of my office," I tell her.

"Well, good morning to you too, Sunshine."

"Get out of my chair and get out of my office."

She flips her blonde hair and rolls her eyes. "Okaaaay-ya. You don't have to be rude."

"You're sitting at my desk—can't get much ruder than that."

She heads for the door. I glance up quickly to see she's wearing an extremely tight mini-skirt that seems to be flattening her butt even more than it's already flattened.

"Sylvia will be hearing about this," she says.

I nearly laugh when she makes the statement like running and telling my mother I kicked her out is going to land me in trouble. She can't be serious…

I sit down, check emails and voicemails. In my office building, I have a secretary who does this for me. At home, I do it all myself.

Around seven-thirty after I've finished my first cup of coffee, I go downstairs for breakfast. I hear a lot of chatter and laughter coming from the kitchen. I know the voices and the people they belong to. I hear Isidora first – she struggles with English. Then there's Minnie. She has one of those laughs that makes you question whether or not she's from another planet. Naomi is chuckling, too. She's heavy-set – always sounds like she's out of breath. And then there's Cherish. Her laugh is softer. Sweeter. Sweet like her voice. Even when she snapped at me yesterday, her voice was sweet. I still don't like it, or her. She's irritated me enough and so I'm making it a point to completely avoid her today.

When I step into the kitchen, all laughter and chatter cease. Minnie puts her head down and leaves the kitchen with a mop.

Isidora looks at me and says, "Buenas dias, Señor," then hurries on about her way.

I glance over at Cherish. She has her hand wrapped around a sports bottle filled with water and ice. She doesn't say a word to me. Doesn't look my way. She has on old, worn jeans and a baggy gray T-shirt that already looks dirty. Her hair is tied up again.

"Mr. St. Claire, I have your breakfast ready, Sir," Naomi says.

"I'll talk to you later, Naomi," Cherish tells her then walks out of the room.

Apparently, her game plan is the same as mine – I'm not acknowledging her and she pretends I don't exist.

Naomi sets a plate in front of me.

"What's this?" I ask her.

"It's an egg-white bagel, Sir, with white cheddar cheese."

"I don't eat bagels."

"Cherry says you do. Said you used to eat them all the time."

I feel my nostrils flare. I used to eat them. Keywords being *used to*. I don't eat them anymore. Bagels were my father's favorite for breakfast. In an effort to feel closer to him, I tried to eat them, too. That was two years ago. Did it for a month and stopped. It didn't work. Didn't make me feel closer to him. Now, I can't stand the smell of bagels.

I take the small plate, dump the bagel in the trash – plate and all – and say, "Don't ever cook bagels in this house."

"My apologies, Sir. I didn't know—"

"Just get me some coffee!"

"Will do, Mr. St. Claire."

Naomi grabs a tall mug, pours in coffee and places the cup on the island in front of me. "Can I get you anything else?"

"No."

I take the cup and head back up to my office, still heated. Now, it's starting to piss me off that I don't know nothing about this Cherish Stevens girl. So, I pull up her personnel record and read through her file:

-Cherish Stevens.
-Born in 1993.
-She lives in Charlotte on Mallard Creek Church Road.
I Google her address. It displays a small white house. I wonder how long ago the photo was taken.
-She doesn't list an emergency contact. I shouldn't be curious as to why, but I am.
-There's not much listed in the way of an

employment history. In fact, I think working for me may be her first *real* job.
-She graduated from high school. Didn't go to college. How is she qualified to be my personal assistant?

Armed with my findings, I head over to the east wing in search of *Mrs. Hawthorne*. She definitely has some explaining to do. I find her sitting at her desk. She lowers her glasses when she sees me standing at her office door. She already looks annoyed and I haven't said a word yet.

"How can I help you?" she asks.

I step into her office. It's been a minute since I've been over on this side. I look at pictures on her wall – pictures of her and dad mostly – then I take a moment to enjoy the view of the pond from her window.

"Cherish Stevens," I say.

"Yes? What about her?" she asks.

"Why'd you hire her?"

"She was qualified for the position."

"Qualified how? This position calls for a Bachelor's Degree."

She chuckles. "Don't be a fool, Monty. Nobody needs a degree of any sort to fetch you coffee and clean up behind you."

"The job description calls for a Bachelor's," I reiterate. "She doesn't have one."

"Well, woopty-freakin'-do. That's what brings you over to my side of the house? A question about your personal assistant's qualifications? Screw a Bachelor's Degree. The girl would floss your teeth if you asked her to. She does everything and then some. Of course, you wouldn't appreciate it, though. You don't appreciate anything."

"I was a *mistake* for you, wasn't I?"

She frowns, looks offended. "What are you talking about, Montgomery?"

"I was a mistake. You don't like me. You *love* Major. Everybody loves Major. He can do no wrong, but when it comes to me—all I see is disgust in your eyes when you look at me."

"That's not true."

"It *is* true! It's been true for a long time."

She sighs. Pushes her glasses back on her face properly and says, "Then you know what, Montgomery—you believe what you want to believe. I've done the best I could by you. The *best* I could! You only care about what *Montgomery* wants. None of us matter to you. I don't matter, your brother doesn't matter—"

"You do matter—"

"No, I don't," she yells, "Because if I did, you wouldn't refer to me as *Mrs. Hawthorne*. You would call me your *mother*! If your father knew the man you've become, he'd be ashamed."

"He made me who I am," I say coldly and without pause, although my heart hurts that I've upset her. I don't know how to fix what I've done. "But thanks for confirming you're ashamed of me. Have a good day."

I leave her office in a hurry and step outside for air. I'm losing it. Losing control. I don't know what's wrong with me, but I know I can't keep living like this.

The landscapers are here again maintaining the property. It's a lot of land. I thought about selling some of it but I like the solitude of not having neighbors. Land offers privacy – something I need a lot of.

I take the steps to the ground and stand in the driveway, looking over at the worker's cars in visitor parking. There's a mini-van, a Mazda, a beat-up Honda Accord and a white Honda Pilot. The Mazda belongs to Cherish.

I find myself walking around the yard again today, same as I did yesterday. I'm not looking for Cherish. I'm just trying to get my mind right so I can do some work, but I spot her near the west entrance, working in yet another flowerbed.

Chapter Seven

Cherish

"Oh, no," I say quietly to myself when I see Montgomery heading toward me.

"No. No. No. Please don't come over here," I say quietly.

I can't handle another run-in with him. What does he want, anyway? Maybe he'll pass me by.

Or, maybe not.

He coming straight for me and when he's close, he stands on the opposite side of the flowerbed watching me work. He doesn't say a thing. Just stands there – same crap he did yesterday. I can't concentrate so my eyes climb his frame until I catch a glimpse of his mean, green gaze and look away.

"What made you think I'd want a bagel this morning?" he asks.

Okay, Cherish. Keep a level head. Don't let this man get to you. Remember what Naomi said...

"I just thought you'd like to try something different. You used to eat bagels back in the day."

"Yeah, that was then. Don't add them to any menus. Got it?"

"Why not?"

"Because I'm asking you *not* to. That's all the explanation you need. And why are you out here working in these flowers again?"

Cherish, DON'T let him get to you. "Just doing my job, Sir."

"Actually, you're not. This isn't one of the duties listed

on your job description, so starting now, I want you to cease doing yard work."

"Are you kidding me?"

He frowns. "No, I'm not *kidding* you. You need to be doing other things. Business-related things. Filing. Typing. Checking my mail and taking my clothes to the cleaners."

"You have nothing that needs to be filed or typed here. Your secretary handles those things for you. As for your clothes, I'm scheduled to drop by the cleaners at two and I always check your post office box at three, you know, *after* the mail is put in there. It wouldn't make much sense to check it before then, now would it?"

I can feel the heat of his gaze intensify before he says, "Pack all of this stuff up and give it to the landscapers. If I see you out here planting flowers, rolling around in the dirt or whatever other nonsense you like to do out here, you're fired."

He turns his back to me and begins to walk away. I know I should let it go, but I can't because I didn't do anything to this man to warrant this kind of attack on me. Two days in a row he's been at my throat and now he's telling me I can't plant flowers – one of the few things that keep me sane while working in this glorified prison.

Just let it go, Cherish. Let it go. Just let it—

"What exactly is your problem?" I ask.

He stops. Turns around. "Excuse me?"

I stand up with my dirty hands and a small shovel. "What's your problem?"

"I don't have a problem. I like things a certain way and I like people to do what they're hired to do."

"I've been doing this for two years. Two! Now, all of a sudden you have a problem with it and apparently with me, too. I don't understand. Is this because you saw me in your closet yesterday? Because you thought the white girl was picking out your clothes. If you want Paige as your assistant then, by all means, go for it."

He takes a few intimidating steps back towards me and

asks, "Why do you think I owe you an explanation?"

I swallow the lump in my throat, stand my ground and respond, "You're telling me *not* to do my job and I take offense to that. You could at least give me a reason."

"I *gave* you a reason. What you're doing is not in your job description."

"Then add it."

"No."

"Why not?"

"There you go again asking questions. I said *no*. That's final. Have a good day, *Cherry*."

He walks away again, wearing the suit *I* picked out for him with a smug look of satisfaction on his face. I had good mind to throw some dirt at him, but I'm not like him. I'm not evil for no reason. All the money in the world and he gets his satisfaction from antagonizing *me*.

I pack up everything – the flowers, the shovels, the soil, the fertilizer – I pack it all up and take it over to Consuela.

"Hey, amiga. What'cha doing?"

"Here, just take this stuff."

"Why? What's wrong?"

"The *boss* says I can't work in the flowers any longer."

"Why not?"

"He says it's not in my job description."

"That's friggin' insane. You do this all the time. Now, all of a sudden, it's a problem?"

"Yep. Anyway, take the flowers."

"Yeah, I'll finish the flowerbed. Don't worry."

"Thanks, Consuela."

I'm walking across the thick, dark green grass toward the house. I have no motivation to do any more work today. I want to leave and by *leave* I mean get in my car, step on the gas and never come back to this awful place. It's the same sentiment I express to Naomi as she prepares Montgomery's lunch.

"No, hun, you can't quit."

"I can't take it, Naomi. I've done nothing but serve this

man to the best of my ability and he's after me like I'm a bad employee."

"He's just going through one of his spells. You know how it is."

"No, I don't know how it is. I'm not crazy and therefore I don't relate to crazy."

She chuckles.

"This is the most he's ever interacted with me and now, I feel like I can't get away from him. I can't take this!"

"Then here's what you do. Call Mrs. Sylvia and take the day off tomorrow. That'll give you a chance to take a breather and get away from him for a while. Ain't no need in messin' up your coins over that man's attitude, honey."

"You're right. And on that note, let me get back to work before *massa* comes-a-lookin'."

Naomi laughs.

***

It makes absolutely no sense that I have to sneak out of this house to get to my car, but that's exactly what I'm doing. I tiptoe to the coat closet, take my purse, ease the front door open and, quietly pull the door closed behind me so it doesn't make a sound. Once I'm inside my car, I feel safe. I made it.

Shrew!

I start it up and get out of dodge, turn up the radio and lose myself in the noise – anything to make me forget about my day.

When I'm home, I fix up a salad – nothing fancy. Tomatoes, lettuce, some shredded cheese and ranch dressing. I watch thirty minutes of TV while I eat and as I'm finishing up my dinner, my mother calls. Two calls from her in two days. It's a new record. I'm sure she's not calling to see how I'm doing. It's always something about my stepfather – the man I refer to as her husband – Webster Gregory – a name I wish I could erase from my memory bank.

I'm not in the mood to talk to her so I let it go to voicemail. I'm sure she won't leave one. She hates leaving messages. She'd prefer to talk to me – to torture me in real time. Unfortunately, I don't prefer to talk to her.

I use what little daylight I have left to go outside and check on my flowers. My babies. Screw Montgomery and his yard! I have a yard of my own – one that I'm very proud of. I have marigolds (yellow and orange), zinnias, hydrangeas, tulips, hostas, petunias – there's a wide variety, all with healthy blooms. It's a hummingbird's paradise.

I pluck off dead leaves and water all the plants and when I'm done outside, I go straight for the bathroom. It's seven-thirty. I have just enough time to shower and get ready for bed.

I don't know why I'm going to bed at eight when I have plans to call out of work tomorrow. I've never called out of work like this before, but I'm not changing my mind. There will be no change of heart in the morning. I'm not going to be Montgomery's superwoman tomorrow. So, I don't set my alarm. I'll get up when I get up.

For now, though, I just lie here, entangled in covers with a lot on my mind. I try to decide what day I want to call my mother back. I ponder over what she has to tell me *this* time about her husband. I think about how much torture I had to endure in that house when I was growing up. Living in dysfunction. And then I think about my Aunt Jolene – the woman who rescued me. I was on a downward spiral before she took me in, gave me this place as a safe haven. Now, she's gone.

I sigh and close my eyes, drifting off to sleep when I hear Montgomery's demanding voice echo loud in my head saying, "GET OUT OF THOSE FLOWERS!"

My eyes fly open in a panic and I sit straight up in the center of my bed. My heart is thumping faster than I can breathe. My pulse races. A cold chill takes over my entire body. Is this man in my house?

I flick on the lamp and look to the right and left to make sure he's not in my bedroom. There's no one here, but the voice was so clear and vivid, it has me shook. I ease off the bed, grab the baseball bat I keep next to the door and tiptoe down the hallway toward the living room. I check the kitchen. I double and triple check the locks on the doors, and then I'm finally able to calm myself down. No one's here and I'm losing my freakin' mind.

Relieved, I lower the bat, grab a bottle of water and return to my bedroom. I lock the door – I usually lock my bedroom door at night even though I'm the only one who lives here – then I move the bat closer to the bed beside the nightstand.

Montgomery St. Claire is going to be the death of me.

Now, I can't sleep because when I close my eyes, I see his face. Before, that was a good thing. I used to have dreams about him and that handsome face of his. That was when I first started working for him – when I didn't know any better and thought he was a normal, down-to-earth kind of guy. Even after discovering he was the exact opposite, I still made excuses for him. Like, maybe it was the pressure of his job that had him throwing papers and yelling at people. It's a lot to run such a huge organization and handle large quantities of money. He projects self-confidence and has everyone thinking he has it all together, but what if he really doesn't? We all have our struggles, right? I often wonder what his are. What makes such a handsome, beautiful soul come across as so broken?

Chapter Eight

Monty

I slap the alarm to silence it and prepare to start my Friday. I shower, brush my teeth, rake my fingers through my hair, a reminder that I need a cut – then I head over to the closet noticing right away there's no suit laid out for me. No shoes, no socks, no necktie, no cufflinks. Nothing.

Either Cherish isn't here, or she's doing this to spite me since I've banned her from the flower garden. I take a step back into the bedroom. I walked right by a minute ago and didn't realize the bed was unmade. My slippers are still beside them. The water bottle I had last night remains on the nightstand. So does the cufflinks and my Rolex. Cherish hasn't done her job this morning.

I smirk. "Okay, so you wanna play dirty, huh, flower girl?"

Little does she know it's nothing to me. I don't care what she does or what special talent she thinks she possesses. Everyone is replaceable. *Everyone*, especially a girl with no college education who makes beds and run errands for a living.

I return to the closet and pick out my own clothes – a black suit, black shirt, black tie, black shoes. I have a feeling I'll be in a dark mood today. May as well dress for the occasion.

I go straight to my office downstairs and notice right away I don't have coffee. I keep walking, heading for the kitchen where no coffee is being made. Nothing is being done, actually.

"Naomi! Where are you?"

Now, I'm frustrated. I don't know where the coffee is stored. When I see Minnie walk into the kitchen, I ask her, "Where's Naomi?"

She pulls white earplugs from her ears and says, "Sorry, Sir. Did you need something?"

"Naomi—where is she? Is she late?"

"No, Sir. Naomi doesn't get in until 6:30 a.m."

"Six-thirty? Are you sure about that, Minnie?" I ask, frowning.

"Yes, Sir. Every morning she's here at 6:30 give or take a few minutes."

"Then who makes the coffee before she gets here? I always have coffee on my desk. This morning, there's nothing."

"Oh. Cherish usually takes care of that, Sir."

"Cherish?" I glare at her, offering her my rage since she's the only one here to receive it.

"Yes, Sir."

"And where is *Cherish*?"

"I'm not sure, Sir."

"Right. Okay, well you make me some coffee until Naomi gets in."

"Yes, Sir," she says.

"And bring a cup to my office. Do you know where my office is?"

"Yes, I think so."

"What do you mean you *think* so? Don't you do the cleaning around here?"

"Yes, Sir, but not for you. I do the common areas and your mother's residence. I don't have access to your residence."

"You do today. I'll leave the entrance unlocked."

I walk away from her – retreat back to my office where I put in a few phone calls about components I need to tweak the taser design. Minnie walks in with a mug a few minutes later. Her hand is shaking so bad, I fear she'll spill coffee all over my desk, so I get up and meet her halfway.

"Sorry. I'm a little nervous."

"I can see that. Hey, before you go, tell me something. If you don't clean my office, who does? Isidora?"

"No, Sir. Cherish cleans your office. She pretty much does everything for you."

"What does *everything* entail?"

"Um, everything involving your residence she cleans and organizes—your bathrooms, closets. She arranges for your cars to be washed once a week even though you don't drive them most days. She prepares a menu for you. Like I said she does everything that concerns you."

"And how does working in flower gardens concern me?"

"Oh," she smiles. "Cherish loves flowers, Sir. You should see her front yard."

"I didn't ask you about *her* yard. I asked about mine. How does working in a flower garden concern me?"

She looks conflicted for a moment then says, "Cherish once told me you stand at your window a lot. Said she wanted to make your view as bright and beautiful as possible. Said flowers make her happy and she was hoping they'd do the same for you."

Now, I'm frowning. "She actually said that?"

"Yes, Sir. She only gardens on your side of the house…just to give you a good view."

I take a sip of coffee and shoo Minnie out of my office. When she's gone, I walk over to the window and look out into the yard. I see all the flowers Cherish has planted. But I'm curious now – I have to see the whole yard to verify Minnie's story. I step outside. The grass is still wet with dew but that doesn't deter me from doing a full lap of the yard. By the time I'm back around to the west entrance, the bottom of my pant legs are wet but I have my answer. None of the other flower beds are as detailed and beautiful as the ones on the west side of the house. Cherish was actually doing something thoughtful for me and I made her stop.

I run upstairs to change suits and when I'm back down, I realize Naomi is here. I can hear her cackling again. When I step into the kitchen, she immediately stops laughing.

"Good morning, Sir," she says.

"Where's Cherish?"

"Uh…I don't know. You might want to check with Mrs. Sylvia."

"You haven't spoken to Cherish today?"

"No, Sir. I'm just gettin' in myself—'bout to get started on your breakfast."

"Don't bother."

"You don't want no breakfast, Sir?"

"No," I tell her, then leave the kitchen, heading for my mother's residence. Once inside, I go straight to her office. I'm not blind to the fact that she's on the phone. I just don't care.

"Where's my assistant today?" I ask.

"Um, I'm going to have to call you back," she tells whoever it is she's talking to, then hangs up. "Have you lost your mind?"

"Where's my assistant?" I ask again.

"Cherish is out today."

"How do you know that?"

"She called me this morning?"

"She called *you*?" I ask, livid. "She's *my* assistant and she called *you*?"

"You think she wants to call you? *Nobody* wants to call you, son." She shakes her head. "You just don't get it."

"Why is my assistant calling you?"

"Because she works for me in case you forgot. I hired Cherish—not you."

"What was her reason for not coming to work?"

"What does it matter? She's off. She has plenty of vacation days and personal leave time if that's what you're concerned about. Seeing as though the girl never takes any time off, she probably has about five weeks worth of time by now."

"That didn't answer my question."

She looks at me with utter disgust and annoyance clouding her features, she says, "I don't know why she's off, Monty. Maybe she had some other business to attend to. *Or* maybe she's just tired of your *bull* and finally couldn't take it anymore. She's probably looking for another job like everybody else around here."

"I'm not going to listen to your insults. I'll find out for myself. Thanks for *nothing*."

I go back to my office, take the keys to Porsche and fire her up, revving the engine. I release the garage door, hit the button to close it back and speed down the long, paved, winding driveway to get to the street. I'm so angry, I can see red and I don't know why. Don't know why I allow myself to get *this* furious over trivial matters. I have no claim over Cherish or what she does with her time. She has every right to call out of work if she wants to, but like a madman, I take offense. I see her absence as retaliation because I banned her from the flowers.

I merge onto the ramp to I-85 South toward Charlotte but I pull over for a moment because my heart is racing. That's not common for me. The last time I felt anything close to it was when I attended my father's funeral. I hold my head and try to get control of myself but it's not working. I feel like I'm losing it. Like a person who shouldn't be driving right now.

The anger building up in my chest encourages me to proceed – to drive to her house and let her know who's the boss since she's obviously forgotten. The five percent rational side of myself tries to make me turn around. To go home and apologize to my mother. To make up for all the wrongs I've done. To use this tightrope I'm walking on as a starting point – a change for the better. To show people that beneath the businessman persona and all the anger, I'm really a good person.

But in the battle between good and bad, bad is winning.

My head hurts. I don't want to go home. I want to check this girl. Put her in her place and find out why she took the day off. When I've accomplished that, then my brain will allow me to continue on with work.

I check the mirrors and start the drive to her house again. I'm on I-85, doing eighty-five even though the speed limit is sixty-five. When a car passes me like I'm going slow, I increase my speed to ninety-five. Pass 'em back. Now, I'm pushing a hundred, weaving in and out of traffic, crossing white lines, passing eighteen wheelers, and dump trucks. When I see the exit for Mallard Creek Road, I floor it and float across three lanes of traffic. When I go for the exit, a pickup truck cuts me off, merges right in front of me. I slam on the brakes. My tires squeal. The car fishtails then goes crazy, sending me back across the lanes opposite of the exit and then—

Chapter Nine

Cherish

I should've done this a long time ago…

It felt so good to sleep in. I haven't had a good, solid night's sleep like that in years. This morning, I got up at nine. Not three. Nine. The sun was already blazing outside. A lukewarm breeze fanned through the thin columns of the porch giving me a pleasant morning to sit on the porch swing and eat a bowl of cereal. I waved at my neighbor – Ms. Kettleworth – who's always breaking her wrinkly old neck, looking over here like I'm her daily dose of entertainment. White lady. Her name should be Ms. *Meddle*worth as much as she stays in my business. She can't help it though. Some people are just naturally nosy. She doesn't mean any harm.

She has a head of gray hair – looks like she slicks it back with baby oil. It removes whatever little body she has in her weak strands. She used to smoke (quit about two years ago) so her skin is decorated with blotches of brown and beige. Her clothes are always sprinkled with cat hair. Even with her dentures in, she pronounces my name *Sherrish* as if she never learned the letters 'C' and 'H' in the word *cherish* makes a 'cha' sound.

She knows my schedule so she came over to ask me what I was doing home. I filled her in on my life for a few minutes, before watering my flowers. Then I came back inside and spruced up the place. I swept and mopped my own floors for a change. I vacuumed. Dusted. It was sort of like being at work, minus the bad vibes. I was totally relaxed and at peace.

AROUND NOON, I settle on the couch with a ham and cheese sandwich. It's interesting what a day off work has done for me. I feel like myself again. Carefree and at ease. There's nothing I can't do or accomplish. Believe it or not, I actually consider calling my mother back. I reach for the phone while the midday news plays in the background. I press Belinda Gregory's name in my contact list and the phone rings. While I wait for her to answer, a BREAKING NEWS headline flashes across the TV screen:

I-85 South shut down because of a one-car accident. All lanes are closed.

A news chopper is showing an aerial view of the scene. There's an overturned vehicle near the cement barrier. It looks bad. Traffic is backed up for miles. Looks like the car is smoking. It's about to catch on fire or still smoldering from a fire that had been put out already. I immediately begin to feel sorry for whoever was driving because they couldn't have survived that.

I hang up the phone when mother doesn't answer. She's probably at work. She works part-time as a receptionist at a dentist office. I refuse to dial her work number. The last time I did that, she nearly had a stroke. Talkin' 'bout she could get in trouble for taking personal calls on the company's phone.

I grab the remote to turn up the volume. The helicopter is still circling the crash scene while the news anchor gives the play-by-play of what's happening. Says this is a single-car accident. Police are investigating what exactly happened. Witnesses say the driver was speeding and lost control. About three state troopers with flashing blue lights on their cruisers have all lanes of traffic blocked. There are two firetrucks. An ambulance is beginning to drive away.

The anchor then says, "If you're just joining us, we have breaking news on I-85 at the Mallard Creek Exit. There's been a single-car accident that currently has all southbound lanes shut down. Police are beginning to divert traffic to the shoulder and around the scene. You will want to avoid this area for at least the next hour or so as traffic is backed up for miles."

Another reporter chimes in, "We just received word that the driver is thirty-three-year-old Montgomery St. Claire of Concord. He's being transported to Atrium Hospital in University City. We do not know his condition at this time."

My heart stops.

I didn't just hear what I think I did, did I? Couldn't have. My mind is playing tricks on me. My hands won't stop shaking. I grab the remote, press rewind and replay the last thirty seconds. I listen intently this time:

"...received word that the driver is thirty-three-year-old Montgomery St. Claire of Concord."

"No. No. Not Montgomery. No..."

I can't breathe.

Can't think.

Can't blink.

And I can't stand up straight without falling over.

This is Montgomery's car that's crushed to a potato chip and flipped upside down on the highway? That's smoldering? That has all lanes blocked? That was *him* in the back of that ambulance? It can't be.

My hands are still trembling. My heart is about to jump out of my chest. This ruthless man who's made my life unbearable for the past two days is also the man I've secretly adored and admired for two years. The mean things he's done to me has no bearing on me in this moment. I'm truly concerned for him.

I have to get to the hospital. I have to see him. I *need* to see him.

* * *

I surprise myself by how fast I'm able to make it to the hospital. I broke laws. Ran lights, but I'm here, looking for Montgomery.

I look for people in nurse's uniforms. All others are just blurs – obstacles in the way of me and the man I'm here for.

"The guy from the I-85 crash, where is he?" I ask in a panic. I feel like sweat is dripping from my face. This isn't real. It can't be. I'm in a bad dream.

"He's in surgery, ma'am."

"Why? Surgery for what, exactly?"

"Are you related to him, ma'am?"

"No. I'm—I'm his assistant. His p-pe-personal assistant. Is he going to be okay?"

"You'll have to wait to talk to the doctor."

"But—"

"Ma'am, please just have a seat here and wait for the doctor."

"Okay. Okay. Um…okay. Thanks," I tell her. I feel no relief. I'm anxious and scared. When I can see through the fog of my brain, I whip out my phone. My hand is shaking so bad, I can't hold the phone steady enough to make a call. I need to call Sylvia. Does she even know?

One of the nurses must witness my struggle. In an act of kindness, she brings me a bottle of water, squeezes my hand and tells me to calm down and wait for the doctor's report. Tells me to pray for my friend. Says no amount of medicine is more powerful than prayer.

"Thank you," I tell her. "I—I have to call his mother. And, and, and…Major. I have to call his brother. I don't know if they know." My hands are steadily shaking.

"Do you want me to call them for you? I'll be glad to."

"No. No. I got it. Thanks."

"If you need anything, I'll be right over here. Okay?"

"Thank you."

She walks away and I take a sip of water and then follow up with deep breaths. I finally dial Sylvia and when she answers, I say, "Sylvia, have you heard?"

"Yes, Cherish. Oh my God! My son," she says, bawling. She sounds so distraught, she makes my eyes fill with sadness.

"I'm at the hospital."

"You're there? How is he? Have they told you anything?"

"No. They don't know yet. He's in surgery."

"Oh, God. Surgery. Oh, God!" She cries harder.

"We're pulling up now, Cherish," Major says. "Come to the front to get Ma so I can go park the car."

"Okay."

I rush to the emergency entrance, to see Sylvia getting out of the car. She's bawling her eyes out. Seeing her in so much pain rattles me. I know her struggles with Montgomery. Know how often they argue, but nothing can thwart a mother's love. It doesn't matter that he was a foster child. That never mattered to her.

I show her to the waiting area, fill her in on everything the nurse told me.

Major comes running in. I can tell he's frazzled though he tries to keep his cool. Probably for our sakes.

"What did they say, Cherish?" Major asks, sitting to the left of me.

Sylvia is on the right.

"They said he's in surgery right now and couldn't tell us much more than that. They won't have an update until he's out."

"Okay."

"Surgery—what kind of surgery?" Sylvia asks.

"We'll find out, Ma," Major tells her, reaching across my lap to hold her hand. "We just gotta be thankful that he's alive at this point."

I nod in agreement. I saw the car. I'm still in shock. I

didn't think anyone would make it out alive.

"How did you find out, Cherish?" Major asks me.

"I was watching the midday news and they switched to a breaking news story about the accident. I didn't know it was Montgomery at first. The car was crushed up so bad, I couldn't make out the model of it. Then they said his name and—I grabbed my keys and floored it here. I apologize if I'm being intrusive. I know I'm not family, but—"

"Nah, don't think like that," he tells me.

"Please don't," Sylvia says. "You *are* family. You wait on Montgomery hand and foot. You're family."

I appreciate this acceptance from them. They know how hard I work for Montgomery. I need the job, but it's never been about the money for me. Since day one, everything I did for Montgomery St. Claire was for him. I recognized how rude he was – how progressively insolent he'd become over the past few months, but I did my job and I did it well.

"Why was he in Charlotte in the first place?" I ask. "Wasn't he working at home today? He typically never leaves to go anywhere before the workday is over."

"He doesn't," Sylvia says, "But he came to my office, livid because he wanted to find out where you were."

"What?" I ask. My heart sinks. Chest nearly caves in.

"He was upset you called out this morning—even more angry that you called *me* instead of him. Said you work for him, you should've called him. We went back-and-forth like we always do and then he wanted to know *why* you took the day off. I told him I wasn't sure and he snapped—said he'd find out for himself. Next thing I know, I heard tires screeching and he was gone."

My body shakes. "Wait—are you telling me this is *my* fault?" I ask with a trembling voice.

"No, Cherish," she says.

"How is it *not* my fault? According to you, he was coming to see me," I say. "*I* did this to him?"

"I don't know for certain if he was coming to see you."

Major puts a hand on my shoulder and says, "Cherish, this isn't your fault. It's nobody's fault."

I hear him, but I'm not listening. This *is* my fault. Had I gone to work today, he wouldn't be here. Wouldn't be in surgery, fighting for his life. Everything would be normal. What have I done?

I look to the left and see Major with his hands interlocked. He wears worry heavy on his face. I look to the right and see Sylvia with her head lowered.

Distraught, I break away from them and run down the hall in full tears, looking for a bathroom through blurred vision. I'm sick to my stomach. What have I done? Who can wake me up from this nightmare?

This can't be happening...

Chapter Ten

Monty
(Subconscious Thoughts)

What goes through the mind of a man who sees his life flash before his eyes? I can tell you what went through mine. When I slammed on the brakes and felt my car fishtailing, I wasn't thinking about my company. Or the car. Or the pure anger I felt on the drive to Charlotte that has resulted in me lying on this operating table. When I saw my life flash before my eyes, I thought of the times when I was happy. I saw my life play out in a series of short segments, sort of like a timeline. I saw a vision of a woman who I believe was my birth mother. I saw my brothers, two of them although I only know one. I saw myself playing basketball with Major. I saw Sylvia – remembered how she cooked for us when she didn't have to. When she could've had chefs and caterers do the job. I recall my father working. Working so hard, he left the rearing of us to mother. He made the money. She made the house a home. I remember the moment I knew I'd rather have my father's talents and his ability to block everything out. I needed that ability.

I was lost as a teen. I shouldn't have been. I should've felt lucky to have been fostered by Caspian and Sylvia Hawthorne, but I didn't. I've always felt like I was missing something mostly because I was raised by people who could do a stellar job of taking care of me financially but never give me their last name. I was lost. I had no identity until working gave me one. Until I became someone because of what I could do. Who I could be. The products I could create. The money I could make.

When my life flashed before my eyes, it was my relationships or lack thereof that haunted me. It was the fact that Sylvia Hawthorne loved me. No matter how awful I was to her, she loved me, but like my father, I didn't have time to love her the way she deserved.

It was the fact that my brother was supposed to look up to me. Instead, he despises me. I let him down.

It was the fact that I, as a thirty-three-year-old man have never experienced love. Real love. Never knew how to. Never loved a woman. Never even considered giving my heart to a woman. Dying today would mean I would never have that chance to love. To have children. To tell my mother I love her and that I'm sorry. To tell my brother to do everything in his power to make sure he doesn't end up like me. To redeem myself. To treat people like *people* instead of servants.

For the first time in my life accolades, the billions I have in the bank or whatever invention I was working on doesn't matter to me. Faced with death, I'm thinking about all the things I regret because accomplishments have already been accomplished. Regrets are open wounds that, shall I perish, I'll never get a chance to heal them. That's what hurts the most when they pulled me out of my crushed car. Hurts more than the cuts on my face, chest and leg. More than my cracked ribs. More than these bruises.

I'm out. I can't feel a thing but I know there's a team of doctors and nurses working on me. While I'm sure I'm supposed to be dead right now, I tell myself that, if I survive this, I'll be a better person like I'm making a deal with the man above, pleading for a chance to right my wrongs. I need that chance.

I need it.

Chapter Eleven

Cherish

After two of the longest hours in history, the doctor finally comes out to give us some news. He says Montgomery is stable. And lucky. *Very* lucky. It could've been much worse, and probably should've been.

"He's stable—wha, wha, what exactly does that mean?" Sylvia stammers.

"He's doing okay," the doctor responds. "He came in with two cracked ribs, bruises, lacerations on his legs and cuts on his face. But, he's alive and he's going to make it."

"Thank you, doctor," Major says reaching to shake his hand.

"Yes, thank you," Sylvia adds. "Thank you so much for saving my son's life."

The doctor gives a modest nod. "You'll be able to see him soon, but right now, he needs to rest. He's on heavy pain medication and he'll be on them for a few days, so he'll be out for a while."

"How soon can we see him?" Sylvia asks desperately.

"Let's give it a few hours."

"Okay. Thank you."

We sit down again. Time doesn't seem to exist when something like this happens, but Major points out that it's after seven in the evening. Suggests we get something to eat.

"How can you eat at a time like this?" Sylvia asks him.

"Mother, the doctor said Monty's stable. I'm more worried about *you* than him right now. You've had nothing to eat or drink since we got here six hours ago."

"I'm fine, Major."

"No, you're—"

"I said I'm fine," she interjects with a raised voice.

"Well, let's just take a walk, Sylvia," I tell her. I take her hand. She accepts.

We walk outside first. It's almost dark. The air is thick and humid – the kind of air that makes it hard for people with respiratory issues to breathe. It doesn't take long for us to make our way back inside the air-conditioned hospital. We walk toward the cafeteria. I'm still holding Sylvia's hand.

Major is behind us talking to somebody on his cell.

"Let's get something to drink," I tell Sylvia as we approach the cafeteria. Like her, I don't have an appetite. My stomach can't handle food right now. Maybe once I lay eyes on Montgomery and confirm he's okay, I'll be better. Until then, we sit and drink watermelon-flavored water lost our thoughts.

Major's phone rings again. He leaves the table to take the call in the hallway.

Sylvia looks at me and says, "You know something, Cherish—I did the best I could with those boys."

"I know you did, Sylvia. Everyone knows that. We see how hard you try with Montgomery."

"But I lost him. Somewhere inside of him is the man I know he can be. A decent man. One who knows how to love. How to treat people. But that man is trapped. He won't come out."

I'm nodding. It's what I've always believed about Montgomery. "You're right. I've always believed that—just never seen it. Montgomery's a good man. You did a fantastic job raising him and no, you didn't lose him, Sylvia. As long as he still has breath in his body, you didn't lose him. He just needs an outlet. Somebody he can talk to. Get things off his chest. Get pain out of his heart because there's plenty of it there."

She nods. Sips water. "He was so angry this morning.

He's always angry."

"Why is he so angry?"

"He's been that way since his father died."

"He was close to him, I take it." Naomi already told me as much but I want to hear it directly from her.

"Yes. He's an exact representation of him. Yet, their relationship wasn't all that great. Yes, Montgomery admired his father's work but their bond was lacking. Foster children or not, they still should've had *that* much. I've always had a motherly bond with them since they were boys, but then again, I wanted children, more so than my husband. I had to nearly beg him to have children. I remember when he finally agreed we could try to have a baby. We tried and tried but I never got pregnant. Don't know why. It just didn't happen. So I talked to him about adoption. Caspian Hawthorne didn't want to hear it. Said if he wasn't raising his own kids, he for sure wasn't going to raise someone else's. Taking in some foster children was the compromise. To my surprise, he agreed, partly because with foster children, you know, the arrangement is supposed to be temporary. You keep them until they can be placed in a permanent home. He thought we'd only have them for a few years. We ended up having them forever."

She smiles. Remembering.

"I was so happy. The older they got, the more I realized they weren't going anywhere. They were *my* children, and I loved them like my children. My husband, on the other hand, he wasn't so fatherly. I believe Montgomery recognized this early on. I think that's why the business interested him so much. He knew it's what interested his father and so that was the only way they could have a connection. Not through love. Through work."

"How did Major turn out so differently?" I inquire. "Aren't they biological siblings?"

"Yes. They have the same mother and father, and I

don't know how Major turned out differently to be honest with you. The only thing I can attribute it to is he didn't spend as much time with my husband. He spent a lot of time with his friends. He and Monty have always had distinct personalities."

"I noticed that soon after I started working for you. Major would always greet me. Montgomery would walk right past me like I was an object instead of a person."

Sylvia shakes her head. "I tried so hard to get through to him, Cherish. I really did."

"I know."

She sips water. "Can I ask you something?"

"Sure."

"You never call out of work. Why did you call out this morning?"

"Because Montgomery had been torturing me for the last couple of days, being nitpicky like I wasn't doing my job to his liking."

"What do you mean?"

"He saw me in his closet and looked at me like I didn't belong. I pick out his suits every morning and he was being so rude to me. Yesterday, he blew up about the breakfast menu and then he told me I couldn't work in the flowers anymore. He was taunting me for no reason at all. Totally unprovoked. I wanted to quit. Naomi talked me into just calling out."

"I'm glad she did. You can't quit. Montgomery needs you around there. He has too much pride to admit that, but deep down, he knows it. I think that's why he was coming to see you. That was so out of character for him. Do you know how many assistants have quit before I hired you?"

"No. How many?"

"Four."

My eyes brighten. "Four!"

"Yes. Four. The last thing he needs is for someone else to quit on him. I argue with him, disagree with him all the time, but I've never quit on my son and I never will."

"I just don't know how to deal with him sometimes—no, scratch that—I don't know how to deal with him at all. Plus, I'm sure I'm the last person he wants to see after everything that has happened."

"That hard persona he exudes is just a cry for help. He needs you more than you know, Cherish. If anyone can help him, it's you."

I frown. "How do you figure that?"

She looks at me like she knows something I don't – like she knows something I *should* know. A faint smile appears then disappears just as quickly. "Because it's obvious you can get to him in ways we can't."

"Obvious to who because nothing gets under his skin?"

"Then why was he coming to see you? Montgomery is not the type to chase after nobody. Employees come and go. What does he care? He doesn't form bonds with anyone. He's lost that ability—at least so I thought. But you—somehow, you got to him."

"Sylvia, I promise I didn't do a thing to him. Montgomery hasn't bothered me or paid any attention to me for two years and—"

"That's what you think."

"No, it's what I *know*. I'm practically invisible."

"Then why on several occasions last summer, I observe him standing at the window watching you leave?"

"Last summer?"

"Yes. So you see…you're not *invisible* after all. You can get to him."

"No," I say, shaking my head. "I doubt if he was looking at me. He was probably plotting his next move on somebody. Like I said, *I'm* invisible."

"Well, whatever the case, I see how hard you work for him, Cherish. I know how much you care about my son."

Actually, she has no idea how much I care. She says it, but I doubt very seriously if she *really* knows. When I made Montgomery this perfect man in my head – a man who could do no wrong, a man who'd give his last for the sake of his family, a man who could love so hard, he rendered you breathless—I fell for *that* man. My made up version of him. The real Montgomery is nothing like that and after this, I imagine he'll be much worse.

"What happened?" Paige says, bursting into the cafeteria, causing a scene with her bleach-blond hair in the wind behind her as she makes a mad dash to the table where Sylvia and I are sitting. I swear if she puts anymore dye in that hair it'll be Casper-The-Friendly-Ghost white.

The color drains from Sylvia's face. She rolls her eyes and says, "Lord have mercy. Who called that child?"

I'm amused, but at the same time, I'm curious about her working relationship with Paige and why Paige feels she's an integral part of the family. Sylvia seems annoyed whenever she's around.

"What happened to Monty, Sylvia?" Paige asks all wide-eyed and open-mouthed.

"From what I understand he lost control of the car. It flipped several times and—"

"No!" she says, placing a hand on her chest. "Is he alright? Please tell me he's alright."

"He's out of surgery. We haven't had a chance to see him yet."

Paige looks at me and frowns. "And what are *you* doing here?"

I narrow my eyes at her. She has some nerve…

"I'm here for support—same reason you're here, right?"

She flashes a fake smile. After all the theatrics when she entered the cafeteria, there isn't a single tear in her eyes or on her face. She's a phony. I never did like that girl.

"Ay...the doc says we can see him now," Major announces, stepping into the cafeteria.

We – myself, Sylvia and Paige – all stand at the same time. Paige out walks us and keeps up with Major.

Sylvia takes my hand again. She needs emotional

support.

WE GET TO the room. The shift nurse informs us we should go in two at a time. Sylvia's hand trembles in mine. She squeezes it tighter.

"I need to see him," Paige says acting all antsy. "I need to make sure he's okay."

Major gives her a choking stare. Seems he doesn't like the broad either. "Ma, why don't you and Paige go in. Me and Cherish will wait out here in the hallway."

Sylvia is still squeezing my hand. "It's okay, Sylvia. Go see him."

She lets go, enters with Paige. My heart breaks when I hear her break down as soon as she steps inside. She's crying, trying to keep it down, but it's hard. I want to yell at Paige for not doing anything to console her. Paige just doesn't have a nurturing side. All she cares about is hair extensions and acrylic nails.

Sylvia cries. Cries for her son. Wails for him. My heart can't take it. I look at Major. "I have to go in there with her," I tell him.

"Please do. Send Paige out. I don't know why she's here, anyway."

I push the door all the way open, walk in to see Sylvia crying over Montgomery. She's a mess. She has every right to be. He's now bruised and broken physically. His outside matches the inside – the broken things we can't see.

Paige is standing on the opposite side of the bed just staring down at Montgomery like he's an inanimate object. She sheds no tears. Just stands in shock, almost like she's afraid of him.

I consider slapping her in the back of the head but instead, I say, "Paige, Major wants you in the hallway."

She turns and walks out.

I go to Sylvia, wrap my arms around her and say, "He's alive, Sylvia. He's breathing. That's what we need to be thankful for right now."

"I know," she snivels. More tears fall. A downpour of them. "But look at him, Cherish. Look at his face."

I look at him. In my mind, I see the Montgomery I'm obsessed with – my version of him – because my mind won't let me see the real version since he's in such a delicate state. I look at his face. I swallow the hurt of seeing him this way. I know I have to keep my tears to myself. I'm here for Sylvia. She needs me. I have to be strong even though I feel like crying right along with her.

I find some inner strength to console her. I tell her he's in good hands. That he's resting and the body has an amazing way of healing itself. I tell her the scars are temporary. The stay in the hospital is also temporary. He's going to make it through this. I haven't seen anything this man can't do. He's strong. He's determined. He's a fighter. Even now.

She kisses him on the forehead and whispers, "I love you, Montgomery."

Makes me think of the things we *wish* we would've told the people we lost before we lost them. She has a second chance to do this. Many people don't get that opportunity.

"Let's go get Major," Sylvia says. "I know he wants to see his brother."

We return to the hallway. Major pulls his mother into his arms. Tells her it's going to be alright. Gives her a tender kiss on the forehead.

I look around for Paige. The heffa's gone.

Sylvia releases Major and says, "Go on in and see him."

Major enters the room while we wait in the hallway.

Sylvia looks at me and says, "Thank you so much for being here, Cherish."

"You're welcome, Sylvia."

Major doesn't stay in the room long. I know him so I can sense his sadness. Can see it in his eyes. He's doing the male thing and fighting his emotions. "The doctor says only one person can stay in the room overnight."

"I'm staying," Sylvia calls out.

I want to stay, too. Want to go back into the room and have *my* time to talk to him. To be alone with him. Since consoling Sylvia, I didn't get a chance to do that.

"I know, Ma. I'm going to go get your bag out of the car. As a matter of fact, why don't you take a walk with me so we can talk," he tells her. "Cherish, can you wait with Monty until we get back?" he asks. He winks like he's telling me he's giving me time to see Montgomery. Alone.

"Of course."

As they walk away, I go back inside the room and look at him. I walk closer to the bed. He's beneath white sheets. There's an IV in his hand. I can see probes on his chest and bandages. I stare at his face. He has stitches above his right eye. Scars are all over his face.

His beautiful face…

I gently trace every scar with my fingertip, even the bruise on his lip. I use the words I told Sylvia moments ago to console myself. I'm grateful he has breath. He's alive. He's got a second chance at life.

I take his hand. Hold it. I look at his face again. Tears come to my eyes. "Why'd you have to get in that car? Why, Montgomery? Why do you have to be so mad all the time? Why can't you just be happy?" I say, in full tears, leaning down to rest my head near his shoulder. "You have everything you've ever dreamed of. Everything. Why did you have to get in that car?" I ask. My tears have gotten the best of me. I know I'm a mess, but I can't help it. It's hard to watch someone throw everything away. Sylvia's right. Somebody needs to get through to him.

"Cherish?"

I jump, startled that Major's back so quickly. I turn around to look at him using both hands to smear tears away from my face. I sniffle. Try to compose myself though I'm still shaken. Still producing tears that I try to blink away.

"It's not your fault," he says. "You know that right?"

"It sure feels like my fault," I tell him. "Where's your mom?"

"She's out in the hallway on the phone."

"Okay. I'm going to say bye to her and go home. Would it be okay if I come back in the morning?"

"Fine by me. I mean, you are his personal assistant, right?"

I flash a pitiful, half-smile. "Right."

Major embraces me. Tells me to try to get some sleep. I tell him the same.

Out in the hallway, I wait for Sylvia to get off the phone. When she does, she looks at me and says, "Are you leaving?"

"Yes. I don't live far...took me about ten minutes to get here. I'll be back early tomorrow morning. Probably around six or so."

"Okay, Cherish. Thank you so much for coming."

"No problem, and if anything changes with him tonight, will you let me know?"

"Of course." She hugs me tight – one of those meaningful, appreciative hugs.

"I'll see you in the morning," I tell her when we part.

"Okay."

I walk away, seeking the exit but I feel like I need to stay. Like I can feel Montgomery's energy pulling me back with every step I take forward.

Chapter Twelve

Monty
(Subconscious Thoughts)

More insight runs through my mind while I'm out of it but there's a question that keeps reverberating throughout the cloudiness of my thoughts: *Who are those people who would be there for you if you found yourself tubed up and near death on a hospital bed?*

If I'm answering this in general, it would be the people closest to you. Your family. Close friends. Maybe even a workmate or two. If I'm answering it specifically for myself, I'd say no one, not because I truly believe that. It's because it's what I deserve.

I know my mother's here. I can feel her presence.

I know my brother's here. He's blood. He has no choice but to love me.

In and out of consciousness, I heard a couple of other voices besides theirs. Maybe the nurses and doctors. Not sure. What I am sure of is, there's no reason why anyone else would step a foot in here to see me.

I can't say I blame them.

I'm not a nice person. Never tried to be. I don't like that about myself. If I'm to be punished for my wrongs, then I deserved to die. Lying here, it has crossed my mind. If I'd died on the highway, I'd be out of my misery and so would everyone else who had to cross my path. There would be no more worries. No more chasing money. No more running a business for a man who didn't love me enough to adopt me as his own. No more of me disappointing people. I'd cease to exist with no memory of all the bad I've done. I'd just be gone.

A voice steers the direction of my subconscious mind. It's my mother. She's here again. I can make out some of what she saying:

"We love you...come home. We're a family and...stick together. I wish...done better...for you and Major. You two are all I have...if I lost you..."

I imagine she's crying. If I could wake up, I'd tell her to stop. There's no need to waste tears over me. I've caused her enough grief already.

Chapter Thirteen

Cherish

I didn't get one full hour of sleep last night. Every time I made an attempt, I saw Montgomery's scarred face. His accident made me realize how fleeting and precious life is. Just the day before, he was so well put together and had the world at his fingertips. Now, he's laid up in a hospital bed, fighting for his life.

This is heavy on my mind this morning – life, and how we take it for granted. Tomorrow isn't promised to no one, yet, I haven't spoken to my mother in so long, I don't even feel connected to her. I called the other day, she didn't answer, so I make it a point to call her now since it's early. She's not at work yet. Probably getting ready for work.

The phone rings, and rings, and rings and then…

"Hello?"

"Hey," I say.

"Who's this?"

"It's your daughter, Ma," I try to say without a hint of derision in my voice but I know I failed.

"Oh." She chuckles. "I ain't heard from you in so long, I done forgot the sound of your voice. Ain't that a shame? You should call your mama more often, girl."

"I tried to call you yesterday, or the day before—I don't remember. You didn't answer. I figured you were at work. I know how you don't like to answer your phone at work."

"Well, I can't. Everybody be breathing down my back enough as it is when I'm on the phone, but when they take personal calls, it's not a problem."

"That's the way it is, I guess," I say pretending to be interested in her work drama. I'm not by any means, but if this is how we break the ice to discuss other issues, then so be it.

"So, how's work going?" she asks me.

"It's fine."

"You still working as a maid for them rich folk?"

"I'm not a *maid*. I'm a personal assistant."

"Potato, potahto...same difference."

"Whatever you say, Ma, but yes. I'm still there. It pays the bills."

"Speaking of paying the bills, your stepfather—"

"Don't call him that," I say interrupting. "He's not my stepfather! He's no kind of *father* to me."

"As I was saying—he's retiring soon. I may not have to work much longer."

"Yippee, good for you," I say as drab and uninterested as I can while my eyes do a full three-sixty.

She sighs. "I understand you don't like him."

"That's an understatement."

"But life goes on, Cherish. Do you think I wanted your father to die? And what was I supposed to do? Stay single forever?"

"No, but you could've at least waited to marry a *decent* man."

She sneers. "Unbelievable. Why is it that every time I'm on the phone with you, you have to say something demeaning about your stepfather?"

"He's not my stepfather!"

"He took care of you."

"Yeah, he sure did, didn't he? That's why I left home and moved with Aunt Jo when I was sixteen, right? Because he took *real* good care of me."

"You know what—I'm not gon' listen to this nonsense."

And then the phone goes silent. She hangs up. That's

how our phone conversations go – it always ends with one of us hanging up on the other. But I tried, right? I take my 'E' for effort and go on about my day.

* * *

At the hospital, I get up to Montgomery's room only to find that Sylvia's not there. I see her bag, but not her. She probably went to the cafeteria to get some breakfast. I take advantage of the alone time with Montgomery to look him over. Nothing's changed since yesterday not that I expected it to. I look at the monitor. His blood pressure is a little elevated, but not enough to set off any alarms. I'm not sure what the other numbers are.

I take his hand into mine again, same as I did last night. I'm feeling his energy. It tells me he's going to be okay. Gosh, I can feel his energy so well, like he's temporarily become a part of me.

"Good morning, Mr. St. Claire," I say, talking to him *normally*. Maybe he needs this sort of interaction to wake up and shake the pain meds. Most likely, he can't hear me, but I don't care. I want him to know that somebody's here. That somebody cares, and he's not alone.

"It's sunny today," I continue. "The high is supposed to be eighty-seven degrees."

I look at his hand. It's big enough to palm my head. Big enough to secure both my wrists.

"I know you're going to make it through this. You're a fighter. You don't give up. I know you're a good man beneath it all, Montgomery, but you fight so hard not to show it. That's what people need the most from you— your kindness. They need to know that behind the suit, there's a human."

I take a breath and keep my tears at bay.

"Good morning," Major says, stepping inside the room wearing a black suit.

"Good morning, Major," I respond, looking at him

before returning my attention to Montgomery. "Did you stay with him last night?" I ask.

"No. Mom stayed."

"Oh. Right. She must've gone down to the cafeteria to get some breakfast, huh?"

"Probably."

Major takes a few more steps over to the bed, on the opposite side as me. I'm still holding Montgomery's hand. I can't take my eyes off of his face. The scars are there but I don't see them. I just see him.

"Cherish."

I look up at Major when he says my name. "Yes?"

"How long have you been in love with my brother?" he asks.

I hold his gaze as if I'd been caught, then I try to backtrack my way out of what I've already told him with my eyes and say, "Um...I'm not."

He smiles. "We both know that's not true," he says, glancing at his brother's hand in mine.

I still won't let it go. "Okay," I begin. "I'm not in love with him. I just—I—I love the person he could be. Someone who doesn't hold on to anger and resentment. Someone who helps others. Who has a good relationship with his mother."

"Oh, so you're in love with me."

I laugh.

He grins.

Major is all of those things. But my soul doesn't pull me to Major the same way it steers me to Montgomery.

He says, "If you really care about him, help him."

"You know, your mother told me the same thing, Major, but how am I supposed to do that? I'm twenty-six—I hardly have my own life together and I'm supposed to *somehow* work magic to whip Montgomery into shape?"

"You care about him, don't you?"

"Yes, but—" I take my attention away from Major to look at Montgomery's face again. "I don't know if I'm strong enough to go through this process with him. As a matter of fact, I was thinking about quitting."

As soon as I finish the statement, I feel Montgomery's hand squeeze mine tight — so tight it makes me cower to withstand it. He has a death grip on me.

"What's wrong with you?" Major asks, frowning.

"Oww. Montgomery's squeezing my hand. Ouch!"

"What?"

"Montgomery's squeezing my hand! Oh my gosh, it's getting tighter."

"Maybe he heard what you said."

"How could he have heard me? He's high on morphine and whatever else they doped him up with." I'm struggling, trying to get my hand out of Montgomery's grasp, but it's to no avail. "Major, he won't let me go. He probably thinks it's my neck. Oww!"

Major laughs. "You think my brother, a hospital patient who survived a horrific car crash, is trying to choke you out?"

"Stop laughing and do something, Major?"

He chuckles. "What do you want *me* to do? I don't have any butter or baby oil." He laughs more.

"Pull his arm or something."

He still finds this amusing. Meanwhile, I'm losing blood circulation in my hand.

Major finally comes around and tries to free me but even he can't break the grip.

"Come on, Major. You didn't eat your Wheaties this morning?"

"Hush, girl. Nobody eats Wheaties anymore."

He's steadily pulling. Ain't nothing happening. Nothing moving.

"At what point did he grab you like this?" Major asks.

"When I said I was quitting."

"Then take it back."

"What?"

"Take it back. Tell him you're not quitting. And *mean*

it."

"Are you serious?"

"Yeah, I'm serious. Tell him."

"Okay. I won't quit. Montgomery, I won't quit. I promise."

And what do you know...

He slowly releases the grip on my hand. I massage life back into my wrist and fingers.

"Does that mean he heard me?"

"Yeah, or he has a very active subconscious mind that's not affected by the medication. That's my brother. He never ceases to amaze me."

"Good morning," Sylvia says as she enters the room holding a cup of coffee.

I'm still rubbing my hand. "Hi, Sylvia."

"Mornin', Ma. You should've been here like five minutes sooner. You would've seen Monty grab Cherish."

"What?"

Major grins.

"Don't pay Major any mind. Monty—I mean Montgomery didn't grab me. He's been just like this— sleeping. Soundly."

"I wish he would open his eyes. If I can just see his eyes, I know he'll be okay," Sylvia says.

"Just talk to him," Major says. "Apparently, he can hear you. Ain't that right, Cherish?"

I narrow my eyes at him.

"Something tells me he'll be awake soon," Major adds.

Sylvia sits down. Sips coffee. She asks Major, "How are things at the office?"

"Everybody's wondering if or when Monty's coming back."

"One step at a time," she says. "It's going to take a while for him to heal."

I offer Sylvia my seat – the one next to Montgomery's bed, but she insists I stay here. I take hold of his hand again, rubbing the pad of my thumbs around his impressive knuckles. He could obliterate someone with them. "How did he do last night?" I ask Sylvia.

"He was just like this. Sleep and out of it. The nurses were in and out checking on him."

I look at him again. It makes me sad that a man so strong, so powerful is lying here helpless. I don't feel any kind of hate for him. I don't have it in my heart to reciprocate his bad behavior. Like Sylvia, I too will feel better when I see those eyes of his. When I know he's out of the woods. I want to see him back to himself again, even if he's the same mean, disgruntled version. *Some* of him is better than *none* at this point. I'll take whatever I can get.

Chapter Fourteen

Monty

I'm groggy and I feel like I've been pressed by a steamroller, but I crack my eyes open to a slither, startled by the light in the room. I close them back and wait a moment. My head is killing me.

"You have to make the decision to be strong," I hear someone say. It's then I realize whoever's talking to me is holding my hand.

I crack my eyes open a little. It's blurry. I can't make out a face – just a figure.

"And if you can't do it for yourself, do it for the people who love you. And people do love your mean butt. Your mother, Major—"

I open my eyes all the way to see this person – this woman talking to me. It's Cherish. She's not looking at me. She's looking at my hand. She's *talking* to my hand. I roll my eyes to the left and the right. No one else is in the room with me. It's just her. I'm in a hospital. I'm not dead. The last thing I remember is flipping my car on the highway. I thought that was it for me.

I close my eyes again and listen to her talk.

"If my mother loved me half as much as your mother loved you, I'd be grateful. But my mother—that's a different story. Yours—you two live under the same roof. Well, I don't know if I can actually say that since the house is so massive and everybody has their own *wing*, but she lives there and you don't eat with her. You only talk to her about business, Montgomery. There's more to life than business deals. That's all you do. Business, and maybe that's why you're so pissed off all the time. Why you're so frustrated, and then you push that frustration off on other people."

She massages my hand and continues, "You could be so much more if you allowed your personality—the part of yourself you keep hidden—to shine through. *So* much more."

I open my eyes again. She's still staring at my hand. She has no idea I'm awake.

To get her attention, I squeeze her hand.

She frowns, looks at me and gasps. Her eyes grow big like she's been caught. She stares. Then she frowns. Looks scared

"Montgomery—I mean, Mr. St. Claire?"

I ease the tension on her hand now that I have her attention.

"I should go get a nurse," she says. "Or your mother. Yes, I should go get your mother. She had to step out to take a phone call. Let me go get her."

She gets up, leaves the room in a hurry.

My mother steps in shortly thereafter, eyes bubbling with tears.

"Oh, Monty," she says throwing her arms around me. I thought I was going to lose you." She's crying. Her tears wet my face. "How do you feel?" she asks.

I want to respond to her, but I'm too weak and drugged to talk. My eyes are drifting. It's a struggle to keep them open.

A nurse comes in figuring it's a good time to check my vitals and level of pain while I'm awake. She asks me to rate my pain – ten being the highest. I'm not in a lot of pain thanks to whatever they have me on, so I rate it a five. She asks me if I want some soup for dinner. My eyes roll over to the clock on the wall. It's six o'clock.

I don't respond. I just want to lie here, go back to sleep and wake up when I'm myself again. When I'm not broken, lying in bed waiting for people to take care of me.

So, that's what I do. I lie here.

SOMEBODY MUST'VE TOLD her to bring soup because it arrives around seven. Mother attempts to feed it to me. I move her hand away.

"Son, don't you want to get out of here?"

What kind of question is that? Of course, I want to get out of here. Who likes hospitals?

"Eat just a little bit."

"No," I say barely above a whisper.

"Don't be stubborn, Montgomery."

She takes another spoonful and offers it to me. I close my eyes. Defiant. I'll eat when *I'm* ready to eat.

"I heard my boy was back," Major says as he steps into the room.

I open my eyes to see my brother. I've never been happier to see him than I am at this moment.

"How you feeling, man?" he asks.

I don't feel like talking so I give him a thumbs up.

"You need to tell him to eat this soup," Mother says.

"Ma, he just woke up. Maybe he doesn't want no soup or anything else just yet."

And I don't eat soup. I have no appetite.

* * *

That all changes, three days later. I'm still on pain medication but not enough to make me want to anything besides sleep. This morning, I feel more alert and hungry. And I don't want this crap they're serving up in this hospital.

"I can go get you something, son."

"No. Don't worry about it," I tell her. "In fact, why don't you go back to work? I'm fine. They're talking about discharging me tomorrow."

"I'm not going back to work until you're out of here."

"I don't need you here!" I snap before I know it.

She frowns. Looks disappointed. She grabs her purse. "You're still the same. You'll never change will you?"

"I'm—I'm sorry," I tell her.

She looks at me as if my words haven't registered with her yet. Those aren't words I use often. I'm sure it's taking her some time to process them.

I sigh heavily. I'm tired of being in this hospital. I feel like, if I can get back into my regular routine, I'll heal faster. Being here makes time move slow. Makes me feel like I'm wasting my time. Makes me angry. I'm hungry and tired of lying down.

"Good morning," Cherish says as she comes into the room holding a bag.

She looks at me as if she expects me to say something. She hasn't been here in three days. I don't say a word. All I do is look at her. The last time she was here, my vision was blurry. Today, I can see her clearly. See that she's not wearing a scarf on her head to hide her braids and she doesn't have on an apron. She's wearing a touch of makeup. Her lips are painted pink with gloss. Her braids frames her face, hangs down past her shoulders. She's wearing a white dress with a yellow flower pattern. She looks like an angel.

"Is he talking today?" she asks my mother.

"Yeah. He—"

"Why don't you talk to me and find out?" I ask her. I don't need my mother answering for me.

She looks at me glances away and says, "Oh. I—I said *good morning* and you didn't say anything in response, Mr. St. Claire."

"Do I *ever* say good morning to you?"

She glances at my mother again.

"Sylvia, can you give us a minute, please?" I ask my mother. She gets up, walks out.

I return my attention to Cherish. "Where you been?"

"What do you mean?" she asks, looking down at the floor.

"I haven't seen you in three days."

"I was at your house, doing my job."

"Your *job* is to be my assistant."

"That's what I'm doing, Mont—Mr. St. Claire, but I can't do my job if you won't let me."

"Your hair is down. I've never seen your hair down. You're always wearing a scarf. And you're dressed up."

"I'm not dressed up," she tells me, looking down at her outfit, her voice riddled with annoyance. "It's a pretty day. I just wanted to wear a dress. What does it matter what I'm wearing?"

"Why don't you look at me when you talk to me? Hunh? Is my face that messed up that you can't look at me?" I ask her.

Being somewhat mobile now, I've been back and forth to the bathroom a few times. I've seen my face. The scars. It's bad, but I didn't think it was so bad that the girl can't hold eye contact with me.

"Come here," I tell her.

She frowns but walks closer to the bed.

"Why can't you look at me?" I ask her again. She's *still* not looking at me. Aggravates me to no end. She's looking at the bed covers. Not at me. "Look at *me*, Cherish."

"Mr. St. Claire, I—"

"Look at me!" I demand.

Her eyes meet mine and something happens. Something I can't explain. Spiritual, maybe. I don't know but it nearly takes my breath away. This transcendent being, this woman – Cherish Stevens – standing before me is looking into my eyes but I feel like she has taken over my soul. She's in my mind. In *me*. She has an ethereal glow about her that illuminates my body. For a second, not only does she see right through me. She *becomes* me and I am her. The spirits inside of our bodies meet and intertwine, co-join and as quickly as it happens, it ends.

I gasp like it's my first experience with breathing. I've never felt anything like this. Never. I've never seen love as it's own entity – as a noun and a verb coexisting in the depths of someone's eyes. It's what I see when I look at her. This girl loves me and I haven't given her a reason to.

"Wow," I utter beneath my breath.

She looks away briefly before looking at me again and starts talking.

"Just so you're aware, I don't see scars when I look at your face, Mr. St. Claire. I just see you. That's what happens when you look at someone to see depth—what they are in the inside. It's how I look at people. How I've always looked at people. I wasn't here for the last three days because I was running errands for you, checking the mail, picking up stuff the workers needed. I—I've been on the fence about coming back to work for you, mostly because you being here is *my* fault," she says with a shaky voice. Her eyes glisten with tears but none fall.

"It's not your fault."

"It is. If you weren't coming to see me—if I hadn't called off work that day—you wouldn't be in this situation."

"You don't know that."

"Whatever the case," she says, taking a deep breath, "I think you should start looking for a new assistant."

"I don't want a new assistant. I want you, Cherish."

She shakes her head. "You hate me."

"I don't hate you."

"You hate everyone."

"I don't hate *you*."

I try to find words to defend myself from her comment, but none comes to mind. Her perception of me is what everyone else thinks of me. Hearing it from her shakes me – makes me realize most of the people who work for me probably felt like they'd be better off if I didn't make it out of here.

"What's in the bag?" I ask her.

She looks at the bag in her hand almost like she forgot she was holding it. "It's soup. Your favorite. Chicken and rice."

I'm not surprised she knows that since she knows everything about me.

She takes it out of the bag, removes the lid and hands it to me along with a spoon. Then she stands, get's the table tray and rolls it over to me.

"Thank you," I tell her.

She frowns. "Say—say what?"

"I said, thank you."

"Oh. I heard you. I just—I thought—I thought I was hearing things, but you're—welcome."

I take a few spoonfuls.

She stands and says, "Anyway, I'll let you eat."

"Where are you going?"

"Back to work. I know you like to eat alone."

"Stay."

"Are you sure?"

"Yes. Besides, we need to talk." I eat more. I'm so hungry, I'm scarfing this soup down. I tell her, "You said you wouldn't quit."

She looks surprised. "You heard me?"

"Yes. I heard you."

"That's why you squeezed my hand so tight?"

"Yes. You promised me you wouldn't quit so why are you considering it?"

"Because I don't know if I can work for you anymore, Mr. St. Claire. You need someone who can handle your personality."

"What I need is for someone to be patient with me. Someone who knows what I need before I need it. That would be *you* in case you were wondering."

"Half the time, I don't even think *you* know what you need."

"Then why don't you help me figure that out, Cherish," I say, dropping the plastic spoon in the empty paper bowl.

97

She instantly gets up, takes it away and trashes it.

"I'll pay you whatever you want."

"I don't want your money, Mr. St. Claire."

"Then what do you want, Ms. Stevens?"

She thinks for a moment and replies, "I want your friendship."

"You want me to be your friend."

"Yes."

I smirk. She would request some crap like that. "Alright. Fine." I reach for her hand.

"What are you doing?"

"Let's shake on it. Seal the deal. This is our verbal contract."

"Okay." She takes my hand, looks into my eyes again.

And the deal is sealed.

Chapter Fifteen

Cherish

Five days later, he's home. I've spent a good deal of time with him in the hospital. I've witnessed his improvements. It'll take weeks before his ribs are healed, but his bruises are slowly healing along with the scars on his face. The doctor says he's supposed to stay in bed mostly, resting for at least two weeks, but Montgomery St. Claire doesn't take directions very well.

I'm back doing my same routine, arriving at his house four in the morning on a Tuesday. I go upstairs to his room and expect to see him in bed but he's in the shower, and apparently, he's done since I hear the water shut off.

He steps out wrapped in a towel. His hair is dripping water.

"What are you doing?" I ask.

"What does it look like I'm doing. I'm getting dressed."

"For what?"

"For the day."

"Mr. St. Claire—"

"Don't call me that anymore! We're *friends* now, remember?" he asks with a slight edge of attitude to his voice.

He's agitated this morning. Frustrated by his limitations. He shouldn't be up in the first place. I take his hand. He snatches it away.

"Montgomery—"

"Get out of my room," he demands.

"No. You told me we were friends."

"Get out of my room!"

99

I glare at him. This man is the king of mind games, but I didn't wake up three-o'clock in the morning to play games with nobody. I was already on the verge of quitting. He's making my decision so much easier.

"If I leave this room, I'm not coming back. Ever!"

"That would be your choice, now wouldn't it?"

"Wow. You're something else." I leave the room as he requested, jog downstairs, take my purse from the closet and drive back home.

I'm done.

He's *been* unstable. I've just been trying to tolerate it. But, since most of my early teenage years was that way – unstable and clouded by dysfunction – I'm not going back. I need what little sanity I have left and I'm not about to let no man drive me into a nuthouse.

It's the same thing I tell Sylvia when she calls to find out where I am. Said Naomi was looking for me because I hadn't left the new menu for this week.

"Tell her to wing it, or maybe use one of the old menus, Sylvia. I can't deal with your son. I tried. Just when I think we're taking a step forward, he takes a million freakin' steps backward. I failed."

"What happened?"

"You heard what the doctor told him, right? He's supposed to be in bed for like two weeks. Well, he decides to get up this morning, take a shower and I don't know what happened in the shower to piss him off, but he was already back to his usual, grumpy self. I was trying to get him to get back in bed. He yelled at me and told me to leave the room. My goodness, that man…have you ever had him tested for bipolar disorder?"

"He doesn't have bipolar disorder, Cherish."

"He has *something* and if he needs some medication, we really need to find out like right now."

"See, that statement right there proves you still care."

I glare at my phone. Is she crazy, too? "Okay, well, tell Naomi what I said. I'm going to enjoy my day. Drama free.

I'll see you around, Sylvia."

It's seven o'clock in the morning now. Naomi tries to call me, but I don't have it in me to answer. Today is the day I draw a line in the sand that separates me from The Hawthorne Estate. I'm free.

I use my newfound freedom to go grocery shopping, since I didn't get a chance to do it this past weekend, being at the hospital with Montgomery and all. I take my time, get items I want, especially what I want to cook today. I'm excited to have the opportunity to do that on a weekday.

I pull up in my driveway around three, taking Food Lion bags from the trunk. My nosy neighbor stops doing her yard work to watch everything I'm doing.

"See you done went and got yaself some groceries."

My eyes roll behind my shades. "Yep. Sure did, Ms. Kettleworth..."

"You home mighty early. I seent-chu pull up and I looked at my watch. I said to myself, I knows it ain't six-thirty—quarter-'til-seven already."

"Yeah, I got off work early today."

"Oh. I see. Lemme ask you sum...when you get off work early like-yat, do you still get paid for it?"

She doesn't need to know I quit. She doesn't need to know anything. "Yes, I still get paid. I'll see you later," I tell her so she can move along.

In the kitchen, I throw my bags up on the table and unpack them. Then I get started on dinner right away. I'm cooking smothered pork chops – haven't had them in forever. I make homemade mashed potatoes and broccoli with cheese to go with it. It was one of my Aunt Jo's favorite dishes. She taught me how to make it.

Aunt Jolene loved cooking. She would cook these elaborate meals every weekend and invite some of the neighbors over – anyone who wanted a plate. I miss those times. Miss her cooking. Her laughter. Her words of wisdom. She was my mother's sister, but they were cut from a different cloth. That's for sure.

* * *

As I sit down to eat dinner alone, I'm thinking about Montgomery in the aspect of being mad at myself for giving up on him so easily. He clearly needs help. My problem is, I don't know how to help him. He's so bent on being mad at the world, and I still don't know why that is. He's got it made. Why can't he see that?

I sigh. Should I go back tomorrow?

No, I can't go back. I put my foot down and told him I wouldn't. He needs to know I'm a woman of my word, and that there are consequences to his actions. He needs to recognize when someone's trying to help him. He needs to…

I digress. I'm hungry, this plate of food in front of me smells good and I'm ready to eat. I close my eyes to pray over the meal and I pray for Montgomery and his family. I pray he finds peace over what ails him and that he seeks help. I say *Amen*, open my eyes. Almost immediately after, the doorbell rings.

I don't have time to be messin' around with Ms. Kettleworth so I ignore it.

It rings twice more, back-to-back.

I get up from the table, take a quick peep out the window and see a black Mercedes parked behind my car.

No way. It can't be. That's Montgomery's car.

I open the door, my heart is racing strictly out of anger and when I confirm it's him standing at my door, I'm prepared to snap and go off. I want to yell, scream and give him a verbal beat down for driving all the way to my house in his condition. Before I can get a word out, he says, "I need your help."

Chapter Sixteen

Monty

She takes me by the hand – I don't snatch it away from her this time. With no questions asked, at least not yet, she shows me to a spare bedroom. I sit on the bed. She lowers herself to her knees to takes off my shoes. Then she tugs at my shirt, slowly moving my arms through each sleeve. She checks my bandages.

"This one is bleeding a little bit," she says, gently touching me.

She hurries away, comes back with gauze, medical tape, cotton balls and alcohol pads. She removes the old bandage. I can officially add caretaker to her other talents and abilities. She dabs the scar with alcohol. I absorb the sting. Let her work. Watch her as she works. As she focuses on taking care of me. Once it's clean to her satisfaction, she wraps it. I'm all bandaged up again.

"Have you *completely* lost your freakin' mind? You're not supposed to be driving."

"At least I made it this time."

She scowls. Her whole face knots up. "That's not funny."

"I didn't mean for it to be funny. It's just the truth. I'm here. *This* time."

"You don't need to be here. You need to be at *your* house lying in *your* acre-sized bed resting per doctor's orders! You're supposed to be drinking water, staying hydrated, eating and making sure you're taking care of yourself. Making sure you change your bandages. You have to give yourself time to heal, Monty."

Monty. It rolls off her tongue naturally like it's what she's always called me. Like, just a day ago, I wasn't *Mr. St. Claire* to her. Her boss. The man she avoids eye contact with.

"Did you hear me?" she asks after she's done reprimanding me. I find her little take-charge attitude comical but she'd never know that by looking at me.

"Yes. I heard you, Cherry," I say since we're on a nickname basis. "Heard you loud and clear."

"Yeah, you heard me but you ain't listening."

"I heard every word you said."

"Sure you did. Can I take a look at your legs?"

"Sure," I tell her. My ribs have yet to heal, but I think I've made it worse today by moving around so much. I can barely stand up straight but I do the best I can, unzip my pants and let my slacks fall to the floor while she studies the area on my thigh where I had to get stitches. She doesn't touch it. She's only looking at the bandage.

"How is it?" I ask her.

"Better than the one on your chest. Did you bring some pain medication?"

"No. My assistant was supposed to pick it up, but she walked off the job this morning."

"If you weren't being so rude, I wouldn't have left."

"How was I being rude? I told you to get out of my room."

"And *that* was rude."

"What if that's what *you* consider to be rudeness but not me? I'm a straightforward guy, Cherish. For that reason, people say I'm rude or hard to deal with."

"Well, I don't like it."

"You will."

She narrows her eyes.

"Once you get to know me," I finish saying.

"How insane does that sound? I worked for you for two years and you come out your mouth with something like that. *Once you get to know me.* If I don't know you by now, what's the point?"

Sitting on the edge of the bed is getting uncomfortable, but I can't resist this conversation. "Why don't you know me?"

"I *do* know you but I *don't* know you...if that makes any sense. You distance yourself from the people who serve you. You won't say a word to us and if you do, it's something cold and terse. The people who've known you the longest are the ones who gave me advice on how to *deal* with you. They said to stay out of your way and do my job. That's what I did. Stayed out of your way. Did my job. I made it a point to know where you were at all times so I didn't have to run into you."

"That's harsh."

She shrugs. "It was my reality, but it didn't hinder me from doing my job." She fluffs some pillows then instructs me to ease back. She helps me get into a comfortable position. Then she walks over to the closet, grabs a blanket and spreads it over my legs. "There. Is that comfortable?"

"It's fine," I tell her, studying her as she takes care of me, remembering the deep bond I felt with her at the hospital. I wonder if she felt it too, or was it all one-sided – a figment of my imagination.

"I'll pick up your prescription in the morning."

"Don't worry about it. I don't need it."

"You couldn't stand up straight just now. You're in pain. You *do* need it," she says.

She's right, of course, but I try to be a man and fight it. Bear it. I can handle pain. I've been doing it all my life.

She powers on the TV hands me the remote and says, "Just in case you're up to watching something. I know you don't watch much television, but you'll need to do something to help pass the time."

I'm watching her. Not the TV.

"What?" she asks, catching my gaze.

"Nothing," I respond even though I want to say thank you, to express my gratitude for everything she's doing for me. For letting me inside of her home after I was rude to her this morning. Just when I think I've mustered up enough courage to say it, she asks, "Have you had anything to eat?"

"No."

"Naomi didn't cook for you?"

"She cooked for *somebody*, but not me. She prepared some nachos."

"Nachos?" She laughs. "You hate nachos."

I watch her giggle herself silly, then ask, "How do you know that?"

"That you hate nachos?" she asks.

"Yes."

She says, "I just know. I've studied you for a long time. I know everything there is to know about you except the things you keep tucked away in there," she says, pointing to my chest. My heart.

"You put Naomi up to it, didn't you?"

She grins. "I promise, I didn't. I would *never* tell Naomi to cook nachos for you."

"That smile on your face doesn't convince me you're telling the truth."

"Only reason I'm smiling is because I told Naomi to use an old menu I made for you since I didn't get around to making a new one. Apparently, she didn't listen to me."

"No, she didn't. So, what's for dinner?"

"I'll bring you a plate."

"You're not going to tell me what you cooked, first?"

"No. Be right back."

A sigh of relief escapes my mouth as I wait for her return. I feel comfortable here. Like this is home, but it's not my home. It's hers. Or maybe my idea of home, of comfort, is having her around.

"Okay, here you go," she says bringing in a tray. There's a glass of water, and a plate with meat, broccoli and mashed potatoes. "It's smothered pork chops. I hope you like it."

"Have you eaten?" I ask her, taking the tray.

"No. I was just about to when you rang the bell."

"Bring your plate in here so you can eat with me."

"Why? Don't you prefer eating alone?"

"Usually, yes, but these are extenuating circumstances."

"Hmm…okay. I'll be right back."

I start on my food while I'm waiting for her to return. The pork chops taste like something a top chef would make at a fancy restaurant. Even the broccoli is well seasoned and the mashed potatoes were made with just the right amount of butter. Everything is delicious.

"Do you like it?" she asks, walking in with her a plate. She sits at the foot of the bed, awaiting my response.

"Yes, it's good. All this time, you should've been my cook instead of Naomi."

"Don't say that. Naomi works hard to prepare your meals."

I eat more, faster than normal until I'm done. Then I drink water and watch her for a minute. I watch the way she chews. I watch how uncomfortable she is sitting on the edge of the bed when she'd be better situated at her dinette. But she's here with me because I requested it. She doesn't *have* to be here. Doesn't have to agree to my requests, but she does. I wonder if she's aware of the power I have over her. She quit this morning, walked out on me and yet still views me as her superior.

She must feel me watching. She looks at me. Narrows her eyes like she's trying to figure out why.

She wipes her mouth with a piece of paper towel. "Can I ask you something?"

"Depends on what it is."

"Okay. I guess I'll take a stab at it, then. Why do you call your mother, Sylvia or Mrs. Hawthorne?"

"You can't ask me that," I tell her.

"I just did."

"Well, it's a family matter. It doesn't concern you, and no, I'm not being *rude* right now. I'm simply telling you it's none of your business."

"Right."

She gets up, takes my tray along with her plate and walks out of the room. She stays gone for a while. I figure she's tending to other matters – her everyday routine. Maybe she's getting ready for bed, or watching TV. I don't know what her days are like. I don't know much of anything about her. What I do know is, we are somehow connected. Even in her dislike of me, she makes an attempt at understanding.

* * *

Around nine, she returns.

Her hair is tied up in a black scarf. She has on a black robe. She walks over to the bed. I'm still propped up against the pillows, the way she left me two hours ago.

"Are you comfortable?" she asks.

"Yes."

"Well, I'm about to go to bed, but I wanted to check to see if you needed anything."

"No, I don't. Thanks."

"Oh, and I need to put some Neosporin on your scars, especially the ones on your face."

"Why?"

"It'll help them heal faster and you won't be able to see the bruises long after they've healed. Is that okay?"

"Sure. Okay," I tell her.

She sits next to me, opens the tube and squeezes some ointment on her fingertip. She carefully massages it on my face, on each scar. I have plenty of them but she takes her time, gives me careful attention.

"That should do it," she whispers. "The bathroom is next to this room."

"I found it already."

"Good. And I left you some towels and a toothbrush."

"Found those, too."

"You've made yourself right at home, I see. Can I get you anything else before I go to bed?"

"It's only nine o'clock. Why are you going to bed so early?"

"Because I always go to bed early."

"My question was *why*?"

"Let's see...I've been working at a job where my hours are 4:00 a.m. 'til 6:00 p.m. Fourteen hours. By the time I get home, it's close to seven. I usually have just enough time to grab something to eat and hit the sack by eight to give myself seven hours to sleep. I wake up at three and do it all over again. I have no life outside of work—outside of you. That's why it felt like such a relief to quit—to walk away and leave it all behind. To know what it's like to work a regular eight-hour shift and actually be appreciated for my hard work."

"I appreciate everything you do for me, Cherish."

"No, you don't, because if you did, you wouldn't complain when one little thing goes wrong, and you definitely wouldn't dismiss me when I ask you a simple question."

"How did I dismiss you?"

"I asked you a question about your mother, Montgomery, and you said it was none of my business. You drove all the way to my house with cracked ribs asking for help and you refuse to talk to me. What exactly is it you need help with? Your scars? Your bruises and bandages? Because the help you need is so much more than physical. You can lie, tell me otherwise, but I know you. I know this hard, rigid persona you display in your lil' business meetings and the way you walk around your house like you're going to fire the first person who looks at you wrong isn't really who you are. People shouldn't have to walk on eggshells around you. Is that what you like? To have people afraid of you? If so, more power to you, but I'm not putting up with it anymore. I'll get your medicine in the morning and drive you back home."

She heads for the door.

"You care about me, don't you?" I ask when she's close to exiting.

She stops turns around and says, "I care about a lot of people."

"That may be true, but I'm talking specifically about me, and don't deny it. If you didn't care, you'd send me to get my own medicine and let me drive myself home, but you're willing to inconvenience yourself to make sure I get there safely."

"Yes, it's called being responsible...like being the designated driver for one of my drunk friends."

"It's much more than that," I tell her.

"How do you figure?"

"Come here," I say in a demanding tone, daring her not to.

She rolls her eyes, caves and walks toward the bed.

"Sit down."

"What do you want, Montgomery?"

"You want to talk. Let's talk."

"Okay," she says. "Why do you call your mother, Sylvia?"

"You mean besides the fact that it's her name?"

"It's disrespectful to call your mother anything besides, *mother* or some variation of it. Like *mom* or *momma*. Ma is even acceptable."

"Sylvia Hawthorne is my foster mother."

"And?"

"Keywords being *foster mother*. Do you know anything about the foster care system, Cherish?"

She shakes her head. "No. Not much."

"Kids go into foster care when they don't have nowhere else to go. I have no idea who my birth parents were. I vaguely remember them. They're both dead but I don't know them. All I know is they didn't want me and Major so we ended up belonging to the state before being placed with Sylvia and Caspian Hawthorne – the rich billionaires who couldn't have children. They were filthy rich when they fostered us. But not once, not *once*, did they file any papers to actually adopt us as their own. To give us their last name. Why do you think my name remains *St. Claire* while hers is *Hawthorne*? You know what that tells me? It tells me she didn't want me."

"You keep saying *she*. What about your father? Did you feel the same way about him?"

"I used to until he took me under his wing."

"Well, I think you should cut your mother some slack the same way you did with your father. He could've adopted you, too."

"Could have but you and I both know decisions like that usually falls under the mother's umbrella."

"Have you spoken to her about it?"

"No. What's the use? I'm a grown man now."

"A grown man who's bitter and angry at the world for how he was raised. A grown man who feels rejected and betrayed by his birth parents *and* his foster parents. Is that why you act the way you do? You feel like you have something to prove? The more you assert yourself, the more you feel like you're *somebody*?"

I'm impressed. She knows me better than I thought she did. I'm impressed by her listening ability and how I can see her seeking understanding. It's in her eyes.

"And you know what the worst part of it is?"

"What?"

"I know for a fact I had an older brother who went to another foster home. I have no idea who he is, what his name is and—" I take a minute. "I'm afraid to go looking because I'm scared of what I might find."

"How do you know about an older brother?"

"Because I remember him. I remember talking to him. I was a child, but I remember."

"Okay. Tell me what I can do to help."

"I don't know. I really have no idea."

"Sleep on it and let me know in the morning."

"Okay," I tell her, although I'm not sure if I'll be in the mood to continue this conversation in the morning. Most likely not.

Chapter Seventeen

Cherish

My nerves are all to pieces. I cannot believe I spoke to Montgomery that way. I can't believe Montgomery St. Claire is at my house! I'm glad he couldn't hear my heart jack-hammering in my chest when I changed his bandage and put the ointment on his face. I'm also glad he's opening up to me. I'm slowly beginning to understand why he's the way he is. He has baggage, but don't we all.

IN THE MORNING, I drive to the pharmacy to pick up Montgomery's prescription. While I'm in Concord, I stop by the estate. He won't survive without being connected to work, so I get his laptop – the one he keeps in the black Hermès briefcase. I also pack a week's worth of clothes – all business-casual stuff because the man doesn't own a pair of jeans. I take his phone charger and anything else I think he might need.

Before I leave, I go to the east wing to talk to Sylvia. She called me last night. Probably wanted to know if I knew where Montgomery was. She's in her office with her head down – looks like she's taking a mental break. She has a head full of thick, gray hair that's pinned like a French roll. I'm sure Montgomery is responsible for most of those grays.

I tap my knuckles against the wooden door three times and say, "Hi, Sylvia."

"Cherish! Montgomery left last night and—"

"He's fine, Sylvia," I say to calm her down. She's one

panic attack away from a stroke. "He's at my house."

"He is?"

"Yes. He drove there—probably gonna be there for a few days because I refuse to let him drive back here until he's well enough."

"Oh—thank goodness. I was so worried. Please take care of him."

"Don't worry. I just picked up his pain meds and I'm headed back now. He was still resting when I left, so I'm sure he'll be ready for lunch by the time I get there."

"Will you please keep me informed about how he's doing?"

"I will. Don't worry, Sylvia."

"I know he's in good hands with you, but I still worry."

"Well, I promise I will call or text you and I will take care of him to the best of my ability."

"Thank you," she says, then smiles warmly. She stands and comes around the desk to give me a hug, squeezing me in her arms. I can feel her appreciation through her touch that gives me a new perspective where Montgomery is concerned. If I tell myself I'm helping him for Sylvia's sake, maybe I won't be quick to give up so easily when he gets on my nerves.

* * *

I unload my car when I'm back home. I have a lot of his things. His clothes, shoes, his favorite robe, the laptop and other items – like that Dolce & Gabanna *The One* cologne and aftershave that smells so good, it almost makes him edible. I have a Rolex. His hairbrush. Toothbrush. Some of his fancy Egyptian towels. I'm sure my small, colorful, scratchy ones are not up to par with his standards.

I set the bags on the couch then walk to the bedroom to look for him. He's still lying there in the same position as when I left. I get closer to make sure he's still breathing and when I confirm he is (thank God) I touch his face and whisper, "Monty."

His eyes open and I promise it's no different than seeing the sun after a few days of rain. It nearly takes my breath away. *Why does he have to be so fine? Why does he have to have this kind of effect on me?*

I find a way to keep it together or at least enough to talk.

"Good morning," I tell him.

He's groggy. He touches his chest. My guess is the pain is bad this morning.

"Sit up a lil' bit so you can take some pain pills," I tell him. "I'll go get some water."

I rush to the kitchen, get a glass of water and then come back with the pills. "Monty, can you sit up?"

He moves a little. Grimaces. He's not talkative. Doesn't even look lively like he did last night. The way he's behaving today has me worried.

I give him the pills. Two of them. He tosses them in his mouth and then I hand him the glass. He drinks, hands the glass back to me.

"Do you want something to eat?"

"No," he says softly, lying down again. He closes his eyes. I'm worried. I promised Sylvia I'd take care of him and I don't know how well I'm doing at the moment.

"Monty, I think I should take you back to the hospital."

"No...not going back there," he mumbles.

"I think you should. What if something is going on that I can't see. You're out of it right now—so different than yesterday."

"Just let me rest. Please."

"But—"

"Please."

I sigh. "Okay. I'm going to check your bandages," I tell him but he doesn't respond. I proceed with the one on his chest. I remove the old bandage and round up everything I need to make a new one. I don't have a wash pail, so I find

115

a big bowl in the kitchen and fill it with warm water. I clean the area on his chest and redo his bandage. I wash his face and apply more Neosporin to his scars. I get a dry towel, spread it across his ribcage, then plug in the heating pad and lay it across the towel. Heat should help to soothe the pain and relax him.

This version of him continues for the rest of the week. He's weak and all he wants to do is sleep, so I continue taking care of him. He doesn't want to eat so I pretty much have to force him to eat a few spoonfuls of chicken broth. I help him travel back and forth to the bathroom. I redo his bandages. Keep his scars clean. I've become his full-time nurse, and I don't mind it. I like taking care of him but I like it even more to feel needed. He knows he needs me. I doubt if he'd trust anyone else to do this – not even a professional nurse.

I've also been keeping Sylvia up-to-date. Every night she calls, sounding almost out of breath as if Montgomery is on his deathbed. I let her know he's fine. That his body needs this rest. He's a strong man, yes, but even strong men need time to heal. Truth be told, I'm more worried about his mental healing than his physical one. The body was made to survive. It knows how to heal itself. The mind, on the other hand, that's a different story. The mind doesn't have that same repairing ability. When the mind is damaged, you can't apply Neosporin to make the damage less noticeable. You have to do things that require mental ability and it's hard to heal something broken with something broken. It's like trying to mend a fractured arm with a broken cast – it just won't work.

Chapter Eighteen

Monty

I've been lying here for so long, I feel like I'm glued to this bed. I glance around. I'm still at Cherish's house. I have no clue what day of the week it is. That's how in-and-out I've been.

I take my phone from the nightstand, pull up the calendar to see that it's Saturday. How did a whole week go by so fast?

At least I'm better today. Still sore, but better. I turn off the heating pad that's on me and remove the towel to make my way to the bathroom. I look at myself in the mirror. I haven't shaved since the accident. My beard is getting thicker. Even the hair on my head is longer than I like it. But that's the least of my worries.

I wash my face. The scars are healing fast thanks to Cherish and her applying that ointment every night, but I'm still not back to my old self.

I walk to the kitchen thinking I'd find Cherish there since I smelled food but she's not. And she's not in the living room, but the front door is open. I walk there and stand at the screen door where I can see her in the front yard, working in a bed of flowers. It's 7:22 a.m. and she's outside working in flowers...

"Good morning," I say loud enough to where I'm certain she can hear me.

She glances up at me. "Well, well, well, the dead has arisen." She walks over to the porch with a little shovel in her gloved hand. I'm somewhat glad to see she's actually wearing gloves. "Hey."

"Hey."

"How do you feel this morning?" she asks.

It crosses my mind to ask if she's inquiring about my well-being just because or if he actually cares about how I am and how I feel. I say, "I feel like I just came out of hibernation."

She smiles, leaves her gardening tools outside and steps inside with me. She looks at my chest. My legs. My face. After her visual inspection to make sure I'm okay, she asks again, "How do you feel?"

I shrug. "I'm not a hundred percent, but I can move around without feeling like I'm about to topple over so that's an improvement."

"No vertigo? No dizziness?"

"No."

"Any soreness?"

"A little, but not to the point where I need medication—at least not at the moment."

"Good. Then let's eat some breakfast."

"You cooked?"

"I did—made some shrimp and grits with biscuits. I figured you'd be hungry today after eating nothing but chicken broth all week."

She pulls out a chair at the table and helps me sit. It's still uncomfortable to sit in a chair but I grin and bear it.

Cherish grabs a bowl, walks over to the stove and fills it with grits. It's still hot. I see steam coming from the pot. She then takes the lid from a pan and adds grits to the bowl. She brings it over to me along with two biscuits on a saucer.

"Thank you."

She pauses. Looks at me. "You're welcome."

She sits down with her food and then says, "There's a lot I need to catch you up on."

"Like what?" I ask, then taste the food. It's so good, I try not to eat it so fast.

"Earlier this week, I went to your house to get you some clothes. I talked to your mother. Told her where you were. She was worried sick."

I keep on eating. "What else?"

"I also brought your laptop in case you wanted to do some work. I wasn't sure how long you'd planned on staying."

"Are you kicking me out?"

"No. You can stay as long as you like, Monty."

"That's good to know."

"Um...what else...let's see...oh! Your secretary called. She wanted to know when you were going to be back. Said you had some big meetings coming up this week."

"They'll have to be rescheduled. I'll inform her about that."

"She sounded like she was in distress."

"Hannah's always like that."

"Oh. Okay, then that's all the updates I have for you."

I finish the grits and right away, she asks if I want more. Once I confirm, she takes my bowl, goes to the stove and fills it again. Brings it to me.

When she sits, I look at her to catch her eyes before I say, "Thank you."

"You're welcome," she says, shying away from my gaze.

That's when I decide to ask her, "What kind of man do you think I am, Cherry?"

She chuckles. "Where did that come from?"

"Just answer it."

"Uh—I cant. I don't know how to."

"Do you think I'm a good person?"

"Yes, I do, but you—um...you know what...maybe we shouldn't be having this conversation."

"We should. Please. Tell me. Don't hold anything back. Just be honest."

"I don't know if you can handle my honesty."

"There's nothing I can't handle. Try me."

"Okay. I think you're a good person, but you try so hard to make people believe you're not. I think you believe that if people are scared of you, they respect you."

"The man I am is the man my father groomed me to be."

"Your foster father," she says to clarify.

"Yes. He left a billion-dollar corporation to me. This is who I have to be to run that company. To make sure the company stays profitable. To carry on my father's legacy."

"That's good and all, but, who are you outside of the company? Like what do you do for fun?"

"I make money."

She laughs. "That's not fun."

"It is for me." I eat more then tell her, "I swim. That's fun."

She shakes her head. "I don't think it is—at least not anymore."

"How do you figure?"

"You used to take laps in the pool every Friday afternoon. If the weather was good you'd be on the outside pool. If it was raining, or cold, you'd use the indoor pool. A few months ago, you stopped."

I stir the grits around then look up at her. "You watch me like a hawk, don't you?"

"Yep. I pretty much know everything you do on a daily basis. I just don't know why you do them. So, why'd you stop?"

"I guess I just got tired of it. I'm taking a break from it."

"I see. You're taking a break from the only thing you *supposedly* do for fun."

Silence falls between us, mostly because she has me backed into a corner with her assessment.

She finishes her breakfast, then says, "I'll probably go out later."

"Go out where?"

"I'm not sure yet, but I've been cooped up in this house all week."

"My fault, huh?"

"I'm not complaining. I'm just saying. It's a beautiful day. I want to do something."

"Then I'm coming with you."

"You can't come with me, Monty."

"I can. You just don't want me to."

"That's not it at all. Why are you trying to make me feel guilty?"

"Why are you trying to make me feel bad for taking up all of your precious time?"

She smiles. That beautiful smile. It takes my breath and makes me clench my jaw at the same time. No woman has ever made me skip a breath.

"Are you okay?" she asks, always attentive to my needs.

"Yeah. I'm fine." I take a sip of water and say, "We could do something fun here."

"Like what?"

I shrug.

She grins, but when she knows I'm serious about my suggestion, she wipes the smile off her face and says, "Okay...um, let's plan on watching a movie later and I'm picking the movie. You down?"

"Yeah. I'm down."

"You say that now..."

"No, really. I'm looking forward to it."

She offers up an inquisitive gaze like she doesn't believe me.

My phone rings. It's Major. I answer, "Hello."

"Yo, what's up, Monty...heard you moved out."

"I didn't move out. I'm just staying with Cherish for a while."

"Ay, lighten up, bro—I'm just teasing. Anyway, how are you feeling?"

"I'm okay."

"Let me speak to Cherish for a minute," he says.

"No," I respond. What does he have to talk to Cherish about? "I'll call you later, man," I tell him, then hang up.

"Everything okay?" Cherish asks.

"Yeah." I get up slowly, holding the edge of the table for support. "I'm going to go lie down for a while."

"Okay. I'll check on you later."

Chapter Nineteen

Cherish

For movie night, I choose *Proud Mary*. I haven't seen the movie but one can never go wrong with Taraji. I'd much rather had gone out to see a movie but here we are, stuck in my living room with popcorn and soda. Monty doesn't look like he's into it. He doesn't look relaxed at all. I have to assume he'd be much more comfortable lying in bed instead of sitting on the couch.

"You don't have to do this if you're not comfortable, Monty," I tell him.

"Do you really think I need you to tell me that?"

"Whoa—" I say, hands up. "I was just saying."

He adjusts his body, attempting to get comfortable again.

"Monty."

"I'm fine, Cherish!"

"No, you're not. You're—" I rub my eyes. Now, I'm getting frustrated. *You know how he is, Cherish. You're doing this for Sylvia, remember?*

I hit the reset button, start over and say, "Come here."

"What?" he asks, frowning.

"Come here—you know—like you tell me to do."

He smirks a little, slides closer to me and says, "Now what?"

"Stretch your legs out that way and rest your head on this pillow," I say, placing one of my couch pillows on my lap.

"You want me to lay on your lap?"

"No. I want you to lay on the pillow. Face up."

"How will I see the movie if I'm face up?"

"Be honest—you weren't watching the movie anyway were you?"

"No," he says, resting his head on the pillow finally. "Ah. So much better."

It's amazing how he's so lean and in shape yet muscular and heavy at the same time. I'm keenly aware of the weight of his head on my lap, just like I'm aware of his smell. Oh gosh, that smell. It's better than the aroma of food. It's like an enhancement to the oxygen I breathe.

And there goes my heart thumping again…

"You could've just gone back in the bedroom and stretched out on the bed," I tell him.

"I didn't feel like being in there. Alone. *Again*."

I glance down at my lap to see his eyes beaming up at me. I study the hair on his face – never seen this much hair on his face before. And the hair on his head is longer. He usually keeps it around an inch. Now, his curly strands are at least two inches. I'm dying to touch it. I want to play in it so bad my hands are twitching, but I resist. He'd probably run if I made an attempt. I'm so not his type.

"Why are you doing this for me?" he asks.

"Doing what?"

"Taking care of me. It *can't* be because you like me."

I smile. "I do like you. I like *this* version of you."

"Oh, the broken down version." He chuckles. "The version that can't move without something hurting."

"No. I just like you more when you're not so venomous."

"Wow. Venomous. That's a bit harsh."

"Okay, well…mad."

"That's not it. And I'm not mad. It's my personality. I told you that."

"I don't believe you."

"I can't make you believe me. All I can do is tell you my truth."

Without even thinking, my fingers dive into his hair.

"What's your truth?" I ask him while massaging his scalp. When I'm aware of what I'm doing, I panic. "Oh my gosh, I'm so sorry. I—I didn't realize I was playing in your hair."

"Sure you didn't…"

"I didn't," I say amused. "I—I—"

"You're stuttering."

"Sorry, it was in my head. I didn't realize I was actually doing it."

"Oh, so you think about playing in my hair a lot, do you?"

"No."

"You just confessed."

"Well, you have nice hair and it's like right in my face, but I'll stop now."

"No. Don't. I like it."

"You do?"

"Yeah. It feels nice."

"I'm surprised you don't have anything rude to say like asking me if my hands are clean."

"Shh," he says. "Do it harder."

I keep massaging, *harder* like he apparently likes it.

He closes his eyes. Moans. Then he says, "You shouldn't like this version of me so much."

"Why not?"

"Because it's not who I really am. When I'm well enough to go back to work—and I think that'll be in a week or so—I won't be *this* person. I'll be the person you don't like."

His words make me sick. All I can hope is that they're not true. That he'll hang on to some sort of compassion when he leaves my house and not go back to the rigid man he was before the accident. It also makes me realize that if I want to do my part to rid him of that flawed personality, maybe I should try a little harder to get through to him.

"Have you spoken to your mother since you've been here?"

"No."

"What about Major?"

"That's who called this morning when we were eating breakfast."

"Really, because if that's the case, you talked to him for all of two seconds."

"I didn't have much to say."

"That's too bad. Don't you love them?"

"Yeah, I love them."

"And that's how you treat people you love?"

"Let me ask you something. When my parents gave me up—me and my brothers—was that love?"

"Maybe it was if they felt they couldn't take care of you."

He sits up, places a hand on his chest when he responds, "Then I guess that makes me a product of my environment. How does a man learn how to love when he's never *been* loved?"

"Gosh, Monty, that's so *not* true."

"You don't know that."

"I know Major and Sylvia loves you."

"You don't know anything," he says with cold eyes, "So don't speak on what you don't know."

"Why are you getting upset now?"

He stands and says, "I think I've done enough talking for one day."

I don't know why I try so hard when he tries so little. The minute I think I'm getting through to him, he reverts back to his old ways. The old Montgomery. I don't think he'll ever change.

I toss the popcorn in the trash, fix my hair, put on a dress and call Major. I need to vent. Need to talk to somebody who understands this dude before I lose my freakin' mind.

We meet up at Sticky Fingers, a barbecue rib joint in Concord across the street from the mall. He walks in looking casual in jeans, a black shirt and a sports jacket. Like Monty, he wears suits on a daily. I'm surprised he didn't come up in here on a Saturday night dressed to kill.

"Hey, girl."

"Hey, Major."

"Your houseguest haven't driven you to check into a mental institution yet?" He laughs.

"I'm getting there. Trust me," I tell him then take a sip of my drink.

He laughs more.

I can get used to being around someone with Major's upbeat spirit. Major is refreshing, especially after being in the house with his twisted brother. Major has been kind to me since I started working at The Hawthorne Estates. He makes me eat lunch sometimes because he knows I have a habit of skipping meals. And he always has a joke. Always lurking around the corner trying to scare me since he knows the place like the back of his hand. I know it now, but back then, it wasn't a thing for me to get lost.

"Nah, you'll be alright," he tells me.

"You think so?"

"Honestly? No," he says and laughs harder. "By the way, you look pretty tonight."

"Thanks."

"I'm surprised Monty let you leave the house looking like this...got these men in here eyeballing you—'bout to leave their wives."

"Shut up, Major? Ain't nobody in here looking at me and your brother definitely ain't looking."

"That's what you think."

"No, it's what I know."

Major flags down the bartender to get a beer, then says, "So, what did he do this time to have you sitting in here getting white-girl wasted?"

"This is the only drink I've had, silly." I take a sip of it. "And as for your brother, I can't get through to him. The guy wrecks his car, cracks his ribs—he almost *died*, Major, and I still can't get through to him. He drives himself to my house, asks for help and he won't let me in. What in the world is wrong? What am *I* doing wrong?"

"Did you ask him about his inner demons?"

"Yes, but does he give me a straight answer? Nope! I can never get to the root of the problem. I mean, he talks about how you two were abandoned by your biological parents, and—"

"He has a point there. We were abandoned."

"But *you're* not bitter. *He* is. Why's that?"

"How do you know I'm not bitter?"

I glance over at him. "You don't walk around acting like the world owes you anything. You smile. I actually know what your teeth look like."

"I got some pretty teeth, don't I?"

He has me laughing again. It's what I do when we're together – a far contrast from Monty.

"Me and my brother may look the same, Cherish, but we're as different as night is from day."

"I know. He hasn't spoken to Sylvia since he left the hospital. Has he even talked to you?"

"I called him this morning, asked him how he was. He was short with me like he was in such a hurry to get off the phone, but that doesn't faze me because I know how Monty is. If you don't want to be let down by him, you can't care as much because I can assure you, he doesn't. All Monty has ever cared about was making money and inventing gadgets, almost like he's trying to be better than dad was."

"It's more to it than that, though. Something is totally wired wrong with him."

"He's always been like that. Trust me. Oh, and then there's some contracts and stuff he had to sign."

"*Had* to? Nobody forces Montgomery St. Claire to do anything."

"Don't have to when money is involved. When dad died, he left me and Monty five million dollars a piece."

"Seriously?"

"Yep, but he gave Monty the option to get his hands

on an additional five billion if he ran the company and honored a specific request by mom."

"What request?"

"That she got to choose a woman for him—more specifically, a wife—and he couldn't back out of it because if he did, he'd forfeit not only the five-billion dollars but the original five million and the company."

"So, he'd have nothing."

"Exactly." Major takes a swig of beer.

"What did he do?"

He chuckles. "What do you think he did? He signed the papers! Got that moola! Next thing I know, Paige is walking around there wearing *Wifey* shirts."

"They're a couple?"

"To be honest with you, I don't know what they are. I just know what went down. What makes me think mom chose Paige for him is, Paige acts like she's entitled around there. It's the strangest thing. She doesn't live there but she does lives in a property owned by the estate. They set her up real nice."

"Is that why Monty doesn't get along with Sylvia so much? Because of Paige?"

Major shrugs. "I'm sure that's part of it, and he could never get over the fact that we weren't officially adopted. I don't see why that makes him so angry but I do know it's been a thorn in his flesh for a while."

"And what about your other brother?"

Major sighs. "Cherish, I'ma be honest—I want to look for him, but each time I think I'm ready I back out. I've gotten to the point of dialing his number but not pressing send."

"Wait—you know who he is?"

"Yeah. His name is Magnus St. Claire. He lives in Charlotte."

"You know all of this and you've never met him?"

"No."

"Have you shared any of this with Monty?"

"No."

"Why not?"

"Because he doesn't care. That's what I'm trying to tell you. Monty does not care, and you best watch yourself if you don't want to get hurt."

"Why do you say that?"

"I'm not blind, Cherish. You've taken a liking to my brother."

"No, I—"

"You can deny it all you want, but when I saw you with him in the hospital that day, I knew for sure. Don't let your infatuation with him land you with a broken heart. He has enough on his plate to deal with already. I hate to sound harsh, but he doesn't have time for you or any other woman."

I sigh. Now, I don't know what to do. The nurturer in me wants to help Monty, but I can't ignore a blatant warning from his brother – someone who knows him better than I do.

"What if I can put a meeting together between you, Monty and Magnus?"

Major looks at me for a moment then finishes his beer. "I won't turn it down."

"Okay. So, I just need to get Monty on board."

"Don't hold your breath."

"Major, at least give him the benefit of the doubt."

He shakes his head.

"Well, I'm going to head back home. I need to make sure Monty's okay."

"See—that's what I'm talking about. You're too invested."

"What do you want me to do, Major? Kick him out on his tail?"

"Listen at you—*kick him out on his tail.*" He smirks. "The man is worth five *billion* dollars. Do you really think he'd be out on his tail? No, he wouldn't. He would hire round-the-clock nurses. He already got maids. Chefs. Let's keep it real for a minute—if the situation was reversed and you were the one in the car accident, do you think Monty would let you live with him? Do you think he would've brought you food in the hospital? Do you think he would've visited you at all?"

My immediate answer to all of Major's questions is no. I don't think Monty would do any of those things for me, but I don't say it out loud. Had I crashed my car and went to the hospital, he wouldn't have shown up to see how I was doing. He wouldn't allow me to stay in his home. Wouldn't wait on me hand and foot. Wouldn't bandage me up. Make sure I was comfortable. Cook for me. Clean for me. Wash my clothes.

"Don't worry, though," Major says. "I'd let you live with me."

I nudge him. "Thanks, Major."

"Yeah, yeah, yeah. How many of those drinks have you had?"

"I told you, just this one."

"You good to drive back home?"

"Yeah. I'm good."

"Okay, girl. I got the check," he says, placing a fifty on the counter.

"Thank you."

"Come on. I'll walk you to your car."

It wasn't nighttime when we arrived, but it is as we prepare to leave. Major walks with a lazy stroll to the car like he's prolonging our time together. Like he's not ready for us to part ways. I fall in stride next to him.

"I'm curious about something," I say. "What are you doing free on a Saturday night, Major?"

"Free?"

"Yeah. You're an eligible bachelor. I'm sure you got women by the boatload."

"You'd be wrong. I don't have time to date."

"No?"

"Nope. I'm just as much involved in the business as the

rest of the family."

"So, am I correct in saying that working for Hawthorne Innovations equates to a lack of a personal life."

"That would be an accurate assessment."

"See, besides biological parents, you and Monty do have something in common."

"Guess we do."

I unlock my car door. He grabs the handle, opens the door for me like a gentleman. "Thank you, Major," I say looking into his green eyes – eyes that match Monty's but doesn't affect me the same way Monty's eyes do. I find it amazing how that works because while I've always viewed Major as a friend, I've gotten certain vibes from him. Like he has a thing for me, but never acted on it, probably because he knows how much I like his brother.

"You're welcome, Cherish." He flashes a faint smile. Then he does something he's never done before. He wraps his arms around me and while he's holding me, he says, "Don't let my brother drive you crazy, girl."

"I won't."

"And if you need anything, you know where to find me," he tells me as he releases me.

"Yes, I do. Thanks, Major."

"You're welcome. Always."

I get in the car.

He says, "Drive safe," before he closes the door.

"I will."

I begin the drive home, purposely driving below the posted speed limit. My mind is so far inundated with everything he's told me about Monty. I'm thinking about their older brother they've never met. And then there's Paige and the contracts Monty had to sign that supposedly tied her to him. I think about Major's warning the most – to not get too attached to Monty. To keep my guard up. I'd bend over backward for Monty, but according to Major, Monty isn't the type to show the same consideration. Let Major tell it and Monty wouldn't even so much as visit me if I were to fall ill. The only person Montgomery St. Claire cares about is Montgomery St. Claire. As much as I don't want to believe that, how can I ignore the advice of the person who grew up with him?

Chapter Twenty

Monty

I battle with a lot. Most things I like to keep private, but this girl wants to know my *entire* life story. Wants to know what makes me who I am. At times, I'm willing to tell her, then when the time comes, I back away. I've been yo-yo-ing all night like this.

Ready.

Not ready.

Ready.

I finally came out of the bedroom to find that she wasn't here. I wasn't aware she'd left. I don't know what time she left or where she went and that bothers me.

After showering, I sit on the sofa alone and watch the movie we were supposed to watch together. I don't make popcorn. I sip water and stare at the screen, forcing myself to watch it. Thirty minutes into it, I hear noise at the front door.

She walks in. My eyes immediately go to her. She has on a dress. A short above-the-knee dress. One with flowers in it again. Pink ones. My eyes follow the length of her legs to her feet. She's wearing thong sandals. Her toes look delicate, decorated with pink polish. Her braids are hanging loose. She's wearing makeup, too – not much – a few touches here and there. The mascara on her lashes enhances her eyes. Blush looks beautiful on her cheeks. The gloss on her lips accentuates their size. She looks beautiful – the way a woman would dress if she was going on a date.

Did she go on a date?

The thought of it nags me like I have claim over her.

She looks at me but doesn't say a word. She walks by the sofa and proceeds toward the hallway where the bedrooms are located.

"Hi," I tell her.

She stops, looks at me briefly wearing a frown. Still, she doesn't say anything.

"Can I talk to you for a minute?"

"No," she responds. "I'm tired. I'm going to bed."

"Cherish—"

Her frown deepens and I hear aggravation in her voice when she asks, "What do you need now? You need me to change a bandage? You need soup? Water? What can I do for you before I go to bed?"

"I don't need anything. I just want to talk to you."

"Well, I know this is a foreign concept for you, but you can't get everything you want." She continues on to her room.

She's upset. It's my fault, so I shouldn't be surprised.

* * *

I can't sleep, and apparently, neither can she. It's around two in the morning when I hear her in the kitchen. I get up, walk there and see her drinking water. She's not wearing a robe this time – just a silk, pink nightie trimmed in white lace. She glances at me. Says nothing.

I look at her and don't know what to say. She usually initiates our conversations.

"I was out of line yesterday," I begin.

"You weren't out of line. You were being yourself. I understand you're straightforward and all that, but I don't have to put up with it, Montgomery. I quit working for you. You came to me. I didn't go running back to the estate. *You* said *you* needed help. When I try to get you to talk to me, you insult me. I don't know *what's* wrong with you. I don't even know why you're here. You don't need me to do anything for you. You're a *billionaire*. Go hire some nurses, therapists, Iyanla Vanzant and whoever else you need to *fix your life* and make you feel like a human again because this guy I'm looking at—this guy standing in *my* kitchen—he's not human. I really don't know *what* you are, *who* you are or what you want from me, but I can't help you."

"Can I speak now?"

"You're a grown man. You don't have to ask me for permission to speak," she fires at me.

"Why are you raising your voice at me?" I ask her.

She hikes up a brow. "Why are you in my house?"

I take a breather. People usually don't speak to me in this manner, so I try not to have a visceral reaction towards her.

"I don't trust a lot of people," I tell her. "That's why I'm here. I trust you."

"But not enough to confide in me."

She's standing in front of the sink. I'm near the table holding on to the edge suffering from a mild case of vertigo this early in the morning. I want to get closer to her but I think the space separating us is needed at the moment.

"I struggle with abandonment," I tell her. "It's the primary reason I'm the way I am. It's why I don't trust people. Why I've never been in love. Never been in any *real* relationship. In my mind, it won't work out because if my—if my own parents didn't want me, who else would? Throwing myself into the company allows me to forget that. To forget how *messed up* I am, because I *am* messed up," I tell her trying not to let my emotions get the best of me. I hate that. Hate being vulnerable.

"When I crashed my car, I didn't care if I lived or died. I didn't want to live. When I woke up in the hospital, I was angry because I didn't want to wake up. I wanted to die. There were things I wanted to accomplish, but I still wanted to die. I wanted to be a better person, I wanted to treat my mother better, I wanted to be a good role model for Major and a better boss. I wanted to show people the real me—the one you say I keep hidden—I wanted a second chance for all those things but I didn't feel like I deserved it."

She gasps, eyes swell with tears. "Monty..."

"I wanted it to be over. But it's not over. I'm here. In pain, trying to make it through. Trying to be *normal*. Trying to live my life like I have it all together. Like I have everything when what I really have is *nothing*. I don't have anything, Cherish. I'm here—at your house—because I need you to help me. I need you to save me," I say feeling a tear roll down my face.

She sniffles. "How am I supposed to do that?"

"No one knows me like you do. Not my brother, not my mother. Only you. I know that about you. I know how hard you work for me. How you go above and beyond for me. I know I'm hard to deal with, but please, *please* don't abandon me when I need you the most."

She walks over to me, wraps me in a hug, careful not to squeeze too hard due to my injuries. "I won't abandon you, Monty. I won't."

Chapter Twenty-One

Cherish

And just like that, he's reeled me back in. I was angry when I came home – ready to kick him to the curb, but he finally decided to talk to me.

I know it took a lot of courage. It breaks my heart to see him so broken. To see a man as strong as him reduced to tears. I walk with him back to the guest bedroom, sit with him, then help him into a reclining position. I make sure he's comfortable.

"Do you need the heating pad tonight?" I ask.

"No."

"Are you in any pain?"

"Physically? No—just a little dizziness."

"That'll probably be gone after you get more rest."

"I hope so."

"Um…you've never opened up that way to me before. I know it took a lot out of you, so I want you to get some rest and we'll talk in the morning over breakfast. Is that okay?"

"Yes."

I FIND HIM in the kitchen bright and early. Surprises me. He usually sleeps in.

"Hey, good morning," I tell him.

He looks over at me. "Good morning."

"I hope you got some sleep last night."

"I did. It felt really good to talk to you."

"I'm glad," I tell him. I place a pan on the stove and

take some cheese and eggs from the fridge. "Cheese and egg omelet. Is that good with you?"

"That's perfect."

While I'm getting the food prepared, he checks his phone. It doesn't take long to cook the omelets. I take our plates to the table and two cups of coffee – one black for him and the other with sugar and cream for myself.

We eat.

He breaks the silence saying, "This is good."

"Thanks."

He takes a sip of coffee. "I've always wondered how my life would've turned out had I been raised by my real parents."

"That's not unusual. Most children who were adopted or fostered probably feel the exact same way."

"I almost feel like I've been living under an identity. Like this person you see is not really who I am."

"I think it will help if you knew why they gave you up."

"How will I find that out when they're both deceased?"

"That, I'm not sure of. I'll have to do some research."

"*You'll* have to do some research?"

"Yes. You poured your heart out to me last night and I promise I'll do everything in my power to help you. Now, as for you giving up—let me tell you something—you don't have that option. You're brilliant—the smartest man I know. You don't have the right to give up when there are so many people who need you."

"Like who?"

"The obvious first of all. Your family. Friends. And you have one of the most profitable companies in North Carolina. Does Hawthorne Innovations donate to any charities? Homeless shelters? Food banks?"

"No. My father didn't believe in that sort of thing. He said they were all scams."

"And what about you? Do you believe that?"

He shrugs. "I never thought about it."

"You need to. Your main problem with yourself is,

you're not happy. You have all this money rolling in, but nothing going out. You need to *give*. Help people. There are kids out there right now who don't know where their next meal is coming from. *They* need you. Giving will make you happy. Knowing you're doing some good in this world is something to be proud of."

He nods.

"And then there's Sylvia…"

He takes a sip of coffee.

"Monty, Sylvia Hawthorne may not be your biological mother, but she does love you. Don't ignore her. Talk to her and don't talk to her like a co-worker. Talk to her like she's your mother because she *is*."

I take a break and eat a little while he digests my suggestions. After a sip of coffee, I say, "What I've come to learn about you is, you keep a lot inside. You hold a lot of resentment. If you don't release it, it'll only build and build and grow legs until you explode. Talk to her."

He nods again.

"And then there's the matter of your family—the people you don't know. If you don't love the people who are right here with you—Major and Sylvia—how will you love the ones you don't know?"

"You're right."

"You said you had an older brother."

"Yeah."

"Do I have your permission to help you find him?"

He stares at me. I can't read him this time. I'm waiting for an answer and he's in a trance.

"Monty?"

He clears his throat. "Yes. You have my permission."

"Good. By the way, you have a follow-up appointment with your primary doctor today."

"What time?"

"Two."

"Alright. That'll give me time to check in with Hannah."

"Okay."

While he's using the kitchen for his make-shift office, I take my laptop and sit out on the front porch. It's hot already – ain't even ten o'clock yet and I see heatwaves dancing across the road. I open a search engine and type: **Magnus St. Claire, Charlotte, North Carolina**. The first listing on the search results is for a company – MJS Communications. I click the link to go there. On the site, there's a page of executives along with pictures. My mouth falls open. Magnus St. Claire, the CEO, looks almost identical to Montgomery and Major. Same illustrious green eyes. Same curly black hair. There's no doubt in my mind that it's his brother. A DNA test isn't needed.

I key the phone number into my cell, fold my laptop closed and walk out into the yard as I press send to dial the number.

"MJS Communications. How may I direct your call?"

"I need to speak to Magnus St. Claire, please."

"Mr. St. Claire doesn't accept unsolicited phone calls, ma'am. May I ask what this is about?"

"Sure. Uh…my name is Cherish Stevens. I know his brothers and they would like to meet him."

"Okay, ma'am…can I get you to hold for a second?"

"Sure." I take a moment to look at my flowers. I glance over to see Ms. Kettleworth's truck is gone, thank goodness. Otherwise, she'd be over here running her mouth.

"Ma'am?"

"Yes, I'm here."

"I'm going to put you through."

Did she just say what I think she said? My nerves are all to pieces. She's actually going to put me through. *Crap! What am I doing?*

"This is Magnus St. Claire. Who am I speaking with?"

And they sound alike, too. Oh…my…goodness.

"Hello?"

"Oh. Hi. This is—this is Cherish Stevens, Mr. St.

Claire. Um…can I ask if you were adopted or in the foster care system at any point in your life?"

"You can, but how is that any of your business?"

"I'm going to get to that. Did you have any siblings who were placed in foster care?"

"I did. I've been talking to my uncle trying to locate them."

"Wow! Okay. Um, I know them."

"You do?"

"Yes. I work for one of them and he's desperate to meet you. They both are."

"What are their names?"

"Monty—I mean—Montgomery and Major St. Claire."

"They live here in Charlotte?"

"No. They live in Concord. Is there any way you can meet us somewhere so you can meet them?"

"You're moving a little too fast aren't you?"

"Yes. I know. I'm sorry. I'm just so excited. They've been waiting for this for a long time and—"

"I'll have my security team clear them and if everything checks out, I'll have them over at my home. Is this a good number to reach you?"

"Yes. This is my cell phone number."

"Okay. You'll hear from me in a few days Ms. Stevens."

"Thank you."

I hang up the phone excited like I'd just found some of my long lost kinfolks, but that's how happy I am for Monty and Major. They deserve to know their family.

THE DOCTOR TELLS Montgomery he's doing better. Says his ribs won't be fully healed until another three to four weeks but as long as he's not overdoing it, he can get around. As for the lacerations, the stitches have already fallen off. The scars on his face are becoming more and more less visible.

"Good job, Montgomery," the doctor says. "You must've assembled yourself a team of nurses."

"No. Not a team." Monty winks at me and smiles.

The doctor looks over at me. I see him although I'm nearly blinded by the brilliance of a rare smile from Montgomery St. Claire, I'm in awe. My goodness, he's beautiful.

"Ah, so you're the caretaker," the doctor says.

"I do the best I can. Montgomery can be difficult to please at times."

"Yet, you do it so well," Monty says.

He smiles again.

Is he—is he flirting with me? Can't be. He's probably just appreciative.

"Alright. That's all for me, folks. I'll need to see you back in about four weeks, Sir."

"I'll be here, I'm sure my caretaker will see to it that I am," he says staring at me more.

The doctor leaves the room.

I'm red-in-the-face embarrassed. "What are you doing?" I ask, amused.

"What do you mean?"

"I mean, you were telling the doctor I took care of you and all that."

"You did, and you did a good job. What? I can't compliment you?"

"No. You never did before."

"We weren't *friends* before. We are now."

I smile again because I think he really means it *this* time, especially since he knows how much I care for him.

Chapter Twenty-Two

Monty

Cherish says I need to learn to love the people who I *know* before getting to know family I've never met. Taking her advice, I called up Major this morning and arranged for him to pick me up for dinner. We end up at Jason's Deli since it's one of the closest restaurants to Cherish's house.

Major gets a salad. I stick with soup.

"You're looking much better these days," he says.

"Gee, thanks."

Major grins. "Seriously. The last time I saw you was shortly after you were released from the hospital."

"Yeah, well, it has been almost three weeks."

"Right. How's Cherish?"

"She's doing good."

"That's good to hear. It hasn't been the same without her around the house."

"What do you mean?" I ask, feeling a jealous streak slice through me. Cherish has always had a better relationship with Major than she's had with me. Everyone seems to get along with Major. I didn't care before. Now that I know her, I do.

"She brings life to the house," he answers. "She knows where everything is."

"Yeah. She does," I say, remembering the relieved look on her face when the doctor told me how my condition had improved.

"And she's as pretty as a picture," he says. "Beautiful inside and out. It's rare to come across a woman like her."

Jealousy burns my chest like acid reflux, but just to find out if my brother has a thing for her, I say, "You act like you're interested."

"Trust me, she's definitely a catch, but it's not *me* she has eyes for."

I get his insinuation but I continue eating while listening to him talk about her. He's right. She's pretty. Inside and out. She's an angel, and I know she has eyes for me. I understand how accommodating she is to my needs. But I'm not in a place where I could give her what she needs from a man. I'm still trying to fix myself and my relationship with my family. That's why I'm here with Major. Following her suggestions.

Not knowing where to begin regarding that, I hesitate at first. Then I hear Cherish's voice pushing me to say what needs to be said. "Listen, I want to—"

"You want to what?" Major asks.

"This isn't easy for me," I say rubbing my head. "I want to apologize for my behavior. I thought that being the CEO and handling problems no one else wanted to handle put me in an elevated position of power, but it has come to my attention that I should be using my platform as an opportunity to *serve* others. Not to belittle them, and I feel like that's what I've been doing with you. I don't want to do that anymore. I don't want to be *that* man. I want to be your brother, first and foremost. Everything, as it relates to the company, comes second."

Major looks to the left, to the right and then back to the left again. He turns all the way around, checks his six, then looks at me and glares. "Who are you?"

I crack a smile.

His glare sharpens.

"Did you at least hear what I said?" I ask.

"Oh, yeah. I heard you. That's why I'm trying to figure out what's going on. I ain't *never* in my *life* heard you say nothing like that."

I smile. That speaks to the power of one beautiful lil'

lady who's changing my life more than she realizes. It actually feels good to say these words to my brother and actually mean it. He's my brother. I love him. Too often, we take family for granted. I don't want to do that with my family any longer.

"Major, can you speak on what I just said?"

He shakes his head. "Not right now. I'm flabbergasted. You're going to have to give me a couple of days just to process this."

"Come on, man."

"This is all Cherish, isn't it?"

I resume eating. "She made some recommendations to me. Yes."

"And you're actually following them?"

"I am. It's a new day, brother. I'm trying to be a better version of myself, starting with you."

"That's good. I applaud you. They say the right woman can change a man for the better."

I grin. "Cherry isn't my woman."

"Who? *Cherry*, you say?"

I laugh at myself. "I mean, Cherish."

"Yeah, she'll be yours soon enough."

"You think so?"

"No. I *know* so."

"How you figure?"

"There's a reason you're drawn to her—just like there's a reason she can get you to do things that you never do. I can't tell you the last time we, as brothers, were out like this to enjoy ourselves over food and drinks. It's been over what? A decade?"

"Something like that."

"It shouldn't be that way, Monty."

"You're absolutely right. That's why I'm looking to change that. And keep in mind, I'm not perfect."

"You're *not*?" he quips.

"If I slip up and revert back to my old habits, cut me some slack."

"I think I can handle that."

* * *

When we arrive back at Cherish's house, Major shuts off the car.

"You're coming in?" I ask.

"Nah. It's late. I just wanted to bring up something about our older brother. I know it's a touchy subject for you and I was wondering if you've given any further thought to maybe finding him."

"I have. What's funny is, I don't know if I have it in me to do all the investigative work, you know."

"If you weren't so secretive about everything, you could hire somebody."

"Yeah, I could."

"Or, you can just let Cherish take care of it. I mentioned something to her about it. She said it was a thorn for you and she wanted to take the lead in finding him."

"She said that?"

"Yep. She's got your back...never seen anything like it."

"Yeah. Me either."

"It's probably time you did something about that."

"Like what?"

"Showing her how much you appreciate her for starters."

"Maybe so. Ay, be careful driving home."

"Yep."

He backs out as I step inside the house. I'm quiet as I enter. If Cherish is sleeping, I don't want to disturb her. The TV is on in the living room – makes me think she's still up. As I get closer to the couch, I can see her lying there, sleeping.

I watch her. Can't take my eyes off of her. I've never seen her so relaxed. She's usually always on the go, taking care of me. Of the house. Of anything that needs to be taken care of. But now, in this moment, is when all the work she's done takes a toll on her. When she falls asleep without making it to her bedroom. Without putting on pajamas and tying up her hair. She has on a skimpy nightshirt, a white see-through one. I try not to stare, but I rarely get to see her body. She keeps it hidden. Now, she's on display for my eyes only. So I take it all in, memorizing the curve of her hips. The firmness of her breasts. The chocolate color of her skin. The way her hair is splayed on the couch. I remember her breathing pattern. Watch her chest rise and fall gracefully. My eyes trace her nose. Her lips. Her chin. Her breasts again. They follow the length of her frame down to her toes. She's beautiful from head to toe. Inside and out. She's my saving grace.

My angel.

I want to scoop her up and take her to her bedroom but I run the risk of injuring myself with crack ribs and all. She'd never forgive me if I did that. So, I do the next best thing – I go to her room to get a blanket – first time I'd ever been in her bedroom. I take a blanket from the bed. As I'm leaving the room, I glance at the dresser and see a picture of a younger version of her with a man who I assume is her father. It makes me realize something – I have no clue who she is. I don't know anything about Cherish. When I'm with her, it's all about me. We never talk about her. Her family. Who she is and what kind of life she had before she started working for the estate.

That shows me how selfish I really am. I've never asked about her family and she's busying herself with helping me put mine back together.

I leave her room and cover her with a blanket. I hate to leave her in the living room alone, so I stay a while. I use one of the pillows that fell on the floor and rest my head on it – keeping my mind occupied by watching TV so I can't think about how hard and uncomfortable this floor is, especially for someone in my condition. It's when I hear

Cherish talking in her sleep. She's consistently mumbling something at first – doesn't make much sense. Sounds like gibberish. Then she yells, "No! Noo! Stop! Don't touch me!"

I sit up to look at her. "Cherish," I whisper, but she's sound asleep with a frown disturbing her otherwise beautiful, majestic face. There's nothing to suggest she's in distress. All I see are her pretty lips and closed eyes.

She's had a bad dream. I would be lying if I said I didn't wonder if there was any significance behind it.

Chapter Twenty-Three

Cherish

I wake up in the morning realizing I'm on the couch. There's a blanket on top of me. The TV is on, but the volume is turned down. I stretch and try to remember how I ended up sleeping here.

Oh, that's right—waiting for Monty to get back. Did he ever come back?

I stretch again and push the blanket off of me to get up off the couch. When my feet touch a body instead of the floor, I scream, snatch my legs back and tremble with fear, only to realize it's Monty.

He sits up, stretches and asks, "What are you screaming about now, girl?"

I'm heated. Scared and heated. "What are you doing down there?"

"I *was* sleeping—"

"You're supposed to be in the bedroom, not on the floor! I could've hurt you."

He laughs. Pisses me off. My heart is beating so fast, I can hardly catch my breath.

"It's not funny, Monty!"

"It *is* funny," he says, still laughing.

It's like music to my ears to hear him in good spirits, but I'm still angry.

He looks at me, amusement still on his handsome face. "Okay, first of all, I slept here because I wanted to be close to you."

"Close to me?"

"Yes."

"Why?"

"Because I wanted to. Second, you're not going to injure me, girl, with your lil' petite self."

"I'm heavier than I look."

"I doubt it."

"I *am*. I used to lift weights."

He laughs more. "The only weights you lift are those garden tools you use when you're playing in your flowers."

I growl, get up off the sofa and snatch my blanket, wrapping it around myself like a towel. "I'll cook breakfast when I'm out of the shower."

"Okay, heavyweight champ."

I roll my eyes at him and head down the hallway smiling. He's loosening up, showing more of his personality. I can't be mad at that.

* * *

My mother calls when I'm at the stove cooking French toast. I know this because Monty picks up my phone and says, "Ay, Belinda's calling you."

I leave the stove to take the phone from his grasp.

"Aren't you at work?" I answer, returning to the stove. In other words, why are you calling me?

"Yeah, I'm here. The boss took the day off. Listen, I'm not going to chat long but just wanted to let you know your stepfather's retirement party is this coming Saturday."

"And? Why are you telling me?" I ask her. I flip over the bread.

"It would mean the world to him if you showed up. We need to put the past in the past and start supporting each other like a family is supposed to."

"Are you—!" I pause before completely losing it, remembering I have an audience of one. When I turn around, Monty's looking intuitively at me while he sits behind his laptop with his hands steepled. I wonder how long he's been looking at me. Did the staring start with my mother's phone call or had he been staring all along, pretending to be engrossed in work? I can never tell with him. He's an intelligent man. Can easily pick up on situations without knowing the whole story. I can literally see him thinking the way he does when he stands at the windows in his office with his billionaire hands in his pockets.

I remove the pan from the stove and decide to take the call out on the porch.

"Helloooo? Are you there? Hellooo?" Mother croons.

Gosh, she gets on my nerves...

"I'm here, Ma."

"What's wrong with your phone, girl? I've been telling you to get rid of that cheap phone service. You've been working all this time and your phone breaks up more than celebrity couples." She cackles.

The side effect of having Webster Gregory for a husband is, his bad joke telling has rubbed off on her. She's even starting to sound like him. *Ugh.* They pronounce words the same now. Makes my stomach turn.

"There's nothing wrong with my phone, and, no, I *will not* be coming to Webster's retirement party."

"Why not? Give me one good reason?"

"Because your husband's still a pervert."

"Cherish—!"

I hang up the phone and step off of the porch, letting the sun warm my body. I close my eyes and angle my head up to the heavens. It's freeing to push bad memories to the back of my mind. My mother has a way of making them come back to the surface. She's the queen of sweeping things under the rug and keeping up appearances. So what if it comes at her only daughter's expense?

"What'cha doin', Sherrish?"

Oh, crap. Ms. Kettleworth...

I can't even get five minutes to myself to bake alone in the sun.

I open my eyes to see the old lady sliding between the bushes that separate our driveways. I swear she stays lurking behind them, waiting for an opportunity to slither her way over here and talk. The woman has a mess of grandkids and nobody to talk to but that funky feline that has her house smelling like cat poop and rotten kitty litter.

"I see yur schedule all thrown off."

"Yeah. I'm just switching some things up."

"Umm-hmm...dats what dey call it now-er-days, eh?"

"What do you mean, Ms. Kettleworth?"

"Oh, don't fart around with me, Sherrish," she says, poking me with her feeble elbow. "I see you done got yurself a man. I seent him. Umm-hmm. Sure did. Good looking feller. Riding up here in a Mer-Mer—what'chu call dem fancy rich-folk cars?" she asks, looking over at Monty's Mercedes.

"It's a Mercedes."

"Yeah. Dat's it. A Mer-shay-dees. Dem cars sure cost a lotta mucho dinero."

"Yeah..." But it ain't nothing for a billionaire. He got the kind of money where he shouldn't be driving himself at all.

"And he's easy on the eyes, too, I tell ya dat."

"Um, yeah. Look, I was just in the middle of cooking breakfast, so I'll talk to you later, Ms. Kettleworth."

"Alright," she says like she's sad I abruptly ended our conversation. I feel bad for her sometimes, but I can't make her family visit her.

I return to the kitchen, catching a glimpse of Monty's laptop screen before returning to the stove. He's staring at a picture of a drawing of some kind.

"Everything okay?" he asks.

"Yep. Fine and dandy."

"Doesn't sound convincing."

"Yeah, well—"

I take some butter from the fridge and a pack of strawberries. I cut them in halves and put some on our plates. I make him coffee. I'm not in the mood for caffeine this morning.

When he sees me walking over to him with his breakfast, he folds his laptop closed and stares at the plate.

"Thank you."

"Welcome," I say. I don't feel like having breakfast with him this morning. I'd rather eat alone but I don't want to be the kind of person I told him *not* to be so I take a seat and just start eating, forcing it down. The faster I eat, the quicker I can get out of here.

I eat a strawberry and glance up at him. He's chewing, looking at me.

I look away.

His eyes, his face still gets to me. Seems to affect me differently when I'm in a somber mood. I was okay before my mother called. Now, I'm inhaling strawberries and whatnot.

I glance up at him again.

His eyebrows raise. Head tilts.

I look away. Eat more strawberries. Retreat to my shell.

"Who's Belinda?" he asks.

How do I answer that? Telling him about my mother opens the door for more questions about my family – something I don't want to discuss.

"Why do you ask?"

He shrugs. "I'm just asking." He takes a sip of coffee, never taking his eyes off me. I imagine this is the same way he does interviewees for high-level positions at his company. "Besides, I realized last night I don't know much about you. So—who's Belinda?"

"She's my mother."

"Oh. She lives here in Charlotte?"

"Yep," I say tight-lipped.

"You don't get along with your mother?"

"Why do you think that?"

"I don't think it. I know it. You just yelled at her before taking the call outside, and when I mentioned it was her on the phone, you cringed."

"I didn't cringe."

"You did, and you're very uncomfortable right now. Something's off."

I ignore his last statement and drink water.

He drops his fork in the plate so it purposely makes a loud clank. He knows it'll get my attention. I look at him. He narrows his green eyes at me. "Wow. You really don't want to talk about her, do you?"

"Not right now I don't."

"Okay, then. Let's talk about your boyfriend."

I crack a smile. "I don't have a boyfriend."

"You got something. Maybe you don't call him a boyfriend, but he's *something*."

"What would make you think that, Monty?"

"Last Saturday, you came home eleven o'clock at night, hair hanging all loose, had on that pretty dress that'll turn any man's head and well, I can tell when a woman is dressing to hang with her girls versus to be with a man."

"Okay, first of all, that was my Saturday outfit. I told you I was going out to do something fun. You talked me into staying home for a movie that we never watched by the way. So, when you flipped your lid and went berserk on me, I got dressed and went out. I wasn't about to waste an outfit staying home."

He chuckles. "You went out where?"

"For a drink."

"*Where* was my question."

"Sticky Fingers."

"In Concord?"

"Yes."

"With who?"

"Your brother."

He frowns. Surprises me because I don't know the reason behind it. Why does it bother him that I was with Major?

He resumes eating, doesn't say a word more. I imagine

he wants to know what me and Major were doing. If we were talking about him, or if we were having a good time together. Laughing and chatting it up. Just me and him.

"You got dolled up to go out on a date with my brother?"

I sigh. He took it there. He doesn't frown. Doesn't sound disappointed. He sounds more like he can't believe it. He puts on his poker face awaiting my response. "It wasn't a *date*, Monty."

"Then what was it?"

"It was two friends having drinks and talking."

"Talking about what?"

"You."

He raises a brow. "Me?"

"Yes."

"Whatever you want to know about me, you can ask me."

"Yeah, *now* I can. Last Saturday, I couldn't ask you nothing. You were about as talkative as a brick wall."

"Sort of how you were just a few minutes ago when I asked you about your mother?"

I pause. I can't tell if he's upset because I compared him to a brick wall, that I spoke to Major about him behind his back or that I was out with him. I don't leave it to him to tell me which. I make the effort to ease the sudden tension mounting between us by saying, "You know what, I'm sorry. I shouldn't have said anything to Major about you."

"What did you want to know?"

"The things you told me on Sunday—that's what I wanted to know. I was trying to figure out the best way to help you. I had no ill intent."

"Do you like him?"

"Major?"

"Yes."

"Yeah. I like him. As a friend."

"The same way you like me," he says.

I can't tell if he meant it as a question or a statement. I look at him, hold his intense gaze and nod since I can't bring myself to speak the lie into existence. If it were up to me, we'd be much more than friends. I don't just *like* Monty – I'm borderline obsessed, but what on earth would I do with a man like him? A man of power and influence. There's no way I could live up to the expectations he'd have of a woman, especially given my inexperience with men.

I never had a man. Don't know what to do with one. For the longest time, I didn't want one – that is until I met Monty. Something about him spoke to me and continues speaking to me. Whispers sweet nothings in my ear. Never did I *ever* think I would be this close to him. Working for him, keeping my distance and fantasizing was one thing. Us being together so often and him living with me in my home is another.

Chapter Twenty-Four

Monty

I've never been a jealous person, partly because I never wanted something someone else had and couldn't obtain it. If I want a car, I go get. A property, I buy it. Clothes – I have plenty of the latest designer suits and shoes.

A woman…

That's something you can't buy. You can't *own* a woman. If I see a man with the woman I want, I can't go buy another one of *her*. That's what bothers me about the slightest possibility that Major and Cherish may have a *thing* going on. Meeting up secretly for drinks and whatnot. If she falls for him, I'll never find another *her*.

And it's a strong possibility that could happen. That *they* could become an item.

Major looks just like me. Only two years separate us by age. He's more outgoing. Friendlier. He doesn't have the same issues I have. He's the nicer version of me. Women like Cherish Stevens don't fall in love with men for their looks. She's more of the personality type. Wants someone with good intentions. A good heart.

To attract someone like her, I'd have to change.

Major doesn't. He's already *that* person. The good-hearted kind.

I don't care that she and Major were discussing me. I care that they were together, having fun. Talking together. Laughing. Doing what people who date do.

Meanwhile, I'm trying to work on myself. To be a man she'd respect. One she could see herself with. I know I'm not that man yet. I desperately want to be. But who am I to hold her back from living? She has no idea I'm feelin' her.

None.

She's so busy tending to my needs, I'm probably more of a burden to her than anything else.

I hear the lightest knuckle tap on the door. She pushes it open, peeps around.

"Hey."

"Hey."

She walks closer to me. Her hair is up in a bun. She has on a pajama set. It's her bedtime. She's doing her final check to see if I need anything.

"I see you already got your water," she says.

"Yep," I say, sitting up a little so I can properly talk to her.

"Do you need anything else?"

"Yeah. I need you to rub that cream on my face."

She laughs.

"Why are you laughing? I'm serious."

"Monty, your scars are barely visible now. Your face is healing well."

"Then why does it miss your fingers."

She smiles again. Her smile is beautiful. When she smiles, I see genuine joy in her eyes. "Your face misses my fingers?" she asks amused.

"Yes."

She chews on her lip, makes my eyes fall to her mouth.

"I'm just playing with you. I'm good, but I do want to talk to you about something."

"Okay. What's up?"

"I've been working on myself and my relationships with people, as you're aware. You laid out a plan for me, I've been following it."

"Okay."

"I want to talk to Syl—my mother—and I was thinking we could do it over dinner."

"Here or over there?"

"Here, if you don't mind."

She smiles. "I don't mind at all. I'll cook. Will it just be her or is Major coming, too?"

"Nah, your boyfriend ain't invited. You can cancel that."

She laughs. "He's not—urrgh—he's not my boyfriend. I don't have a boyfriend."

"Why is that? You're obviously beautiful, have a heart of gold. You're smart, you can cook. You're everything a man would need."

I can tell she's searching for an answer but when one escapes her, she says, "Let's get back to this meal. What would you like for me to cook?"

"You can cook whatever you want."

"Okay. I'll think on it and go to the store tomorrow."

"Sounds like a plan."

"And you're going to help me cook it, too," she says.

"I don't cook, sweetheart."

"I know you don't. You've probably never cooked a meal in your privileged life, huh?"

"That's one of the perks of being rich, baby. I get people to do things for me."

"Well, you're going to get those hands dirty tomorrow."

"Is that right?"

"Yes. That's right. Get some sleep. If you need me, you know where to find me, *boss*," she says walking away from me. My eyes follow the length of her body like it always does. Lingers on her hips. Her hair. Her feet. I often wonder if she feels the heat from my eyes – if she notices the way I look at her or if she sees me just like she does my brother. We're *friends*. I made that suggestion because before, we were nothing. She was my employee. Now, she's so much more. She's the woman who's saving my life. The woman teaching me how to love and showing me the importance of my family. I will always be grateful to her for that.

Chapter Twenty-Five

Cherish

I can't get the grocery bags out of my trunk and here comes Ms. Kettleworth, wearing a straw hat that looks like it came straight off the head of a scarecrow. She has a can of sardines in her hand. Her cat, Butterball, is clawing at her heels – big ol' freakin' cat – meowing and carrying on...pecking at her ankles like it's in starvation mode.

"You done went and got yaself food, ain't you, Sherrish?" she asks so loud, I know the people who live across the street heard her.

"Yep. Had to replenish the fridge."

"You say what?" she asks loudly, turning her head to point her ear toward my mouth.

"I said, I had to replenish the fridge."

"Oh. The fridge bare again, hunh? Didn't you just fill dat thang up last week? Dat man you got in there must be 'bout to eat you out of a house and home."

I chuckle. "He *does* have quite the appetite."

"You say what now? I 'pologize. I'm missing a hearing aid...didn't quite hear ya."

"Nevermind, Ms. Kettleworth. I'll see you later—"

"What'chu cookin' for him this evening, hun?" she asks, thwarting my escape. Danggit!

"Um, I think I'm going to make some Ziti."

"You say—you say you fixin' up some Zeebi—what in the world is dat?"

"No, Ms. Kettleworth. Ziti."

"I heard you, hun. Zeebi. Sounds zotic."

Lawd have mercy. I ain't got time for this...

"It's not *exotic*. It's kinda like spaghetti, just with different noodles."

"Sounds like it might be good. Zeebi. Ain't never heard of no Zeebi."

"You know what, I'll save you some. How about that?"

"Oh, you ain't gotta do dat. These sardines'll serve me just right." She licks the sardine oil from her fingers then says, "I sure wish I knowed you were going to the store though. I would've told you to bring some cat food back."

"Yeah, you need to buy some ASAP. Your cat looks like he's 'bout to claw you up real good for that sardine can."

"Well, guess what, Sherrish. I ain't sharing. Scat! Scat!" she says. Butterball doesn't run. Not while she's holding that sardine can...

She's shoveling sardines in her mouth by the spoonful. The fishy smell is taking off thanks to the heat of the day. And her cat is scratching his way up her dusty old shoes and dirty jeans, trying to get his share.

"Scat! Scat!" she tells it. "Fat ol' cat. Eats er'thang in its path like a tornader. I bet'chu that's what happened to my hearing aid."

I don't mean to laugh, but it couldn't be helped. This woman is nuts. "I doubt if the cat ate your...your hearing aid, Ms. Kettleworth."

"Say what, hun!"

Oh, Jeez...

"I said, I don't think your cat ate your hearing aid," I shout.

"Well, somebody broke in and stole it then I tell ya dat."

I'm giggling so hard, I can hardly speak when I say, "Somebody broke...broke into your house...to...to steal *one* hearing aid and left the other one in your ear?"

"They most certainly did. I paid good money for dem hearing aids, too."

"Well, maybe you can get another pair if you file it with

your insurance."

"Insurance? Ha! Honey, I ain't had insurance since 1998. Mess cost too much money."

"What about Medicare?"

"Medicare don't *care* 'bout me. Just another way for the gov'ment to fill they greedy pockets. But don't you worry 'bout me, Sherrish. I can buy a brand spankin' new pair of ears from the Walgreens right 'round the corner."

If she insists on wearing drugstore hearing aids, who am I to stop her? "Well, I'll see you later. I need to put this food up, Ms. Kettleworth."

"Okay, and one more thang, Sherrish."

I roll my eyes before I turn around and say politely, "Yes, ma'am?"

"Now, you knows I try to mind my own business 'round here but I done seen a white Chevy rolling real slow past your house a couple of times. I ain't thank nuttin' of it the first time, but I'd be doggone if it didn't roll by just before you pulled up with dem there groceries."

"Oh, it's probably nothing," I tell her, although I feel sick suddenly. I know someone who drives a white Chevy Impala. My stepfather. Webster Gregory.

"Will you let me know if you see it again?" I ask her.

"Sure will."

Montgomery comes out of the house before I can make it to the porch. He's dressed in a button-up shirt – a white one and a pair of black slacks like we're going out to dinner. His hair looks extra curly. He hasn't shaved since he's been here with me and the facial hair looks good against his light skin tone. He looks like a whole entire snack.

Oh, my heart...

He's breathtaking without even trying to be.

"Hey, if I knew you were out here, I'd come to get the bags," he tells me.

"Oh, it's okay. I only have a—um," He's wearing that cologne. Dolce & Gabanna. Smells like he just jumped out

163

of the shower and sprayed it on his body. That hot body that's been healing so well.

"Um—" I still can't find words.

He takes the bags out of my hands.

"And who do we have here?" Ms. Kettleworth asks, looking at Montgomery. Looks like he's blushing, but her face is so discolored and damaged from years of smoking, I don't know what she's doing. This could very well be the prelude to a stroke.

Montgomery looks at me before returning his attention to her to introduce himself. That's a huge leap for him. "Hi. I'm Montgomery."

"Pleased to meet your 'quaintance fine, Sir. I'm Ms. Kettleworth." She drops the sardine can – the overweight cat runs off with it – then she reaches to shake Montgomery's free hand.

"Nice to meet you," he says.

"Alright, Ms. Kettleworth. I'll see you later," I say.

"Okay, hun. Eat enough Zeebi for me and I'll let you know if I see that car 'round here again."

"Okay. Thanks."

As we walk up the steps to the porch, Montgomery asks, "What car? What is she talking about?"

"Oh, nothing. That's Ms. Kettleworth—my nosy neighbor I was telling you about."

"She looks bad."

"And yet you still shook her hand. I'm so proud of you."

"Proud?" he asks setting the bags on the counter.

"Come on, Monty—you know just as well as I do you would've never done that in the past."

He shrugs. "Probably not."

"But you did. Kudos to you. Just make sure you wash your hands because she was eating sardines. Your hand probably smells like fish oil."

He takes a whiff of his hand and sure enough, goes straight to the sink and washes his hands for a full two minutes. He dries them and says, "So, what do we need to do first?"

"Well, you need to get out of that white shirt if you don't want sauce splashed all over it."

"I'm good. If I get sauce on it I'll just change."

"Yeah, because it's no big deal if you ruin a five-hundred-dollar shirt."

"It's not," he says all cocky. He's getting his swagger back. Makes me wonder how he'll be when he's fully healed and won't need me any longer.

I give him the assignment of cooking sweet Italian sausage and ground beef. I take the harder tasks — chopping onions and boiling noodles to the correct firmness. Then I caramelize the onions before preparing the sauce. I find the biggest pot I have, pour in the spaghetti sauce, fire-roasted tomatoes and add the onions. Now, I need the meat.

"How's it going over there?" I ask him. "Do you need some help?"

"No. I got this," he says tending to two pans.

"How long before it's ready, Monty?" I ask him.

"You're asking a man who's never cooked a thing in his life if something's done."

I laugh. "You gotta eyeball it."

We reach for the handle of the pan at the same time. His hand lands on top of mine. Skip the heat from the stove. The heat I feel with him is unbearable. All kinds of energy flows from him to me. I wonder if he feels it, too? Then again, why would he?

"Sorry," he says, moving his hand.

"That's okay," I say like it had no effect on me.

"It's done," I tell him. "Good job, chef."

"Whatever. You're doing the hard work. You gave me the easy stuff."

"No, no, no. It's a *team* effort. I can't make the sauce properly without the meat."

I pour off the grease, then add it to the sauce. When

the noodles are ready, I strain them and dump them in a casserole dish. I add the sauce along with a thick layer of mozzarella cheese and place it in the oven.

I wipe sweat from my head using my forearm. Montgomery is propped up against the counter looking at me. "Is there anything else I can help you with?"

"Um—I think I can handle it from here. Did you text your mother to make sure she was still coming?"

"Yes. Said she'll be here at five."

"Five!"

"Yes."

"I thought she wasn't going to be here until six?" I say in a panic. "I haven't even made the salad yet."

"It's fine, Cherry. Calm down."

"I am calm," I say, looking for my best bowl – the glass one I never use.

"No, you're not. You look like you're about to pass out. Hey—"

"I'm fine, Monty."

"No, you're not," he says, wrapping an arm around me, pulling me to him. Next thing I know, I'm spinning, standing in front of him. Facing him. Looking up at the smirk on his face that tries to hide beneath the cover of his thick beard.

I'm soaking it all up – getting all the testosterone and all the feels that only a man can exude to make a woman's body ache. Well, in my case, only him. No other man could ever make me feel this way. "Monty," I say, looking to the right and the left, too timid to connect my gaze to his.

"I need your attention," he says.

"Monty…"

"Do I have your attention, Ms. Stevens?"

I look at him, can see the smile on his face now. Oh gosh, he's so handsome I can't stand it.

"Ms. Stevens?"

"Yes?"

MONTY

"Look at me."

I look at him. His eyes are my weakness. I'm drowning in them. "Wha—wha—what are you doing?"

"Forcing you to calm down."

And you think being pinned between your body and the counter is a calming mechanism...

"I am ca-ca-calm. I told you that."

He chuckles.

"You're not calm. You're stuttering. You don't stutter under normal circumstances, now stop it. You have nothing to be stressed about. It's only Sylvia coming over."

"I just want to make sure everything's perfect. It's more than just about Sylvia. It's about *you* and Sylvia. I'm not doing this for her. I mean, I am but it's mostly for you. I'm doing it for you, and I want it to be perfect."

He smiles, then it goes away, replaced by a more serious look when he strokes his thumb down my face. My body shivers beneath his touch. "It will be, Cherish. It already is. Even if we don't have a salad. Now, what I want you to do is breathe."

"I am breathing."

"No, you're not. You're panicking. Over some lettuce and tomatoes." He comes closer to me. We're chest to chest when he says, "I feel your heart thumping. I'm close enough where I can hear how hard you're breathing, baby. Stop stressing."

Cute. He thinks the meal prep is the cause of my stress.

It's not the meal prep, Monty. It's you. The way you smell. The way the heat of your body feels against mine. Make me all tingly and stuff. It's the way you're looking at me like I'm the only woman in the world – like you want me. I know you don't, but a girl can dream.

"Yeah. You're right," I tell him, hoping he'd let me go. He doesn't. Instead, he lifts me from the floor and places me on the counter with one effortless motion. I'm light as a feather in his grasp. Now that I'm almost face-to-face with him, courtesy of the height of my kitchen counters,

167

he looks at me and says, "I just want you to know how much I appreciate everything you're doing for me and everything you've done."

Am I imagining this?

"Cherish?"

"Oh, you're welcome, Monty."

"I mean it. I appreciate everything. You've taught me to appreciate people and what they do for me. Going forward, I'll be more conscientious of my workers. But you—there's just something extra special about you."

"There's nothing *special* about me."

"There is. No one can take care of me like you, Cherish Stevens."

The way he's looking at my lips makes me think he wants to kiss me.

"Oh, please. I'm sure there're plenty of women out there vying to take care of you."

"Probably, but there's only one I want," he says.

I try not to twist his words. Try not to trick myself into believing they mean something. He didn't say he wanted *me*. He said it in the context of me being the only woman he trusts to take care of him. But there's something about the way he's looking at my lips...

"Maybe I should get started on the salad now," I say.

"That's probably a good idea."

* * *

Sylvia arrives. I greet her at the door with a hug. She hasn't seen Montgomery since he's been here and when he comes walking into the living room, she's reduced to tears.

"Oh, son, I love you so much," she says, her arms wrapped around him so tight, I don't think she'll ever let him go.

"Stop crying. I'm okay," he tells her.

I go ahead to the kitchen to give them some privacy. I'm preparing their plates, instantly deciding I'm not going to be a part of this conversation. Monty needs this time alone with his mother and she needs it with him just as equally. I don't want to get in the way of that. I want them to say what needs to be said without a third party being eyewitnesses to their innermost thoughts.

I relay this to Montgomery when he walks in the kitchen and he says, "No. I want you here."

"Monty—"

"It's not up for discussion, Cherish."

Monty has a way of being assertive when he doesn't get his way. I know this about him now, but I won't accept it this time. "It *is* up for discussion," I toss back.

Sylvia stays quiet and takes a seat at the table.

"Let's talk." Montgomery secures me by the arm and leads me down the hallway to my bedroom then closes the door. "What are you doing?" he asks.

"I'm being respectful of you and your mother. She has things she needs to get off of her chest and so do you. I don't want to be in the middle of that, Monty."

"You've *been* in the middle of it, Cherish. If it wasn't for you, she wouldn't be here right now because guess what? I didn't have the desire to fix things between me and her. That was all you. Now you're backing out on me?"

"No—"

"Then what do you call it?"

"I'm giving you privacy."

"I don't want privacy. I want your support. I need it. I need *you*."

We stare at each other. I'm more shocked than anything because I know he's a strong man. He's fully capable of having this discussion with Sylvia without me there. But he doesn't want to.

"Monty, you have my support."

"Then why are we having this discussion? Hunh?"

I grit my teeth.

This man, this man…

He's going to be the death of me.

I take his hand and say, "Let's go." I open the door and we head back to the kitchen.

We all sit around the table with plates. Sylvia comments on how good the food is.

"Thanks, Sylvia. Monty helped me cook the Ziti."

"Really?"

"Yes, he did."

"Monty hasn't cooked a day in his life."

"Now he has, so you can't say that anymore."

He looks at me and smiles. Then, with the straightest face I've ever seen on him, even more so than before the accident when he was a cruel dictator around the estate, he looks at Sylvia and says, "Let's get down to business. Why don't you love me?"

"What?"

"We're here to resolve our issues, and my main issue with you is, I don't feel that you love me. Or Major."

"Son, that couldn't be further from the truth."

I feel helpless. I can't jump in and remediate. I'm just a fly on the wall trying to understand both perspectives, but leaning more toward Monty's because, well—I love him. There. I said it. I love him and I'm no longer willing to deny what my heart feels. I love Montgomery St. Claire and it hurts me to see him sad. Pains me to think he feels this way about Sylvia when I can clearly see how much she loves him.

"If you loved me, I'd have your last name. I don't have your last name. Major doesn't have your last name. You never adopted us. You fostered us, hoping the social workers would find us a permanent residence but they never did. So, you were stuck with us, but we weren't good enough to be adopted."

"I wanted to adopt you. The first day I laid eyes on you and Major, I wanted to adopt you both then and there, but your father—"

"Please don't blame this on dad."

"Son—"

"He's not here to defend himself."

"Monty, I'm sorry, but I have to tell you the truth whether it's hard to hear or not. If we're truly going to get to the bottom of this, you need to hear my side of the story."

I can see Monty struggling. Can feel his strong rigid vibes that used to paralyze me when I worked at the estate – before I knew him as well as I do now. To help him through this, place a hand on his thigh. Still frowning, he looks at me. "It's okay, Monty," I whisper.

He places his hand on mine and says, "Okay. Let me hear your side of the story," he tells Sylvia.

"Son, I wanted children. I desperately wanted children but your father and I couldn't have any. We looked at alternative treatments, but by that time came around, we were exhausted. He was tired of trying so he kept himself occupied with work. I suggested we adopt a baby. He refused. Said he wanted children of his own. The only other option for me was to become a foster parent. I nearly begged him to get on board with that idea. At first, he didn't like it. Told me I could only take one of you. I convinced him I wasn't going to split you two up, so we took you both—you and Major. As the years went by and we knew you two weren't going to be adopted, I asked your father to make it official. Told him I wanted to adopt you. He didn't want to. Said he loved you all the same— didn't matter what your last names were. He wanted you to keep your name. Wanted you to have that connection to your roots in case you ever wanted to go looking for your relatives. It had nothing to do with a lack of love. I fought to keep you two together and even though we were well off, I made sure your upbringing was as normal as I possibly could."

She pauses. I look at Monty. His head is down. He's not saying anything. He's thinking about what he wants to say. That, I can tell. "Monty," I whisper to get his attention. Then I say, "Tell her what's on your heart." I interlock my hand with his, assuring him of my support.

He draws in a deep breath, looks at her and says, "As a child, you don't fully know what's going on, you know, being in a situation where you're being placed in different homes. You don't understand the reason your parents gave you away. But as you get older, as *I* got older, I realized they didn't want me. That somebody actually *gave* me away like—just handed me away as easily as I can hand you this fork. I never got over that and I don't think I ever will. That's why I'm the way I am. Why I feel like when you and dad took us in, it was confusing because it's like you wanted us, but you really didn't. We were being handed off again, waiting to be handed off to someone else. I remember as a teen thinking I didn't want to get too attached to you or dad because the time would come when we would have to move to another house. That fear subsided when I graduated. I was grown. I could go where I wanted, choose my own path. I chose to learn the business because I felt like—"

He pauses. Takes a breath. His lips trembles just slightly.

"I felt like it would be the only thing that would keep dad from dismissing me as the *foster* child he raised. I felt like it would make me his son even though I didn't deserve to be his son."

"Montgomery," Sylvia says, with tears streaming down her face.

"How do I qualify to be *his* son—the great Caspian Hawthorne—when my own father didn't want me? Why did you want to be my mother when my *real* mother threw me away?"

His hand shakes. My heart breaks for him. It's how I know I love this man. I only want the best for him. Want him to be happy because his happiness makes me happy. Right now, he's not happy. He's broken.

Sylvia gets up, sits beside him and puts an arm around him. "Monty, I don't know what happened to your biological parents, so I can't answer that, son. All I know is, I love you. I always have. I raised you and Major. I wish things were different for you. I do, but I don't regret taking you in. You and Major—you're the best thing that's ever happened to me and I will love you 'til the day I die. Love you like I've always loved you."

He nods. "I'm sorry," he tells her. "Sorry for the way I've treated you."

"It's okay, son," she says.

"No, it's not okay," he says looking at her. "I'm sorry and I want you to know that. And I love you too, Mother." He releases my hand to embrace her in a full hug.

I smile. Finally. She's his *mother* again.

He clears his throat when they separate and says, "Now, that we've cleared that up, let's eat."

"I'll re-warm the food," I say getting up to take their plates to the microwave.

Chapter Twenty-Six

Monty

It's freeing to rid myself of the pain my past has caused me. I have a long way to go but getting back on good terms with my brother and now my mother is a great start.

And it's all because of her.

Cherish Stevens.

She's cleaning the kitchen. I'm perched against the doorway my hands in my pockets watching her work. She's washing the casserole pan, wiping down the counters and putting away dishes.

She turns around, surprised to see me standing here at first, but then a smile comes to her face. A face I've come to enjoy over the last few weeks. "Hey. Everything okay?"

I hear her question, but I'm so enthralled by this amazing woman who's come into my life that I can't fix my mouth to make words. I only stare, take in her beauty. Appreciate her for being accommodating of me. For being my support through this difficult time in my life.

"Monty," she says and smiles.

She owes me nothing. She doesn't have to do a thing for me. I haven't offered her any compensation and she hasn't demanded anything of me but respect. She does what she does out of the goodness of her heart. This beautiful girl has paused her life for three weeks for me and I'm not blind to it. I know why. There could only be one reason she'd do this for me.

Only one.

She smiles again. Narrows her eyes. "Monty?"

I take a few steps over to her, stand in her immediate

space while she's holding a dishcloth.

"What's wrong?" she whispers.

"Why do you think something's wrong, sweetheart?" I brush my knuckles down her soft, warm cheek. Her eyes close at my touch. Her breaths are short and quick. She nibbles on her lip but stops just as quickly as she started to my chagrin. .

I take my hand away from her face.

Her eyes open, peering into mine.

That soul exchange phenomenon happens again.

She glances away like she always does when she looks into my eyes. Then she's right back, looking. Losing herself in my gaze.

Time stands still.

I'm too much in awe to say anything. My heart swells with joy to be in her presence. To know how this woman feels for me without her having to say it. Her actions have told me all I need to know. That's why it's so easy for me to open my heart to her – to let her see all of my faults and fears – all the things that make me who I am.

Time stands still.

My gaze doesn't let up. In my mind, I think of ways I can repay her for all she's done for me. That somehow turns into images of us making love in this kitchen. I've never thought of her this way before, but it's all I can think about lately – about hoisting her up on this counter while my body is embedded so deep inside of her, I make her thoughts dissipate. Make her brain turn to mush. Make her moan with pleasure. I can already taste her lips. Her mouth. I can feel the warmth of her body. Her heartbeat thumping. Chest to chest with me, we'll share sweat and heat. She'll cry her moans until they become screams. She'll scream so loud, her nosy neighbor will call 9-1-1 to request a wellness check.

But I pace myself. She's too special of a woman to rush anything with her. Besides, there's plenty I don't know about her. A lot of things.

"Monty," she whispers again in a sweet voice that instantly makes me want to change my mind. The counter is looking better and better.

"Yes?"

"Are you okay?"

"I'm fine. Are you okay?"

She smiles. My heart dances.

"Yes. I'm okay."

"It's been a long day, hasn't it?"

"Yes. It has, and I'm *so* proud of you."

"Why?" I ask for no other reason than wanting to see her lips move when she answers me – to give me another minute to decide if I want to catch her off guard and devour them.

"You worked things out with your mom. You opened up and got a lot of your problems out. It takes a lot of courage to do what you did."

It also takes a lot of courage to resist your lips right now. Instead of going for them, I leave a kiss on her temple. "I couldn't have done it without you."

She smiles. Blushes.

"Do you need any help in here?" I ask her.

"No. I'm done. I'm just about ready to take a shower and crash."

"Me, too."

"Have a good night."

"I will. You do the same, Cherry," I say and walk away from her quickly to avoid pushing my lips to her temple again. Why? Because they might divert and drive towards her mouth instead and I know if I ever kiss her lips, I'll never want to stop. So, I walk away. Don't want to, but I do. "Oh, by the way," I say before exiting the kitchen, "I'm taking you out tomorrow night and I want you to wear something pretty like you do when you go out with my brother."

She smiles. That's something I can take with me to bed.

Chapter Twenty-Seven

Cherish

I get up early in the morning to water my flowers since I didn't get a chance to do it yesterday evening. I glance over at Ms. Kettleworth's house. The front door is wide open. I run back inside to get the plate of baked Ziti I saved for her and walk it over. I step up on the porch.

Meow, meow. Butterball is circling my leg like a shark. "Hey, Butterball. Where's your—um—your mommy?"

Meow. Meow!

"Ms. Kettleworth, are you up?" When I don't hear anything, I say her name louder, remembering she'd lost one of her hearing aids.

"Sherrish, what you doing over here so early this morning doing all dat hootin' and hollerin'?"

"Sorry. I didn't know if you heard me, Ms. Kettleworth. I know you had lost your hearing aid."

"I found it. It fell off in the bed."

"Oh. Okay. I just came by to bring you some Ziti."

Her eyes light up. "You brought me some Zeebi?"

"Yes. I told you I would. I hope you like it."

"I'm sure I will, hun. I'ma eat this for dinner tonight. I'll tell you how I like it. I most certainly will."

"Okay."

"How'd your lil' shindig go last night? I saw a lady come over. She was driving a nice car, too. One of dem spaceship lookin' thing-a-ma-jobbers. That's what I call 'em. Spaceships. Doggone thangs run off bat'tries and a push from the lord."

I grin. "I went good. The lady you saw is

Montgomery's mother. She came over for dinner."

"Well ain't dat nice. That's how you do it, Sherrish. Get in good with the mum and you'll have dat man wrapped 'round your finger and fo' long, you'll have a ring on dat same finger."

"We don't have that kind of relationship, Ms. Kettleworth. Montgomery is a friend. I'm helping him."

"Friend." She releases a sneaky grin. "He's a mighty good-looking friend. How you stay trapped in a house with a man dat looks like him and call him a *friend* is beyond me, hun. I might be old and can't hear worth a lick, but these here eyes—ain't nothing wrong with my eyes."

"Yeah, he is easy on the eyes. I'll admit that much."

My cell phone rings. I check to see who it is. It's Magnus St. Claire. I've been waiting for his call. "Ms. Kettleworth, I have to take this. I'll talk to you later."

"Okay. Thanks for the Zeebi, hun."

"You're welcome," I say, walking back to my yard, then I answer the phone, "Hello."

"Cherish?"

I'm amazed that it's *him* and not his secretary. He said he would call me back. Looks like he's a man of his word. "Yes, this is Cherish."

"Hi. It's Magnus St. Claire. How are you this morning?"

"I'm doing well. I'm glad you returned my call."

"I'm glad you called me. I want to schedule a meeting with Montgomery and Major as soon as possible."

"So, do you think they're your brothers?"

"I don't *think* it. I *know* it, and I cannot thank you enough for reaching out to me. I don't know any of my family. I just found out I had an uncle – my father's brother – who's alive and he has four sons."

"Wow. More family?"

"Yes, and I haven't met them as of yet. What do you think about me trying to get everybody together at the same time?"

"Oh, um…you know what…I know Montgomery well, and I believe it would be very overwhelming for him to meet everybody. I think he would just like to know his big brother for now."

"Okay. That's fine. How does next Saturday sound?"

"I'm sure it will be fine, but let me run it by Montgomery first and I'll confirm it with you."

"Okay. Thank you."

"Thank you. Talk to you soon. Bye." I hang up and—

"Boo!"

"Aaah!" I scream. Monty snuck up behind me and poked his index fingers into my sides. Now, he's laughing, looking all cute and whatnot. I laugh, too. This is not something he usually does. He's not playful – that's more of Major's speed. To see him loosen up like this is refreshing.

"Stop sneaking up on me like that, Monty."

"Stop talking about me behind my back."

"I wasn't talking—"

"I just heard my name come out of your mouth. Now, what do you have to *run by* me?" he asks and does that super sexy lip bite. I wonder if he knows how much of a turn-on it is.

"Okay, um—do you remember me asking you about your brother?"

"Major?"

"No. Your older brother. The one you and Major lost contact with after being separated into different foster homes."

"Yes. I remember you asking me about him. What's up?"

"That was him on the phone just now."

"Are you serious?"

"Yes. His name is Magnus. Does that ring a bell?"

He shakes his head. "No. It doesn't. You were just on the phone with him?"

"Yes. He wants to know if next Saturday is a good day

to meet."

"Seriously?"

"Yes, Monty."

"How did—"

"I just did a little digging."

"And are you sure that's him?"

"Positive. Here, look at this," I say, pulling up the screenshot I took of Magnus, straight from his company's website. I hand Monty my phone. "Y'all look alike. You, him and Major. Same complexion. Same hair. Same green eyes. My guess would be you have the same biological parents."

He hands the phone back to me and says, "That's amazing." He smiles. "You actually found him."

"I told you I'd look."

"I really didn't expect you to."

"Why not?"

"I just didn't. You got enough on your plate with me."

"You ain't never lied about that."

He smiles.

"What do you think about meeting him?"

"Let me think it over. I'll get back to you."

Chapter Twenty-Eight

Monty

She wears a dress that forms to her figure-eight body. It's black — matches my suit. Her hair is swinging loose. I love her braids. She's not the woman that works for me tonight. She's just a woman. A beautiful, mind-blowing, down-to-earth human being.

It baffles me how I never noticed this about her in the two years she's worked for me. I've noticed her beauty, but never took the time to appreciate it like I'm doing now. Staring at her. Ogling her. Making her blush while I commit her face and its many pretty features to memory.

As we're eating, I say, "You know what I don't like about you?"

"What don't you like about me, Monty?"

"The fact that I hardly know you."

"You know me."

"No, I don't."

"You know me well enough to stay with me for nearly a month."

"Yes, because I know you're trustworthy. I don't know you in the sense that I don't know much about your personal life. Like, where did you grow up?"

"In Charlotte."

"Are you an only child?"

"Yes."

"No siblings?"

"No."

"And your parents?"

"What about them?"

"Are you close with them?"

"My father died when I was ten and in a way, my mother died with him."

"How so?"

"She changed. She hasn't been the same since. She remarried, but still—no one could ever replace dad."

"I see. Sorry to hear about your father, by the way."

"Thanks."

"How was life for you growing up?"

"It was perfect when my dad was alive. We did mostly everything together. I think my mother was jealous of that because I was her little girl, you know. She expected me to do little girl things. Instead, I was more into sports and watching him work on his car."

"I imagine you took it hard when he passed."

"I did. He was—he was my dad. I still miss him."

"That's understandable."

She takes a sip of wine then asks, "Is that all you want to know about me?"

"No, but I don't want to bombard you with questions."

"I can handle it."

"Oh, can you?"

"Yes. Ask away."

"Okay. Why aren't you married?"

She laughs. "You skip straight to marriage, huh? You don't ask why I'm single. You ask why I'm *not* married."

"Yeah, so answer it."

"I don't date."

"Why's that?"

"Because I'm always occupied. With my work schedule, I don't have time to date."

"So, it's *my* fault."

"In a way it is. Yes."

She looks away from me like she always does, getting her thoughts together. Thinking of which way to take the conversation so the heat is off of her. She doesn't like being in the spotlight, I conclude. It's why she usually hides behind baggy clothes, aprons and head scarves. She doesn't want to be seen. Doesn't want to attract anyone.

Tonight, she's seen.

Seen by all the men in here who sneaks glances, but she's unaware. Her own beauty escapes her. It's why I desire to know more about her. Her upbringing. Values. Things her mother taught her about being a woman in this world where all too often black women are undervalued, not taken seriously or not respected as queens. Was she taught to stay hidden or to reach for the stars? To be a personal assistant or the woman who owned a company of personal assistants? To look a person in the eye when they talked to you or shy away?

She takes another sip of wine. Glances up at me. Looks away.

"I have something for you," I tell her.

"You do?"

"Yes. I do." I take a rectangular white box from my pocket, place it on the table.

She smiles and frowns at the same time. "What's this, Monty?"

"Open it."

She pulls the red bow, takes off the top and I watch her eyes widen when she sees the diamond, white gold tennis bracelet. She looks up at me. Her smile leaves. The frown remains. "Monty, I can't accept this."

She bases her decision on how much she thinks the bracelet is worth, I imagine. She doesn't know it cost ten thousand dollars. She only knows it's expensive. *To her.*

"Sure you can," I tell her.

"It's beautiful, but—"

"You don't think you're worth it?"

"I—I don't know."

"You are," I tell her. "You're worth much more. In fact, I have something else." I hand her an envelope."

"And what's this?"

"It's your pay for the last three and a half weeks."

"You don't need to *pay* me. I've still been getting my direct deposits every week. You've been paying me all along."

"I know, but you've been my nurse, my therapist, my personal chef and private investigator for nearly a month and you should be properly compensated for your time. Take it."

She takes the envelope, opens it and looks at the check. "A hundred thousand dollars! Are you—crazy? This is way too much money."

"Who determines if something is too much? The giver of the gift or the receiver of the gift?"

"Monty—"

"If I told you it was too much work to change my bandages and rub that greasy stuff all over my face, would you have stopped doing it?"

"No."

"Then, in the same token, you can't refuse my gift. Thank you for everything."

"You're welcome, Monty, but I don't understand. Why are you talking like you're going somewhere?"

"Because I am," I tell her. "I'm going back home tomorrow."

"Oh," she says.

I can see her disappointment, but she pushes it aside and forces a smile.

"I guess it's time now, huh?"

"It is. I have to get back to work. I'm already behind three weeks."

She nods.

"Are you okay?"

"With you leaving? Yes. I mean, you, um—I'm happy you're well enough to want to get back to work."

If she's happy, she doesn't look it.

"Um, I wanted to know if you'd consider coming back to work for me? I know I was a jerk to you before, but thanks to you, I've changed. At least, *I* think I've changed."

"You *have* changed."

"And I really could use your help," I tell her. It's true. I could use her help, but my reason for wanting her to continue working for me is a personal one. I couldn't imagine not seeing her every day. I can't have this line drawn between us where we go our separate ways. I want her around. Need her energy. Need to be able to lay eyes on this beautiful face whenever I want.

I sip wine and look at her. She has yet to answer me. It makes me think she's against the idea.

"Okay," she says.

"Yeah?" I ask to confirm.

"Yes."

"Good."

She smiles, but I still see hints of sadness in her eyes.

Chapter Twenty-Nine

Monty

I get up in the morning to shower, pack up my clothes and gather other items I've left lying around her house. It's around ten when I finish putting everything in the car. I sit on the bed and hang my head. This is bittersweet. I didn't think it would be, but it is. I never imagined I could grow this attached to a woman, but truth be told, I have. Leaving her is messing with my head.

She doesn't come out of her bedroom. Not for breakfast, to water her flowers or sit on the front porch like she usually does. I don't hear a peep, but I know she's not still sleeping. She's not the type to sleep in. Like me, she's an early riser so where is she this morning?

I go to her room, tap on the door and twist the knob. The door is locked, but I hear her say, "Yes?"

"I'm about to go, Cherish."

Moments later, she comes to the door. She's dressed in a baggy T-shirt and sweatpants.

"Hey."

"Hey."

"You already packed up your stuff?"

"Yes."

She draws in a breath. "Oh."

"I didn't want to leave without saying bye to you."

She nods, tries to smile, but she can't blink away the tears that form in her eyes.

"Please don't cry," I tell her.

"I'm sorry. I can't help it," she sobs.

I embrace her, hold her close to my chest while she

cries.

"Are you sure you'll be okay?" she asks.

"Yes, sweetheart. I'll be fine. And you'll see me on Monday, right?"

She sniffles. Nods. "Yes."

"Then stop crying. Thanks to you, I'm healed."

More sniffles come. "You're not completely healed. The doctor says it takes six weeks for your ribs to heal, Monty."

"I know. I'll take it easy."

More tears fall from her eyes. I cup her chin and prompt her to look at me. I'm staring into the eyes of a woman who loves me. Who'll do anything for me. There's no doubt in my mind about that. "Cherish."

"Yes."

"I'll be okay."

She nods. "Okay," she says sadly.

I take a final, long hug then leave a kiss on her temple. "I'll see you on Monday. Okay?"

"Okay."

With that, I head outside, get in my car and drive away, feeling a sense of loss with each mile I'm away from her house. My life has changed drastically. I'm not the same man I once was. I'm a *better* man. A *better* person. Major was right. A good woman will do that for a man – prompt him to make his own changes without demanding him to, and not only prompt him but walks with him as he makes those changes. It's what Cherish has done for me. I'll be forever indebted to her for that.

* * *

Back home, I feel like a different man – almost like I went to rehab and came out refreshed. I unpack my clothes and do a quick walk-through. None of the workers are here today. They don't work on weekends. Saturday and Sunday are my days to fend for myself.

My residence looks as good as it did when I left it. Neat and clean. Everything in order. Nothing out of place. After getting settled, I take a trip to the barber. He comments on how lucky I am to have survived a car crash as severe as the one I was in. Said I looked as good as new, but I told him it was a long road getting here. He asks what kind of cut I want. I tell him the usual, but to leave about two inches of length since I know a certain woman who likes it. Then we go right back into our normal conversations about business. While he's talking, I'm thinking about what Cherish is doing right now. It's close to two in the afternoon on a Saturday. Last Saturday, I remember her doing laundry. Maybe that's what she's doing now. Laundry.

When I'm back at the estate, I go to visit mother. She's at her residence, greets me with a hug when she sees me and comments how good I look. How well I've healed. Said Cherish took good care of me. She would be correct in that assessment.

After visiting her, I head back over to the west wing and spend some time in the office, studying a drawing of the taser. I examine it for flaws – make sure the handle is not the same width as the handle of a gun so if these were tested in the field, there would be no confusion between the two.

I read through some old emails. There are a ton of meetings I've missed. Calls I need to return – most of which will happen on Monday.

* * *

Sunday comes around and I'm feeling like relaxing today. I spend some time in the indoor pool, working muscles that have been dormant for some time. It takes some exertion, but I'm able to form pretty good strokes swimming back and forth across the length of this pool.

When I'm out, I take a shower to wash off the chlorine. When I'm done, I wrap the towel around my waist and stare in the mirror, looking at the scar on my chest. It's healed, hiding behind chest hair, barely visible. The scar on my leg is healed but still looks pretty bad – a forever tattoo to remind me of the time I almost died.

I head down the hallway to the den – a room that's rarely used by me – and turn on the TV. While I'm sitting there, I can picture Cherish lying against my chest while we share a tub of popcorn and take in a movie. I can see myself playing in her braids. Feeling her warm skin. I'd have a front-row seat to her smiles and the way she looks at me.

I miss her.

I miss her so much I've been fighting the desire to drive to her house. I think about calling to wish her a good night like I've done so many times before but we both need the space to get ourselves together. To get back in work mode. Tomorrow, I'm her boss and she's my employee again – that's if she comes back.

Chapter Thirty

Cherish

I arrive at The Hawthorne Estate at 4:00 a.m. nervous as can be. Why? Because it feels like everything is back to normal. Monty is back at his home. His throne. His kingdom. This is the place where he's always in work mode. Focused. Likes everything in a certain kind of way. He plays no games with his work. I'm worried he'll fall back into his regular routine of being domineering and arrogant – being rude to the workers. Will *that* Monty emerge, or will the Monty I've come to know over the last three weeks make an appearance? The kind-hearted one. The one whose smile could make a woman faint.

When I step into his bedroom, I notice the bed is made. There are no slippers. No water bottle on his desk. Did he make his own bed? Clean his own room?

The bathroom door is closed. I don't hear the shower, but I imagine he's in there, getting ready to take a shower. Standing naked with his hairy, bare chest, looking like Wolverine with all that hair.

Shrew. I fan myself. Is it hot in here or is it just me?

"It's just you, silly. Pick out the man's clothes for the day and get to work," I mumble.

After giving myself a pep talk, I head on to the closet to pick out a suit for him. It's where I run into another distraction. His scent. It engulfs me, takes me captive as if his very arms are encircled around me. Those strong, muscular arms.

My goodness…

How am I supposed to work under these

circumstances?

"Focus, Cherish."

I fan through the suits. The dark ones. I know he'll be in hardcore work mode today so I go to the power black suits. Ones that still has the tags on it. The never-been-worn suits made by Givenchy and Saint Laurent.

I take one off the rack, look it over and hang it back up having second thoughts. It's a beautiful day. The sun is shining. I don't want him in a dark suit today. I choose a khaki-colored one and pair it with a light teal shirt and brown Louis Vuitton leather shoes — all items he's never worn before. I lay out the tie, the cufflinks, the socks — take my time doing so hoping that by some chance, he'd want to see me today. Maybe he'd cut his shower short just to corner me in his closet.

That doesn't happen. I get no surprise visit from him. Bummer...

I leave, feigning disappointment and go downstairs to make coffee. Then I take out my notepad and get started preparing a breakfast, lunch and dinner menu for the week. As I'm sitting at the table, I hear Minnie, Naomi and Isidora talking as they make their way back to the kitchen where I am. I look up and catch their surprised gazes when they look at me.

"Cherry!" Naomi says and wobbles over to me. She wraps both arms around my neck while I'm still sitting.

"It's good to see you, too, Naomi. How are you?"

"I'm good, darlin'. How are *you*?"

"I'm okay."

Minnie and Isidora follow up with their own smothering hugs for me.

"Good to see you, hun," Minnie says.

"Si, si. Muy Bueno," Isidora says, smiling from ear-to-ear.

I must admit — it feels good to be missed. I wish I was missed by Monty, too.

"We didn't think you were ever going to come back,"

Naomi says. "Mrs. Hawthorne didn't know, either. That woman was so worried—lawd have mercy that po' woman."

"I know, but she's better now."

Tying on her apron, Naomi responds, "But lemme tell you something...once she found out Mr. St. Claire was with you, she calmed right on down."

I smile. I don't know why Sylvia trusts me so much, but she does. She has from the beginning when she hired me.

"And what were you doing with Mr. St. Claire for three weeks and some change in that lil' house of yours? Answer me that," Naomi says. She throws a dish towel across her right shoulder.

"I was just making sure he was okay. You know, eating properly, staying hydrated, not re-injuring himself."

"That was a bad accident," Minnie said. "We didn't think he was gon' pull through."

"Yeah, it was rough," I say, "But Mont—I mean Mr. St. Claire is a strong man with a strong mind and strong will. He can survive anything."

"Hey, y'all hear that," Naomi says. "Ol' Cherry here is on a flirt-name basis with Mr. St. Claire, or shall I say Montgomery."

"A *flirt*-name basis, Naomi?" I ask trying not to laugh. "And I didn't say his first name."

"You almost said it. I heard it. You *almost* let it slip...makes me wonder how close y'all *really* got over these last few weeks."

"I was thinking the same thing," Minnie says.

Isidora goes about her business working.

"Okay, it was nothing like whatever you're thinking it was," I say writing down his lunch for today. I get up, go to the pantry to check if there are some multi-grain muffins. I place them on the counter.

To get Naomi and Minnie refocused on work, I say, "Hey, Naomi, go ahead and whip up Mr. St. Claire's breakfast before he comes down here."

"Too late. I'm already down here."

His voice reverberates through me like I'm a conductor of it. I turn around to look at him. My throat goes dry. I can only muster half of a blink. His unflinching gaze is on me something fierce. He's just staring.

I'm staring back.

I'm studying him for everything that looks different from when I last saw him Saturday morning. His scars are barely visible. *I* can only see them because I know where every one of them is located. I'm sure Naomi and Minnie won't notice.

He's been to the barber. His hair is shaped up and I'm thrilled to see he's kept some length. And the beard...

Mmm, mmm, mmm...

It's lined up and cut low – trimmed black hair against caramel skin and a set of lips I remember feeling against my temple. And the khaki suit I chose for him this morning – he's decided to wear it and it looks amazing on him. Fits his body so well. A body I *know* well after taking care of him.

He's back. Montgomery St. Claire, the man I've been crushing on for two years. I feel a shockwave of current electrify me in his presence. He's the ultimate figure of masculinity and sensuality and he knows it.

"Good morning," he says but he's only looking at me.

Naomi throws a hand over her chest probably because this is the first time she's ever heard him say a greeting. "Well, I'll be—" she says. "Good morning, Sir. How are you this morning?"

"I'm doing well thanks to my guardian angel."

He's still looking at me. I disconnect from his gaze and say, "I'll get you some coffee, Sir."

He walks over near me and says, "Hold off on the coffee for now."

"Oh," I say. "Yes, Sir." Why am I so nervous right now? I glance up at him as he's sliding his hands inside of his pockets.

"Cherish?"

"Yes, Sir," I answer, my eyes greedily feasting on his handsome face. It's only been two days since he left but gosh I miss him. I miss him so much, it's making me feel extremely emotional right now. I do a good job of hiding it. I think. I fight to remain professional. I'm back at work. I'm sure professionalism is what he expects of me.

He grimaces a little. "May I have a word with you, please?"

Did I hear him correctly? Did he ask to speak to me?

"Um—wha—what was that, Sir?" I ask.

"May I have a word with you, please?" he asks again and then walks out of the kitchen before I can give him an answer.

"You hear that, Minnie," Naomi whispers. "He wants a *word* with her."

"I heard it," Minnie said. "Bet that ain't all he wants..."

"Y'all stop it," I whisper to them. "I'm probably in trouble," I say trying to steer them away from their current thought path.

"Yeah, you in trouble alright. He was looking at you like he could take a bite," Naomi says. "Guess I ain't gotta fix him no breakfast after all."

"Naomi, stop it."

"You best to go on in there before he circles back," Minnie says.

I'm too nervous to laugh so I leave the kitchen to find Monty standing by the downstairs conference room with his arms crossed.

"Hey," I say when I'm close to him.

"Hey." He opens the door to the conference room, gestures for me to enter. Then he closes the door. Locks it.

"How are you this morning?" he asks.

"I'm fine," I say, trying to free myself of his gaze by glancing away.

He walks over to me and angles my head up with a nudge of his index finger. "That's better."

"Um...how—how are you?" I ask.

He lowers his hand away from my face now that he's captured my full attention.

"I've been better," he answers.

Immediately, I start to panic. "What's wrong?" I ask, looking him over.

"I didn't get much sleep over the weekend?"

"No?"

"No."

"It's not vertigo again, is it?"

"No. Actually, it's all your fault."

"*My* fault?"

"Yes, Cherish." He cups my face in his hands. "I miss you."

"You do?"

He gives me a single nod before strumming my lips with his thumb. When he licks his lips, I think I'm just about going to die. He leans down, places a gentle kiss on my trembling lips. "You don't know how much I miss you," he says against my lips.

His breath smells like mint and chloroform – it's about to render me unconscious. I'm helpless. I don't know what to say or do. I'm in his arms. At his mercy. This man has me feeling emotions I've never felt before. Emotions I never thought I could feel after what happened to me.

He places a kiss on the tip of my nose. Middle of my forehead. The area below my left ear. He whispers, "Don't ever call me, Sir, Mr. St. Claire of anything else that sounds formal. Understood?"

"But, Monty, I have to."

"No, you don't." His eyes are locked on my lips. Hands still caressing my face. He smells good – the aromatic smell of cologne, soap and shampoo – has me in a tizzy.

"I do. I don't want the other workers thinking I'm getting special treatment," I explain, but from the expression on his face, I know my explanation is going in one ear and out the other.

"To be frank, I don't care what they think."

The forward, arrogant side of him is emerging. He wasn't backing down off of this. My goal was to convince him otherwise. "Monty—"

"I love you."

I frown. "What?"

"You heard me. I said I love you."

Tears well up in my eyes. Other than from my father – my *real* father – I'd never heard those words from a man's mouth directed towards me. I try to turn away from him, but he's still holding my head.

"Don't look away from me," he says, holding me steady.

Since I can't move, I close my eyes, squeeze out some of the wetness, feeling tears run down my face.

"Cherish, open your eyes and look at me."

I sniffle. I feel his thumbs acting as wipers for my tears.

"Cherish, please look at me."

I obey him this time. More tears roll down my face when I finally open my eyes. He says, "It'll be difficult for you to hide the fact that you love me. And I *know* you love me. You've never said it and you don't have to say it. Your actions say it for you. I feel it when I look at you. See it in your eyes, baby. Feel it in your touch. In the way you take care of me. I want you to know that I love you the same. I've never been in love, but I'm in love with you and I've never even touched you. I don't even know you well enough to be having these kinds of feelings for you. Never made love to you. Don't know what our bodies feel like pressed together in passion, but I know what our spirits feel like intertwined. Feels like I've *already* made love to you. So, believe me when I say I don't care if they know. You're mine. You will always be mine, and I'm never letting you go. Do you hear me?"

I nod and gasp, and gasp some more.

"Do you love me?"

I nod again.

"Then, tell me."

My lips quiver.

"You need some help?" he asks, flashing that super white, sexy smile. "Okay, repeat after me. Monty—"

"Monty," I say smiling and crying at the same time.

"I love you," he says, prompting me.

"I love you." A smile glows on my face. The tears no longer matter.

He dips his head to kiss me again, only this time, I feel his tongue slide into my mouth.

My knees buckle. He lifts me as effortlessly as air while we're still kissing. His tongue explores my mouth. I don't know if I'm doing this right – kissing that is – but he's so dominant, I don't need to do much but sit here and take it. And that's what I do. I savor his tongue thinking of all the times I dreamed of this. It's surreal.

He takes his mouth away from me and says, "I'm going to be busy today. Really busy, so I probably won't see you anymore, but I want you to come find me before you leave. Okay?"

"Yes."

"I mean it, Cherry. Don't leave without seeing me first."

"Okay. I won't," I tell him. "And don't pick me up again. No heavy lifting per doctor's orders, remember?"

"It's not the first time I've picked you up with your lil' self."

He takes a final kiss, pressing his lips to mine, then I exit the conference room while he remains. As I'm exiting, Major is headed in my direction, going for the conference room. He looks at me in an examining way.

"Hey, you alright?" he asks.

"Yeah," I say, sniffling. "I'm fine."

"Are you sure?"

I smile and say, "Yes. I'm sure," but he's not buying it since he sees evidence of crying.

"Okay, what did my brother do to you?"

"I didn't do anything to her," Monty says stepping out of the conference room. "She's fine."

"Yes. I'm fine. I'll see y'all later."

"Okay. See ya, Cherish," Major tells me.

I'm so gone in the head, I'm floating. I've never used drugs, but this has got to be what it feels like to be high. I don't know how I'm supposed to get any work done like this.

Chapter Thirty-One

Monty

"What's going on with Cherish?" Major asks, looking worried – more worried than I think he should be for a man who doesn't have feelings for her. I asked him as much. He confirmed they were friends. Nothing more. Said Cherish only had eyes for me. It's *his* eyes I'm concerned about.

"Good morning," Mother says, walking into the room.

"Good morning," I tell her.

"Good morning, Ma," Major says.

"How does it feel to be back?" she asks.

"It feels good. A little overwhelming, but one day at a time, right?"

"Yep. One day at a time and one problem at a time," Major says.

"To give you an update on where I am physically, I should be back to one-hundred percent in about three weeks. I can work and *will* work every day. I've already started back on the taser project and I've been setting up meetings all week. By the way, I'll be working at the headquarters for the rest of the week."

"I will, too," Major says.

"Good, because there's something I want you to work on."

"What's that?"

"Hawthorne Innovations has no community involvement."

Mother chimes in to say, "Your father was adamant about not donating to any charities. He said they were all scams. All looking to make a profit off of people's hard earned money."

"Is that what you believe?" I ask her.

"No. Not at all. I think we should do all we can to support our community."

"I agree," I tell her. "That's why I want Major to put together a charity ball."

Mother's face lights up.

Major has the opposite reaction. Frowning, he asks, "You want to do a charity event?"

"Yes. We can invite our clients, suppliers – not all – just about eighty or so people. Formal attire. I think the first charity should be to further cancer research. We'll do this in honor of dad."

Mother nods. "He'll be so proud."

"Yes, he would," Major adds.

"And one more thing—Cherish has taken it upon herself to look for our older brother and she's found him. Magnus St. Claire. He lives in Charlotte."

Mother brings her hand to her mouth. "I can't believe it."

"Me either," I say looking at Major. "He wants to meet us on Saturday."

Major nods. "That's fine with me."

"This is wonderful," Mother says. "Everything seems to be falling right into place. I'm so proud of you, Monty. Of *both* of you."

"Thanks, Mother."

"Well, I have a call at nine that I need to get ready for, so I need to get going," Mother says, "But keep up the excellent work."

"Okay. I'll talk to you later," I tell her. I'm glad she has to leave for a call because it gives me more time to talk to Major about Cherish.

"I can't believe you want to do this charity thing," he says.

"Yes, I do."

"This has Cherish's name written all over it."

I smile but don't confirm or deny.

"The only drawback is the timing. People usually plan for events like this a year in advance," Major points out. "You're asking me to put together something in two weeks."

"You can do it. Plus, who'd want to miss a chance to mingle with the St. Claires? People have been dying to come to the estate. Well, now here's their chance."

"That's true."

"Ay, before you leave, I need to talk to you about something."

"What's up?"

"Cherish," I say and look at him just to get a reaction. He doesn't react.

"What about her?" he asks.

"Do you like her?" I probe. I need to get to the bottom of his relationship with Cherish. I don't want any animosity between us. Our family is healing from brokenness. I don't want to do anything to set us back.

Major's green eyes narrow. "You do realize we've had this conversation before, right?"

"Partially."

Major shakes his head. "No. I recall telling you straight up that Cherish didn't like me like *that*."

"Yes, but what about you? Do you like her like *that*?"

"Why do you ask?" Major probes. "You're in love with her, aren't you?"

I don't answer – just stare back at him, waiting for him to answer *my* question. He doesn't answer immediately. He leans back in his chair and takes a moment to think it through, then he says, "I'll be honest with you. I liked her from the jump—when she first started working here and I've been friends with her for just as long. She's never liked me in that way. She's always liked you. From the beginning, she's liked you. When I realized that, I accepted it. Accepted her as a friend. I know how she feels for you and I wouldn't do anything to come between that."

I take him at his word. He has no reason to lie, I surmise.

"But what do you plan on doing about Paige?" he asks.

"What do you mean?"

He looks puzzled. "Correct me if I'm wrong, Monty, but didn't you have to sign away your life to get that money and the CEO title?"

"I didn't sign away my life. I—"

"Then you must not know about the marriage clause?"

"Mother told me. I told her to fudge it—left it up to her to handle the details. I didn't care whose name she put on there. It doesn't change how I feel for Cherish."

"I know it's Paige," Major says. "That's why she throws herself at you every chance she gets."

"That's funny. When I was in the hospital, bruised and battered, I don't recall seeing her."

"She stopped by. *One* time." Major grins.

"And when I spent the last three weeks recovering at Cherish's house, I didn't get a call from her. A text message. Nothing."

"I'm just saying—it looks bad on paper. And I know Cherish."

Jealousy tightens my forehead. "You do, do you?"

"Yes. I know her better than you do, and I know she's not going to go for a man who's married *just on paper* or otherwise."

"Whatever the case, I'll speak to mother about it. There has to be a way to reverse whatever she did."

"I hope so."

Chapter Thirty-Two

Cherish

He wanted me to come see him before I left, so I make my way upstairs. I see him standing at the window, his back to me. His mind is flooded with thoughts. Staring out the window is one way he processes those thoughts.

"Monty."

He turns around, sees me and smiles. It's one of those smiles that seems to hide something. He's had a rough day, but in true Monty fashion, he buries it — at least for the moment while I'm in his presence.

He begins his walk over to me, every stride makes my legs weak. He says, "You're about to go?"

"Yes. Are you okay?"

"Yes," he replies but I know he's not. I can sense these things about him now.

"I'll be at the office tomorrow."

"Yes. You told me," I say, and I'm glad he did tell me. It's given me time to coordinate with his secretary to have a welcome back party for him upon his return. Whether most of the people there like him or not, they don't have to worry about their paychecks not coming on a regular basis, so at least they should be happy to see he's alive and well.

After convincing Hannah it was okay, and that Monty wouldn't be irritated by the sight of balloons and banners, she agreed to run out and buy the essentials. I took care of the food, then reimbursed her for what she spent on the decorations.

"I'm going to miss seeing you around here this week,"

he says.

"You'll see me first thing in the morning as long as you don't lay out my clothes and make a run for it like you usually go."

I chuckle. "I didn't want to make a run for it this morning. I lingered, hoping you'd finish your shower early."

"Really?"

"Yep."

"I thought about it—finishing my shower early so I could run into you in my closet."

"Why didn't you?"

"You don't want to know," he says and folds his bottom lip beneath a top row of sexy teeth. He embraces me. I feel the love in his squeeze. "See you tomorrow."

We separate. He leaves a small kiss on my lips. "See you tomorrow."

* * *

Today was perhaps the best day of my life. It's the day I found out the man I love loves me back. I feel high. Stuff like this never happens to me. I'm always the unnoticed girl – not the woman who catches the magnificent eyes of a man so handsome, smart and talented.

I need to be pinched. I can't believe this is real.

I pull in the driveway at my house prepared to jump right into my dinner-shower-bed routine – but as I climb the stairs to the porch, I turn around to see a white Chevrolet pulling up behind my car.

It's him.

Webster.

For the life of me, I can't imagine why my stepfather is at my house. I'm not a scared little girl anymore and this shovel next to me is a tool I know how to use well. I wouldn't think twice about breaking it across his back.

When he gets out of the car, I yell, "Leave, or I'm

calling the police."

"Call 'em," he says.

I see the years have done a number on him. He has a round potbelly and a head full of salt and pepper hair. It doesn't help that the shirt he has on is a size too small.

"Leave my house!"

He ignores me. "You gon' stop feeding your mama these lies about me, girl. That's what I *do* know," he says waving his index finger that looks about the size of a boiled hotdog.

"What lies? She's married to a pervert. A child molester. She should know that, but you done brainwashed her into thinking *I'm* the liar. One day, she'll find out and leave your ugly, fat self."

"Oh, you gon' insult me now, huh?" he says, slamming his car door closed heading in my direction with balled fists.

Around the same time, Ms. Kettleworth slides between the bushes like a navy seal on a secret mission, cocks back a shotgun and says, "Now, you hold tight right there, cowboy. I do believe the lady asked you to get off her prop'ty."

He looks at Ms. Kettleworth then back at me and smirks. "Is this a joke?"

"Take another step forward and you'll see who winds up laughing. Now, I advise you to get yur portly hind pots back in that car 'cause I'm locked and ready to slide a hot one in ya. The poe-poe won't touch me when I tell 'em it was self-defense. It's up to you which way this thang gon' go."

Webster looks at me with flared nostrils and says, "This ain't over, girl. You best to shut your mouth," he says then gets in his car and peels out.

Ms. Kettleworth lowers the gun and walks over to me. "Are you okay, hun?"

"Um...I—I don't know," I respond. "He's never threatened me before."

"Who was dat?"

"He's my stepfather."

"I ain't never heard you mention nothing 'bout no stepfather before."

"I know. I don't acknowledge him as a stepfather. When I was a child, he—"

"Honey, you don't have to talk about it. I heard you call him a child molester. I ain't never been one for math, but I can put two and two together. What I don't know is why he's mad at you and driving by yur house so frequently. I don't like that one bit. No ma'am. Not one bit. You might either want to get yurself a 'straining order or one of these babies," she says, holding up her shotgun. "Now, go on in yur house and relax, Sherrish. I'm on watch for the rest of the night. You ain't gotta worry 'bout him coming back tonight."

"Okay. Thank you, Ms. Kettleworth."

"Not a problem."

When I'm inside, the adrenaline starts to wear off and the panic sets in. That dizzying feeling of not believing what just happened has me using furniture for support to make my way to the kitchen where I grab a glass and fill it with water. I drink, hoping it'll help me breathe right again. My heart is hammering. My mind is taking me to places I don't want to be. Remembering what he did to me. I thought I'd buried it. Now, it's all coming back.

I go to bed at my normal time, doze off and as if triggered by his presence, I'm hit with a nightmare…

I'm twelve, lying in bed. Must've been around one in the morning. Mom was long asleep. I was sleeping, too, until I felt his hands rub me awake, touching my chest. Rubbing my stomach. When it first happened, I thought he was trying to comfort me for some reason. I didn't understand what was going on. I think I was more in shock than anything else.

The next night, the same thing happened. He came into my room after mom fell asleep and touched me, only this time, he slid his hand down my pajamas.

I screamed, but he covered my mouth with his hand. Told me if I ever told Mama, he'd hurt her. Told me to be a "good girl" while he touched me. Told me to touch him and when I refused, he would choke me. This went on for three months. Three months, I lived in terror hoping my mother would see the change in me. See how depressed I was. But she was happy. He treated her well as long as I behaved.

Then one day when she ran out, he came in my room, touched me again but touching wasn't satisfying him any longer. He climbed on top of me and...

I wake up screaming. My nightshirt is soaked in sweat. My body trembles in fear. I sit up on the bed and grab my bat, looking all around the room for him.

I'm afraid.

I'm in tears.

I'm the twelve-year-old girl who couldn't defend herself all over again.

Chapter Thirty-Three

Monty

I was looking forward to going to the office again, getting back in the swing of things but then Cherish called in sick this morning. Called my mother. Not me.

We're close enough now where if she wasn't coming to work, she could call me directly. She has all my contact information – cell phone, email – she has unrestricted access to me, but she called my mother.

I call her. It goes to voicemail.

I call again. I get voicemail *again*.

I send her a text:

Montgomery: Call me as soon as you see this message.

That was three hours ago and I have no call or text from her. It's after 8:00 a.m. now and I'm back at the office. When I walk in, I'm greeted by a 'Welcome Back' banner. There are balloons and party snacks all around. I didn't expect this kind of welcome from people who hate my guts.

"Good morning, Hannah," I say to my secretary.

"I'm sorry?" she says like a question and frowns.

It's when I realize the issue – I usually never speak to anyone in the office. Not even my own secretary. I'm not that man anymore. I'm actually proud of that. "Good morning, Hannah."

"Oh. Um—" she frowns. "Good morning. How are

you this morning?"

"I'm doing okay. What's all this?"

She whips her blonde hair to the side and adjusts her glasses. "This is a little welcome back celebration for you."

I smile, appreciating the gesture. "Thank you for putting it together. Looks like it was quite the undertaking."

"Oh, it was no problem at all."

"Be sure to submit a reimbursement for it," I say continuing on to my office.

"Oh, there's no need. Cherish took care of it all."

I stop in my tracks. "Who?" I ask, turning to look at her.

"Cherish Stevens. I was under the impression you knew her."

"Yes. I know her. Thanks, Hannah."

I step into my office and see a bouquet of flowers. They instantly remind me of Cherish since I know how much she loves gardening. I pull the note attached. It reads:

They came from my flower garden. Welcome back, boss. - Cherish

I settle at my desk and call her again. Can't reach her. Now, I'm getting worried. Has me thinking about how I don't know her family. I can't reach out to anyone related to her because I don't know anyone related to her.

When my phone rings, I'm relieved to see it's her calling me.

"Where are you?" I answer quickly.

"I'm home."

"*Why* are you home? What's going on, Cherish?"

"I don't feel good today, Monty," she says. She sounds different. Her voice is soft and slow. She's not upbeat like she usually is. It only adds to my anxiety.

"Be more specific, Cherish. *What* doesn't feel good?

209

Do you have a headache? A stomach ache?"

"I just don't feel good in general, Monty. I didn't sleep well last night."

Her answer makes me think she had a nightmare like she had when I was at her house. When she'd fallen asleep on the sofa. It's something else I don't know anything about. Are nightmares common for her? Is there a reason behind them?

"Why are you being elusive with me?"

"Monty, why are you asking so many questions?"

"Because I'm worried about you, and why didn't you call me? We've been through this before. My mother hired you, yes, but you work for me and I would like to think we're close enough now to where you'd feel comfortable doing that."

She doesn't say a word. Irritates me to no end.

"Cherish?"

"I'm here."

"Talk to me."

"I'll be at work tomorrow," she says like that'll be enough to satisfy me. It doesn't. I want to know how she's really doing today, what she's doing today and how *sick* she really is.

"I'm going to leave work early and bring you some soup or something."

"No. That's not necessary. I don't want you to interrupt your day for me."

"You interrupted your *life* for me. I think I can give you a day."

"Monty, please. I'll be fine. I'll see you tomorrow, okay. I have to go."

And she hangs up.

Chapter Thirty-Four

Cherish

Last night, I was afraid to go to sleep. I did a walk through three times, making sure all the doors and windows were locked. The slightest noise startled me, making it difficult to relax. When I finally did fall asleep, around two or so, I must've hit the pillow pretty hard because I forgot to set my alarm and now it's six o'clock.

I'm going to be late for work.

I look at my phone. Monty has already called three times.

I call him back and say, "I'm so sorry. I overslept. I'll be there soon."

"Take your time," he tells me.

He doesn't sound irritated or upset. In fact, I can't decipher his mood over the phone.

When I finally arrive at his house around 7:30, I expected him to be at the office, but he comes walking down the massive front steps as I'm parking. He's dressed to the nines. All black. Suit, shirt, shoes, hair.

"Good morning," he tells me.

"Good morning. Sorry I'm late."

"I don't care about you being late, Cherish. I care about you."

He reaches to touch my face. I turn away so his hand doesn't make the connection. I need it more than anything – the connection – but right now, I don't know if I can handle it. Don't know if his hands can truly console me after what I've been through.

He grimaces. "Why'd you just do that?"

211

"Do what?"

"Pull away from me."

"I don't know—look, I—"

His large hand grips my forearm. There's no breaking away from it. "What's wrong with you?"

"Nothing's wrong."

"Don't lie to me. Something's wrong. I can feel it. This isn't you."

My heavy sigh surprises me. "Okay, well, it's personal, so—"

"Personal?" he says, frowning like I've offended him. "Did you really just say *personal*? After everything I've shared with you about my screwed up life, you want to pull the personal card on me."

"It's really complicated, Monty, and I don't want to drag you into it. Okay?"

He stares at me for what seems like an eternity, then says, "Okay. Then here's what I want you to do. I want you to go home. You're taking the rest of the week off."

"I can't do that."

"I'll find someone else to cover your shift. You look like you need some time."

Time was the last thing I needed. I need to stay busy – to keep my mind occupied with something other than being stalked and harassed by my stepfather.

"And I need you to be back to yourself again before we go to visit Magnus."

"I'm not going."

"What?" he asks frowning.

"I think it's something extremely emotional you three should share together. I was there when you made amends with your mother. I don't think I need to be there for this."

He doesn't like my answer, but he takes it. He releases my arm, turns away from me and stares out into the expanse of his front yard – green acres upon green acres. I've become complex to him. He doesn't know what to do, and if that's the case, we have that in common.

He turns around and bites back disappointment and says, "Okay."

I know he's upset, but at the same time, he's trying to be accommodating. Trying to understand me instead of having his way.

"I'm on my way to the office. I'll see you later."

He walks back to the house.

I get in my car and drive away.

Chapter Thirty-Five

Monty

Saturday evening, me and Major are preparing to go to our long-lost brother's house. Magnus lives off of Providence Road in the Myers Park Neighborhood area of Charlotte.

I grab my keys ready to go and get this show on the road when Major says, "Hold on a minute, lead foot. I got this." He takes his keys out of his pocket.

"I can drive, Major."

"I know you can, but I want to get there in one piece, so—"

"That's not funny."

"I didn't mean for it to be funny. I'm driving. By the way, are we going to pick up Cherish?" Major asks.

"Cherish isn't coming."

"Oh," he says, starting the car. "I thought she would since she put all of this together."

"She's not coming," I say. "I wanted her to come, but she's been distancing herself from me since Tuesday. I'm not sure what happened."

"She called off work on Tuesday, right?"

"Yeah and got to work late Wednesday."

"What went down between y'all on Monday when I saw her coming out of the conference room. She looked like she'd been crying."

"I kissed her. Told her I loved her."

"Wow! Never thought I'd see the day."

"What do you mean?"

"You don't connect with people enough to love them.

Are you sure it's love?"

"I'm sure," I say glancing out the window.

"I'm just throwing this out there, but if you love her, Monty, then maybe she shouldn't be working for you."

"I don't consider what she does *working* for me necessarily. She does for me what a wife would do for her husband."

"In other words, if you were married, you'd consider your wife to be more of your personal assistant instead of your equal."

"No. Not like that. She would be my equal. She would be my *everything*. The way I feel for her is messing with my head. I don't know her all that well, but I know I love her."

"What do you love about her exactly?" he asks.

"Her smile. Her work ethic. Her drive. Determination. She's a phenomenal woman."

"Yet, you didn't notice her for two whole years."

"That's not true. I noticed her. I just never said anything to her."

"Why not?"

"I didn't want to. I'm not like you—I don't develop friendships with people on a whim. I'm more reserved."

"You ain't all that reserved. You were at her so hard before the accident, you had her sneaking around the house trying to avoid running into you."

"I know."

"Why were you at her like that?"

"I think it was the fact she talked to me in a way that most people fear."

"So, she's a challenge."

"She's—she's different from everything I know. From all the women I know and I really hate that she's not coming with us tonight."

"Maybe she didn't think it was appropriate."

"That's exactly what she said, but I told her it was okay—that I wanted her to come and she wouldn't consider it. Something's wrong and I don't like the fact that I don't know her well enough to pinpoint what the problem might be. I don't know her friends or family. I don't know anything about her."

"I know she's an only child," Major says.

"Well, I do know that much. I know she lost her father at an early age."

"Yep, and she's not on good terms with her mother."

I glance over at my brother. "How do you know that?"

"We've talked about it. Me and Cherish used to talk all the time, but it was always general stuff. If you really want to find out what's bothering her, I would suggest either being patient and talking to her about it like a *real* boyfriend or talking to her neighbor, Ms. Kettleworth."

"*Real* boyfriend. You're funny. And how do you know Ms. Kettleworth?"

"I took Cherish home one day last year. The old lady came out of nowhere, standing in the yard in a pair of dirty overalls and stringy hair, looking all in the car. Freaked me out for a minute until Cherish told me who she was."

This conversation between me and Major so far lets me know he's a lot closer to Cherish than he led on. He knows where she lives. Knows her neighbor. They used to talk *all the time*, he said. It irks me.

"Did you tell Cherish about Paige?" I ask him.

"No. Why would I do that?"

"I don't know. I'm just trying to find out why she hasn't been herself this week."

"Nah, I haven't said a word. Maybe mother told her."

"I thought about that, but I don't see why she would have a reason to."

"Just talk to Cherish. She's easy to talk to. It's one of the things I adore about her," he says. I don't know if he's trying to get under my skin but it's working.

I change the subject by asking, "What do you expect from this meeting with Magnus?"

"Well, first of all, you probably shouldn't be looking at

it like a meeting. After all, he *is* our brother."

"Yeah. A brother we don't know. I have no idea what he's like."

"I know a lil' something about him. He owns a company called MJS Communications, based out of Charlotte—one he started, so he has good business sense."

"Is he married? Does he have kids? Has he ever tried searching for us?" I ask.

"That, I don't know, but we're here so we'll find out soon enough."

Major goes up the long driveway to reveal a mansion, a little smaller than mine. Gorgeous house with well-kept grounds.

We park, walk up to the door, ring the bell. A woman answers the door. Says her name is Lucille. My guess is she's the housekeeper.

"Amazing," she says staring at us like we're movie stars. "Come on in, gentleman."

"Thank you," I tell her.

We follow her through a grand entrance on to an even grander living room until we get to the dining room.

I'm stricken with a bout of anxiety, wondering what we're dealing with. I'm usually cool and carefree. In this case, things are different. We're dealing with a long-lost brother. Old family matters. Wounds that haven't healed. Then there's Magnus. What if I don't like him? What if he doesn't like us? How did he grow up? Did he always have money? Who were his foster parents? Are they still alive? Does he remember mom and dad?

I hear voices. Must be Magnus talking to Lucille. Me and Major don't say a word. Just sip on cucumber water that's been provided for us. We hear the voices get closer.

And closer.

And then...

"Good evening."

I turn to look at the man whose voice sounds like mine to see that he also looks like me. Looks like the three of us could be triplets. We have the same features – green eyes, black hair. Same height. Same complexion. Looking at him is like looking in the mirror.

I have no doubt he's my brother. I'm in such shock, I can't move. I just sit and stare. Major does the same.

"Hi. I'm Magnus."

Major get up, walks over to him. They slap hands then hug – not the half-hug that men do – but a hug of a person who has finally reconnected with a long lost sibling.

Their embrace doesn't end. It lingers.

Lingers as they fight back tears like men do even though the circumstances call for it.

Their embrace tightens.

I swallow the lump in my throat.

We're brothers.

We're family.

We're broken.

Joined by blood, but broken.

I join them – my brothers – dividing this hug into thirds as we all struggle to hold in our tears until our throats hurt from tightening.

It's when I realize we're men who've been damaged. No fault of our own, but it's what life has handed us – the hand we were dealt. And now we're here. Together. We've found each other.

We're brothers again.

OVER DINNER, WE get to know Magnus in more detail. He's married to a woman named Shiloh. They have twins on the way. He tells us about MJS Communications and how successful his company is. We have that in common. Successful business ventures.

We eventually get to the meat of the conversation by diving into the past when Major asks, "So, were you in a foster home as well?"

"I was."

"Interesting. It's funny how the mind works. I used to think you were the only one our parents kept and they gave me and Montgomery away. It gave me a reason to dislike you. To never take that extra step to find you."

"And all along I was in foster care. My foster mother died about a year and a half ago. What about you two?"

"We were in foster care as well," I tell him. "Our foster parents were Caspian and Sylvia Hawthorne. He died three years ago. Our foster mother, Sylvia, is still alive and well."

Magnus nods.

I notice right away he and I are a lot alike, more so than me and Major. Magnus doesn't come across as the casual, laid back kind. He's more of the let's-get-stuff-done type. He doesn't smile much. Just want to get right down to business.

"It was difficult growing up without that parental support, and I'm talking biological parents," Magnus says.

"It was," Major adds. "It makes you feel unwanted."

I nod in agreement then say, "It plays with your mind because you're a man and you want to be strong like a man is supposed to be but that feeling of being unwanted always lingers in the back of your mind. And for me, no matter how much money I made or how much I did to advance my company, I still carried that awful feeling that my parents didn't want me."

"I felt the same way," Magnus said. "But Mason helped me put some things in perspective."

"Mason?" Major asks. "Who's that?"

"He's our biological father's brother, so in other words—"

"He's our uncle," I say.

"Yes. I just found out about him. We talk on the phone often now and I've met up with him a few times. He gives me some background on the family. Told me our father's name was Micah St. Claire. Biological mother, Abigail Miller who's also deceased. I think after she died, Micah turned us over to the state. Probably couldn't handle the responsibility of being a single man with three boys. Anyway, me and Mason have been trying to get everybody together for months, but our schedules are always off."

"Everybody like who?" I ask.

"Well, Mason has four sons—our first cousins—Ramsey, Royal, Romulus and Regal. Also, according to Mason, after our mother died, dad got himself together and remarried, moved to South Carolina where he lived with his *new* wife and three kids until he passed."

"What?" I ask, my heart racing. "Are you telling me we have half-siblings?"

"According to Mason, yes."

"Wow," Major says. "This is insane."

"Do we have any way of reaching them?"

"Mason and Micah weren't close so Mason didn't get to know Micah's new wife or their children. All he knew was that the wife's name was Zayda. Said she had two sons who he thought were twins and a daughter."

"We need to find them," Major says.

"One step at a time, Major," I say. "We just found Magnus."

Magnus cracks an easy smile. He looks at both of us in a quizzical way then asks, "How are your lives?"

The question sounds odd to me. It leaves the door wide open to start talking about anything. Then again, that's exactly what we need – to know everything about each other. But I also recognize it won't happen in one evening over dinner.

"My life is okay," I answer. "Our foster parents were wealthy. Pretty much left us billionaires."

Magnus nods. "I researched Hawthorne Innovations. Very impressive."

"Yeah, well, I can't take credit for something my father built," I tell him.

Major shakes his head. "Don't listen to him, Magnus. Dad taught Monty everything he knows."

"What about you?" Magnus asks Major. "What do you

do?"

"I work for the business as well. I'm not an inventor, though. I'm on the marketing side of things."

"Either of you married?" he asks.

"No," Major says.

He looks at me and I answer the same, my mind instantly going to those documents I signed. And Paige. And Cherish.

"I was married before Shiloh. Had a son, too, but they both died. I hit a low point in my life after that, and then Shiloh came along. That's why I asked you two how your lives were. I wasn't necessarily talking about money, because I know you have money. I have more money than I could ever spend and I was suicidal because my life wasn't what it should've been. I had the world at my fingertips, yet, I had nothing. I know we have a lot of catching up to do, but as the oldest, I feel it's my duty to offer you some advice."

"Which is?" Major asks.

"The money means nothing. The prestige, the accolades, the spotlights in business magazines – it's futile if your relationships are not in order. And I'm talking all kinds of relationships – mother, brother, friends, girlfriends. You can try, but you can't replace people with money."

I nod, understanding this fact recently thanks to Cherish. The more I think about her tonight, the more I wish she was here. The more I wish she was here, the more I wonder why she's not.

"Monty," Major says tapping his wine glass with a fork to get my attention.

"Oh, sorry. I zoned out there for a minute. What's up?"

"I just asked if you wanted more wine," Magnus says.

"I'll pass," I tell him. I glance at my watch. It's already after ten. We've been talking for over four hours. "I think we should pause this conversation and pick it up again real soon."

"Yeah. You're right," Magnus says. "I didn't realize it was so late."

Major stands. "That's what happens when you reconnect with your long-lost brother. Time flies by and we still haven't scratched the surface."

Magnus stands and I join them.

"Next time, you'll get to meet Shiloh. She wasn't feeling well, so she ate early and went to bed."

"No problem," I tell him. "We got you now, bruh. There's no getting rid of us now."

"I wouldn't want it any other way."

Magnus walks us to the door where we embrace again and make promises to keep in touch. They're not empty promises. We've been apart too long to let more time separate between us.

"When I nail down this meeting with Mason and his family, I'll let you know."

"Does Mason live in Charlotte, too?" Major asks.

"Yes, but all his sons live in Cornelius—you know the Lake Norman area."

"Right. I'm familiar," I tell him. "Ay, let us know when we can meet and we'll go from there."

* * *

On the drive home we're quiet, soaking it all in. Then Major asks, "So, what did you think about Magnus?"

"He's cool."

"Yeah, I thought so. He's a lot like you."

"And you determined that in a few hours."

"Sure did. Don't tell me you didn't see it, too."

"I did. He is a lot like me."

"It's crazy about the half brothers and sister. I never thought of that possibility."

"Me either."

"How do you feel about meeting them?"

"I definitely *want* to meet them. Absolutely."

Major sighs. "It all seems wrong, you know. He raised them but neglected us."

"Yeah, it is wrong, but I'm realizing you can't judge anyone without first walking in their shoes. And most times, you *still* can't judge them. I don't know why our parents did what they did, but maybe in the grand scheme of things, we were better off. And, we can take a lesson from it."

"Yeah, and what lesson is that?"

"To not do what they did. I would never give my children up," I say. "Never."

"Children? *You* want *children*?"

A grin comes to my lips. "Why'd you ask it like that?"

"I honestly didn't think you had the patience or temperament for kids."

"Gee. Thanks, bruh."

"I'm serious. I didn't. Your life has always been the company."

"Yeah, well, you heard what Magnus said—the money, wealth, fame, prestige—it doesn't matter in the end."

"Yeah. I can't believe he was suicidal."

"You never know what people are going through," I say thinking about Cherish again. I have no idea what she's going through, but I have every intention of finding out.

Chapter Thirty-Six

Cherish

Tonight's dream was more gut-twisting than the one from Friday night. Again, I'm soaked with sweat and anxiety when I wake up. My heart beating rapidly as I relived the feeling Webster's nasty hands on me. This time I'm so shook, I'm in tears. I thought for sure I was over this, being an independent twenty-six-year-old woman and all, but how can I get over something that has never been properly dealt with?

It resides with me. Haunts me. Even though I try to block it out and make myself forget, it always finds a way to resurface.

I get up again, get my bat, turn on the lamp next to my bed and do a full search of my house. There's no one here – I'm sure of it – but the dream was so vivid, so *real* I feel like I need to make sure no one's here.

I can hardly breathe.

I feel sick.

Sick and dirty.

I'm steadily sweating.

I take deep breaths in an attempt to self regulate. If I don't, I'm sure I'll have a panic attack and pass out right here. No one would find me – not even nosy Ms. Kettleworth.

"It was just a dream, Cherish," I tell myself. "It was a dream."

It's three o'clock in the morning and I have to repeat this to myself several times before I'm able to calm down enough to go to the kitchen and get a glass of water. I drink it, then drop my head in full tears. Why do I do this to myself? I'm still his victim. All these years later, he still torments me.

I've researched the issue. I know the statistics:

One in three girls are sexually abused before the age of eighteen.
I was twelve.
Thirty percent of sexual abuse is never reported.
I reported it to my mother. She didn't believe me. Chose him over me and never reported it to the authorities. Some mother, huh?
Ninety percent of sexual abuse victims know the perpetrator.
I only knew him because my mother married him.
There are nearly half a million registered sex offenders in the United States.
This scared the life out of me. Still does sometimes. It's why I never wanted to be with anyone. What if *he* turned out to be one of *them*?
Pedophiles are usually repeat offenders.
Makes me wonder who else Webster assaulted before he got his hands on.

Other statistics found that teens who are sexually assaulted usually become promiscuous and have a higher chance of committing suicide. I've never had thoughts of suicide, although I have asked myself a million times why this had to happen to me. I also didn't become promiscuous – looking for sex as a form of love. For me, it was the opposite. It made me distrust men. I was perfectly fine being in the shadows – not being one of those *it* girls the guys always tried to talk to. I didn't want that kind of attention. I didn't want any attention. I just wanted to work and go home.

That's it.

Work, and go home.

So, I made that my life. I worked myself to death, went home and did it all over again the next day. I couldn't care less about a man or a relationship.

That all changed when I first saw Monty. I think, in the beginning, I was more curious about him than anything else. I'd never seen him with a woman. He was always alone outside of anything involving work and mad all the time. I didn't consider Monty a threat to my personal safety, nor his brother. They weren't like Webster. They were upstanding, respectful men – men I learned to trust.

Now, that these nightmares are haunting me, I don't even know if I can trust *them* anymore. Don't know if I can stand the thought of Monty holding my hand, kissing me or touching my face like he likes to do because how can I ever truly trust a man when all I can think about is how the man who was supposed to care for me and be a father figure for me ended up on top of me in my bedroom while my mother was asleep down the hallway?

It sickens me.

I'm so sick, I run to the bathroom to vomit. I have no idea what to do about this. I don't know when the feeling will go away. Even when it does, another bad dream will set it off all over again.

I rinse out my mouth and brush my teeth. Afterward, I stare at myself in the mirror. I'm damaged goods. I'm certain once Monty finds out what happened to me, he won't be so *thrilled* to be with me. To be honest, I know I was never his type. I don't fit the mold of the kind of woman he should be with. I don't know which fork is the salad fork. I don't swish wine around in my glass and sniff it before I drink. I don't put a napkin in my lap when I eat. I don't know rich folk etiquette. I don't wear big fancy hats and go to tea parties for fun. You won't catch me fake-laughing or pretending I like someone that I can't stand. I'm not uppity. My clothes don't cost thousands of dollars. I don't buy cars for fun and I don't have people to tend to my every need.

I'm just the woman who cleans Monty's residence and makes sure he looks like Montgomery St. Claire, the billionaire, when he leaves the house.

* * *

In the morning, when the sun illuminates the outdoors and I hear birds chirping and singing their favorite songs, I get in my car and drive. I have no idea where I'm going. I just need to get out of the house. I start with breakfast then work my way over to the nail salon. A little self-care should help relax me and take my mind off of everything, so that's what I do. I get a manicure.

I'm not ready to go home when I'm done so I go to the AMC at Concord Mills Mall and watch a movie, stuffing my mouth with popcorn, sitting off to the back where no one is near me.

I'm safe here. Safe from my own thoughts. I just eat and distract myself by following the plot of this movie.

Chapter Thirty-Seven

Monty

I pull up in the driveway, crushed when I don't see her car. It's a Sunday night, already close to nine. She's usually home on Sundays since she goes to bed early for work. Somehow I doubt she has plans to come to work tomorrow.

The house is dark. The porch light isn't on. That tells me she left during the day – doesn't give a clue where she might have gone, but she's not here.

I think about calling her, but she hasn't called or talked to me since Wednesday. She's not going to take a call from me.

Major seems to think I may find some answers from Ms. Kettleworth, so I get out of my car and walk over there to Ms. Kettleworth's house. I tap on the door. It opens a little – makes a creaking noise.

"Who's there?" I hear the old woman ask.

"It's Montgomery St. Claire, ma'am."

"Oh," she sings, comes to the door and says, "Well, looky-looky. How you doin', Montgom'ry?"

"I'm—I'm doing good," I tell her, trying not to be distracted by the pieces of food in the corners of her mouth. "Hey, uh—I'm looking for Cherish."

"Yur lookin' fo' Sherrish? Don't tell me you done up and lost yur girlfriend."

I smile. "She's not my girlfriend," I tell her since technically she's not. We never got a chance to confirm what we were.

"Ain't no need in you trying to pull the wool over my

eyes, Montgom'ry. I know you fancy dat gal."

"Ms. Kettleworth, do you have any idea where she could be right now?"

"No. That chile high-tailed it out of dat house so fast, I bet you she didn't even take a piss fo' she left."

She chuckles.

"Has she been gone all day?"

"Yes, Sir—since 'round 'bout nine sum this mornin'."

"Let me ask you something—ah—have you noticed anything strange going on with her lately? Has she talked to you about anything?"

"Sherrish like to keep her business to herself."

"Right, but since you're her neighbor, I thought maybe you would know *something*."

"Well, I can tell you this here—her stepfather been driving by here back and forth. He saw her car in the driveway Monday night—pulled up right behind her. Next thang I know, she's yelling at him telling him to leave her driveway. He's yelling back at her, telling her to stop lying on him 'bout sum. Sherrish called him a child molester and he got so mad, the man balled his fists like he was gon' charge at her. So, I reached in the back of my truck and pulled out my shotgun—told him to leave. He ain't been back since. I told Sherrish she might want to get herself one of dem 'straining orders. Ain't nothing but a piece of paper, but I believe harassment should be documented."

And now I know the reason for Cherish's sudden change of behavior. I don't want to think it but what other conclusion am I to arrive at given the play-by-play from Ms. Kettleworth? If Cherish called her stepfather a child molester, most likely she was one of his victims.

It would explain a lot. It would explain why she's never had a boyfriend. Why she doesn't date. Why she hides herself behind loose clothes, aprons and head ties. It's because she *is* hiding. She doesn't want to be seen. She has issues with men because of the act of one man – someone she thought she could trust. A man who'd—

I can't bring myself to think it. I hope it's not true but I don't see how it can't be. I'm so lost in thought that I completely forget I'm standing on Ms. Kettleworth's porch until she says, "Now, Montgom'ry, you best get on back in dat Mer-shay-dees of yurs fo' dem skeeter hawks come swimming 'round you for blood."

I don't know what the old lady is yapping about but I thank her for the information and go on back to my car, waiting for Cherish to return home.

* * *

It's a little after ten when she pulls into the driveway. She almost breaks into a sprint to run to her house where she unlocks the door and enters before I can reach the porch.

"Cherish." I reach for the screen door. It's locked.

"What do you want?" she asks me from a small crack in the main door.

You'd think I was a stranger by the way she was acting.

"Can I come in?"

"No," she answers quickly. "What do you want?"

"I want to talk to you."

"About what? Work? I'm not coming back."

I can see fear and pain in her eyes. She's scared to death. Of *me*. I've never done anything to hurt her and I never would, but she's afraid. I say, "I know what's wrong with you and I want to help you."

"I don't need help. I just need to be left alone."

"You need to talk to someone, Cherish. I know what your father did to you."

"You don't know anything!" she yells. "Just leave and go back to your life."

"I know he hurt you."

"Go, Monty! You'd be better off," she says.

"How you figure?"

"You don't need anyone to pick out your clothes or tell

you what to eat for breakfast."

"Is that all you think you *do* for me? Is that all you think you *are* to me?"

"That's what I've always been. I'm your personal assistant. Nothing more."

"You know that's not true," I say feeling like I've been stabbed in the heart. I love this woman and she's killing me with her words. She's killing *herself* by refusing to acknowledge what happened to her.

"I have to go," she says, her voice distorted. She's on the verge of tears. She closes the door. Locks it. Shuts me out like I'm a stranger.

TINA MARTIN

Chapter Thirty-Eight

Cherish

A few days later, I get a call from Sylvia. She's full of questions. She's asking me where I am. What's going on? Why am I not there? What's wrong with Montgomery? She wants to know if we got into a fight. If he did something or said something slick. She tells me to remember he's a work in progress. Reminds me to not give up on him.

"Sylvia—"

"And he's come a long way in such a short period of time, Cherish. A long way."

"Sylvia."

"Yes. Please tell me something."

"I can't work for Monty anymore."

"Why not? What did he do?"

"It's not him. It's—it's me. I'm going through something right now and I can't see my way out of it yet."

"What is it? Do you need money?"

"No, I don't need money," I tell her. "Why do people with money think money solves everything?"

"I don't think it solves everything but if you need it—"

"No, I don't need money."

"Then tell me what you need, Cherish."

"I don't know what I need. I just know what I don't need and right now, I can't work. I can't function. I need some time."

"Okay. I don't understand, but okay. Just please make sure you come to the charity event on Saturday. Major put it together. It's something Monty suggested. Please tell me you'll make it."

"I don't know, Sylvia. I don't want to tell you I'm

coming and then I change my mind. Look, I need to go. I'll talk to you later."

OVER THE NEXT few days, I stay held up in my house reading articles about how to cope with traumatic experiences – articles I've read before. Remedies I already know about like exercise, not isolating myself, taking care of my health, breathing techniques, getting plenty of sleep, eating a good diet and avoiding alcohol.

Alcohol has never been a problem for me, so I'm not concerned about that one. The thing I need the most is sleep. So, I sleep during the day when I feel safe and at night, I'm up watching TV. It's what I'm doing when I get a call from Major.

I don't answer. Haven't talked to him in a while. I'm sure he's calling on Monty's behalf.

He calls again. I answer this time.

"Hey."

"Hey, girl. What's up?"

"Nothing."

"I haven't seen you at work. Mom said you quit. Monty's irritable—slowly creeping back to his old self again."

"Oh, no," I say.

"He misses you, Cherish. We all do. Me, Mom, Naomi, Isidora, Minnie, even the landscapers been asking where you are. What's up with you?"

"It's personal, Major. I feel like I need this mental break for myself before I have a freakin' breakdown."

"You mean like my brother had."

"Yeah. Like that."

"He exposed so much of himself to you. Did he not?"

"He did."

"So, whatever's bothering you, why are you having such a hard time talking to him?"

"Because it's not easy to talk about."

He blows a breath, becoming frustrated with me. He's never been frustrated with me. "Look, all I know is my brother has taken a liking to you in a way I didn't think was possible. He's changed. I'm sure this charity benefit he had me put together this Saturday was your idea, was it not?"

"He came up with it. I just told him the company should do more to give back."

"So, basically, it was your idea."

"It—" Just when I thought I had it in me to argue against it, I digress.

"My brother respects you. He loves you and I truly believe if you don't show up Saturday it will crush him. Tell me you'll be there."

"Major—"

"Just tell me you'll be there, Cherish."

"I'll be there."

"Are you saying that just to be saying it, or—?"

"I'll be there."

"Good. I hope you find peace in whatever you're going through, but just remember you're not alone. I don't want you to ever think that. If you don't want to talk to Monty, I'm always available. Or mother. Or Naomi."

"Thanks, Major."

"You're welcome. I'll see you on Saturday."

"Okay. See ya."

Chapter Thirty-Nine

Monty

There are about sixty people floating around the bottom level of the estate dressed in gowns and tuxedos. Most are wearing black like this shindig is an all-black affair. They're mingling and drinking champagne. Eating appetizers. Networking. The salad bar, drink stations and live jazz band are nice touches. In such a short period of time, Major came through with an amazingly well-planned evening.

There's no stage so I climb the staircase about halfway up to make an announcement concerning donations. Before I do, I scan the room looking for Cherish. Major said he thought she might make it. Mom wasn't so sure. An hour into the evening, her attendance doesn't look so promising.

I signal the band to kill the music.

"Good evening, everyone," I say to get people's attention. "I hope everyone is having a good time and enjoying themselves this evening."

They clap and cheer, confirming they are.

"I want to thank you all for coming out to the first charity event hosted by the St. Claires at The Hawthorne Estates. All donations tonight will go toward cancer research and I'll triple whatever money is raised this evening. Many of you don't know this but my father, Caspian Hawthorne, the great man who started Hawthorne Innovations died of cancer. He—"

I pause when I see her – my angel – walking into the room. She's at the back of the crowd, in a strapless black gown. With such pretty skin and a beautiful collarbone, she doesn't need jewelry. Her braids are pinned up, exposing the shape of her face. She's breathtaking. Literally. I can't find my breath to form words.

I take my gaze away from her and rack my brain to remember what I was talking about.

Right.

My father...

I continue, "He would still be alive and well today if he didn't have the disease. Cancer affects millions of people globally. Cancer doesn't care how rich or poor you are. It just happens. It can happen to any one of us."

I glance over at Cherish again. She's as attentive as the rest of the crowd is.

"I never considered doing anything like this before, mostly because my father who was my mentor thought charities like this were a front to collect money and not to actually help people. But he was wrong. My father was an intelligent man, but on this particular topic, he was wrong. We can do good by helping others with our generous donations, and that's what I want to accomplish this evening. So reach into your pockets and dig even further into your hearts and let's help someone win their battle with cancer. Thank you very much."

I take the stairs back down as the guests clap, but my mind is on one thing – getting over to Cherish's table. It's why when I see Paige coming my way carrying two glasses of champagne, I cringe.

"Well, hello there, bachelor," she slurs. "I got a lil' something for you."

She tries to hand me a glass. I don't accept it. I've had one glass of champagne already and don't plan on having another.

"No, thanks," I tell her. "I've reached my limit."

"Then one more ain't gonna do you no harm. Believe it or not, this is my fourth one."

Oh, I believe it....

She's already wobbling in her heels. "I would advise you not to have anymore."

"Oh, stop being such a party pooper." She laughs wild and crazy – makes a few guests uneasy.

I walk over to mother and say discreetly, "Find a way to get Paige out of here."

"Why?"

"She's a lil' tipsy."

"Oh, no."

"Why'd you invite her, anyway?" I ask.

"I thought it would be good for her to mingle and meet some of the area's elite professionals."

"Well, she's not behaving like an *elite* professional."

"Okay. I'll call her an Uber."

"Good."

"By the way, I know you really wanted Cherish to be here. I thought she would make it, but—"

"She's here. She came in while I was addressing the crowd. Excuse me," I say walking away from her. Major steps in my path and says, "Nice speech."

"Thanks."

"Ay, listen, I tried my best to get Cherish to come."

"Then, like this charity ball, you did a good job, bruh. She's here."

"She's here?"

"Yes—came in during the speech. That's where I'm headed. To find her."

The jazz band plays a song that fills the floor with dancers. I weave through them.

"Nice work, Mr. St. Claire," one lady comments.

"You have a lovely home," another one says.

I thank them and keep it moving.

Finally, I make it to the back of the room but I don't see Cherish. I look to the right, to the left and finally, my eyes have the pleasure of landing on her. She's sitting at a table alone like she's lost. In a way, I think she is.

I walk her way knowing I've pretty much left the ball in

her court. Told her to come to me when she wanted to talk. But I eat my words and go to her instead. It's how I know I care deeply for her.

She looks up, sees me. She frowns a little.

I stretch out my hand and say, "Dance with me."

Chapter Forty

Cherish

I hesitate to take his hand. I've spent the last two weeks in a bubble trying to make sense of my life and get ahead of reliving what had happened to me. The only reason I showed up today is because I realize I can't take this out on him. Monty's done nothing wrong to me. He doesn't have Webster-like tendencies.

"Cherish."

I look up at him. His hand is extended, waiting for me to reach out for it. He could just grab my hand if he wanted to, but he wants *me* to make the decision whether to dance with him.

I reach for his hand, feel my hand trembling in his large one and he leads me over to the dance floor where he places his other hand on my side. Then we sway. At an affair like this where all the affluent guests are millionaire status or better, I'm surprised he asked me to dance. There are plenty of women who are standing around, looking at us — mostly white women wearing real pearls and ugly shoes that look like they cost a fortune.

But it's lil' ol' me dancing with him. Inhaling him. Enjoying the feel of my hand in his hand.

I don't say a word.

He doesn't say a thing.

He's rocking a black tuxedo with a crisp white shirt and a black bowtie. I've never seen him wear a bowtie. It looks good on him, but then again, anything looks good on him. The mere sight of him still intoxicates me. I wonder if he can hear my heartbeat pounding as loud as I can hear it in my ears. Or if he can feel my hand shaking. Probably so being that he's squeezed it a few times.

I get into my head as we slowly glide from side-to-side to the jazz rendition of Brian McKnight's *Love of My Life*. I know people are watching us – watching him look at me. I don't have to look up at him to know his eyes are on me. I can feel it. Feel the heat warming the top of my head. Even with heels on, we're not face-to-face.

These women are staring fiercely, waiting to get his attention. One thing I know about people with money is they tend to settle down with someone of the same wealth and influence. No doubt that's why these hussies came to the charity event – hoping to impress Monty by acting like they care about people with cancer.

I wonder if these women know who I am – that I work for him. I'm not one of *them*. I'm not rich. Not of the affluent community of entrepreneurs and philanthropists. I'm just a woman. With excess baggage.

Aside from my own negative thoughts, being in his arms feels perfect. He's perfect. The way he smells. The way his body moves when he dances. The way he's so attentive to me. I feel like I'm the only person in the room. Maybe he really does love me the way he said he did. And I let two weeks come between us…

I'm consumed with guilt at that thought. My throat tightens as I fight the emotions I'm battling.

We sway from side-to-side.

His hand tightens on mine again.

He leans down next to my ear, inhales a long breath of my scent and exhales like it has a calming effect on him then whispers in a soothing tone straight into my ear, "I miss you."

He breathes deeply again. In and out.

My cheeks flush with heat. I'm sure they're blush-red.

"I miss you so much, Cherish. Ah," he moans. "I miss you, girl," he says again as if I didn't hear him the first time. He's probably waiting for me to acknowledge him, look at him or return the sentiment.

I do none of the above.

I'm staring down at the floor. I've never been good at eye contact, fearing someone would see the shame I hide behind my vision.

He releases my hand and brings his hand to my face. I don't duck away this time. I close my eyes at the contact. Let his hand warm my body.

My lips tremble when his thumb touches them.

I open my eyes to see him staring back at me. He's given me all of his attention.

Now, he has all of mine. I fight the tendency to break eye contact and look back into his eyes. His beautiful eyes.

"I miss you so much, Cherish."

"I miss you, too, Monty," I say and bury my forehead in his chest. I feel his arms close around me and it doesn't freak me out. I feel safe here. I feel home.

"Let's go somewhere and talk," he says.

"No. I don't want to take you away from your event."

"I'm not as committed to this as much as I am to you. Come with me," he says, then whisks me away from the dance floor. We climb the stairs and walk toward his bedroom. He opens the door, enters after me and closes it.

There's a party and live band downstairs, but up here in his bedroom it's virtually quiet. We walk over to the chairs near the windows and sit, our legs angled toward each other.

"The last time I reached to touch you, you moved away from me. You've never done that before. *That* time, you did, and you had this look in your eyes like you were scared of me and I know that can't be the case. I lived with you for an entire month. I know you're not scared of me. *That* day, you were. Even the day I came by to talk to you—you wouldn't let me in. You had the screen door locked talking to me like I was a stranger. I knew something was off. I knew that wasn't you. So, I want you to tell me what that was."

"I want to, Monty, but it's hard to talk about," I say as tears blur my vision. "I don't talk about it to anyone."

"I know. I was the same way, remember? I needed help but didn't want to be vulnerable with you. Didn't want to appear weak."

"There's nothing weak about you."

"No, there isn't, baby and the same applies to you. You're stronger than you realize, but whatever is going on with you, nothing will change if nothing changes. You have to face it head-on. Talk about it. The same way I opened up to you, is the same way you need to open up to me."

I cringe. I've always concluded if I never told anyone what happened to me, it never really happened. I almost convinced myself of that. I wanted to feel normal. I didn't want to be a statistic. The embarrassment of people knowing kept my lips sealed.

And just what would Monty think about me if knew? He'd never look at me the same. I'd be the ruined girl. The one who needs professional help.

"But it's not the same, Monty," I say offering one last retort.

"It may not be the same, but it's something that's bothering you like I had something bothering me. We've already lost two weeks, Cherish. I don't want to lose more time."

I draw in a breath and prepare myself to say what he's waiting to hear. "This is not easy."

"I know."

My hand shakes. I glance up at him. The shame of what I'm about to say disturbs me to my core. I'm so shaken, I don't think the words will come out but I try.

"My dad died when I was nine years old. I was young—didn't really understand death. I just knew he wasn't around anymore. I remember being at the funeral. Remember people wearing all black. People crying and carrying on. Mama cried. I cried. I wanted my father back.

I loved him. I still love him. Still miss him. Mama couldn't function afterward. She tried to get her life back on track, but she was a mess. Losing someone you love is one of those things you never fully get over. I know you feel that way about your stepfather."

He nods.

I continue, "Mama wasn't the same. I didn't know what to call it back then, but I think she had something like a nervous breakdown. She couldn't work. Didn't eat. She rarely got any sleep. Didn't cook. Clean. It's like she ceased to exist when we lost my dad. This went on for the better part of a year. Then she met someone. Webster Gregory. She was happy again. He would take her out, wine and dine her and they got married pretty quickly. Everything was going good, at first, but I wasn't too thrilled with the idea of having a new man around because I always saw him as a replacement for my father. I never tried to get close to him. I hardly even talked to him. Mama scolded me for that. Told me I needed to respect him. Said my father was gone and Webster was my *new* dad. She told me if I tried, I could love him as much as I loved my dad. Of course, I looked at her like she was insane. No one could replace my dad. When I turned twelve, I remember Webster giving me funny looks. Weird stares. I didn't think anything of it. It was just creepy. Then one night, he came into my bedroom. It must've been early in the morning because it was still dark outside and I was still sleeping. I woke up to his hands on my chest. I tried to scream, he covered my mouth. Told me if I said a word, he'd hurt my mother. So, I didn't say anything. It was happening so frequently, my body became numb to it. Then finally, the touching wasn't enough. Mama went out with some of her friends one day. I was in my room with headphones on listening to music when he barged in, locked the door behind himself and grabbed me. I can still feel the weight of his body on top of me when he—when he—"

Montgomery releases my hands and pulls me into his lap. "I'm so sorry, Cherish."

I cry as he holds me. I find the cradle of his neck and cry all I want. I cry for all the years I've held this in. I cry because my mother didn't believe me. I cry because I don't know if that monster did this to anyone else.

"Why didn't you tell your mother?"

"I was scared he would hurt her like he said he would. All those times he touched me, I kept it to myself. After he forced himself on me, I told her. She didn't believe me. She sided with him. After that, he didn't touch me again, but I still had to live in fear in the same house with him until I couldn't tolerate his dirty looks anymore. I ran away—went to live with my Aunt Jolene in the same house where I live today and I never went back."

He relaxes me by stroking my back, helping me calm down. "That's a lot to hold in."

"It is," I say.

"You are a strong woman."

"Sometimes, I don't feel like I am."

"You have to be a strong woman to endure what you've endured, and you know what, baby. It's going to be okay. I'll see to it that no man ever hurts you again."

Chapter Forty-One

Monty

In all my years of living, killing someone has never crossed my mind until now – in these hours that have passed since Cherish told me what her stepfather did to her. I don't know the man and I want him dead by the strength of my bare hands. Webster Gregory needs to pay for what he's done. So what if I catch a murder charge?

I sit on the bed and stare at the face of this beautiful, sleeping woman – the only woman that's ever laid on my bed, and think about how I can't do anything to jeopardize our chances of living a happy life together. And she *will* be happy. I'll make sure of it. I have to.

I love her.

Nothing about her confession makes me love her any less. It makes me want to love her more – to show her what love is. Makes me angry that men like Webster Gregory walk this earth every day, preying on young girls.

She confirmed everything I didn't want to think in my head. I knew somebody hurt her. I didn't know who exactly until Ms. Kettleworth gave me the rundown on what happened at Cherish's house when her stepfather showed up. He was still bothering her, even as an adult.

Not anymore.

When she's up in the morning, I tell her to take her time waking up and getting ready for the day. It's a Sunday. A dreary one. Rain pounds the roof while thunder pops and crackles in the sky. We're not going out today. I've hired a chef to make us brunch. It'll be ready at eleven. Right now, it's a few minutes after nine and she's just getting up.

She stretches, still wearing the black dress she had on last night at the charity ball. She yawns. Her puffy eyelids are proof of her sadness – of things she confessed to me last night. She looks at me. Smiles. I smile back.

"I hope you slept well."

"I did. It was the first night in a week I didn't have a nightmare. Guess I'll have to stay here for the rest of my life."

"I have no objections to that."

She smiles, but I wonder if she knows I'm serious.

"These dreams—do they happen often?"

"Only when something triggers the memory of what happened."

"And what triggered it this time?" I ask, curious to know everything now that I'm all in.

"He came to my house."

"Your stepfather?"

"Yes. Ms. Kettleworth told me she kept seeing this white car driving by, but it never stopped probably because I wasn't home. The one time he saw my car in the driveway, he stopped."

"For what?"

"Mom told me he was having a retirement party. Asked me to come. I forget exactly what I said to her, but I probably called him a child molester or something. She must've run back and told him because he pulled up and started yelling that I needed to stop lying on him to my mother. I can't even believe she would call me to invite me to come to his retirement party. She had the nerve to say I was being disrespectful. Said Webster took care of us when dad no longer could."

Cherish massages her temples. "It's just baffling to me. How does a mother choose a man over her own child?"

"You may never know the answer to that question, sweetheart. Just like I may never know why my parents gave me up. It's a tough pill to swallow. In life, we don't get all the answers sometimes, but I still think you should talk to your mother."

"I've tried talking to her, Monty. It's like she's brainwashed. She's not the same woman she was when dad was alive."

"And you're not the same either. You need each other more than you know. I know it's easier to write her off, but you won't get *any* answers that way."

"I know. You're right."

Her eyes linger on me like she wants to say or ask something but she doesn't. She stretches her arms up high in the air and looks around at the bed.

"What?" I ask, prompting her to relay her thoughts.

"I'm sitting on your bed thinking about how, when I used to come in here to straighten up your room, the side of the bed I'm lying on right now is the only side you ever slept on. The other side is always left untouched."

"You got a problem with that?"

She smiles. "No. It was just an observation. You must be a calm sleeper. No tossing and turning."

"No, not much. After last night, I know for a fact you're the opposite."

"You watched me sleep, Monty?"

"I did. I wanted to make sure you didn't have any bad dreams. You did a lot of tossing and turning, but no bad dreams."

"Yeah. It felt good to sleep through the night and not freak out thinking my stepfather was coming to get me."

"You definitely don't have to worry about that, sweetie. I won't let anything happen to you."

* * *

The rain becomes an all-out downpour. We're sitting at the cove in my bedroom surrounded by windows. We can see the rain. Can hear it bearing down, banging on the window panes.

For brunch, we have waffles, ham and cheese sliders, salad, fresh fruit, danishes, coffee and juice. I get right down to business and ask, "What are your next steps where your stepfather is concerned?"

"I don't know. I just want him to stay away from me."

"Have you thought about a restraining order?"

"I have. Ms. Kettleworth actually suggested that, but won't that just make him angrier? I don't want him to retaliate and come after me."

"I think it's important his behavior is documented at this stage. He's already terrorized you as a child. I won't allow him to continue bothering you as an adult. As a safety precaution, I'm going to install a security system at your house."

"I don't think I need that, Monty."

"Whether you think you need it or not, you're getting it."

She eats a strawberry. My eyes land on her lips but I move them quickly to her eyes because I know if I continue to watch them, I'll end up eating them along with the strawberry she's munching on.

"So, here's what I want to happen," I tell her. "Tomorrow, we'll go to the police station and file a restraining order."

"Wait, shouldn't I think this through first?"

"What's there to think about?"

"The fact that my mother is still married to this man. What if he tries to retaliate and do something to harm her?"

"Then, you need to talk to your mother. Does she work?"

"Yes. She's a receptionist."

"What are her hours?"

"She starts at 7:30 and gets off around one."

"Then we'll be there so you can talk to her."

"She won't listen to anything I have to say, Monty. I've been telling her for years about Webster."

"Did you tell her he came to your house and threatened you?"

"No."

"Then that's what she needs to know before you mention the restraining order."

She sighs. "Okay, but I at least need some time to think it through first."

"That's fine." I eat waffles and sip coffee, watching her eat ham and cheese. "Oh, and by the way, you don't work for me anymore."

"I don't?"

"No. You don't."

Her eyebrows raise. She stops eating and asks, "You're firing me?"

"That's exactly what I'm doing."

"Why? Because I've been missing for two weeks."

"No."

She looks puzzled, returns the sandwich to her plate. "Then why?"

"Because you're my girl and I don't want you working for me anymore."

She blushes. Looks away from me. "I'm your girl?"

"Yes."

"Are you sure about that?"

"What do you mean?"

"Come on, Monty. You hardly knew I existed and now I'm your girl? It's one thing to be appreciative of everything I've done to take care of you, but it's another to assume you're in love with me just because I helped you."

"It's during the time you helped me when I got to know you as a person. Got to know your heart. Before then, I didn't know you, Cherish."

"Yeah, and you didn't like me."

"I didn't like anybody. It wasn't specific to you, baby."

"True. You got a point there."

"But that was then. This is now. I love you. There's no doubt in my heart about that."

She smiles beautifully. "I love you, too, Monty," she says, but I have a nagging gut feeling she doesn't believe those same words that left my mouth.

* * *

She's relaxed after brunch. So am I. We're still sitting by the window. The rain doesn't let up. It's a dreary day – perfect day to be indoors – especially with her.

"I should probably get going," she says.

I don't try to hide the frown that appears on my face when I ask, "Going where?"

"Home."

It was on the tip of my tongue to say *this is your home*, but I don't want to be presumptuous so I say, "It's raining hard out there, Cherish. Stay until it slacks off a bit."

"Okay, but I'm not going to be good company for you. I'm exhausted."

"Then let's take a nap," I say gesturing toward the bed.

She grins. "You don't take naps."

"I don't, but I'll take one with you."

She walks over to the bed, stretches her body and lies flat on her back. I open the windows. The sound of the downpour fills the room, along with the smell of rain. This is perfect.

I get on the bed, lay next to her and slide so close, my nose almost touches hers. She smiles then closes her eyes. She has a look of contentment on her face like this is where she's supposed to be. She doesn't look terrified. Doesn't appear uncomfortable. She looks like a woman who knows she's with a man whom she can feel safe and protected with.

I brush my fingertips down the side of her delicate face. She releases a soft hum that has the power to relax me the same way she's relaxed. She opens her eyes – it's like she's opened her soul – and looks at me.

I say, "I didn't get a chance to tell you—I met

Magnus."

Her eyes light up "How'd that go?"

"It went well. It was an emotional experience. I never thought I'd get to meet him."

"Why not? You could've hired a private investigator to track him down."

"I know, but sometimes, fear of what you'll find makes you hesitant to go looking."

"Yeah. I get that."

"But I'm glad I met him. He said my father's brother, Mason St. Claire, who's still alive has four sons. And get this—Mason told him I have half-siblings. Three of them."

"That's amazing."

"It is. He hasn't tracked them down yet, though."

"I'm sure he will." She yawns. "Tell me more about Magnus."

"He's married. His wife is pregnant with twins. He told us he lost his first wife and child in a car accident."

"That's awful."

"It is, but he seems to have come around now. He has a billion-dollar company called MJS Communications. He wants us to meet up again soon, with the cousins this time."

"That would be nice."

"It would. For the longest time, I thought it was just me and Major in his world. I'm glad to know I have some family out here."

"I'm happy you found them."

"And it's all because of you."

"No. Give yourself some credit. You went. You didn't have to."

"I suppose, but I'm grateful to have you."

She cracks a small smile. Her eyes close as she succumbs to sleep.

Chapter Forty-Two

Cherish

Old habits die hard. A week later, I find myself still getting up at three, arriving at Monty's house at four and laying out his clothes. It's weird, but I miss doing this for him since he banned me from working for him, only I don't feel like I'm working now. I feel like I'm taking care of my man.

My man...

It's what he is to me now. The man who I thought could never see me – someone I always believed was out of my reach is *my* man.

This past week, he's come to my house every day after leaving work. He came by to make sure the alarm system was installed correctly. Every evening we ate dinner together. We even watched a movie together, finally.

Monty is amazing. He knows about my past and so he's careful not to touch me in a way he thinks will disturb me. He wants more. I can feel it, but he doesn't have a problem taking it slow. His self-control is impressive.

"And just what do you think you're doing?" he asks.

I turn around to see him standing there, bottom half wrapped in a towel.

"What are you doing, Cherry?" he asks again.

"I'm finding you a suit."

"That's not your job anymore," he says with a straight poker face as he walks over to me. "I thought I made that clear."

"I know, but you have a big day today with testing that taser and all. I just want to make sure you look fly."

All I see is a wall of muscles coming my way. I see the healed scar on his chest, remembering back to when it was a wound. To when I changed his bandages. To when I helped him heal wounds that weren't visible.

He stops in front of me, pulls the scarf off of my head and takes off the barrette that was keeping my braids in a ponytail. He buries his fingers in my hair and plows his tongue into my mouth. He hasn't kissed me this hard since our first ever kiss in the conference room downstairs. Whatever the case, I close my eyes and absorb it. When I'm with him, I'm *with* him and try my best not to think about nothing else but him. My only *experience* with a man was a bad one. I try to not allow it to control my life, especially when this man is so freakin' yummy, I don't know how I could ever turn him down.

After he gets his fill, he gives me my tongue back along with one of those pointed stares of his and says, "Good morning," then bites his lip.

I could just die.

"Good morning."

"You chose a black suit."

"Of course. It's one of your power suits—lets people know you mean business."

"Let me let you in on a little secret—people know I mean business when I step in the room. It doesn't matter what I have on."

"I don't doubt that not one bit."

He kisses my forehead then says, "I need to get dressed."

"Go ahead. I already laid out your suit. Oh, let me grab you some socks."

I walk over to the drawer where they're kept then walk them back over to him. He's still wrapped in a towel, and the thing moves again.

"What are you doing?" I ask, looking at his midsection then back up to him. He has a sneaky smile on his face.

"What are you talking about?"

"You're making the towel move again like you did the very first time you caught me in your closet."

The towel jerks again and he bites his lip. Amusement is in his eyes.

"I'm about to get dressed, so if you don't get out of here, you're going to see what's making it move."

"Alright. I'm out of here," I say. "I'll wait in the bedroom."

He comes out after about ten minutes – looks amazing. Smells like a slice of heaven.

"Here goes nothing," he says, slapping his hands together.

"Would you like some coffee?"

"No. I'll get some from the office," he says, sitting on the bed next to me. He rubs his hands together.

"You're nervous. I don't think I've ever seen you nervous before."

"You're probably the only person who can recognize when I'm nervous since you know me so well now." He takes my hand, interlocks our fingers and brings my hand to his mouth. Kisses it. Sends a warm sensation throughout my body.

"What am I supposed to do while you're gone?"

"Whatever you want as long as it doesn't involve work."

"Then who's going to clean your bathroom and change out your bath towels?"

"Not you," he says standing, pulling my hand so I stand up with him. He wraps his arm around my neck and says, "Don't let me hear Naomi or anybody else telling me you were in here working."

"Okay, *daddy*."

He kisses me again, briefly this time, and says, "I'll see you later."

"Okay."

* * *

Once he leaves, I go to the kitchen to talk to the crew. Naomi is here early, sitting around shooting the breeze. Isidora has a broom in her hand and Minnie is tying on an apron.

"Well, well, well, looka here, looka here," Naomi says. "If it ain't the lady of the house."

"Stop it," I say, blushing. I can't hide the smile on my face or the light in my eyes. I'm in love and they all know it.

"Did I just hear you call *her* the woman of the house?" Paige asks as she walks into the kitchen looking at me like she's somehow greater than I am. The last time I saw her, she was nearly about to puke at Montgomery's charity event. Now, she's here with her blond hair neatly flat-ironed. The black pantsuit she has on looks like it's about to burst at the seams.

"I beg your pardon," Naomi says to Paige.

None of the staff likes her. I'm actually surprised Sylvia would hire someone so stuck up and snooty.

"I said, it sounded like you called Cherish the woman of the house," she repeats.

"Don't talk about me like I'm not right here," I tell her.

She huffs and mumbles, "You won't be here for long…"

"What was that?" I ask.

She smiles. "Nothing. And FYI, Naomi, the woman of *this* house would possess the kind of class suitable for a king."

Naomi snorts, then laughs out loud. Her infectious cackle has us laughing with her – me, Minnie and Isidora.

When she can finally stop laughing, Naomi says, "So— so lemme get this straight. You think you got class. *You?* I saw you, just the other day picking your nose." She laughs harder.

"Whatever. Why don't you cook something and try not to eat it?"

"Paige, will you stop?" I tell her.

Naomi says, "She doesn't have to stop. It's obvious she doesn't know how tight that suit is she's got on."

Paige rolls her eyes and stomps out.

"What an entitled lil' piss pot..." Minnie says.

"Idiota," Isidora says.

"She thinks she's something don't she?" Naomi says. "See, the problem is, she knows Mr. St. Claire likes you, Cherry, and she don't know what to do about it. Thought that white privilege was gon' work on mister's heart, but he only has eyes for you."

I force myself not to smile and ask, "Why do you think Montgomery has eyes for me?" I ask the question because I thought me and Monty were being discreet whenever we were affectionate, but apparently not discreet enough.

"We know these things," Naomi said waggling her brows. "A little birdie told me he's been going to your house every day this week after work. Plus, that day he called you into that conference room—woo—we've all been speculating on what went down that morning."

"Nothing went down," I tell them.

"Cherry, stop that lying," Naomi says. "It's first thang in the morning and you already doing the devil's work. We know some kind of wham-bam-a-lam went down in there. Mister always looking at you like he hungry."

"Mmm, hmm," Minnie says.

I laugh harder, then I say, "I'll talk to y'all later. I have to go home and catch up on some sleep."

"You do that, *lady of the house*," Naomi says, teasing me.

"Yeah. Catch up on some sleep before your *man* comes over," Minnie adds.

I smile and make my exit. I feel bad about leaving them but Monty has banned me from working so what else am I supposed to do?

At home, I get back in bed and as I lie there, Paige crosses my mind. This morning's incident reminded me of a conversation I had with Major. He said Paige was suddenly a different person after Monty signed the contracts to secure Hawthorne Innovations. Sylvia had hired her and Paige supposedly lived in a Hawthorne property not far from the estate. What if there's some truth to that? What else could explain the way Paige walks around like she owns the place? And why suddenly does she feel threatened by me? I've never done anything to the girl, well except catch the eye of the man who *she* thinks is hers.

Chapter Forty-Three

Monty

The taser works exactly like I want it. Of most importance is the handle specifications. The grip is made with uneven ridges that make it easily identifiable without having to look at it – distinguishes it from a gun. It's what I set out to accomplish and it's done. I'm satisfied that the product can finally go to market testing. That it could possibly save lives.

"How do you think it went?" Major asks.

"I'm pleased. It exactly what I wanted."

"Another billion-dollar idea. Good job, man."

"Yeah. Thanks. I got somebody I want to try it out on right now," I say thinking about Cherish's stepfather.

Major chuckles. "What's the latest with you and Cherish?"

A smile automatically comes to my face. "I already told you how I feel about her."

"Okay, then, what's the latest on meeting with mother to see about those papers you signed."

I narrow my eyes at him. His concern irritates me. "Why do you think you have to hold my hand through this process, Major? I know what I'm doing."

"It's not *you* I'm worried about."

"You're worried about Cherish?"

"I am."

"Why?"

"Because she's my friend, and she's a good person, Monty. I don't want her to get hurt."

"Why would I hurt her, Major? She literally saved my

life. And it's really starting to bother me how much you think about her. Are you in love with her?"

"I'm not in love with her, but she's in love with you and I'm concerned how she'll react when she finds out about you and Paige."

"I don't even know anything about the girl."

"All the more reason for you to go to mom's office and have a talk with her. The longer you put it off, the worse it's going to be for Cherish."

He's right. He's a pain in my rear end, but he's right. I walk away from him and go straight to mother's office. At headquarters, her office is on the same floor as mine, just on the opposite end of the building.

She looks up and her eyes brighten when she sees me enter through the glass doors.

"Well, hello, Monty."

"Hey," I say closing the door.

"The testing went good today. I know you're pleased."

"Very much so."

"I was sitting here thinking about how proud your father would be right now. If that man didn't make you a replica of him…"

I think about how much he taught me and how Caspian Hawthorne loved me and Major as if we were his. Otherwise, he wouldn't have been so patient, especially with me since I wanted to learn the business. He could've turned me away – told me to do my own thing, but he patiently taught me. And then, he left the business to me. But there are other aspects of what went down after he died I didn't quite understand, and it's not anyone's fault but mine. I didn't care to understand. Back then, all I cared about was making sure I took Hawthorne Innovations to the next level. All that concerned me was the money.

"You look like you have something on your mind," she tells me, then gestures for me to take a seat. I do so, cross one leg over the other and lean back in the chair that sits in front of her desk.

"I've had a lot on my mind lately," I tell her. "Especially concerning all that paperwork from when I took over the company."

"Oh, now you want to talk about it, huh? When I first brought it to you, you just signed everything. Didn't look it over or read nothing."

"I know. I didn't care back then."

"But you do now?"

"Yes."

"Why? You have everything you want now. You have the business, you have the money. You own half of the real estate, and—"

"Let me interrupt for a minute. Did dad make the stipulation that you got to choose my wife or did you make that call?"

"That was your father's idea, and he didn't tell me to choose a woman for you. He wanted you to choose one."

"Why? Why would he do that to me?"

"You were too business-driven to do it for yourself. He was afraid you'd die alone without ever experiencing love."

"And out of all the women you could've chosen for me, you chose *her*. I don't understand that."

"What's there not to understand? The choice was yours, son. You told me to make the decision for you."

"Yeah, I did, didn't I," I say. "So, what would happen if I wanted to change it?"

"Trust me, you don't want to do that. Changing anything on those documents puts you in breach of contract which means you'll lose everything – the money, the business, the house. You'll be left with nothing and everything your father worked for would go up in smoke."

"There has to be a way it can be amended."

"I'm sorry, son, but it's ironclad. If you want to change it, you'd have to sign an amendment form and then we'd have to meet with the lawyers to reverse everything."

For a moment, I feel like I'm not breathing. I can't believe this is my life. I'm stuck being married to a woman

I don't love. A woman I can't stand.

"Does she know?" I ask.

"No. It'll be up to you to tell her."

The idea of it all disturbs me to the point that I get up and leave her office. I take the elevator down to the ground floor and stand outside, soaking in the sun trying to determine my next move. Do I tell Cherish I'm married and all the circumstances surrounding Paige or do I say nothing?

I can't ignore the issue and say nothing. Can't do that to her. And if I want a future with Cherish, I have to cut any ties to Paige. Doing so would mean I forfeit everything.

Cherish is not the type of woman who would accept the fact that I'm a married man. Circumstances don't matter. Her moral compass won't allow her to be with me and if I can't be with her...

I don't want the thought of it to take over my mind.

* * *

I spent the rest of the day agonizing over this. I can't blame my mother. Can't blame anyone but myself. It's ten o'clock and I'm still at the office trying to come up with a scenario where I can get everything I want, including Cherish. Nothing is making sense.

I'm exhausted. Hungry, but I couldn't eat if I had a big plate of food in front of me. All I want is to be near my angel. I pack up, drive to her house. Her car is in the driveway. The porch light is on. I let myself in and deactivate the alarm. Since the alarm has been installed on her house, she feels more secure. She doesn't lock her bedroom door any longer. She's somewhat back to normal – whatever normal means.

I walk into her room. The bedside lamp is on. She's asleep but her sleep doesn't look planned. Her hair is loose and wild. She's lying on top of the covers. She has on a thin, spaghetti strap pajama top. No pajamas. Just panties. Looks like they're the same flimsy fabric as her top.

As I'm removing my clothes, my eyes trace her frame. Her chocolate legs. Toned arms. And her hair – I want to swim in it. She looks so peaceful, I don't want to disturb her, but I have to. I need to kiss her lips. Need to feel the love she has for me before I tell her about Paige. I know it's selfish. I normally wouldn't do something like this, but I can't shake the need. Not this time.

"Cherish." I say her name in a whisper hoping my voice will be enough to keep her calm since she has no idea I'm here. I don't want to scare her. Don't want her to think I'm an intruder. "Cherish."

"Hmm," she hums and turns over, adjusting her position. Her eyes never open. Her hair falls differently. She's out.

I ease on the bed, stroke her hair for a moment and call her name again. Her eyes open this time.

She stretches. "Monty?" She glances around the room. "What are you doing here?"

"I wanted to see you."

She stretches, rises up to an elbow. "You wanted to—"

Before she can say another word, I stuff my tongue into her mouth. I kiss her deeply. Make every lick, every stroke count for something. I savor her tongue. Make love to it.

She hums.

Moans and hums.

I crawl on top of her until her back is flat on the bed again, my weight holding her in place.

She moans as we kiss. I feel her hands on my back. They're hot. A fire has been set to me.

I deepen the kiss, allow my tongue to linger in her mouth, while her hands explore and grip my muscles.

I hear desire and need in her moans.

I need her.

I'm selfish. Greedy. I want her.

"Mmm," I say, pulling my mouth away from hers. I stare down at her for a moment, losing myself in her big, brown eyes when I say, "I love you, Cherish. No matter what, I'll always love you."

"What?" she asks, frowning.

I ignore her, leave kisses all around her neck, making her body shiver.

"Monty," she whispers.

"Yes, baby?" I say before flicking my tongue across her earlobe.

"Ahh," she hums. Her body shivers but she manages to ask, "What does that mean?"

Her question irritates me, yet makes me want her even more. It proves how much she really knows me. "What are you talking about?" I ask.

"I'm talking about what you just said. *No matter what, you'll always love me.* What does that mean?"

"It means what I said."

"But why are you saying it like *that*—like something's about to go down. What's wrong, Monty?"

"Everything's okay, sweetheart. Just kiss me."

"Monty—"

"Kiss me," I request, as my lips touch hers.

She releases her worries and gives me her lips. I take them, devour them. My body feels like it's glued to hers. Meshed with hers. I've never kissed lips so sweet. Never knew I could crave a woman so much. That I could love a woman like this. She means everything to me – the woman who's put me in touch with my true emotions. The woman that made me *feel*. Made me come alive and from beneath the rock that had been restricting me from happiness. I love her. What am I supposed to do without her?

Chapter Forty-Four

Cherish

I open my eyes in the morning and see Monty beaming back at me. He's just standing there, leaning up against my dresser, watching me.

He doesn't blink.

Doesn't smile.

He's stoic.

I knew something was bothering him last night. This confirms it.

He's fully dressed. Has on a suit, but not the jacket. His arms are crossed.

He frowns.

"Monty?"

"Yes."

"Good morning," I say.

He uncrosses his arms, slides them into his pockets. "Morning."

I crack a smile. "Why are you just standing there?"

"We need to talk."

A chill automatically runs through me.

"O-okay."

"I'll be in the kitchen," he says, then walks out of the room.

I guess he's going to wait for me in the kitchen...

I get out of bed, brush my teeth, wash my face and slide into a robe. About fifteen minutes later, I join him in the kitchen. He's sitting at the dinette. I pull out a chair and brace myself for whatever it is he needs to tell me. He's clearly at a quandary so I know it's not good and what really bothers me is, I have no idea what it could be. We're fine. Everything is good between us – at least I thought it was.

"Hey. What's up?" I ask in an upbeat tone, trying to keep the mood light, but I don't think it's working.

No, it's not working.

He looks up at me and I can see trouble in his eyes. He says, "I—uh—"

He doesn't know where to begin. Monty isn't usually this way. He knows what he wants to say and just says it. His being extra careful is a sign he's treading softly.

He makes another attempt and says, "I signed some documents as a part of my father's will to gain control of the company and in it, I had to choose a wife."

He breaks eye contact with me and looks down at the floor while shaking his head. "It had to be done. I wasn't with anyone then and I didn't care about a woman or being in a relationship. I didn't care about anything but the company and the money, so I tasked mother with taking care of it for me, and—"

"She chose Paige for you," I say because it's all making sense now. Paige walks around like she's the queen because, well—she is.

"How did you—?"

"I figured some things out on my own, Monty," I say. The severity of what he's saying hasn't hit me yet.

"I can get out of it by reversing everything. I would have to give up my inheritance—the company, the money—everything."

"Give it to who?"

"The money would be dispersed across charities, I imagine. The company would be sold and the money from the sale would also go to charity."

I'm getting upset now, because he came to my house last night and spent the majority of the night kissing me, telling me how much he loved me, holding me and talking me to sleep – all the while he was harboring this secret. He belongs to someone else.

It stings. No, it hurts. I know in my heart that I will never love another man as much as I love Monty. Never. So, my life *after* him will be mediocre at best. Not extraordinary. Could I fall for someone again? Probably, but whoever the poor guy is will never know true love because I will never be able to truly love him. I love Montgomery St. Claire.

But he's married.

That changes everything.

"Why are you telling me this now, Monty?"

"I'm trying to be transparent with you. I didn't know I would feel the way that I do about you, Cherish."

"I'll ask you again—why are you telling me this?"

"You're upset."

"Why wouldn't I be upset?" I ask frowning.

"All of that paperwork had slipped my mind until Major brought it to my attention."

"Right. So, now what?" I ask blinking the wetness away from my eyes. I'm too pissed to cry.

"I want to talk this through with you."

I get up from the table and cross my arms. "There's nothing to talk about, Monty. Even if you were crazy enough to give up everything for me, I wouldn't let you."

"You wouldn't *let* me," he fires back.

"No."

"And how is it do you think you have control over my decisions?"

"It's not about having *control*. It's about doing what's right. Your father was your world. You loved and admired him. He left everything to you. He wouldn't want his company—everything he built—thrown away because of—of a personal assistant."

"Don't say that."

"And I'm not the kind of woman who'd sneak around with a married man, so—"

"Cherish—"

"It's the truth! You *are* a married man. Are you not?"

"On paper, yes, but I don't love her. I love you."

It's a painful experience to hear him say he loves me when my heart is breaking because of him. To relive all the time we spent together. The way he kisses me. Touches me. The way he looks at me. I'm at a loss.

"Say something," he tells me. He's still sitting, looking up at me.

"I don't know what's left to say. There's really nothing to say. It doesn't matter how much you love me. You're married." My arms are still crossed. I think it's a way of guarding my damaged heart from him. I'm already starting the process of distancing myself even though he's in my house.

He stands and begins walking towards me. Every cell, every atom, every drop of blood inside of me freezes.

He comes to a stop in front of me, tries to touch my face but I turn away. I'm still in heart-protection-mode although the damage has already been done.

"You should go," I say.

He grimaces. "Do you think this is easy for me?"

"Just go. Please."

He respects my wishes and leaves. I break down upon hearing the front door close because out of it has walked the man of my dreams. I thought he was my future. The man who'd father my children. The man who I would spend the rest of my life with. I had so many hopes for us, even though I knew he was too good to be true.

Chapter Forty-Five

Monty

I take Friday off work to spare my employees the wrath of the previous version of myself. I can't get Cherish out of my mind. Can't believe how reckless I was with my life before her. All I do now is sit around and wish things were different.

Saturday, I get a call from Magnus. He assures me he hasn't forgotten about setting up a meet-and-greet with our Uncle Mason and cousins, but he's been on baby watch. His wife could be called in at any time.

I relay this message to Major when he disturbs me while I'm swimming laps in the outdoor pool. Then he says, "You swam like fifty laps nonstop. What's eating at you, bruh?"

"Nothing," I say. I swim a lap back across. Swimming gives me time to think about my next move, only I've been swimming for the last hour and I don't have a clue what that next move might be. I come up again, taking deep inhales of air after holding my breath for so long to see Major has walked the length of the pool to where I am.

"Are you sure it's nothing?" he asks.

I'm still catching my breath. Water is dripping from my hair. "Yeah. I'm sure."

"Alright, well, I guess I'll leave you to your Olympic swimming in that case."

"Wait—let me ask you something. If you were in my shoes and mother presented you the offer of obtaining the company and five-billion dollars but you had to choose a wife beforehand, would you have done it?"

"I don't know, man. That's a tough call. I know how dedicated you are to the company. If I was as dedicated as you, maybe I would have. I don't know. Did mother at least come to you before she made her pick?"

"She did. She asked me if I had any input and I told her I didn't care."

"Why would you *not* care about something as serious as marriage?"

"Because I had no intentions on actually being a husband to whoever she picked. I didn't care. I was married to my work. Nothing else was more important than that to me. Now, it's come back to haunt me."

"I assume you talked to mother about it already."

"I did—I told Cherish about Paige. I told her everything a couple of days ago."

"And?"

I pull myself up out of the pool and sit on the edge, my feet still in the water. "And I haven't heard from her in a couple of days. It broke her heart. *I* broke her heart."

I feel pain in my chest at the sound of saying that out loud.

"You haven't tried to call her?"

"No. I don't know what to do at this point."

"That's why you're out here tiring yourself out?"

"I can't focus on anything else, so—"

"You should go see her—at least make sure she's okay."

"I don't know if I should. The day I told her, she asked me to leave. She hasn't asked me to come back."

"Then take the initiative. One thing's for certain. Nothing is going to get resolved if you don't talk to each other."

"Trust me, I want to talk to her, but I don't want to go to her without any indication from her end that she's ready to talk to me. I have to tread softly."

"What! Okay, who are you?"

I grin. "I know her well, Major."

"And I know *you* well. I know how aggressive you can be when you want."

"But there are things about her past that's driving my decision-making process right now. I have to take this one step at a time. I don't want to bombard her."

"I hate to say this, but I think now's the time for you to be more aggressive. If you want her, *show* her you want her. There has to be a way to fix this Paige crap."

"Yeah, I just haven't found it yet, but trust me—I'm working on it. Cherish is too good of a woman for me to let go. I can't let her go. I love her too much."

Chapter Forty-Six

Cherish

It's been five days. Five, long days. I haven't heard his voice. Seen his face. His eyes. Those amazing eyes. Oh, gosh, those eyes. I miss laughing with him, seeing him smile. I miss being around his family.

At the same time, I hate that I miss him. How am I supposed to get over him and move on with my life?

I busy myself with taking care of my flowers since I don't have a job to go to. I'm not hard up for money. I have savings and Monty had given me a check after he was well. My finances will be fine. My heart on the other hand – not so much.

"What you doing there, Sherrish?"

I turn around to see Ms. Kettleworth behind me holding an ax. If it was anybody else, it would've freaked me out, but I know the old lady has issues.

I ask, "What are you doing with an ax, Ms. Kettleworth?"

"I done killed me a snake earlier this mornin'."

"What!"

"Yep, a black one. A shiny black one and I probably would've missed him if Butterball wasn't following right down 'hind him. I told Butterball, I say now, don't you worry. Mama's gon' take care of it. I ran out in the back and the ax is the first thang I saw. I hauled dat thang back and chopped dat sucker into fours...serves him right, too. I left it lying right there so the others know what they gon' get if they slither over here on my prop'ty."

She laughs like a crazy person off meds, then says,

271

"You ain't seen no snakes over here have you, Sherrish?"

"The only snake I saw in my yard was my stepfather."

Ms. Kettleworth laughs.

"No, but I haven't seen any snakes. I always put some snake repellant around the perimeter of my house. I got some left if you want to try some."

"Nah. Long as I got this here ax, I'ma have me a choppin' good time."

I smile at her nonsense and continue pulling weeds out of my roses.

"So you're working out'chea in yur flowers today, huh?"

"Yeah. Just killing time."

"You don't go to work anymore?"

"No. I'm taking a lil' break," I tell her.

"I ain't seent yur boyfriend by here either. He used to be here all the time. Now, he's like my teeth—nowhere to be found."

I chuckle. "Yeah, we're, sort of—um—"

"Broken up?"

"Something like that."

"What happened?"

"I don't want to bore you with details about it, Ms. Kettleworth. It just wasn't meant to be. Some things aren't."

"Aw...that's too bad, hun. He was mighty, mighty handsome."

"Yep."

"He got dem eyes that'll hyp'tize somebody."

I crack a smile. "He does."

"He most certainly does...they sho got me...had me caught in a spell a few times."

I pull more weeds, loosen the dirt and start on the next flower bed.

"So, what happened to him? Don't tell me you done let some hussy take him."

"It's a little more complicated than that."

"Look, all I know is, y'all seemed like a pretty dang good couple. I was happy when I first saw him over here. I said to myself, Sherrish done got herself a man. Lemme tell you sum—you don't want to get old like me and then start looking for a man. Time flies, Sherrish. Believe me when I say dat. One minute you're running on the beach in a bikini and the next, you got skin hanging loose, flappin' whichever way and your best friend is an overweight cat. Ain't no man looking for an old lady with loose skin and no teeth. Find a man while you still got yur teeth, Sherrish. That's the key."

I laugh. "*That's* the key?"

"You bet yur skinny britches it is. Now quit tending to dem flowers and go tend to dat beautiful man of yurs."

She walks off with the ax and goes back over to her yard. She comes back just as quickly and hollers, "Oh, one more thing, Sherrish—make sure you keep yur car doors locked at all times. Neighbor 'cross the street said somebody done broke in her car last night. I checked my truck and sho 'nuff somebody broke in it, too."

I laugh to myself. The woman never puts the windows up on her truck unless it rains. I wouldn't be surprised if she had a bird's nest in there.

"Ms. Kettleworth, you always leave your windows down on your truck."

"Whether dey down or up, if somebody been in my truck, they were crushpassing."

"You mean, trespassing?"

"Yeah. Dat's what I said. If somebody comes on yur prop'ty and they ain't 'sposed to be there, is dat not called crushpassing?"

I chuckle a little and say, "Yes. You're right."

"I knows I'm right. Now, keep an eye out and get you one of these bad boys," she says holding the ax up in the air like a torch.

She moseys on back to her house.

LATER AFTER I'M done playing around in my flowers, I take a shower and consider doing something to get out of the house to help disrupt the boredom. I get dressed. I have nowhere to go but I'm dressed in jeans and a black T-shirt. I get my purse, sit on the sofa and think about Monty like I always do. I get up, walk to the bedroom where he used to sleep – my guest bedroom – and I can still feel his presence in the room. I sit on the bed, run my fingers across the comforter but it doesn't *comfort* me.

I'm happy for the distraction my phone provides when it beeps. It's a text message from Major:

Major: Hey, girl. How are you?
Cherish: I'm okay. You?
Major: I'm good. Long time, no speak.
Cherish: I know.

Now he's calling…
Crap!
I don't want to answer because I know he's going to say something about Montgomery, but I decide to answer, anyway. He didn't do anything to me. His *brother* did.

"Hello."

"Hey, Cherish. What's going on? How you livin'?"

"You mean now that I'm jobless? Ain't nothing going on. I'm an old lady these days, spending my days digging in flowers and entertaining my seventy-year-old neighbor."

He chuckles. "You could come by and visit us. Naomi and the girls miss you. Said they haven't seen you in a while. They're all concerned and quite frankly, so am I."

"I can't come there for obvious reasons. I'm sure you're well aware of them."

"Okay, so, you and Monty are not on the same page— does that mean you write everybody else off?"

"That's not what I'm doing, Major."

"That's *exactly* what you're doing."

"You know what—you're quick to make judgments on things you know nothing about," I tell him.

"I know everything," he replies. "Who do you think told Monty to find out his status with Paige? I did. Do you know why? Because I didn't want you to get hurt."

"Yeah, and how'd that work out?"

He's quiet for a moment, then asks, "Am I to conclude we were only friends because of Monty because I seem to recall being your friend before Monty knew you existed?"

"You *are* a friend to me, Major. This is just a complicated time right now."

"Yeah. It's not like I don't know what that's like."

"Gosh, you are impossible sometimes. You and Monty have that in common."

"And you're a little stubborn."

"I'm not stubborn. I'm—I'm hurting."

"Who hurt you? Me?"

"No, but I—" I take a breath. Now, I wish I didn't answer the phone. "What do you want, Major?"

"Monty's not here. Why don't you come by?"

"Sounds like a setup."

"It's not. Well, it kinda is but not in the way you think. I told Naomi to make extra sandwiches because I would convince you to come by at least for an hour or so."

"Okay. Fine. I'll leave now."

"Good."

* * *

When I arrive at the estate, they're all sitting out back by the pool at one of the umbrella tables on their lunch break. Naomi prepared ham and turkey subs and sweet tea. There are chips – barbecue and plain – and pickles, the kind Monty likes.

"How's everything been, Cherry?" Naomi asks.

All eyes land on me. Isidora raises her brows. Minnie stares intently. Major takes a bite of his sandwich, eating like he's trying to get out of starvation mode.

"I've been okay. I take it everybody knows what happened?"

"Yeah," Minnie says, crestfallen. "We know. I wish things were different for you, Cherish. We sure miss you around here."

"And so does mister," Naomi says. "He's lost without you."

"I doubt that. He has Paige."

"That's not fair to say," Major says. "You know how Monty feels about you, Cherish."

"He can't stand Paige," Naomi says. "Nobody here likes that girl."

I take a sip of tea and try to eat a little more.

Naomi asks, "When is Mrs. Sylvia coming back, Major?"

"She's supposed to be back tomorrow. I'll have to call her later to confirm."

"Where is she?" I ask.

"She took a vacation—she'll be back on Friday but didn't tell nobody where she was going. I think Monty got her stressed out again."

Speaking of Monty...

I nearly lose lung function when I see him walking toward us. I haven't seen him in days and he's walking out here, wearing a navy blue suit – the man has all the swagger in the world.

"I thought you said he was at the office today?" I ask, looking at Major.

"He was...must've came home for something."

"You told him I was here, didn't you?"

"No, I didn't."

"Major, I'm going to kill you," I say between gritted teeth.

"I promise you, I didn't. He has a connection to you," Major says. "An internal one."

"He also has surveillance," Minnie says. "I bet he saw

you the moment you rang the bell."

They stop talking when he's closer.

"Good afternoon everyone," he says.

They all respond while I sit there chewing hoping he doesn't bother me.

Hope goes right out the window when he grabs a chair from the neighboring table and places it beside my chair. I can feel him looking at me. The heat of him, his smell, his overbearing male presence has the hair standing up on my arms.

I'm not ready for this. Not at all.

Chapter Forty-Seven

Monty

"Good afternoon, Cherish," I say directly to her since noticing she didn't speak to me. She's the only one I want to hear from. I wasn't looking at anyone else. Just her.

"Hi," she says dryly, then sips tea.

I watch her for a moment trying to determine her mood. "How have you been?"

She frowns a little, makes no effort to look at me when she responds, "You know how I've been. You don't have to ask."

"I haven't seen or heard from you in five days. How am I supposed to know how you are?"

She stands, tells the others she's leaving. I leave, too, following her to the front driveway before she can reach her car.

I reach for her arm. She snatches it away from me.

"Cherish."

"What do you want, Monty?" she asks, looking at me.

We're steps away from her car. "I want to talk to you. Want to know how you are. How you're doing. That's all I asked and it solicited *this* kind of reaction from you?"

"Why wouldn't it?"

"Look—I know things didn't go as planned between us, but at the very least, we could still be friends."

She frowns. "Friends?"

"Yes."

She shakes her head and looks offended that I made the suggestion. "We can't be friends."

"Cherish—"

"I know you can't help it. The billionaire in you is used to getting everything he wants, but no, I can't be your friend. I don't *want* to be your friend. I will not stand by and watch you love another woman. I won't do that to myself."

"You know I don't love her. I—" I pause. My words are falling on deaf ears. I'm not getting through to her now. She's scorned. Angry. She has every right to be.

"You've been dealt a life—deal with it," she tells me. "Who knows, maybe you and Paige will be happy together. Have you thought about giving it a real shot instead of resisting it? That maybe your mother truly knows what's best for you. Sylvia's a smart woman. Maybe she sees something in Paige you don't. Maybe a man with your status and level of success needs a white woman on his arm. Maybe it'll help you further your career—open doors that might've remained closed. All I know is, I can't be around to watch it happen."

She gets into her car, drives away, taking my heart with her.

"Ay, you alright?" Major asks as he gets closer.

"No. I'm not. I'm not alright with any of this. How can I be? I—"

I can't say anymore. Words are just words and I'm tired of talking about how much I love this woman and how much I want to be with her. It's time to do something about it.

Chapter Forty-Eight

Cherish

I can't sleep. It's one o'clock in the morning and I'm wide awake thinking about Monty. After running into him again, those old feelings stir inside of me. I love him, he loves me but we can't be together. That's the crux of my problem. If two people love each other, nothing should stand in between that. No one should *settle* for a person because they couldn't have the one they *really* wanted. I don't want to settle. If I can't have Monty, I'll just be another Ms. Kettleworth.

As I'm slowly drifting off to sleep, I hear a thump that makes my eyes fly open. I glance around my room, make sure my bat is next to the bed. I sit up, listen keenly for any further noises. I don't hear a thing. It's probably the house settling, at least that's what I tell myself hoping to stop the frantic beats of my heart. Ms. Kettleworth has me on edge now talking about somebody breaking into cars in the neighborhood. I'm being extra vigilant now – the way I used to be before I met Monty.

I know it's not him at my door, disturbing me. If it was, it wouldn't be the first time he came over unannounced in the middle of the night but that was before he told me about Paige. There's no need for him to come over here now.

There's another thump – sounds like it came from the front of the house. Now, I'm a little scared. I ease off the bed, grab my bat and tiptoe to my bedroom door. As I grab the knob to open it, I hear a loud crash. The alarm sounds, blaring so loud, it probably wakes the entire block.

Somebody's breaking into my house. Somebody's breaking into my house!

The alarm is steadily going nuts. I'm hiding in my room in pajamas and a bat wishing I had Ms. Kettleworth's ax or shotgun.

My hands are trembling. *Someone's breaking into my house.*

My cell phone is ringing now. All the noise in this house – the alarm, my cell phone has me on edge. I don't know if someone is in my house because I'm too afraid to come out of the room. What if it's a burglar? The car break-in guy? What if it's—Webster?

The piercing sound of the alarm seems to get louder – so loud I can't hear any commotion in the living room. I unlock my bedroom door, peep out into the hallway. I walk a few quiet steps and can clearly see that my front door is kicked in. The door is wide open. Frame busted.

Now, I'm freaked out. I run back to my bedroom, close and lock the door. The intruder could still be here, but I didn't see anyone. Didn't hear anyone.

My phone is ringing again. I run over to the nightstand to grab it with my trembling hand. It's the security company. I whisper, "Somebody's in my house. Somebody kicked in the front door and broke into my house! Please send the police. Please. Hurry!"

"Okay. Stay calm ma'am. The police are already on their way."

"Okay," I whisper, then get a call-waiting beep.

"Stay on the line with me."

"O-okay. I'm here."

Montgomery is on my call-waiting. The security company probably called him, too, since he's the one who had this system installed.

My hands are still shaking. I'm still on the phone. Door still locked. Bat still next to me. I hear sirens now. I hear the police announce themselves. I hang up the phone and yell, "I'm in here!"

I unlock the bedroom door and wait for them. They

TINA MARTIN

are checking the rest of the house and once they clear it, they come to talk to me. I tell them what happened. That I was in bed and heard a loud crash. Then the alarm went off.

My hands are still shaking at the gravity of what's happened while I'm standing in the living room talking to them. I can see the splintered wood from where the door frame cracked. The screen had been ripped out of the screen door.

"Ma'am, can you stay at a friend's or relative's house tonight?"

"I—I—I don't know." Tears come to my eyes. Who could've done this?

"Sherrish! Sherrish!" Ms. Kettleworth is standing on the front porch.

"Who are you?" one of the officers ask.

"She's my neighbor," I tell him.

"What happened, hun?"

I walk out there while the police talk amongst themselves in the living room and say, "Somebody kicked in my door."

"Oh my—are you alright?"

"I—I guess. I don't know. Why would somebody target my house, Ms. Kettleworth?"

"That's a good question. Doesn't look like they bothered yur car at all, whoever it was. And of course the po-leese show up *after* er'thang's over. That's why I keeps my shotgun. You keep on waitin' on the po-leese to get here…you'd be laid out dead."

In the darkness, I see the headlights of a black Mercedes pull into my driveway. It's Monty's car. He gets out, runs up to the house and grabs me into his arms, holding me so close to his chest, he nearly cuts off my air circulation. "My God, girl. I tried to call you a million times. Are you okay?"

It's when I break down. When the tears flow. When the adrenaline slowly starts to leave and now I'm left with the realization that somebody kicked in my door and disrupted my life.

"Cherish, baby, look at me," he says placing his hands on my face. "Are you hurt?"

"No, I'm—I—I'm not hurt."

"What happened?" he asks, wiping tears from my face. He looks panicked and scared. I've never seen him this way.

"I was lying in bed about to go to sleep and—and somebody kicked—kicked in the front door."

"Do you think it was Webster?"

"I—I—I don't know, Monty. He's never done anything like that before."

"Ms. Kettleworth, did you see anything?" he asks her.

"No, but like I told Sherrish—neighbor 'cross the street said somebody broke in her car, and somebody been in my truck, too. I tell you what—wish whoever did this would've come to my house. I would've laid him out right where he stood."

Monty goes to talk to the officers. He looks frustrated with their responses to his questions about dusting for prints and checking through the neighborhood for possible eyewitnesses. They assure him they'll do everything they can to find out who's behind this. They take a statement from Ms. Kettleworth and then they leave.

Montgomery comes over to me and says, "Pack a bag. You're coming with me."

"Okay," I say because I know I can't stay here. Truth be told, I don't know if I'll ever be able to again. Right now, I can't be here. I grab the smaller of my suitcases, throw in clothes, undergarments, shoes – I don't know all of what I tossed in there. I'm just ready to get out of here.

Monty tries his best to secure the broken front door. I'm sitting in the car, waiting for him to finish up. My hands are still shaking. I can't believe this happened to me.

* * *

When we're at Monty's house, he tells me to take a warm shower to help settle my nerves. I stay in there for a good twenty minutes, shaking and crying, getting it out of my system.

When I step into his bedroom, he's sitting by the windows. He tells me to join him.

"I made you some tea."

"Thanks," I say then take a sip.

"Are you sure you're okay, Cherish?"

"Yes. As okay as I'm going to be until they figure out who did this."

"When the security company called to notify me of the alarm, I couldn't breathe. Then when I couldn't reach you—"

He scrubs his hands down his face. "I don't know what I would do if anything ever happened to you, and I'm not willing to find out. I know things are messed up between us right now, but that doesn't diminish the love I have for you. I'll always love you, no matter what, and I will do everything in my power to protect you. I know I hurt you. I know I did, but I give you my word I'll do what I have to do to make it right."

"No," I tell him. "If it means giving up your livelihood and your father's company—no."

"In my heart, it's already done, baby."

I shake my head. "I can't let you do that, Monty."

"Everything I have is nothing to me if I don't have you." He swallows the lump in his throat and says, "You don't know the thoughts running through my head when I jumped in my car and floored it to your house. And then when I pulled up at your house and saw blue lights…" His lips tremble. "I thought something bad had happened to you. That won't happen again because you're *going* to be with me. Always."

We stare at each other. I'm not up for the challenge of

challenging him tonight. I'm traumatized. He's shaken. The best thing I can do is drink this tea, calm down and accept the security of being this close to my protector.

Chapter Forty-Nine

Monty

My baby.

That's who she is. I stayed up all night watching her sleep, making sure she was okay and didn't have any bad dreams. Incidents like those that occurred last night could be enough to send her into another spell of bad dreams and insomnia. But I watched her sleep like a baby.

She slept soundly. Quietly. Like a woman who had no worries. That's who I want her to be with me. A woman without worries. I want her to be my woman. My wife. I'm prepared to do whatever I need to do to make that happen.

I call an emergency meeting in the conference room downstairs since mother's back. Major is already here. I'm waiting for her to arrive.

"Must be important," Major says, then yawns. "I can't remember the last time you called a meeting this early in the morning."

"Yeah. It's important."

"Whatever this is about, I hope you tread softly with mother. She was really upset the last time y'all met up?"

"Why?"

"I don't know."

"Then why would you assume she's upset with me?"

"Because the day after she met with you, she was out in the backyard walking back and forth, holding her head."

I grin. "You never think mother's frustration has anything to do with you, huh?"

"Of course not. Parents always expect more from the

eldest. Sorry, bro."

"I don't know what I've done to irritate her, but—" I shrug.

"Just try to keep a level head, man. You and mother just got back on good terms. Don't impede progress."

"I have no desire to."

The door opens. Mother enters saying, "Good morning."

"Hello, Mother," Major says.

"Good morning," I tell her. "How was your vacation?"

She drops a stack of papers on the table and takes a seat. "My vacation was short. Too short. I need another week. At any rate, how can I help you this morning, son?"

"Um—first I want to say that I enjoy my work mostly because it's what dad taught me. I feel proud to carry on his company, to take it to the next level. It's important to me. It's my dream, well it used to be. I asked you why dad wanted marriage for me. You said he wanted me to know what love was. It's amazing he knew that about me. Knew I'd never been in love before. No high school crushes. No woman in college I was infatuated by. My focus has always been this job. But now, I have to walk away from it. That's why I called this meeting. I want to know exactly what happens to the company if I walk away. What happens to everything dad built?"

Mother shakes her head. "Why are you even considering this, son? I don't understand. I really don't."

"What don't you understand, Mother? You said dad wanted me to experience love, correct?"

"Yes."

"Then how can that be accomplished when I'm married to a woman I *don't* love."

"A woman you don't love?" she hisses. Her forehead is in a flurry of knots. "I knew I should've stayed on vacation," she says. "That *woman* you *don't love* took you into her home, literally patched you up and stuck by your side until you were well again."

"What?" I ask, looking at her like she's crazy.

"And she'd do anything for you. Has she not proven that time and time again? And you don't even want to be with her. I don't understand you, Montgomery."

"Wait—who are you talking about?"

"I'm talking about Cherish Stevens!"

"Cherish?" I ask.

"Yes. Who did you think I was talking about?"

I glance over at Major then back to her. It's when I realize I'd never confirmed who Mother chose for me. I assumed it was Paige because of things Major told me and the fact that Paige walks around here with her nose in the air like everything in my house is hers. Like I owe her for some reason.

I look at my mother. Keeping my breathing calm and even, I say, "I thought the woman you picked for me was Paige."

"That's the same thing I thought," Major adds.

She frowns, snaps her head back and says, "Paige? Why on God's green earth would you think I'd choose her?"

"You hired her without consulting me. You let her live in one of our properties rent-free, gave her a company car—"

"Yes, because she was *broke* before she started working here. She's good at what she does, but she's not so good at life. I wanted her for the job so I let her live in one of our properties for a low rental fee and I didn't *give* her a company car. I rented a car for her until she made enough money to buy her own car which she's already done. And she has her own apartment now—she no longer lives in our property. And by the way, son, she's not the only person I hired without consulting you."

She hands me a folder. I open it and flip through the pages. I read about the land ownership, the company and then I come across a section that talks about the marriage. I flip to the next document and see an actual marriage license that was filed a little over a year ago. My name is listed and below, it lists my spouse's name: Cherish Stevens.

I look up at her in disbelief and ask, "Cherish is my wife? She's the woman you chose for me?"

"Yes. I thought you knew that."

"How would I have known that, Mother? This is my first time ever laying eyes on this document."

"Then, I don't know why I thought you knew, but goodness you're going to give your Mother a heart attack. Do you know that?"

A feeling of overwhelming joy creates a bubble around me. I say, "That's why you were upset with me?" I ask her. "All this time, you thought I knew."

"When you came to my office and said you wanted to amend it, it broke my heart because I know Cherish is perfect for you."

"How would you have known that so long ago before I even said five words to Cherish?"

"Because I'm observant. When I hired Cherish, I noticed how quiet and mild she was. She was the exact opposite of you personality wise. She always did her work, went above and beyond to take care of your needs. One day—um…I want to say about three months after she was hired—you were on your way to the office, running late, and she was standing at the window watching you drive away. The next day, she came to work early to lay out your suits, hoping it would help you with your time and she'd had been doing so ever since. You complained about your meals—she started making menus. You needed clothes dry-cleaned—she took on that. My point is, she was willing to do anything to make your life better. And the way she looked at you—my goodness—I could see the love in her eyes whenever she laid eyes on you. She'd try to play it off, but I could tell."

"How?'

"Because it's the same way I—the same way I used to look at your father." She sniffles. Tears fall from her eyes.

"Before he was the working man who neglected his family for the sake of his company, your father and I were a lot closer. The company took him away from me long before cancer did. He realized that a little too late. That's one of the main reasons he wanted you to get married. He wanted you to have love in your life. If you were willing to give it all up for her, I know you love her."

Major gets up, walks around the table to sit next to Mother. He puts an arm around her. "Don't cry, Ma. Everything is going to be alright now."

I close my eyes and surrender myself into relief knowing that the woman upstairs, lying in my bed is mine. My wife. I don't ask Mother what she had to do to make this all legal. I really don't care what she did. I only have one more question for her. "How did you get Cherish to sign this without knowing what it was for?"

"Cherish trusts me. I brought her some papers, told them they were job-related and I needed her signature. She signed them. Didn't ask any questions."

"Congratulations, Monty," Major says. "You got your girl."

"Yes," I say feeling my heart do backflips. It's such a huge weight lifted off of me. I actually feel lighter. I feel free.

Major laughs and says, "If you're this good at playing matchmaker, I'ma need you to find me a wife, Ma."

She laughs. "I don't think you need my help in that area, Major."

I stand up because there's only one thing on my mind and that's getting upstairs to my girl. My woman. This meeting is adjourned.

"Wait, son. There are some other things we need to discuss."

"Okay, Mother, but can we talk about it later?"

"Why later? Why are you rushing off?" she asks, smiling.

"You know what the rush is, Ma. He's going to see his

girl," Major says.

"Just make sure you drive the speed limit and be careful," Mother tells me.

"No worries. She's already here. Upstairs, sleeping."

Major raises his brows.

"Whatever you're thinking, Major, get it out of your head. There was an incident at her house and as a safety precaution, I brought her home with me."

"What kind of incident?" they both ask at the same time. They care about her as much as I do.

"Nothing for you two to worry about. Now, if you would excuse me, I have some pressing business to take care of."

Before going upstairs, I go to the kitchen.

"Good morning, Mr. St. Claire," Naomi says. "You look like you're in a good mood."

"Good morning, Naomi. I *am* in a good mood. This is perhaps the best day of my life."

"Oh, really now?"

"Yes. Look, I need breakfast for two this morning."

She smiles and says, "Yes, Sir. I'm making some French toast and bacon. Shall I add anything else to the list?"

"Yes. Add some fruit, coffee, cream, sugar and anything else you think Cherish may like."

Her smile widens at the mention of Cherish's name. "Yes, Sir. I'll get right on it."

"Thank you. I'll be back around ten."

"It'll be ready," she sings.

I head upstairs, checking my watch at the same time. It's almost nine. I open the bedroom door. Cherish isn't in bed, but it's made to perfection how she always used to do it. The shower jets tell me where she is so I sit in a chair by the window and patiently wait for her to come out of the bathroom.

I grow antsy when I hear the shower go off, lean back in my chair, hoping she's the type to step out of the bathroom, wrapped in a towel.

I get my wish when the door opens. She's wrapped like a burrito in one of my extra large towels. Her braids are in a high ponytail.

She looks at me and smiles.

I'm in love.

In love with my caretaker. My assistant. My nurse. My best friend. My confidant. My reason for happiness. My strength.

I'm in love with...

My *wife*.

She's my wife.

She doesn't know it, but she's mine.

My wife.

My flower girl.

My *everything*.

"Good morning," she says making sure the towel is secure and nervously crossing her arms to add extra support. "I didn't know you were in here."

I get up slowly, walk over to her and ask, "Did you sleep well?"

"I did."

She looks up at me, holds my gaze and says, "Are you okay?"

"Why do you ask?" I inquire while glancing at her lips, trying to decide the precise moment I want them in my mouth.

"You look like you have a lot on your mind."

"I always do." *Especially when, most of the time, the subject is you.*

"I know you're probably busy today—"

"Yes, I am."

"Good. Then, I'm going to get dressed and run back over to the house...see if I can get somebody to fix the door."

"I already have somebody going out there this morning to fix it."

"You do?"

"Yes. I do, and by the way, I don't want you over there unless I'm with you."

"I'll be fine."

I touch her face. My body pulsates with desire. "Read my lips, Cherish. I do not want you over there unless I'm with you."

She looks at me for a moment then asks, "Why are you being so stubborn?"

"I could ask you the same thing."

"Okay," she says, grabbing my wrists, attempting to pull my hands from her face but to no avail. It's when I go in for her lips. Before she can register what's happening, I'm chomping on her tongue, playing ping pong with her tonsils while she moans and makes attempts to control her breathing.

She pulls back.

I inch forward and work my tongue in every corner of her mouth like I'm trying to eat her. I could kiss her forever. I don't want this to end.

She pulls back again, stealing her lips away from me. "Monty—"

"I love you."

She grimaces. "We've been through this, Monty."

"I love you," I say again.

"I love you, too, but with the circumstances the way they are—"

"Get dressed so we can talk." She also needs to get dressed before I snatch the towel off and show her what I mean when I say I love her. I'm trying to pace myself. She's making it hard.

Literally.

She grabs her clothes, goes back to the bathroom.

I take the opportunity to go downstairs get our breakfast tray from Naomi, then I'm back up. She comes out of the bathroom around the same time.

I pull out a chair for her. She sits down and looks at the food.

"Wow. Naomi went all-out."

"Yeah. She likes you."

"You—you told her to cook this for me?"

"For us. Yes." I take off my suit jacket and lay it over the armrest of my chair.

"While I was in the bathroom, I was thinking that I probably shouldn't be here."

"Then why are you here?"

"Because of what happened last night, obviously. I was scared, and I'm not scared with you."

"That's good to know."

"But I—"

"Eat," I tell her.

"I will, but I'm trying to express myself right now, Monty," she says in one long, frustrated breath.

I eat a piece of toast while she's processing her thoughts. She comes out with, "I don't want to be this close to you."

I grin. "*You* don't even believe that, so why'd you say it?"

"I do believe it. I can't be with someone who's already taken." She stabs a pineapple chunk and chews it slowly. She's still thinking.

A wave of silence surrounds us while we eat. We suffer five long minutes of this unnecessary tension until I ask, "How close are you with my mother?"

"We're okay. I mean, we're not best friends. She hired me so in a way I look at her as my superior and as a friend, too."

"Do you recall about a year and a few months ago, she came to you with some papers to sign?"

"Yeah."

"And you signed them?"

"I did. I needed my job. Why wouldn't I have?"

"Did you read through them?"

"No. Sylvia asked me to sign them—told me they were employment papers and legally she needed them for my personnel record, so I signed them. Didn't give it a second thought. Why?"

"Let me give you a bit of advice. Don't sign anything without reading it first. You could get yourself in a world of trouble, sweetheart."

"Am I in trouble?"

I crack a smile. "Yes. Yes, you are but in a good way."

She sips coffee. "What are you trying to tell me, Monty?"

I wipe my hands, take the folder I got from mother off the floor and remove the only document that's relevant. It's our marriage license. I hand it to her, watch her look it over. She frowns, glances up at me. Frowns more. Looks at me again. "What's this?"

"It's proof of what you signed."

She looks it over again. "It's proof of what I si—"

Her brown eyes roll up to look at me again. "This is— you said—this—"

"It's a marriage license. All this time, I thought my mother chose Paige when really, the woman she chose for me was you. It was you all along."

She shakes her head like she's defiant. I thought the news would bring her relief. Right now, she appears to be in shock.

"Isn't this what you want?" I inquire.

She looks at me, opens her mouth and nothing comes out. No words. No sounds.

"Cherish?"

"Huh?"

"Okay, you need to talk to me because this is not the reaction I was expecting."

"I know I—I guess I'm having a hard time believing it. I—I'm your wife?"

"Yes."

She lowers the paper to the table.

"Are you not happy about that?" I ask, not masking the frustration in my tone, especially since I thought *I'm* what she wanted.

"I—I uh…"

"Cherish?"

"I hear you. I'm just trying to process this."

"Wow. And here I was thinking this would be good news. Guess I was wrong."

"You're not wrong, Monty. I'm speechless. I—I don't know what to say. All this time I thought you and Paige—I never thought this could happen to me. Stuff like this usually doesn't happen to me. I'm the woman who gets overlooked. The woman no one sees. I'm not the lucky woman who somehow gets magically married to the man of her dreams."

"Well, now you are."

She blinks away tears and asks, "We're married?"

"Yes."

"We've been married all this time?"

"Yes."

"And you're okay with that?"

"Heck yeah. You're the only woman I want, Cherish. The only woman I love."

She covers her face with her hands and cries.

"Baby," I say, falling to my knees in front of her. I move her hands away from her face, tell her to stop crying. Her tears leave stains on my heart.

She places her trembling hands on my face, looks me in my eyes and whispers, "Are you really mine?"

"All yours," I respond.

She leans in close to me, touches her lips to mine, then goes in for a kiss – first time she's ever initiated a kiss with me.

I stand up, pull her into my arms and hold her close to me feeling a sense of completeness.

"I hate to leave, sweetheart, but I have meetings that I can't cancel. We'll continue this over dinner tonight, Mrs. St. Claire."

"I'm looking forward to it," she says, then rises up on

her tiptoes to kiss me again.

Chapter Fifty

Cherish

Monty pulls out all the stops. An afternoon business meeting took him to Uptown, so instead of driving back to Concord, he sent a limo for me. Before that, he had a dress delivered – a long backless red one that came with a twelve-thousand dollar price tag. I wear my braids down because I know he likes that. I also wear the diamond bracelet he'd given me as a 'thank you' gift.

He's standing on the sidewalk when the driver pulls up. My heart races as I watch him waiting for me. I still can't believe he's mine. This is my life. *He's* waiting for *me*.

Montgomery opens the door, then reaches for my hand.

"Good evening," he says.

"Good evening," I reply. I'm wondering why he's being all serious. I don't get to see that handsome smile he possesses. It's as if he's still in business mode. Tonight, *I'm* his business.

We're escorted to a private room at The Capital, the most elegant restaurant I've ever stepped a foot in. There's one table in the center of the floor. White candles serve as its centerpiece in the dimly-lit room.

"This is beautiful, Monty."

"Not as beautiful as you in that dress," he says. He catches me off guard when his hand touches the bare skin of my back. My body jumps beneath his touch. I gasp...wonder if he hears it.

"Sorry. I didn't mean to startle you."

So he did hear me...

"It's okay."

He pulls out a chair, gestures for me to sit. Once I do, he unbuttons the buttons on his suit jacket, then sits down.

"How was your day?" he asks.

All I see are flames in his green eyes. I tell myself they're from the candles burning in the center of the table but by the way he's looking at me, I can't be so sure. They're probably from an internal source.

"Uh—" I stutter, then immediately think about if my conversation habits are a turnoff from him since he's more accustomed to extreme professionalism from highly educated individuals with college degrees that cost a fortune. "My day was okay. After breakfast, I talked to Naomi for a while. Don't get upset but I was bored so I worked out in the flowers."

"As much as you love flowers, I don't consider that work for you." He nods and reaches for a bottle of champagne. He fills our glasses. "Drink."

I follow his order, pick up the glass, hoping a sip would take the edge off. Somehow, I downed the whole thing. I reach for the bottle to get more but he intercepts and pours it for me.

"Thank you."

"My pleasure."

"Um—do they have menus?" I ask, then chastise myself. *It's a restaurant, silly. Of course they have menus.*

"They do, but we don't need them. I've prearranged everything for us."

"You did?"

"Yes, to ensure we'd have as little interruptions as possible."

"Oh." I tap my fingers on the tabletop. *What now, Cherish? Say something.* I want to reach for the champagne again, but I don't want him to think I need to be drunk to endure an intimate dinner with him.

"Ask me how my day was, Cherish," he says as if

sensing my distress and underdeveloped one-on-one ability to hold a romantic conversation.

I smile. He doesn't. Just sips.

"Okay. How was your day, Monty?"

"My day was excellent. Everything about it was. Every deal, every phone call, every meeting went good. I already have millions of dollars in contracts for a device that hasn't made it through production yet."

"The taser?"

"Yes. The taser."

He taps his index finger on the table and stares at me like he has some kind of a nervous tick but I know him. He ain't nervous about nothing.

"That's excellent. Congratulations, Monty."

"You know what's interesting about the whole thing?"

"The contracts you mean?"

"Yes. The contracts."

"What's that?"

"It brought me no pleasure."

"Hunh?"

"I'm usually over the moon when there's this level of excitement for one of my inventions. This time, not so much. Ask me why?"

"Why?" I ask glancing up at him.

"Because you're my only source of pleasure now."

A waiter comes in and breaks up our stare down. He has food on a cart that he's wheeled in – seared tenderloins and lobster tails. There's a vegetable medley, mashed potatoes and potato salad.

The waiter leaves in a hurry, doesn't bother us much as if he knows not to. He'd been forewarned.

Montgomery takes my plate and places it on the table in front of me. Then he takes his.

"I don't eat lobster," I tell him.

"Have you ever tried it?"

"No."

"Then now is a good time. Go for it."

"Go for it how?"

"Take a piece, dip it in butter."

"Okay…" I say reluctantly but still follow his instructions, surprised that lobster is not as bad as I thought it would be.

"Is it good?"

"Yes."

"As I was saying before, you are my only source of pleasure. In every meeting today, you were at the forefront of my mind. Every time I thought of you, I smiled."

He cuts a piece of meat, then says, "We need to discuss some things."

"What things?"

"Like what happened to you. What your stepfather did to you."

I automatically frown. I don't want to interrupt our dinner with this. "Do we need to talk about this right now?"

"Yes."

"This is such a romantic dinner. I don't want to ruin it by talking about that, Monty."

"We're not ruining anything. We're just two grown people talking."

I try more lobster. I don't particularly want to go down this road, but I suck it up and keep an open mind about it. It's obviously been on his mind if he wants to talk about it now.

After a sip of water, I ask, "What do you want to know?"

"Was he your only experience with a man?"

The question hits me hard. "Molestation is not an *experience*."

"That's not what I mean. I want to know if there was anyone before or after him."

"But you're making it sound like he's an old relationship. He *violated* me."

"Believe me, that damages me every time I think about

it. It's why I'm asking you the question, Cherish. I want to know exactly what I'm dealing with."

"What does *that* mean?" I ask, feeling highly uncomfortable and offended by his line of questioning. "You know what, don't answer that. I don't want to talk about this anymore. Can we talk about something else, please?"

"No," he says. "I need to be able to have this discussion with you."

"Even if I don't want to talk about it?"

"Yes. You've been carrying it around for too long and as your *husband,* it is my duty to make sure you can overcome it. It is my responsibility now."

"Why?"

"Because I love you, and I want to help you, Cherish."

I'm done eating. The food is still there, but I can't make myself eat another bite.

I should be grateful he's asking. That he cares, but the anger welling up inside of me has me on the defensive. I've already told him I didn't want to talk about it. Why does this horrible thing that happened to me have to ruin my life and a relationship that I so desperately want? A man I so deeply love? And if I love him so deeply, why do I feel like I could reach across this table and choke him? And if he loves me, why won't he respect my wishes when I say I don't want to talk about it?

"No. There were no other men. When that happened to me, I retreated into a shell. I felt used. I didn't think no decent man would want me, especially not a man like you. Honestly, I still don't understand your attraction to me."

"That's why your reaction was so off when I told you about the marriage certificate this morning? You don't want this, do you?" he asks. His green eyes darken a shade.

"I do want it. I'm having a hard time trying to figure out why *you* want me when I'm—damaged. Physically and emotionally. You know why I stayed single so long, Monty? It's because I didn't think any man would want me when he found out what happened to me. When he learned about the baggage I carried. You don't have to love me because of what I did for you. I would've done it, anyway. I didn't need a hundred-thousand-dollar check, a twelve-thousand-dollar gown, a diamond tennis bracelet and I didn't need your love in return."

"Well, that's too bad, ain't it, because you have it and you'll always have it. There is no other woman for me. It's only you. I don't see you as damaged. I see a woman I'm in love with. I see a woman I've wanted for a long time. I show incredible restraint with you. I tread softly with you because, in my mind, I'm giving you time to heal. To get accustomed to my presence. So I tell myself to wait. To always wait. To keep my needs at bay and I've done that. But I want you. I wanted you the first day I laid eyes on you. I wanted you then and I want you now. I want you so bad, sometimes I can't breathe. I want to be buried inside of you so deep, we'd need specially trained surgeons to pry us apart. I want the taste of you on my tongue. I want to make you yell cry and smile all in one breath. I want to hear you call out for me until you know I don't see you as a woman who's damaged. I see you as a woman I'm in love with. I love you, Cherish St. Claire, and if you don't believe my words, trust and believe I can show you better than I can tell you."

His gaze locks on me. Solidifies.

"Then, show me."

With his eyes still on me, he throws back the rest of his champagne, stands up and says, "Let's go."

"We're not going to finish dinner?"

"No."

* * *

We hardly talk in the car. There's plenty of tension and sexual undercurrents but limited conversation. He doesn't listen to music to pass the time. I imagine he's thinking of

303

all the things he wants to do to me – all that pent up desire inside of him is dying to be released.

He opens the door for me when we're in the garage and follows me upstairs.

Upon entering the bedroom, I take off my shoes.

He takes off his suit jacket and loosens his necktie. Unbuttons his shirt.

I walk to the bathroom and look at myself as I take off my earrings. It's when I see him appear behind me with that thick, muscly chest. He rests his chin on my shoulder while hugging me from behind. I close my eyes and delight in the feeling of being held this way. I feel his chest hair brushing against my bare back thanks to this dress. I squeeze his forearms and close my eyes again. Gosh, he smells good. My body shivers just by the smell of him. It nearly convulses when he whispers in my ear, "You're not damaged. But you do need an attitude adjustment, baby. Open your eyes."

I open them and see his green ones beaming back at me by way of the mirror.

"I'm going to talk with actions tonight. I'll show you how much I love you, Cherish. Show you how bad I need you," he says then latches on to my earlobe. He nibbles then sucks it into his mouth, using his other hand to lower the left strap of my dress. His lips make a smacking noise when he releases my ear after a hard suck. He lowers the right strap of my dress and glides his tongue down my shoulder blade before grazing the area with his teeth.

I gasp, throw my head back and accept the foreign feelings taking over my body. I'm hyper-aware of where his hands are. His mouth. His tongue. It's rolling across the nape of my neck. His right hand is tugging at my dress until it falls to the floor. That same hand covers my breast, squeezes gently. We both gasp at the same time. It's as overwhelming for him as it is for me.

He spins me around. I can no longer see myself in the mirror. I just see him – those enticing eyes, lips, face – my goodness. I'm going to die a thousand deaths in this bathroom.

He looks at me. Stares. I look away. He lifts my chin. "If you're uncomfortable with anything I'm doing, I want you to tell me to stop. Do you understand?"

"Yes."

"I mean it, Cherish."

"Okay."

He bites his lip briefly before he cups my head in his hands. His grip is strong when he tells me to open my mouth. He traces my lips with the tip of his tongue before sliding it into my mouth rolling it all around, tangling it with mine, breathing heavily and squeezing my head tighter. I'm not sure if he realizes how tight he's holding me. His lips taste so good in my mouth. I don't care that he's squeezing the life out of me. He kisses like an expert. Kisses me so good, I feel his love for me in every pull. He takes my lips like they're his. They may as well be. His mouth is hot. His tongue is on fire. When I pull his lips into my mouth, I want to bite them. They taste so good. So good I nearly shed a tear when he stops kissing me. I'm desperate for more and that surprises me. I thought I'd be scared to be with a man this way, but I'm not. My body is yearning for him. I need to know what it feels like to be made love to.

"You okay?" he asks.

"Yes."

We're still standing in the bathroom, in front of his-and-her vanities. He leaves kisses on my neck, sucks gently then harder.

Soft, then hard.

I gasp.

He does this over and over again.

I gasp more.

He presses his lips to mine briefly to recapture my attention before lowering himself to my chest. He rolls the pad of his index finger across the buds of my softness. He takes his fingers away and does acrobatics with his tongue.

My legs shake. He's making me weaker and weaker as he feasts like he's having an after-dinner dessert. Then he does something that sends voltage through my veins. He moves his hands to the juncture of my thighs, teasing me until I think I'm going to experience too much pleasure to handle.

My legs shake. "Monty…" I gasp.

He stops. "Are you okay?"

I nod.

He takes a kiss while his thumbs breach the waistband of my undergarments. "Are you sure you're okay?"

"Ye-yes."

He tugs at them, pulls them down and goes down with them.

All the way down.

He lifts my feet one-by-one to remove them, then kisses his way up my legs moving from one to the other until his large hands are gripping and squeezing my backside. He's on his knees, looking up at me.

I gasp.

"Cherish."

"Yes?"

"Does this bother you?"

I shake my head slowly and bite my lip when I feel his mouth on me. My body convulses.

"Monty," I pant and grab a fistful of his curls. I close my eyes and get a grip on the counter while more deep waves pass through me. I've never felt these feelings before. They have my mind so gone, I didn't realize Monty had scooped me up and taken me to the bed.

That's where I am now.

The bed.

Looking at him. He has a satisfied look on his face, but his eyes are filled with hunger. His hairy chest, tight hard abs and caramel skin offers satisfaction to my eyes. The man is a walking aphrodisiac.

And now he's lowering his boxers. I glance at him, then look away like it's a part of him I'm not supposed to see. I look again.

My goodness gracious!

I look into his eyes, then back to *that* part of him, feasting on it with wide eyes to capture the scope of it all. Where does he hide all that beneath those fancy suit pants?

He gets protection from his nightstand then climbs up on the bed, moving my legs apart with his knees, spreading them to his liking. He eyes my body. Bites his lip like he's deciding what to do first. He lowers his body so our warmth connects and takes a kiss. Takes my tongue. We duel for control of the other's lips.

He's winning.

I feel like I'm going to swallow his whole face with how deeply he's kissing me.

He breaks the kiss, wraps those large hands around my wrists and says, "I want you to tell me when you're ready."

"When I'm...when I'm ready?" I pant. "When I'm ready for what?"

"To feel me inside of you. I want you to be sure. I want you to tell me when."

"I'm ready now, Monty," I tell him sounding desperate. In a way, I am. I don't know how we will fit together and I don't care. I just want it, and him. I'm certain he has the skills to make it work and even if it doesn't *work*, at least I'll die happy.

Without hesitation, he's inside of me. Goes deep. He's made my body his home. I think I can handle it.

I think I can, I think I can.

I squeeze my eyes to assist me to that end. I can feel every movement he makes. His member solidifies in me like it's found a new home. Like it's never leaving.

He gives me smooth, deep strokes – gives me so much pressure, I feel like a pipe that's about to burst.

Oh the way he expertly moves his body...

I was ready for this, but then again, I wasn't ready. This

man, lawd this man....

He withdraws in a way that makes me pull him back. I don't know how I'm handling him, but I'm not ready for him to leave.

Turns out he wasn't leaving.

He was resetting himself to go deeper – deeper than he was before. All this while his tongue is inside of my mouth. His kisses match the intensity of his strokes. They're deep and direct. He drives me close to my end, denies me pleasure – drawing out my desire and prolonging his own.

"Monty," I whisper, my face flushed with sweat. I feel the warmth of his sweat dripping on me, mingling with mine. I want more of it. This noise our sweaty bodies make sounds like music to my ears.

"Yes, baby," he finally answers me, twenty strokes later. He stops moving, giving me his full attention. "I love you, sweetheart."

"I love you, too."

"I will never forget what you've done for me. You saved me, baby. You mean the world to me. Thank you for trusting me with your body. With your life."

Tears come to my eyes. Emotions overtake me.

Monty hits me with those excruciatingly slow strokes again, driving me to the edge only this time, he doesn't pull back. I dig into his back. He grunts, groans, arches his back.

"Oh, Monty!" I cry out. He groans and relieves his body of the pressure. He doesn't want to stop.

He repositions himself and thrusts his tongue into my mouth. Our connection deepens on both ends. All I can do is moan, dig my nails into his shoulders and handle it. It's overwhelming to be loved like this. It's so good because it's *him*. My crush. My lover. My protector. My husband.

He has endless stamina, endurance and determination. And those soft groans of his tells me he likes making love to me. The way his mouth captures my lips tells me the same.

"Monty," I whisper against his lips.

"Yes, baby?"

"What are you doing to me?"

"Showing you how much I love you. Isn't this what you asked for?"

"Yes."

"It's what you're getting. Me. All of me. Mind, body and soul. I love you, girl. Look at me."

I stare up into his sparkling green eyes, feeling him heavy on top of me.

He moves. I whimper.

He drives his body. I cry out his name. He likes that. Likes to hear his name oozing out of my screams.

I pinch my eyes closed when he increases this pace. I want to scream and cry, maybe a combination of both. The pleasure is so great, my mind is confused in the way it should react.

I gasp.

"Aw…Cherish."

I hear him whisper my name.

I open my eyes again. Our eyes lock. I see his soul. He's lost in mine. He utters a groan that peaks my desire. Over and over again he's doing it until he meets my mouth with his sweet, damp lips and whispers, "Let go."

"Oh, Monty."

"Let go, baby. It'll feel so good when you let go," he says.

I let go and descend into an abyss of pleasure. And he's there with me.

Falling.

"You okay?" he asks as I'm panting.

Still catching my breath, I'm unable to speak at the moment.

"Cherish, are you okay?"

"Yes, Monty. I'm more than okay."

"Good."

He goes to the bathroom, comes back still naked and pulls me into his arms.

"I didn't expect this would happen so soon," he confesses. "I thought I could resist you long enough until you were moved in with me."

I position myself to rest on this thick, muscular chest. With my index finger, I follow the healed scar that remains there after the accident. I kiss him there.

"Why did you want to do that? Why did you want to wait?"

"I didn't want to rush you, but you get to me, girl. All that talking you were doing in the restaurant, asking me why I wanted you, telling me you never thought anybody would love you and all that—I wanted to throw you up on that table then and there. As much as I love you, I can't stand to hear you talk that way."

"I know that now."

"Do you?"

"Yes," I say feeling his curly hair beneath my fingers.

"I love making love to you, Cherish."

"I love making love to you, too, Monty."

"That's good to know since I plan on having you every time the opportunity presents itself."

"Every time?" I ask.

"Yes."

I press my lips to his and close my eyes. My heart is full, flooded with love.

Chapter Fifty-One

Monty

We sleep until noon. Actually, I'm up at noon. She's still sleeping soundly. I take a moment to look at her again. I love watching her when she's not aware of it. When I can focus on her beauty and think of the many things she means to me. I think of all the days she worked for me, all the time she spent making sure I had everything I needed to start my day when what I needed all along was her. Now that I have her, I intend on showing her how much she means to me. It's my turn to serve her. To love her like she needs to be loved. To love her so deeply, she forgets about her past and looks forward to a future of us living together in peace and happiness.

While she sleeps, I arrange for lunch to be delivered. It's a beautiful day. The temperature is around eighty-two degrees. The sky is a perfect hue of blue. Lunch by the pool is something she'd like.

Before it arrives, I go to my mother's residence just to see her. To speak. She opens the door and says, "Hello, son."

"Good afternoon, Mother."

"Come on in. How are you doing?"

"I've never been better."

She smiles. "Glad to hear it. How's my daughter-in-law?"

"She's perfect," I say as a smile grows on my face.

"You're in love," she says. "I can see it."

"I am in love. I'm still amazed at how you knew Cherish would be my one. She's everything I need."

"I know."

"Is that why you hired her?"

"No. I didn't hand pick her for you. In the beginning, I hired her because she had the qualifications for the job. I didn't know she would fall for you. Shoot, I didn't think anyone would fall for you. You were so mean to everybody. Paige tried hard to get your attention, but you ain't give that girl a second look. And, honestly, she's probably more interested in your money and lifestyle than anything else. But Cherish—"

She smiles.

"She loves you for you."

"I know." I sit next to mother on the sofa and say, "Life is crazy. This is crazy."

"What is?"

"All this time I thought you were against me. At one point, I thought you hated me."

She takes my hand, interlocks our fingers. "I've always loved you as my own. I couldn't have children, but as far as I'm concerned, we're blood. You and your brother were always my priority. I love you dearly, son."

"I love you, too, Mother." After a few passing moments of quietness, I say, "I want to have a wedding. Here. I want Cherish to have her day. I want to see her in a gown walking down the aisle toward me. I want pictures. I want the world to know I'm taken. Want them to know how much I love her."

"That would be wonderful."

"I was thinking it could be here."

"Absolutely! Have you told her about it yet?"

"No. Not yet. I want to propose first." I chuckle. "I'm doing everything backward, but I want us to have those moments. I'm meeting with a jeweler on Monday."

"Backward or not, I think it's a great idea. I can hire a wedding planner to take care of everything."

"That would be good."

"Then I'll get right on it."

* * *

Lunch arrives. I have the caterers set it up in the back while I run up to see if Cherish is out of bed. It's close to two o'clock.

I walk into the bedroom and she's sitting on the bed in a white lace bra and panties set, rubbing lotion on her legs. Up and down she goes. Her body looks moisturized and ripe for the plucking. Arousal stops me in my tracks. I want her again, can already picture her legs up in the air at the foot of the bed. Can hear my name screaming off of her lips.

"Monty."

I slide my hands in the pockets of my slacks and quietly chastise myself for wanting her this much. I have no control. What's wrong with me?

She looks up at me. "Are you okay?"

"Yes."

"I was just talking to you—you didn't say anything."

"Put your dress on and let's go eat," I tell her.

She laughs. "Well, good afternoon to you, too."

My eyes narrow.

"Are you in a bad mood this morning?" she asks.

"No."

"Then why are you not talking to me?"

"It's not intentional. I—"

"You what?"

"I'm standing here imagining you naked where you're sitting. Me on top of you. Inside of you. Making love to you. I can hear your screams. Can feel your fingernails in my back. Can feel your body tremble when you—" I pause. "Put your dress on, sweetheart. I have caterers delivering our lunch."

"Okay."

She stands. It's when I see her panties are thongs that fit her hourglass shape so well. The green dress pairs well

313

with the rich, chocolate tone of her skin.

The dress glides down her body, falls to her knees. She gathers her hair into a ponytail, then walks over to me. Her arms encircle me. She squeezes. I embrace her. I try not to pull her close because I already want her. If our bodies stay close for too long, we won't make it downstairs.

"Let's go eat," I say. Maybe sitting down to lunch to talk will be the break I need to tame my desire.

"IT'S BEAUTIFUL OUT here," she says but all I can see are her lips wrapped around a strawberry. She smiles.

I'm jealous of that strawberry...

I take a sip of water hoping to smolder the fire that burns within me. It doesn't help. Maybe an afternoon swim will.

"Monty, what do you do for fun besides swim?"

"Swim in you," I tell her.

She gnaws on her lip, then takes a sip of lemonade. "Answer my question," she says.

"I did answer your question," I say, hiding my amusement.

"But you're *you*. You're a billionaire. Don't you want to travel? Go to exotic places? Make new experiences?"

"I do, more so now that I have someone to share it all with. And I have traveled. I have vacation homes in the Caribbean, The Bahamas, Mexico, Hawaii, Australia, the African coast – I've also been to all those places but only once when I inspected the vacation homes for purchase."

"And you've never been back?"

"No. What about you, Cherry? Do you want to travel?"

"I think so."

"You think? You're not sure?"

She mulls it over and says, "I do want to travel."

"And what about children? Do you want children?"

"Umm—"

"You don't want children," I say with a straight face

when I'm worried that she doesn't. I want children. I need her to want them, too, but at the same time, I know if she doesn't, it's not a deal breaker. I'm willing to make whatever compromises I need to make to keep her, even if that means sacrificing what *I* want.

"I do. I'm just worried I won't be so good at it. I didn't have a great example."

"But you're not her. You're a nurturer. You care about people. And you're passionate. That's what stimulates me—your passion and who you are as a person. I've never met a woman like you, and yes I do want you to have my children."

She takes a sip of juice. "It would be an honor for me to have your children."

"An honor."

"Yes."

I chuckle. "You act like I'm royalty, baby."

"You *are* royalty. You're my king. You're the man I never thought I'd have. A man I didn't think I—"

She smiles to cover her emotions. "A man I didn't think I deserved."

I slide my chair over to hers and say, "Cherish, don't let what happened to you devalue you, sweetheart. It doesn't define you. You are as valuable, as beautiful as sweet as you always were. *I'm* the one who's lucky to have *you*. Remember that."

"Thank you, Monty."

"You're welcome, always," I tell her. Her past, the abuse, her relationship with her mother, the loss of her father runs deep and affects her even now. I know how it is to lose a father. I know how it is to have a strained relationship with my mother. She helped me fix my issues. Now, it's time for me to return the favor. But how can I do that when every time I see her, I want her? Want to love all the pain out of her? Want to make her forget she has problems?

Chapter Fifty-Two

Cherish

It's a thing a beauty to watch him swim. The way his arms extend forward. The way he stretches his body to lengthen his strokes. His muscles glide through the water. His body is so lean, so fit and strong, he has no issues with swimming stroke after stroke. It's probably where he gets his endurance. I've never seen anyone hold their breath for so long.

I pull up my dress and sit on the edge with my feet dangling in the water. We're at the indoor pool since it's too hot outside to actually enjoy the water. He swims up to me, looking sexy as sin. The water does something special to his eyes. Makes him look like he has super powers. Wait, this is Montgomery St. Claire I'm talking about. He *does* have superpowers.

"Where did those bruises on your back come from?"

"The accident," he says.

"No. I know the location of every bruise from your accident. These are new."

He smiles. "Oh, you mean the ones near my shoulders?"

"Yes."

"You did that."

"I did?"

"Yes, when we made love. You don't remember?"

"Oh my gosh, Monty…why didn't you tell me to stop?"

He shrugged. "Because I liked it."

I narrow my eyes at him. "You liked it?"

"Yes," he says then bites his lip. "Are you getting in?" he asks, splashing water on my legs.

"I don't have a suit."

"You have on a bra and panties beneath that dress, don't you? There's no difference between that and a two-piece bikini. Come on," he says tugging at my feet. "Take off your dress."

"Monty, stop," I say smiling.

"Come on," he says, splashing more water.

"Noo. I can't swim like you."

"You don't have to swim like me. Just get in the water."

I pull my dress up over my head. He does that lip biting thing. I leave the dress on the floor and gather myself to stand.

"Hey, where are you going?" he asks.

"I'm going to the steps to get in."

"Girl, if you don't get your butt back over here."

"Monty."

"Come here."

"Monty, I can get in over there."

"Don't make me get out of this water."

My laughter echoes in the pool room. "Okay. Fine."

I sit down again. Slowly, I inch into the water, into his arms. We're on the eight-foot side of the pool.

"Your whole body is tense."

"I can't remember the last time I've been in a pool."

"The water feels nice, though, right?"

"Yes. Lukewarm. It's perfect."

We drift. His arms are around me. "Are you going to show me how to stroke?" I ask.

"I thought I did that last night?"

I laugh. So does he.

"You don't know how to swim?"

"I can swim a little but only under water. I can't do the strokes like you."

"I'm pretty sure you could stroke it like me, baby."

"Are we still talking about swimming?"

"We are. What did you think we were talking about, Cherish?" he asks, keeping a straight, serious face.

My smile fades, then slowly reappears. You know how you can know someone yet not *really* know them, but know that person is *your* person? Montgomery is *my* person. My husband. My life partner. I don't know everything there is to know about him. I desire to know those things, but I know it'll take time. Years. A lifetime. In the meantime, I go with the flow. With the waves of this pool. I drift with him to the five feet side of the pool where I can actually feel my feet on the bottom.

"Is that better?" he asks.

"Yes."

He drops below the surface of the water. I feel his teeth chomping at my thigh.

"Monty!"

He comes up again, doesn't shake water away from his face or nothing. He just comes up. Eyes open.

"Do you swim with your eyes open?"

"Yes."

"The chlorine doesn't irritate your eyes?"

"No. I'm used to it."

"Oh."

"Let me see you swim," he says.

"I'm not as good as you."

"You don't have to be. Show me what you got."

"Okay. Here goes nothing." I close my eyes, go under and swim blindly beneath the water with my hands out in front of me. When I touch the wall, I come up and brush water away from my face, more specifically my eyes.

He's clapping. "Good job."

"Thanks," I say, feeling refreshed as water drips from my braids. "I haven't done that in so long. Oh my gosh."

He swims toward me, stands and wades the rest of the way. "It feels good, though, doesn't it?"

"It does."

His hands are resting on the edge, caging me in front of him. He leans down, licks my lips in a quick swipe and looks at me with those eyes.

He's fully aware of their power over me.

Suddenly I grow nervous. I know he wants me. I can feel the heat between us boiling this water.

"Kiss me," he says.

I stare up into his eyes. Glances at his lips. Rising up on my tiptoes, I aim for his lips. He meets me the rest of the way and our lips collide. His lips are strong. Sensual and strong. He bathes my mouth. Sucks on my lips. Pops the clasp of my bra and his hands go to my breasts.

He looks at me while he's touching me deciphering my comfortability level with it. I'm anxious, but at the same time, I like his touch. But what if someone catches us?

"Monty?"

"Yes?"

"What if someone walks in?"

"This is my residence. The doors are locked. Nobody's walking in." He moves his hands and dips his mouth to my chest.

Oh, the sweet, sensuous torture...

The water boils.

He releases me to take off his swim trunks then disappears beneath the water, sliding my underwear down the length of my legs, removing them completely, then coming up again with them like they're his trophy.

"I want you."

I nervously chew on my lip. "Monty..."

"Right here. Right now."

"Right now?"

"Yes," he says, lifting me slightly, the water helping – not that he needs any help.

"Do you want me, Cherry?"

"Yes," I say and almost immediately, he fills me.

I grab on tight to him and hold on. My moans bounce

off the walls and echoes in this room. His groans chase them. They're more frequent than before. Than last night. Maybe it's the water. Or, maybe it's his need to be connected this way with me again. Whatever the case, he's audible, grinding into me while he tears down the walls of my reserve. I'm crumbling already.

With our bodies still locked together in passion, he uses the edge of the pool to drift to the deeper end near a silver ladder. Our heads are barely above the water. The water makes me breathe heavier. The way he's inside of me is having the same effect.

He grabs the ladder, still managing to keep me in place with his other hand gripping my backside.

"Hold your breath and wrap your legs around my waist."

"Monty," I say, fearing what he's contemplating. Why he wanted us on the deeper end of the pool.

"Hold your breath."

"I don't know if I can do that while we're—"

"Hold your breath, babygirl," he says again. "On three we go under. One, two…"

I pull in a deep breath before he says three and we go under. I don't know how I'm able to, but I open my eyes and watch him. He's looking at me, holding his breath while he's stroking me against the tiled pool wall. He's so strong, so powerful. So beautiful. This otherworldly connection has me transcending into a portal of unending pleasure where lovers die and are resurrected to experience death all over again.

I crumble. My legs tremble then lock around him. I remember to hold my breath when sensations of pleasure burst into me. Rocks me. Makes me want to breathe, but I can't. I'll drown. In a way, I already have.

I watch the distress on his face, see his eyes close.

He brings us up above the water. We gasp for air, refilling our deprived lungs. We breathe and breathe some more.

We're both hungry for air, panting, struggling to get breath. The moans I wasn't able to make below water are now echoing along with his grunts and groans. We're still connected. He's still filling me.

"Aw...Cherish...that was so good. Tell me you liked it."

"I liked it."

"Are you okay?" he asks.

"Yes," I say, still breathing heavily. My eyes burn a little from the water, but I've never experienced anything like that in my life. It scared the life out of me, and I enjoyed every minute of it.

Chapter Fifty-Three

Monty

When the jeweler stopped by, it didn't take me long to pick her ring. I'm not the kind of person to buy a fancy, expensive ring just for the sake of buying an expensive ring – used to be – not anymore. This ring had to mean something and this particular one spoke to me. I wasn't paying attention to the $175,000 price tag – only to the way it would look on Cherish's finger. It's a five-carat cushion cut, halo diamond ring. It's perfect for her. As a finishing touch, I'm having our initials engraved on the band.

She was still sleeping when I left for the office this morning. I had every intention of working from my home office today, but I can't control myself around her. I'd want her again, and after making love in the pool and again last night, she needs a break.

I left her a note to call me when she was up. She'd probably do so anyway, but she had another one of those dreams last night. The disturbing ones. She didn't wake up in a cold sweat. She didn't wake up at all, but I could tell she was struggling. Kept yelling the word, *stop*. Sounded like she was crying, but she wasn't. Then she got quiet again. Was back to sleeping peacefully.

It makes me wonder if making love to her is provoking this. If she correlates our lovemaking to the things her stepfather did to her. I don't want that for my baby. I don't want to do anything to hurt her. This issue with her stepfather needs to be addressed immediately.

* * *

Around lunchtime, I get a call from Magnus. He tells me Mason wants us to meet at his house Friday night. Says everyone will be there, gives me the address and we hang up. I dial Cherish's cell but there's no answer. I call again. Nothing.

I call Naomi. She answers, "Hello."

"Good morning, Naomi."

"Good morning, Mr. St. Claire. You coming home for lunch today, Sir?"

"I hadn't planned on it. I was actually calling you to ask if you talked to Cherish this morning."

"Oh, yes, Sir. She came down 'round ten."

"And where is she now?"

"Oh, I don't know. She did leave, though. I just don't know where she went."

"Do you know if she had her cell phone with her?"

"She doesn't have it, Sir—left it right here on the table after breakfast. I thought she would realize it and turn around but she didn't come back for it."

"So, she's been gone since eleven o'clock?"

"Yeah. About that time."

"Okay. Thank you."

"You're welcome, Sir. Is everything okay?"

"Yes. I apologize if I alarmed you. How are things there?"

"Everything's fine."

"Good."

I hang up with Naomi and Major walks into my office and says, "What's up, man? I'm surprised to see you in the office today."

"Why's that?"

"You and wifey are inseparable these days."

I smile. "To be in love with one's wife is a good thing, Major. You remember that when you find yours."

"I will."

"Hey, I spoke with Magnus this morning. He said Mason wants to have a meet-and-greet at his place on Friday. Is that good?"

He shrugs. "Yeah. I ain't doing nothing."

"Good, because I already told him we'd be there."

"Should we invite mom?" he asks.

"I don't know. I mean, she's not related to any of them. Do you think she'd want to come?"

"I don't know. I suppose we could ask. By the way...are you staying all day?"

"I was, but something came up," I tell him, purposely leaving Cherish's name out of the equation.

"Everything cool?"

"Yeah—just something I need to handle." I glance at my watch and say, "I'm out of here around two."

"Alright. I'll see you later."

Chapter Fifty-Four

Cherish

This is the first time I've been back at the house since the break-in. The door is repaired, but I notice right away the alarm doesn't go off. It's been off since the repairman was there to fix the door. I've been so busy with Monty I didn't think to turn it back on.

I walk in and feel like a visitor instead of the person who lives here. My home has been violated. I don't think I'll ever feel the same here.

I get more of my clothes. Montgomery hasn't discussed a timeline for me to move in with him officially but in the meantime, I need a few more pieces of clothing, some shoes and personal items. I grab a plastic bag, toss in a few shirts, pants and a pair of flats. I take a couple of pairs of earrings and then I grab my purse and get ready to leave.

Until...

I remember to get my favorite picture of me and my dad from the dresser. I walk back into my bedroom, look at the dresser, but there is no picture. I check the floor, behind the dresser. Under the bed. In the living room. My picture is gone.

I try not to panic. Maybe I took it earlier and just don't remember. That night was so nerve-racking, I'm not sure what I did. So I get my stuff and head for the door. I set the alarm, lock the door and on the way to my car, Ms. Kettleworth appears.

"Well, howdy, Sherrish."

"Hey, Ms. Kettleworth. How have you been?"

"Oh, honey, you know I'm just fine and dandy. What

'bout you? I ain't seen you 'round here. How you doin?"

"I'm okay."

"You been staying with Montgom'ry ain't cha?"

"Yes," I say smiling. I have. "And I should be getting back. I know he's tried to call me and I left my phone."

"Now, listen here, honey—don't you be no stranger. Done got yourself dat fine, rich man and run off."

I chuckle. "I won't be a stranger, Ms. Kettleworth, but I do have to go. I'll talk to you later."

* * *

I'm back at the estate. I open the back door of my car to get my bag and as I head up the walkway, I see Montgomery come out of the massive, wooden doors. He's home early, still in his suit. It's my first time laying eyes on him today.

He usually keeps a straight face, but this particular face looks a little *too* straight. If I'm reading him right, he's angry.

"Where have you been?" he asks.

"I went to get more clothes. I left my phone—"

"You went to get more *clothes*? Meaning you went to the house by yourself? Is that what you're telling me right now? Please don't let that be what you're telling me right now, Cherish."

"Monty—"

"I *told* you *not* to go there without me."

"Monty, it's not a big deal."

"It *is* a big deal!" He yells, his nostrils flared. "It's a big deal to me! What I asked of you was not that difficult. I said if you want to go there, *ask* me to come with you! What's so hard about that? Huh?"

"You were working!"

"So what? Do you think my job is more important to me than you are?"

He's heated. I can see figurative steam rising from the

326

top of his curls.

"What's the job to me without you!" he snaps, raising his voice the loudest I've ever heard it. "You risk your life to go over there for some clothes—"

"How am I risking my life, Monty?" I ask him.

He glares at me. "Somebody kicked in your front door! Do you not remember that?"

"Of course, I remember that!"

"You don't know who did it. You assume it's your stepfather, but you don't know and the police have not arrested anyone. Yet, you go there alone to get some clothes?"

"I was in and out. I didn't think it would be a big deal."

"I can buy you clothes. I can buy you all the clothes you want but I can't buy another you!"

He retreats, shakes his head and walks back toward the house, leaving me standing in the driveway. I done messed up now.

Chapter Fifty-Five

Monty

I'm standing at the window in my office, looking out into the yard at the flowers this woman planted for me. Now, every time I see them, they remind me of her. It's a reminder of how much she loves me. How much she cares.

I'm convinced that love is insanity. It's romantic and fulfilling, but it's ninety-five percent insanity. Why? Because when you love someone, you give them so much of yourself. So much of your heart. You make yourself vulnerable to everything. You open yourself up to experience their problems more so than your own. You ride their highs and descend with them to their lows. You think about that person constantly. Daydream about them. Think of ways to make them happy. Ways to cure their sadness. You protect them at all costs. You live for them. You'd die for them.

I'm just understanding this in my mid-thirties since this is the first time I've been in love. Cherish has completely infiltrated my life, made me reset my priorities and rethink everything I thought I wanted. While work is important to me, it's not more important than she is. Apparently, I need to do a better job of convincing her of that.

I take a moment alone in my office to allow my frustration to subside before I go to look for her. I step into the kitchen. Naomi is in the middle of dinner preparations.

"Good afternoon, Sir."

"Good afternoon, Naomi. Where's Cherish?"

"I just saw her walk by with a basket of clothes. She might be in the laundry room."

"Okay. Thanks," I tell her and proceed in that direction. I open the door. I see Cherish pouring laundry detergent in the washer. She turns around, looks at me and continues working.

She says, "I heard you loud and clear earlier, Monty. You don't have to yell at me anymore."

She closes the washer, presses a button to start the cycle.

My fingers ache. I can feel the muscles in my jaw twitching. *Talk to her. Explain yourself. No yelling. No frustration. Let the love shine through. The insanity. Give her the assurance she needs. Let her know you love her, how deeply that love runs and how worried you are for her.*

These are all the things I want to say, but now that I'm looking at her, standing in front of her, I decide not to.

She turns around, appears shocked to see how close I've crept up behind her. Before she can say a word, I bury my tongue in her mouth while at the same time hiking up her skirt.

I'm hungry for her. I need her. Need her to understand how much I care. How deep my love runs. I need to be inside of her. I release my belt, unzip my pants and lower my boxers. I lift her so she's pressed against the washer and with one smooth stroke, her body receives me. She's moaning. Panting. Her legs close around me. Her arms wrap around my neck.

Insanity.

I could've waited. Taken her upstairs. Taken things slow. But I'm here, in the laundry room, taking it fast while she holds on to me.

I savor her tongue like a delicacy while the rhythm of this washer drives me.

She moans. The anguish on her face is delayed, but it's coming. I can feel it coming. And then I see it – see the moment she loses it. When the first spasms hit. When her eyes slam closed and her face tightens. Her body shakes. Her mouth falls open, head goes back. She screams her pleasure to the ceiling and I spill my love inside of her. It seems to take forever – this transference – but she gets it all. I groan and whisper her name.

I'm still giving.

She's still taking.

My name drags between her lips. I love it when she moans my name. Love it when I feel her body cave in my arms.

I fill her mouth with my tongue to silence her moans. When I've successfully digested them, I look at her. Our bodies are still connected. Her legs still locked around me. I still have her pressed to the washer.

I say, "I'm sorry."

"I'm sorry, too. I didn't mean to upset you, Monty."

I withdraw from her, pull up my boxers and pants then fasten my belt.

She lowers her dress.

I remind myself of what I need to do:

Talk to her. Explain yourself. No yelling. No frustration. Let the love shine through. The insanity. Give her the assurance she needs. Let her know you love her, how deeply that love runs and how worried you are for her.

We're still standing near the washer. We're clothed. Bodies healed, but mentally, we remain distant. I want to change that.

Explain yourself. No yelling. No frustration. Let the love shine through.

"Cherish, when I told you not to go to your house alone—to ask me to come along—I wasn't being controlling, sweetheart. I was protecting you. Your home was broken into and when I got the call that night about the alarm going off, you don't know the panic, the fear that gripped me. I can't lose you. I can't."

The insanity.

"You mean more to me than I think you realize, but

now you need to know. I'm so in love with you, so far gone I don't know who I am without you. You've completely flipped my life upside down. It's only because of you that I know how it feels to be loved and I will fight to the death for you. Give my life for you. I would do anything for you."

Tears escape her eyes. I can't stand the sight of them so I wipe them away.

Give her the assurance she needs.

"We're one now. You and me. We're no longer two entities. You don't have a life independent of me anymore and this problem that exists between you, your mother and your stepfather is one that I've inherited. We'll get through this together because that's what married people do. We navigate through life together. I need you to understand that I'm not going anywhere."

Let her know you love her, how deeply that love runs and how worried you are for her.

I take her hand and put it flat on my chest. On my heart. "Do you feel that?"

She nods.

"That's you. Do you understand that, Cherish?"

She nods again.

"Talk to me. Let me hear you say it."

"I understand."

I lift her chin so she looks at me. "Do you?"

"Yes. I do."

"I worry about you. You have problems with your mother that needs to be addressed. You live in fear of your stepfather. This needs to be taken care of."

"I know."

"Okay, so take the rest of the day to think about how you want to move forward and after we make love tonight, we'll talk."

She smiles. "*After* we make love?"

"Yes."

"We just did."

"I know, but I'll want you again. You know that. And not against the washer, this time, but in my bed. In *our* bed where I can slow down and have you just the way I want you."

I kiss her lips again and we leave the laundry room.

When we pass through the kitchen, Naomi and Minnie immediately stop what they're doing to stare at us. Analyzing us.

"Is everything okay?" Minnie asks, looking more at Cherish than she is at me.

"Yes," Cherish responds. "Everything is fine."

"Yes, we're fine," I say. "Just had to straighten some things out."

Chapter Fifty-Six

Cherish

Monty doesn't just make love to me. He breaks down my cells, my DNA, my soul until I am no more and then he repairs me. Rebuilds me. He puts me back together again, only to restart the entire process from the beginning. That's what he did tonight. Three times he did this, and now I'm love-drunk, sweat-drenched and sleepy. But he wants to talk about stuff. Stuff I'm not interested in after coming down from several trips to euphoria.

"Monty, can't we talk about this later?" I slur. I make his chest my pillow tonight like I do every night.

"No, baby."

"But—"

"We need to talk about it now. You know you still have those dreams. You don't wake up all the time, but you still have them. You can't go on like this. It needs to be dealt with."

"Well, I did think about it. A little. Whenever I try to talk to my mother on the phone, she ends up hanging up on me or I hang up on her. So, on Wednesday, I was thinking that I could go to her job and talk to her in person if I can catch her in the parking lot before she leaves."

"That'll be good. That way, you won't have to worry about running into your stepfather."

"Right."

Now, I'm lying here thinking about the break-in, wondering if my stepfather was behind it. I think about the missing picture. I don't recall bringing it here. The picture

333

is actually missing.

"What are you going to say to her?" Monty asks as his fingers stroke my back.

"I'm not sure yet."

"What time does she get off work?"

I lift my head to kiss his chest. I roll the tip of my tongue around on his skin.

"Mmm…you better stop before I keep you up for another hour."

I laugh. I know he'll do it. "She's off work at one."

"I'll come with you."

"You don't have to."

"I want to."

"I don't know if I want you to witness what a conversation is like with my mother. It's awkward and forced and—well, awkward.…"

"Similar to the way conversations with my mother used to be. You coached me through that—gave me a better approach when it came to her. Maybe I can return the favor."

"Okay. We'll see how it goes. You said Wednesday, correct?"

"Yes, babe."

"I'll have to remember to get my secretary to block my calendar that day."

"You know besides your mother, Major, Paige and Hannah, I don't know anyone you work with."

"You can come to my office any time you want."

"I don't want to disturb you."

"Disturb me? Did you hear *anything* I said to you in the laundry room?"

"You mean, while you were thrashing me?"

He rotates his body so he's on top of me. "Thrashing you, you say?"

I giggle. "Yeah. Thrashing me against the washer."

He nips at my neck. Pulls my swollen lips into his mouth. I feel him solidifying against my thigh, digging into me with steel. "I'm going to thrash you again."

"Monty, you said you were going to let me sleep."

"I was until I discovered you weren't paying attention earlier."

"I was paying attention," I say giggling. My body shivers when he rolls his tongue on my neck.

"Then how could you possibly think coming to my office is a disturbance when I told you—you're my priority?"

The smile falls away from my face as I stare into the eyes of this man who loves me. It's the moment I realize everything he told me was true. I'm his heart. He'd do anything for me.

"Cherish?"

"Yes?"

"Why are you—?"

I lift my head to silence him, kissing his lips with deliberate power, hoping the connection leaves a mark. Hoping it tells him I get it now. He loves me. I love him the same.

He opens the drawer on his nightstand, grabs protection and he's back over to me.

My legs open for him automatically and while he's kissing me, he moves inside of me. My shriek is lost in his mouth. We'd made love for an hour straight already once tonight, but every time he enters me, he makes an impact.

"Mmm...I can't get enough of you," he hums. Strokes to sell it. Gassing me up. Making me think I have some special power over him.

He strokes. I whimper. He strokes more. I whimper more. I look into his eyes. They make me do things. Makes me lift my hips from the mattress and meet him stroke for stroke.

"I like that, baby. Keep doing it," he says. He groans. "That's it. Keep—ahh. Mmm."

"Monty!" I scream.

He groans, throws his head back and tumbles with me

to paradise.

Chapter Fifty-Seven

Monty

I'm at the office but I spend most of the day coordinating the dinner I have planned for Cherish tonight. I could've hired someone to do it for me, but I want to do it so I can have control over every aspect of it. Nothing will go wrong tonight.

I arrange for a chef to come by to cook a feast fit for my queen. She knows this night will be special, but she doesn't know she's getting a *true* proposal or a ring. Doesn't know I'll officially declare to everyone she's mine.

I press the speakerphone button to dial her cell from my desk. It rings twice, then she answers, "Hey, you."

Just the sound of her voice is enough to make me want her.

"Hey, baby. What are you doing right now?"

"I was just talking to Naomi."

"Listen, I'm having dinner prepared for us tonight. I want you to wear that black dress."

"Oh. I was going to ask you about that. Did you pick that out for me?"

"I did"

"You're making it a habit of picking out clothes for me, I see."

"You spent two years doing it for me. Think of it as me returning the favor. I should be able to pick out your clothes, right?"

"Can't argue with you there."

"No, you can't. Wear it tonight. Just the dress. Nothing else."

"Nothing else, meaning…"

"No bra. No panties. I want you naked beneath it."

"Really now?" she asks. I imagine she's biting her lip right about now.

"Yes."

"And why's that, Monty?"

"The less you have on, the less I have to take off and I *will* be taking it off."

"Why do you sound so serious?"

"Because I am."

"You're making me nervous."

"You should be. I'll see you this evening. I have meetings until five-thirty."

"Okay."

"I love you, girl."

"I love you, Monty."

* * *

Naomi keeps Cherish occupied until seven. In that time, I have our family and friends gather in the dining room. Minnie, Isidora, Mother, Major and Consuela are all here. The food is spread out on the table. I'm standing, waiting for my girl to walk in.

She comes around the corner.

My heart drums. Can't I see her and not want to immediately jump her bones?

Her braids are hanging loose. Her body looks so good in that dress, I consider taking her upstairs before I bust my zipper.

I breathe. Pace myself through this.

"Come on in, Cherish," I tell her.

She comes to me, gives me one of those subdued, cordial hugs then says, "Hey, everybody."

They speak and tell her how beautiful she looks. She looks at me and whispers, "What's all this, Monty?"

"It's dinner for my lady. A special dinner." I leave a kiss

on her temple, then take her hand and lead her over to my chair at the head of the table. I sit down and tug at her hand so she knows to sit on my lap.

I feed her. Literally. She playfully takes turns doing the same to me. People can't eat for watching us.

Cherish turns her head to look at me. She whispers, "Maybe I should sit in a chair instead of on your lap."

"No."

She finds my stubbornness humorous. When I slip my hand under her dress, her laughter ceases. She stares me in the eyes as if to ask what I'm doing. I touch more. She fights to hold in a gasp.

"Cherish, why don't you tell everyone how long you've been in love with me," I tell her.

We have everyone's attention now.

Her cheeks flush.

I'm still touching her. No one is aware.

She bites down on her lip and lowers the croissant she has in her hand to the plate.

"Um, I—"

"Aw…look at her," Naomi says. "She's blushing. You're embarrassing her, Mr. St. Claire."

"She can handle it," I say, slowly strumming a song on her guitar strings.

Consuela says, "Well, seems like the cat got her tongue, but let me tell y'all…Cherish has loved him from the beginning. I remember when I first met Cherish. She was out there working in those flowers and I remember thinking to myself, doesn't she know that's my job."

The women laugh.

Consuela continues, "But then I realized why she was doing it. I never told her I knew, but I knew. Then, one day, I saw her staring at Mr. St. Claire and I mean she was in a trance! Couldn't look away. I said her name like five times and she still didn't hear me."

"Is that right Cherish?" I ask her.

She turns to look at me again, face flushed. My fingers

continue playing a song. "Monty," she whispers.

"Yes?" I answer with a straight face, holding keen eye contact with her.

She bites down on her lip. Words fail her. She turns to face everyone and forces out, "Um, Consuela is right. I—" She fights a gasp. Tries to talk again, "I did love Monty from the beginning. I just—I—I—I thought he was mean. When I watched him leave for work, he was always so well put together. Everything about him was perfect. And he was so beautiful. So handsome. He's the kind of man that women, myself included, gawk over. The kind of man you want but know he's out of your league, so you're just satisfied with being able to *see* him every day. I never thought he would actually like me. Never thought I was the kind of woman who'd catch his eye, but I'm glad by some miracle I did because I love him so much."

She gasps, covers her face. Her body trembles on my lap. She holds in a scream. They think she's emotional over her words, and she is, but she's also in the middle of ecstasy – overcome by the weight of body spasms hitting her.

"Aw, look at her," Mother says.

"That's a woman in love," Minnie adds.

"It is, isn't it?" I ask, moving my hand away from her. I prompt her to stand. Her legs are so weak, she holds the edge of the table.

I stand and say, "I invited you all here because you're not just workers. You're friends, more so of Cherish than you are with me. She adores you and I wanted you to know I adore her. I love this woman. For those of you who don't know, Cherish is my wife now but we didn't have a ceremony. I want to fix that. She means so much to me, I want her to have everything she deserves. So—"

I drop down to a knee, take her hand and look up at her. Tears run down her face. I say, "Cherish, I never knew how good love could be until I met you. You've changed my life. You taught me how to love. I will always be grateful to you for that. I love you from the depths of my soul. I love you more than I love myself, and I want to spend the rest of my life with you. Will you marry me?"

She nods and says, "Yes."

I slide the ring on her finger and stand to kiss my woman. I kiss her good – like there's nobody in this room but us. I imagine they're clapping and cheering but my tongue is so far down her throat, I'm not paying them any attention.

Cherish has all my attention.

My wife.

My lover, and I want her. Now.

I pull her lips with my mouth when I end the kiss. Still holding eye contact with her, I say to our guests, "Excuse us for a minute."

I take her hand and lead her straight to our bedroom. It's at the edge of the bed, where I loosen my belt and bury my length inside of her. She moans.

She holds on to me and moans.

"I can never get enough of you," I growl. I lose myself in pleasure listening to her sounds. Feeling her muscles contract around me. I love it when she does that, and then she screams her pleasure and I find release soon after.

I secure my clothes while she steps into the bathroom. She comes out and asks, "Are we going back downstairs?"

"Yes."

"We've been up here for twenty minutes. They know what we've been doing?"

I shrug. "I don't care, and neither should you." I kiss her lips. "Let's go."

All eyes are on us when we return to dinner. Naomi asks, "Is everything okay?"

"Everything is fine," I say, pulling up a chair so Cherish can sit next to me and enjoy her dinner.

Mother says, "I'm taking care of the arrangements for the wedding ceremony. It's going to be next Saturday at three. How does that sound?"

"Sounds good to me," I say. "Is that okay with you, baby?"

"Yes," Cherish says. "But I don't have a dress or anything."

Mother smiles. "No worries. We have an unlimited budget. You'll have a dress in no time. Oh, and be sure to let your mother know about it."

"Uh-okay," Cherish says.

Mother doesn't know the history Cherish has with her mother and stepfather. Now is not the time or place for her to find that out. I can tell just the mention of her mother is bringing her anxiety.

I lean over and whisper, "It'll be okay, baby."

She smiles and resumes eating her food.

Chapter Fifty-Eight

Cherish

I'm up around nine. I get dressed in a pair of black pants, a red sleeveless top and a pair of black flats. I'm going to see Monty this morning. It will be my first visit to Hawthorne Innovations' headquarters. I'm all set and ready to go, but I can't find my car keys.

I run downstairs with my purse and check the kitchen counter. Nothing.

"Good morning, Cherry."

"Good morning, Naomi," I say in a frenzy. "Have you seen my car keys by any chance?"

"Your husband told me he sent you a text about that."

"About my keys?" I ask as I dig around in my purse for my cell phone.

"Yes."

When I find it, I see a text from Monty that says:

Monty: Good morning, sexy. Your car is in the garage. Keys are already inside. Love you.

"What?" I say quietly. I glance up at Naomi. She's smiling. Now, I know something's up.

When I go to the garage, I'm greeted by a shiny, red Mercedes with a massive white bow on the hood. My mouth falls open. "Oh my gosh, Monty!" I scream like he's actually here. I check it out, take off the bow and dial his office number.

"Please tell me you're here already," he answers.

"No. I'm still home, standing in the garage looking at the car. You bought this for me?"

"Yes."

"Oh my gosh, Monty! Thank you."

"Is it to your liking?"

"Are you kidding? It's so—wow! I love it!"

"Okay, then get your pretty lil' self in it and come on over. I've been waiting for you."

"Okay, I'm getting in now. I'm so nervous."

"Why are you nervous?"

"You bought me a freakin' car."

He chuckles. "And that makes you nervous?"

"A little bit. And I've never been to your office. Nobody there knows me, well besides Hannah."

"There's nothing to be nervous about. Just come on over here."

"Okay."

I plug the address into my GPS and back out of the garage. The building is only twenty minutes away from here. I'll be there in no time.

* * *

When I arrive, I see Monty standing at the main entrance, as fine as he wants to be.

Lawd have mercy...

I still can't believe he's mine.

I park in visitor parking, get out the car and nearly break into a sprint to get to him like I haven't seen him in ages. Like we didn't just make love in the shower last night until we both had trouble standing upright. I embrace him. Squeeze him. He squeezes me and then we kiss for what seems like an eternity. After he's satisfied, he takes my hand.

We get on the elevator to go up. There're a few people on here besides us, but that doesn't stop him from cornering me, kissing me more while the bell dings, letting people on and off.

He doesn't care who's getting on. Doesn't care who sees us. When I'm with him, the rest of the world ceases to exist.

On the tenth floor, we exit hand-in-hand. We walk toward his secretary's desk. He says, "Hannah, this is my wife, Cherish."

She stands, greets me with a smile and says, "It's nice to put a face to a name finally. It's a pleasure to meet you, Cherish."

"Nice to meet you as well," I say.

We continue on to his office. I'm amazed when I step inside. Don't know why because I should be accustomed to elegance by now. His office is immaculate. It's decorated with the finest quality Cherrywood furniture. I gravitate to the pictures on the wall – images of him that will add to the story in my mind of who he is. I see a picture of him and an older man. I'm sure it's his adoptive father – the only father he's ever known. Mr. Caspian Hawthorne. I find it interesting how they look alike but aren't related by blood. Being together for so long probably made them that way.

I see pictures of him and Major. One with him and his mother. Others with him and other businessmen and famous people – football players and prominent figures in the community.

"What are you doing, girl?" he asks, his arms swallowing me from behind.

"I'm admiring your pictures."

"You can admire me in person. I'm right here."

I turn around to look at him. "Yes, I can but now that I've finally made it to your office, I want to know exactly what you do."

"I told you that already," he says narrowing those enchanting eyes at me. "You're not paying attention, Mrs. St. Claire."

"Okay, okay. You told me, yes. Now, *show* me."

For a moment, I think he's going to kiss me but he says, "Okay. Come on."

I follow him to his massive desk. It's spotless. There's no clutter. It looks like the thing was polished with some Old English.

Instead of pulling up a chair for me, he pulls me onto his lap. I'm wearing pants, so there won't be a repeat of yesterday evening at dinner but Monty can be pretty slick when he wants to be.

He opens his laptop. It looks top-of-the-line like he had it specially designed for his use. He pulls up a picture. Tells me it's a taser and how he came up with the concept of making government grade tasers that vibrates when you touch the handle to help police officers distinguish between their gun and the taser. He says these types of accidents happen too often and as a society, we need to do all we can to show the world that black lives matter besides marching whenever there's a 'new' news story. He wants to remove the excuse of an officer reaching for the wrong weapon. As he talks, I listen closely. I can tell he's passionate about his work. He finds great meaning in what he's doing.

I ask, "What made you come up with the idea for the vibration aspect of it, though?"

"Just thinking outside of the box. The key to any good invention is asking yourself if what you want to invent will solve a problem. If the answer is no, it's probably not a good idea. All the greats would tell you the same if they were still alive. So would my father."

"This is very interesting."

"You think so?"

"I do. It takes a lot of creativity. Right off the bat, you don't really come across as the creative type. Business, yes, but not creative."

"It does take creativity to come up with this stuff. It's one of the things my father was a master at. Whenever I was with him working on a project, I could see his brain firing off ideas. He kept a portfolio of them."

"Can I see it?"

"Sure," he says. He takes a notebook from the bottom desk drawer and hands it to me. I page through it and see the incredible ideas and sketches. "These are nice."

"Yeah. They are."

"Did he make all of these?"

"Most of them. There are about five or six he didn't get a chance to complete."

I place the portfolio on his desk and ask, "Are you going to complete them?"

"I thought about it, but I'm not sure. It's too soon. I wanted to work on these with him. It'll be difficult to work on them knowing he's no longer here."

"But I'm sure it'll bring you great satisfaction knowing you completed something he started."

"Yeah. Maybe one day."

He smiles and says, "Let me show you around."

I stand and he puts the portfolio back in the drawer. We walk down the hallway. He shows me a prototype of the taser. I grip it by the handle and it automatically vibrates.

"Ooh...this is neat," I say, then release and grab it again.

"Okay, okay...that's enough. Give it here. I'm getting jealous."

"Jealous how?" I say, securing the taser behind my back.

He flashes a wicked-sexy smile and says, "You've never grabbed my *handle* like that."

"Yeah, that's only because I need to use *two* hands to grab that monster."

He chuckles. "Let's test that theory," he says reaching for his zipper.

"Don't you whip that thing out in here."

He laughs. "Nobody's here but us," he says, stepping in front of me. He kisses me. Slow. Methodically. I hear myself whimper. Hear him moan. "Alright, let's go before we tear up this lab," he tells me.

"Yes. Let's go."

We proceed down a level. He takes me by Major's office but he's working from home today.

We visit various departments – accounting, sales, logistics and marketing. He shows me the gym, tells me his father was passionate about exercise and fitness, but unfortunately, his good health was no match for cancer. He's always mellow when he talks about his dad. I never know if I should chime in or not.

WE LEAVE THE office and go straight to the dentist office where my mother works – on McCullough Drive in University City. Monty is riding shotgun. He left his car at the office.

We pull up and park. Monty has on a pair of gold-lense Cartier sunglasses, laid all the way back in the passenger seat like he's about to do a drive-by. Looks like a sexy assassin.

He looks over at me and asks, "Are you ready?"

"No. I'm not ready. Not at all. I wish I didn't have to do this."

"You can do it. If you can deal with me, you can deal with and *handle* just about anything."

He definitely has a point there…

"You're right," I say, my sweaty palms still gripping the steering wheel even though we're not driving anywhere. We're just sitting here. On a stakeout…

I glance at my watch growing antsy. "She should've been out by now."

"Do you see her car?"

"Yes. That black Honda Accord right there."

"Is that her?" he asks looking toward the front doors of the building.

I look to where he's looking and see Mama walking fast

to the car with a bag on her shoulder.

My stomach is in knots. "Yes. That's her." I get out of the car. I hear Monty's door open and close, but my head is so cloudy, I don't tell him to wait in the car. I meant to. I don't want him to witness this conversation because I know it's going to be a bad one. My mother has never had my back. Only Webster's. There's no reason for me to think she'll have it now.

She looks my way, sees me walking toward her and frowns – not the reaction a mother should have upon laying eyes on her child – her *only* child.

Since I already know this isn't going to go well, I snap out of my fogginess and say to Monty, "Hey, why don't you wait in the car?"

"No, I'm not waiting in the car. I'll try to stay quiet, but if I say something you don't like, just *tell* me to be quiet."

"I can't tell you to be quiet. You're my husband," I whisper back at him.

"What are you doing here?" my mother asks like I'm a stranger. Like I have no right to visit her, or like the parking lot is off limits to me.

"Hi, Mom."

"I said, what are you doing here?"

"I need to talk to you."

"If it's about your stepfather, I don't want to hear it." She reaches for the car door handle.

"Ma, just wait a minute."

"Why! I refuse to listen to this—this *rubbish* you're spewing. I told you, lil' girl...I'm sick of it! Sick!" She grabs the door handle again.

"Excuse me," Monty says, stepping closer to me. "Please let her speak."

Mama throws a hand on her hip. "And who are you supposed to be?"

"I'm her husband, and she's not a *little* girl. She's a grown woman and you're *supposed* to be her mother."

"I *am* her mother."

"Then listen to what she has to say, you know, like a *loving* mother would."

My mother glares at him, then looks back at me. "You done got married?" she asks as she looks Monty from head to toe.

"Yes."

She returns her gaze to me. "Go on and say what you gotta say so I can go."

"Ma, I hate to keep bringing this up. I just don't understand why you don't believe me. Webster is lying to you. All those things I said he did to me, he *did* them and I think you know it. You're just covering for him like you're scared he's going to leave you. You're willing to put up with a man like him just to say you got somebody because you can't stand the thought of losing another man after dad."

"That's not true."

"It is true. You've never been able to get over dad. In a way, neither have I because if he was still here, at least he would've protected me. I would've never crossed paths with Webster."

She looks sad. Just when I think I'm getting through to her, she shakes her head. "I hear what you're saying but he's my husband, Cherish. He says he didn't do anything to you. Who am I supposed to believe?"

"How about your own flesh and blood? I'm telling you the truth, Ma. And recently, he came to my house and threatened me. My neighbor had to run him off with her gun. Then he kicked in my front door in the middle of the night. The police haven't arrested anyone for the break-in yet, but my gut tells me it was him. And he stole—" Tears come to my eyes no matter how hard I tried not to cry, but the fact is, I can't find the photo of me and my dad and I know he took it. Took it to hurt me.

I get myself together enough to finish talking but I garble my words when I say, "He stole my picture. The one of me and dad. I can't find it anywhere. I know he took it. Why don't you check his car? Or in the garage? He took it, Ma."

"Yeah, look, I gotta go," she says. She gets into the car and drives off.

I stand there, frozen in time, watching her leave.

My mother.

She'd abandoned me a long time ago. I lived with her, and still, I know what it's like to not have a mother.

"Cherish," Monty says.

I turn to look at him. I've lost my mother and it's time I come to the realization that she'll put the interest of Webster ahead of mine every single time.

"Come on, baby. Let's go," he says. He takes the keys out of my hand and drives straight home.

I go upstairs, sit on the bed and hang my head. I feel much worse now. I shouldn't have gone through with it. Should've left things like they were – her not talking to me and me not talking to her. That was our comfort zone. Pretending nothing ever happened and living our lives.

Monty sits beside me. He says nothing at first, just feels out the moment then asks, "Are you okay?"

"I'm fine," I say, although I know he doesn't believe me. In his defense, I don't sound believable. I sound miserable and confused. Broken and disoriented.

"Why didn't you tell me about the picture?"

I shrug. "I didn't want to bother you with it."

"Bother me? It wouldn't be a bother. You know that."

I am aware of that, but he's done enough for me already. Certainly he'll grow tired of always catering to what I need as if he doesn't have a billion-dollar corporation to run. He has his own share of problems to be carrying the additional weight of mine on his shoulders.

"When did you realize it was missing?"

"When I went over there to get some clothes."

"That was after the break-in, right?"

"Yes. When I was over there, I looked for the picture. I think Webster came and took it. We didn't know anyone was in the house because the alarm wasn't set after the door got fixed."

Monty takes my hand and assures me everything will be alright. He tells me to take a hot, late-afternoon shower so I can relax for the rest of the day.

After the shower, he pampers me with a foot rub that feels so good, it nearly puts me to sleep. He massages my legs, my back. Shoulders. Arms. Tells me I'm still tense and he wants me to relax. Then, when he's rubbed and squeezed every part of my body, he tucks me in.

"Get some rest," he says. "When you wake up, I'll have dinner waiting."

"Thanks, Monty."

"You're welcome, sweetheart."

Chapter Fifty-Nine

Cherish

I open my eyes to see his peering back at me. I'm groggy but so relaxed, I don't want to move a muscle.

"Hey," he says.

"Hey."

"What time is it?"

He glances at his watch. "It's a little after seven."

He leans over to kiss my forehead then asks, "How do you feel?"

"I feel relaxed. I so needed this after the conversation with my mother."

"I know." His thumb brushes across my cheek like a flutter. "Dinner is waiting for us in the dining room."

"Just us?"

He smiles. "Yes. Just us, this time."

"Okay." I stretch my arms above my head and extend my legs as far as they can go. "I'll be down in a minute."

I fix my hair, throw on a pair of leggings and a crop top then head downstairs. When I walk into the dining room, Monty eyes me up and down. His gaze lingers on my belly button before our eyes meet.

He smiles. "New top?"

"No. You've just never seen me wear it before."

"I like it," he says. He stands, pulls out my chair. I sit adjacent to him.

"Thank you."

"You're welcome."

The food is already here. I have no idea what it is. Something fancy that smells good with salad, rolls and a bunch of other stuff we probably won't get around to. Monty likes variety.

"What is that for the main course?" I ask.

"It's veal parmigiana." He points to a long, square dish and says, "That's risotto and to complement that is sausage, roasted shrimp and fried chicken."

"This is a lot of food."

"It is, but I like to keep my bases covered in case there's something you don't like."

He places a roll on my plate then picks up a dish of what looks to be butter formed in little balls and infused with green herbs.

"Butter?" I say.

"Yes."

I take a few pieces and try it with the bread.

So good…

I could sit here and eat bread and butter for dinner and be completely satisfied. I take another roll and butter it.

He chuckles.

"What?" I ask with a mouth full.

"All this food on the table and you're stuffing yourself with bread."

"It shouldn't be so good." I take a sip of water to wash it down.

"I'm teasing. Eat all you want. It'll keep that round butt of yours nice and thick the way I like it."

He proceeds to serve me a sample of everything on the table. That's *one* way to ensure I keep it *thick*…

"Thank you," I tell him.

"You're welcome, baby."

I take a bite of the parmigiana and moan how good it is.

"You can save all that moaning for later on tonight," he tells me.

I swat at his arm. "Hey, thank you for coming with me earlier to see my mom. I'm sorry you had to witness that, though."

"That's okay. Toward the end, I got the impression she might've believed you."

"Seriously? You didn't see how fast she bolted?"

"I did but at the same time, I was reading her expressions. There's a lot she doesn't say that you can figure out if you watch her."

"Is that what you do with people? Watch them and try to figure them out?"

"I'm a businessman, baby. I have to be good at reading people."

"Then if you're so good at reading people, why didn't you know I had a crush on you when I started working here?"

He glances up at me before he pours wine in his glass. "Who says I didn't know?"

"I do."

"Of course, I knew. I know when a woman is feeling me."

"You knew but you didn't act on it."

He sips. Licks his lips. Lowers the glass to the table. His fingers are still gripping the stem when his eyes roll up to look at me. "No. I didn't act on it."

"Why not?"

"I was busy working."

"And being rude," I toss back.

"Believe it or not, my rudeness was protection for you."

"How so?"

I glance her way. She's so innocently beautiful my heart sings her praises. I've made love to her too many times to count and still can't get enough. It's her mind, her state of being, her virtuousness that has me deeply in love with her. It's how she struggles with adversity and keeps on moving forward. She's not a quitter. She's a hard worker. A fighter. We have that in common. She's the representation of who I am. I see myself through her eyes.

Well?" she asks as she waits for me to answer her

question.

I say, "I wasn't the kind of man to find a woman and settle down with her. If I was with a woman one night, the next morning she meant nothing to me. I wasn't into relationships. Being callous towards you was my way of pushing you away from me, hoping you'd get the message."

"Oh, I got the message alright. That's why I quit, but if that's what you wanted me to do all along, why'd you come looking for me that day you—you were in the accident?"

That still haunts me. Some of my nightmares are about that wreck and him being in the hospital but I don't have it in me to tell him that.

"I didn't want you to quit. I wanted you to stay away from me."

"That's what I was doing. Since the closet incident, I tried hard to stay out of your way, but then you came looking for me that day when I was working in the flower garden. Why?"

"Because I needed to see you. Eat your food, baby."

A small smile touches my lips. I resume eating at his request, trying the sausage and risotto, discovering it makes a great combination.

He eats chicken, then shrimp. He takes a napkin, wipes his mouth and says, "Friday, me and Major are going to meet Magnus at my uncle's house. I want you to come with me."

"I would love to."

He looks at me in a way that tells me he wants me again. He picks up the glass instead. Drinks more wine.

"Tomorrow, I think we should go get the rest of your things. I want you completely moved in."

I nod but feel a level of sadness since I know I'll be leaving the house for good. My Aunt Jolene's home. It saved me in many ways. Saved me from abuse. It was my safe haven. It was my home.

"Do you want to put it up for sale?"

"I don't know, Monty. It has sentimental value. I don't know if I should sell it."

"Just think about what you want to do and let me know. I'll support you in whatever you decide."

"I hate that I have to leave all of my flowers behind, too."

"Baby, I'll buy you all the flowers you've ever dreamed of."

"I know you will, Monty, but those flowers are special. When I was going through it, they saved me. I know that sounds stupid, but—"

"It doesn't sound stupid. It makes perfect sense."

"It does?" I ask.

"Of course. It was your outlet. I'm glad you had one."

I drink wine and eat shrimp.

He says, "If you'd like, I can get the landscapers to go over there and bring some of them over here. You can plant them anywhere you like. You can make your own personal flower garden if you want."

"I would love that."

"Then it's so ordered," he says.

I smile. I love it when he behaves like a king. My king. *It's so ordered.*

Chapter Sixty

Monty

We spend most of Thursday at her house. She tells the movers what to pack and what should stay. I have the landscapers come over to dig up some flowers. Cherish chooses the ones she wants. She also informs me she's not ready to sell the house. She wants to keep it for now.

Ms. Kettleworth comes hobbling over in her favorite pair of jean overalls – looks like the same ones I always see her wearing. She's already talked to Cherish for a while this morning but I'm glad she's making her way over here again because as wacky as she is, she's been a friend to Cherish and anyone who's a friend of hers is a friend of mine.

"Howdy," she says.

"How are you today, Ms. Kettleworth?"

"I was doing dandy 'til I heard all the commotion out'chere, Mr. Montgom'ry. I had to step out on the porch to see what was going on and by golly, Sherrish is moving out."

"Yes, she is."

"I knew it. I knew you were going to sweep Sherrish off her pretty feet! Did she tell you what I said about teeth? Did she?" she asks and nudges me with her elbow three times.

"No."

"Ah ha! She took my advice. This ol' lady still knows the tricks of the trade, I tell ya dat."

I have no clue what she's talking about. I just grin and play along. I take an envelope from my pocket and hand it to her.

"What's this, Montgom'ry?"

"Open it."

She tears the envelope open and removes the check. Her eyes grow big. She looks like she's about to faint. She catches her balance, then asks, "What's this for?"

"I wanted to show my appreciation for everything you've done for Cherish."

"Well, Montgom'ry, I ain't do what I did 'specting payment."

"I know, but I still want to show my gratitude."

"You can show yur gratitude by buying me a can of tuna and an extra-large bag of cat food."

"With that money, I'm sure you can buy plenty of cat food, Ms. Kettleworth."

"For that Butterball, I tell ya...I'm gon' need it. I 'preciate it Montgom'ry."

"You're very welcome."

"Don't y'all be no strangers."

"We won't."

* * *

When I meet Mason, right away I can tell he's a St. Claire. His eyes are green like mine and we have other features that came packaged in our DNA – features that'll be passed down to future generations.

We hug for what feels like an eternity. He's the closest person to my biological father and somehow I can feel him here in spirit. This is a new beginning for me. For all of us.

He has tears in his eyes when the hug ends and even more when he embraces Major.

Magnus and Shiloh arrive after us and when he steps into the foyer, Mason says, "Good to see you again, Magnus."

They embrace, then he attempts to give Shiloh a hug, but she's very pregnant, so he settles for a side hug.

His wife, my Aunt Bernadette, hugs us and then she

says, "You know what—let's get introductions out of the way so we can start behaving like a *real* family instead of strangers. Come on in here. Everybody else is waiting in the living room."

I take Cherish's hand and when we step into the living room, I'm in awe. All these people – my cousins their wives and children, whole families – are waiting to meet us.

"I'm Montgomery and this is my wife Cherish."

Magnus has never met the cousins. He introduces Shiloh and tells the family he has twins on the way.

Major throws up his hand offering a single wave as he introduces himself.

Then one of the cousins says, "It's a pleasure to meet you all. I'm Ramsey St. Claire, and this beautiful woman next to me is my wife, Gianna. This pretty shy lil' girl I'm holding is our daughter, Rianne." Rianne climbs up on her father, hiding her face in the crevice of his neck.

The next one stand and says, "Hi. I'm Royal and this is my wife, Gemma."

"Hi," Gemma says. "Oh, and by the way, me and Gianna are sisters."

"Neat," Major says.

A third cousin says, "I'm Romulus and this stunning lady next to me is not only my best friend, but she's my wife and my baby mama, Siderra. We have a four-month-old son named Egan who's fast asleep right now."

"Hi," Siderra says. "I'm the *baby mama*." She laughs.

The last cousin looks more animated than the other three. He says, "What up cousins? I'm Regal, the smartest of the bunch."

Ramsey shakes his head.

"Here we go," the woman standing next to Regal says.

Regal introduces her as Felicity, his wife. He says, "I call her WB, but y'all call her Felicity."

Felicity laughs.

"That little girl who's been staring at you with those

big, pretty eyes since you came in is my daughter Rayne and we have a son on the way."

Felicity puts on hand on her stomach.

"Congratulations," I tell them.

"Yes, congratulations," Cherish says.

"Thank you," Regal says. He looks at his daughter and says, "Hey, Rayne, don't just stare. Say something."

I look at the girl. Her cheeks are red. Eyes brown and big. She looks like a real-life doll.

"Hi," she finally says. "I'm Rayne."

"Aw, she's so sweet," Cherish says.

"Thank you," Felicity says.

"Don't let that innocent voice fool you. The girl ain't got a shy bone in her body," Regal says. "She's *feisty*, like her mama."

"Hush, Regal," Felicity tells him.

"You hush before I come after those lips."

Bernadette chuckles. "Major, Magnus, Montgomery, Shiloh and Cherish—did I get it right?"

"Yes, ma'am," Major says.

"Y'all gotta excuse Regal. He ain't got to sense."

"Lies," Regal says.

The family erupts in laughter.

"She's not lying," Ramsey tells us.

"Look," Regal says. "Stick with me and I'll teach you everything you need to know about the St. Claire click. First of all, welcome to the fam. It's a blessing we found each other. From what I hear, we have Shiloh and Cherish to thank for that."

"Yes," Magnus says. "I have *so* much to thank her for." He kisses Shiloh on the cheek.

Magnus continues, "And if Cherish had never reached out to me, I wouldn't have met my brothers—Major and Montgomery—so thank you, Cherish."

"You're welcome."

"Let's get you a chair, Shiloh," Mason says. "As a matter of fact, come on. Let's sit at the dinner table.

Bernadette has been cooking all day."

"Oh, I smelled it when I came in," Regal says.

I can already see there aren't enough seats. Mason sets up a folding table in the dining room and brings more chairs.

I pull out a chair for Cherish. "Are you comfortable?" I whisper.

"Yes. I'm okay. How are you holding up?" she asks.

"I'm good."

After everyone takes a seat, Regal stands up again. "Now, as I was saying, here's what y'all need to know about this family. Get some pen and paper if you need to because this is important. Everybody ready?"

"Yeah, *ready* for you to sit down," Romulus says.

Everyone laughs.

Regal continues, "Number one—Mrs. Gianna over there owns a bakery and I swear she sprinkles crack in those cupcakes. They're highly addictive."

Laughter fills the dining room.

Ramsey says, "Let me translate what my brother is *trying* to say. My wife is an excellent baker and her cupcakes are as addictive as she is."

"Thanks, Ramsey."

He places a kiss on her cheek.

Regal continues, "Gemma acts all innocent and sweet but she's married to bad boy Royal, so right off the bat, you know that sweet, innocent thing she's got going on is all a front."

Gemma's tickled. "Royal is not a bad boy."

"Yes, he is. Look at him. Got the beard and everything going on."

"We all have beards," Ramsey says. "Even you, Regal."

Everyone laughs again.

It's the first time I realize we have beards. Must be a St. Claire thing.

Royal take a sip of water like he's unfazed.

Regal then turns his attention to his brother Romulus

and says, "And then there's Rom...he and Siderra have been *friends with benefits* for quite some time now—they thought they had us fooled."

Siderra laughs. "Don't listen to Regal, y'all."

"Last, but certainly not least is my wife, Felicity," he says. "She runs a matchmaking company – Wedded Bliss. She doesn't just set people up—she marries fools off. Major, I noticed you came solo. If you're in the market for an insta-wife, Felicity can fix you up. She put Ramsey and Gianna together."

"That's partially true," Ramsey says.

Bernadette brings out food. There's nothing like food to relax this crowd. I quickly discover that my aunt can throw down in the kitchen. Everything's good. No matter how long you've been apart from family, a reunion has a way of bringing it all back together. Of making you feel welcome. It's how I feel sitting in this room with people who share my last name.

My family.

My heart is full. There's nothing like being surrounded by people you know who loves you by default because of your relation to them. I'm glad I get to share this moment with Cherish.

* * *

After dinner, we mingle and eat dessert. The women are in the living room talking about marriage and babies while the men remain in the dining room, seated around the table.

Mason says, "I sure wish Micah was here to witness this."

Magnus nods. "It would be nice. It would bring so much closure to have a discussion with him face-to-face. I know it can't happen, but—"

"I'd give anything for that opportunity," I say. "I've personally struggled with it, partly because when our foster parents took us in, they never adopted us. It gave me a sense that we were being rejected all over again. I'm not sure if you've felt that way Major." I glance to my left to look at Major. I'm not sure if he heard my question. He's checked out.

"I can definitely relate," Magnus says. "No matter how successful I was, my upbringing always haunted me. As men, we're conditioned to let things roll off our backs, but it got to me. Made me work harder to do more—to *be* more as if success would compensate for my parent's decision to put me in foster care. It doesn't work. All it did for me was cause more pain. In fact, if I wasn't such a workaholic, my wife and child would be alive and well today."

"Wait—you were married before?" Ramsey asks.

"I was," Magnus answers. "They died in a car accident."

"Sorry to hear that, man," Ramsey says. His brother Romulus, Regal and Royal express the same sentiment, as do I. Major's still in La La Land.

"But with the help of Shiloh, I've moved on. She came into my life at my lowest point and completely turned it upside down. I don't know what I would do without her."

"We're similar in that regard," Ramsey says. "I was engaged and my fiancée died of cancer. It shook me because there was nothing I could do about it. Her death hit me pretty hard. I hadn't intended on being with anyone after that, but I met Gianna, started over and we have our baby girl and I'm happy."

"I think the key to overcoming this foster parent situation is never giving up and not being afraid to start over," Romulus says.

Regal gestures with a beer in his hand and says, "If there was ever a lesson to be learned in all of this, that would be it."

I glance over at Major again. He's still sitting there expressionless lounged back in his chair, not trying to participate in the conversation. He gets up, excuses himself, heads out of the room.

"Is he good?" Royal asks, looking at me.

"I don't know. He doesn't talk about this much," I answer.

"You two grew up together, right?" Romulus asks.

"Yep. Magnus was placed first, then Sylvia and Caspian Hawthorne came along and took me and Major in."

"Caspian Hawthorne—why does that name sound familiar?" Ramsey asks.

"He's gone now, but he was pretty famous around here. He was an inventor."

"That's right—Hawthorne Innovations," Ramsey says. "Great work has come out of there. Your father was a master at his craft."

"Thanks, man. I appreciate that."

Regal finishes his beer then says, "So, instead of staying down memory lane, we need to make memories of our own. So, who plays golf?"

"I don't," Magnus answers.

"Me either," I tell him.

Regal asks, "What do you do to relax...to get out of the office and just let it all hang out?"

I chuckle. "I work, take my wife on dates. Swim. That's about it," I tell him.

"I'm the same way," Magnus says. "I work, but since being married, me and Shiloh do more things together...never tried my hand at golf, though."

"You should," Ramsey says. "I think it'll be a great way for us to get acquainted with each other."

"I'm down," I say. While it's not my thing, any opportunity to bond with my cousins and brothers is an opportunity I don't want to miss.

"I'll give it a shot, too, but it'll have to wait until after the babies are here," Magnus says.

"Do you know what you're having?" Ramsey asks.

"Yes. A girl and a boy."

"That's awesome. Congratulations, man," Royal says.

"Yeah, it's good to get 'em in a package deal," Regal says. "That way they grow up together."

"Oh, and if you ever need sitters, me and Gem are the designated babysitters of the family," Royal tells me.

"I think Bernadette will fight you for that title," Mason says. He's been standing near the opening that separates the dining room from the kitchen. "I was telling Magnus twins run in the family."

"Then where's my twin, Pop?" Regal asks.

Mason chuckles. I'm sure he's accustomed to his son's antics.

He responds, "*One* of you is quite enough, Regal." He chuckles. "Hey, where did Major run off to? Did he leave?"

"I think he just stepped outside for a minute," I tell him.

Mason says, "Just so you know, Montgomery, I've reached out to Zayda...haven't heard anything back yet."

"Who's Zayda?" Regal asks. I know who she is because Magnus has already told me about her – my biological father's second wife. I'm surprised Mason hasn't told his sons.

He does so now – explains it to everyone. They're amazed to discover they have more cousins while I process the fact I have two additional brothers and a sister I don't know. I'm still in a state of awe sitting among these men. Strong St. Claire men. Magnus lost a wife and a child. Ramsey lost a fiancée. My uncle Mason lost a brother. Me and Major lost our parents. I don't know the rest of their stories, but I know whatever they are, they came out victorious. It seems to be the St. Claire way.

"I'm not giving up," Mason says. "We've done come too far to give up now."

"Yes, we have," I say. "Yes, we have."

Chapter Sixty-One

Cherish

I've never had many friends, but through marriage, I now have friends *and* family. After talking to them for a while, I discover I have the most in common with Gianna. I learned about her struggles of growing up without much parental support – just her taking care of her sister alone. I admire her drive, being a busy mom to a two-year-old little girl and still able to run a bakery.

Siderra talks about Romulus a lot and how much her son is like his daddy.

Felicity is glowing. She's carrying her baby well. Tells me she's having a boy. Says she hopes he has her personality because Regal is a wild one.

Gemma doesn't have children, but she loves them. Makes me wonder why she doesn't have any of her own.

Shiloh has *two* babies on the way. There's nothing big on her but her stomach.

She asks me, "Are you and Montgomery going to have children?"

"We will eventually. We're actually having a wedding ceremony next Saturday."

"A wedding ceremony?" Felicity says. "I thought y'all were already married."

"It's a long story," I begin. "But in a nutshell, we were legally married on paper before we had a ceremony."

"Oh," Felicity says. "And that ring is phenomenal."

"It is," Siderra adds. "I had to put my sunglasses on to look at it."

The women laugh.

I say, "So, since we didn't have a ceremony before, Monty surprised me with one after."

"Where's it going to be?" Gemma asks.

"It's going to be at our home in Concord."

"Can we come?"

"I'm sure you can. Let me confirm it with Monty. I'll be right back."

I get up to go to the dining room when I catch sight of Major standing on the porch. I step outside. It's dark, but the porch light provides more than enough light.

"Hey, Major."

"Hey," he says. He doesn't make an attempt to turn around to say it. Immediately, I notice something's wrong.

"You okay?"

"Yeah. I'm fine."

"That didn't sound believable," I say standing next to him now. "What's wrong?"

"You know, I really don't like how well you know me."

The pain in his eyes prompts me to throw an arm around him. "This is difficult for you, isn't it?"

"It's a lot to take in. And everyone here is married. It's easy for Monty and Magnus to embrace all of this. Monty has you. Magnus has Shiloh. They have support."

"So do you, Major. I support you and you know Monty does."

He cracks a smile, looks at me, then stares off into the night.

"Major, we used to talk all the time before me and Monty became an item. We still can, you know."

"I know. Thanks, Cherish. I appreciate that."

I give him a pat on the back, before going back inside in search of hubby. When I turn around, I see Monty standing at the door like he'd been there for a while, watching. His hands are in his pockets. He smiles, opens the door so I can enter.

"Hey," I say.

"Hey. I was coming to check on Major, but I saw you

talking and didn't want to interrupt."

"It's not an interruption. You could've come out."

"How is he?"

"Um…I don't really know." I *do* know, I just don't feel it's my place to tell him everything Major has told me. They're brothers. I'm sure they'll have the conversation at some point. "How are you doing?"

"I'm good."

"It sounds like a lot of male bonding is going on in there."

"There is, but we have a long way to go."

"At least you're off to a good start."

He nods.

"Hey, so I told the girls about our wedding. They wanted to know if they could come."

"Of course."

"Really?"

"Yes. They're family, and I want them to know how much I love you."

He pulls me close, slides his tongue into my mouth. Alcohol and desire please my tastebuds. The combination makes me tingle. Gives me goosebumps. Has me thinking about cold water to get rid of this hot flash.

"Mmm," I say.

"We have to leave soon," he tells me.

"Why?" I ask, but I already know why.

He grabs my hand and lowers it to this zipper. "Need I say more?"

"Monty! You can't be up in here all aroused like this."

"That's why we need to go."

"Well, let me tell the girls about the ceremony."

"Okay. I'll let the fellas know about it."

WE LEAVE. MAJOR is quiet on the drive home while me and Monty discuss the events of the night.

Monty's on cloud nine. I can tell he's riding a high. I

always know when his sense of excitement is elevated.

Major is at ground zero.

It baffles me how their reactions are so vastly different. I actually thought Major would handle this better than Monty would. I was wrong.

Monty parks in the garage. The car can barely come to a stop and Major is already hopping out the back, heading for his residence.

"I'll talk to him later," Monty says.

"Please do. He needs it."

We retreat to our residence. I can't get out of my clothes and Monty is all over me. He's so smooth. Meticulous. I'm naked before I realize it. He's inside of me before my mind can warn the rest of my body to prepare for 'the monster'. My hands grip his shoulders as he pushes into me and retreats, doing this so many times my head spins like I have a sudden case of vertigo. His mouth works wonders on my lips, on my breasts on – on every part of my body.

He strokes my mind blank. My body is in a frenzy. He goes deeper, cradles my head in his hand and rides, moving his body like he's swimming beneath water.

Our bodies explode into a beautiful, catastrophic ending.

Monty groans his pleasure against my lips, tells me he loves me as he empties his love inside of me. I'm hot. Intensely so.

My breathing is labored. Muscles contracts and contracts some more, gripping him. Not wanting to let go. Taking all he has to offer. It's good 'til the last drop.

Sleep came easily after that and all was well until I wake up at 4:00 a.m. screaming. I'm cold. Sweaty and cold.

Monty tries to put his arm around me but I pull away and look at him like he's a stranger.

"It's okay, Cherish," he says.

His voice calms me. Makes me realize it's him in the midst of my troubles and I latch on and hold on to him like he's my lifeline. Like I'm in the middle of a raging river and he's the life preserver that'll save me from drowning.

Here I am suffering from yet another bad dream courtesy of Webster. Monty holds me, assuring me it'll be alright. That my nightmare is over.

But it'll never be over for me until I get some kind of justice.

Chapter Sixty-Two

Cherish

Justice.

What would that look like for me? I'm happily married to my dream man and my life is pretty much a fairytale except for what happened in my past. At what point do I let it go and be happy? I thought I had let it go, but it keeps reappearing in my dreams and I have no control over that. The damage is in my mind. It's something my subconscious won't let go of. Doesn't matter how happy I am or how many times my husband makes love to me. It's always there, waiting to interrupt my life.

Monty has to be frustrated. If love isn't enough to make me forget, what is?

I sit up in bed and stretch, remembering how frightened I was last night. It rattles me still even though I'm no longer dreaming. It's no longer night. The sun shines bright through the windows. Monty isn't in the room.

"Good morning."

I turn to the sound of his voice. He's walking into the bedroom with a tray.

"Good morning, Monty."

He brings it over to me, places it on the bed. "You had a rough night, so I thought I'd make you breakfast."

"Wait—you prepared all of this?" I asked, looking at the food. There's yogurt and granola and strawberries. Eggs. Bacon. Steaming hot grits.

"Yes, I did. I want you to eat and relax."

"Wow. Thank you." I start with the yogurt, then say,

"I'm sorry I keep having these dreams, Monty. I know it's a burden on you."

"No. The burden on me is knowing what you had to go through. I need to come up with a solution so we can put this behind us."

My phone vibrates. I take it from the nightstand to discover I have three back-to-back text messages. They're all from my mother.

Belinda: They arrested your father. Said he broke into your house. You ought to be ashamed!

Belinda: You know this is ALL YOUR FAULT! I don't have $5,000 to bail him out.

Belinda: You got him into this mess. You should be the one to get him out!

I didn't realize my hands were shaking until Monty put his hand on top of mine.

"What's wrong?" he asks. He takes the phone from my grasp. Reads the messages for himself.

"They got him," he tells me. "Don't worry about what your mother has to say."

My hands are still shaking.

Monty takes the tray away and pulls me into his arms. "They got him, baby, and he should be thanking his lucky stars because I was tempted to go handle him myself."

"I need to—to—to call her."

"No, you don't."

"I do, Monty. I need her to know I'm telling the truth. It's all I ever wanted. For her to believe me. He's in jail. Now's my chance."

He sighs.

I don't know why I'm obsessed with her believing me when I've always maintained she's known all along. Maybe without him being around, she won't have anyone in her ear, brainwashing her against me. Calling me a liar.

"I don't like the way she's talking to you in these text

messages, Cherry."

"She's just lashing out. I need to talk to her," I say, jumping up out of bed.

"Cherish."

"Monty, I *have* to go. Please."

"Okay, just wait a minute," he says, hooking an arm around me before I can reach the bathroom. He rotates my body so that I'm looking at him. "You need to settle down for a minute."

"I'm fine."

"You're shaking. Breathe."

I take a moment to pull in some breaths and slowly breathe them out. Monty holds my hands. Helps me through.

"If you really want to go over there, I'm taking you."

"I'm good with that."

I breathe.

In and out.

"Get dressed and we'll go."

"Okay."

I breathe some more.

When he releases my hand, I take the quickest shower in history, get dressed and we hop on 85 South, heading for Charlotte. When we pull up in the driveway at Mom's house, all kinds of feelings and emotions come over me. I grab Monty's right hand with my left and squeeze. This is the first time I've been back here since I was a teenager.

My mother storms out of the house before I can get out of the car. I release Monty's hand and open the door.

"She looks angry," he says.

"I'll be fine," I tell him. I get out, close the door and walk toward her.

"Where is it?" she asks.

"Where's what?"

"The money. Isn't that why you're here?"

"Ma, why on earth do you think I would bring you some money to get that man out of jail after everything he did to me?"

She folds her arms. "I don't believe you. You've got some nerve."

She's struck a *nerve* with me. I thought I'd be able to stay calm but screw it. I say, "And so do you to let a man molest your daughter and not make an attempt to put a stop to it. Not one!"

"He didn't molest—"

"He did!" I snap, yelling at the top of my lungs. I yell so loud, my head feels like it's about to explode. "And he broke into my house. Not only did he break in, but he came back and stole a picture of me and my *real* dad. It's probably in his car. Go get the keys and look."

She glares at me.

"Don't you want to put an end to this? Go get the keys! Check the car!"

"I will, and when you see that he ain't got no *picture* of yours, I want you to give me the money to bail him out."

She stomps away. I look back at the car to see Montgomery standing on the driver side like my personal bodyguard with his arms folded, waiting for something to jump off.

Mama comes back with keys, unlocks doors to Webster's white Chevrolet and releases the trunk. She looks all around, moving some tools, a crowbar and a few cans of Valvoline.

"Ain't nothing in here," she says. "I don't see no—"

She pauses. My guess is she sees something.

I take a step closer as she picks up a few oily towels and there's the eight-by-ten picture frame – the picture of me and my father. The glass is shattered, but the picture remains intact. I snatch it from her.

"Now do you believe me?" I ask her. "And don't say I put that there. I didn't. He did it! He—" The tears come. "You know what he did to me, Ma. Why did you protect him all these years while I suffered? Were you that *desperate* to—to have someone after dad died that you'd let this man abuse me?"

I feel Monty's arms circle around me. I'm in full tears. My mother is too ashamed to look at me. She's crying, too.

"I didn't want to believe it was true," she says. "I wanted you to have a father again. I wanted to have a husband. I didn't think I would ever want another man after your dad but when Webster came along, I thought he was good enough. I knew I would never love him as much as I loved your father, but he was there, and he's always denied touching you, and I—I had a feeling he was lying."

"Then why didn't you do anything about it, Ma? I came to you and told you. I begged you...all you did was send me back to my room. I had to move in with Aunt Jolene to get away from him. I honestly don't know which was worse—the abuse or the fact that my own mother didn't believe me. Didn't have my back. I'm your daughter, your only child and you believed him over me."

She still can't face me. Her back is to me. She's standing at the opened trunk wiping tears.

Monty leans down and whispers in my ear, "I know you're angry. I can feel it in your energy but I want you to go talk to her. I know it's difficult, baby, but the only way you're going to move past this is to forgive her."

I turn around and look at him. He wipes my tears away. I smile, finding strength in his eyes. If he can repair his relationship with his mother, then so can I.

Emboldened by the courage and encouragement of my husband, I walk over to Mama and take her hand. Before I can get a word out, she breaks down and starts crying harder. "I'm so sorry, Cherish," she says. "I'm so sorry."

I embrace her, hold her trembling body in my arms as we empty our pain. Whatever she's done, she's still my mother and Monty's right – I need to forgive her.

"I'm sorry," she says again.

I have no words to say at the moment. I only embrace her. We still need to talk, but now isn't the time. We need to hold each other. To reconnect as mother and daughter.

To put glue in the cracks that have severely broken us.

She invites me inside the house, but I can't go in. I won't. My wounds are still open. The memories still haunt me. We talk outside. She apologizes over and over again, says she's going to end her relationship with Webster. She asks me if I want to report him to the police for what he did to me. Says she'll have my back one-hundred percent. The only thing is, I don't know if I want to travel down that road. It'll be his word against mine. I have no evidence of the crime he committed against me so many years ago, and I don't want to be involved in a lengthy legal process where I'd have to see him.

I only want this to be over.

Chapter Sixty-Three

Monty

I take her to lunch when we leave her mother's. After we're seated, she looks at me and says, "Shrew. That was tough."

"It was, but you're tougher. I'm proud of you."

She smiles. "Thank you. I don't know how I would've done it without you."

"Give yourself the credit."

"Nope," she says shaking her head. "I had so much anger in my heart towards her. Even though I went there to talk to her, to try to convince her I was being truthful, I wouldn't have been able to forgive her if it wasn't for the way you forgave your mother. I found so much strength in your example. If you could do it, so could I."

"Amazing how that works, isn't it?"

"It is," she says.

I get up and walk over to sit in the booth beside her. I take her hand, look at the ring I put there and say, "I am profoundly proud of you. In awe of you."

"Stop trying to make me cry in this restaurant, Monty. I've cried enough for today already."

"I'm not trying to make you cry, but it's true. You came into my life at a time I needed you. I wasn't aware I needed anyone or anything. That's the price I paid for being a billionaire. I always felt like I didn't have to rely on anyone. That I didn't need anyone, but I needed you. I still do. And today, you showed me a woman with a forgiving heart. You showed me your strength. I know without a shadow of a doubt we can get through anything together."

She leans close, pushes her lips to my face.

"You and your mother have a long way to go, but today was a good start."

"Yes, it was. I don't know if I will ever feel comfortable going back in that house, though."

"That's understandable."

"And another thing I was thinking about is, what if Webster bails out of jail and comes after my mother or me?"

"If she wants, I can have all of her locks changed, install a security system. I can buy her a house in Concord, close to us if she'd be willing to relocate. And as for you, you don't have to worry about him coming after you. I always protect what's mine. If that shotgun Ms. Kettleworth had was enough to run him out of your yard that day, then I know he doesn't want to see what kind of heat I'm packing. In fact, I don't want you to worry about your mother. I'll reach out to her today and see what avenues she wants to take to secure herself. Maybe it's time for a move, especially since that house has so many bad memories for you. You wouldn't be able to visit her there."

"I wouldn't. It would be good if she was willing to relocate."

"I don't want you to be worried about anything. We have our wedding ceremony coming up in a week. That's what we're going to focus on from now until Saturday. Sunday morning, we're flying out to the Seychelles Islands."

"We are?"

"Yes. I'm ready to travel now, so get ready, travel buddy."

She smiles. "You said we're going where?"

"The Seychelles Islands."

"Where's that?"

"There is a cluster of islands off the East African coast in the Indian Ocean. I have an eight-bedroom, oceanfront home there that I've only visited once when I made the purchase. I haven't been back, but I have it maintained regularly. It's all set for our two-week stay."

"We're staying for two weeks?"

"Yes. I'll have you all to myself for two full weeks. No distractions. No interruptions. No business meetings, no work, no mama drama. Just us secluded in paradise. How does that sound?"

"It sounds like a dream."

"Good. That's how I want to make you feel every day of your life. Like you're living in a dream."

I can't help but latch on to her lips. The waitress is placing our lunch plates on the table but I can't let go. They're too good to let go. *She's* too good to let go, and that's why I know I want an eternity with her.

* * *

At home, we go for a swim just for the fun of it *and* to relieve the tension of the day. Then she naps. While she does so, I go to my mother's residence to talk to her about the ceremony.

She smiles as she opens the door. "Hello, son."

"How are you doing, Mother?"

"I'm well…just got off the phone with Siderra St. Claire. They've all called me. Gianna, Gemma, Felicity…all very nice people."

"I thought you were going to come with us yesterday to meet them in person."

"I know. Last minute I decided not to. I wanted you and Major to have your time with them. I'll meet them at the wedding since it seems they're *all* coming. Felicity says her daughter can be the flower girl."

"I'm sure Cherish will be okay with that."

"Gianna's bringing cupcakes. Gemma and Felicity are going to get here early to help with the setup. I told them I hired professionals, but they insisted."

"Whatever they want to do to help, I say let them. It'll help make our kinship more real. Plus, most of the women are around Cherish's age. She'll need their support and advice as we mature as a couple."

"That's true. How was it meeting them? What is it four of them?"

"Four cousins, yes, and they're all married. Magnus was there, too with his wife. We all got along fine. They're a good bunch of people. Regal suggested the fellas get together to play golf."

"Yeah. Some good ol' male bonding time would be good. Do they all have children? I know at least one of them does."

"All the couples have kids except for one. Magnus and his wife are expecting twins."

"What about you and Cherish?"

I chuckle. "No, we're not expecting twins."

"You know what I meant. Are you going to have children?"

"We will."

"Oh, by the way, I fired Paige."

I grin. "'Bout time."

Mother laughs.

"What did she do?"

"I caught her talking down to the staff. Minnie was about to hit that girl over the head with a mop." She laughs. "I came downstairs just in time."

"Yeah, we don't need that kind of attitude around here."

"Funny you should say that. You used to ignore the staff like they had the plague—Naomi, Minnie, Isidora..."

"I know."

"What changed?"

"You know that changed."

"I don't think I do," she teases, smiling with her eyes. "Tell me."

"I fell in love with a woman who made me realize the

way I treated others was a reflection of how I felt about myself. Cherish has really changed my life."

"She's a blessing—that's for sure."

"Yes. She's a blessing."

Chapter Sixty-Four
A Week Later – The Wedding Ceremony

Monty

Her dress is the color of homemade vanilla. It matches the color of my tuxedo. On her, it looks like vanilla pudding against her chocolate complexion. Yes, my mind is going there. I could eat her up right now as she walks down the aisle looking like a fudge sundae, stepping on pink and red rose petals that Rayne dropped there moments ago. My bride is wearing a gold, diamond-studded tiara. Her black hair is curled in long spirals. It's the first time I've seen her without braids. I can get used to playing in all that hair.

On either side of the aisle are our family and friends – some old, but most of them new. They're the people who matter to us. The ones who will be a part of our lives as we embark on this new journey of love.

She steps over to me. I take her trembling hands into mine. She already has tears in her eyes.

The minister gets to ministering about us. Asks who gives Cherish away.

Her mother stands and says, "I do."

It's a moment I'm sure Cherish will never forget, especially considering just a week ago, she was still at odds with her mother.

We repeat our vows after him and then I have a few words of my own I want to say to her. I didn't write anything down, didn't rehearse a speech. I made up my mind I would say whatever came to my heart in that moment.

Staring in her lovely eyes, I begin, "Before you, I thought my life was ideal. Full. Complete. I thought I had everything I needed. That's why I was confused when my heart kept pulling me to you. I didn't understand that, and so I fought it because that's the only logical thing to do when your mind and heart aren't in sync. Then I realized how simple it would be to give into the unknown feeling that had taken over me—the overwhelming feeling of *needing* someone when I thought I had everything. But I didn't have you, so truthfully, I had nothing. Material wealth can never compare to you. I would give it all away for you...would give my life for you," I say getting choked up.

I take a moment, clear my throat and continue, "Thank you for making me see what's important. For loving me despite my many flaws. For being a positive influence in my life and helping me correct the error of my ways. For being a *real* woman, my strong, black queen who've overcome so many adversities and yet still have the heart to love a flawed man like me. I will *always* be yours, and you will always be mine—my lover, my friend, my wife, my everything. I love you, Cherish."

"I love you, too, Monty," she says through tears.

Keeping in line with doing things backward, we kiss before we're announced as husband and wife.

As if on queue, we hear three loud pops like someone had planned fireworks. I know mother wouldn't plan fireworks in the daylight hours. I later find out the noise came from Ms. Kettleworth's truck backfiring as she parked on the front lawn.

After we take pictures, she's one of the first to congratulate us. She says, "You done did it now, Sherrish."

Cherish hugs the old lady. She's happy to see her. "Hey, Ms. Kettleworth. Don't you look snazzy." She gives her a hug.

It's the first time I've seen Ms. Kettleworth in nice

clothes.

"Figured I'd fix myself up just in case Montgom'ry got a single pawpaw hobbling 'round here."

I chuckle. "I don't, but hey, look around. You never know."

"Oh, I plan on it…didn't shampoo this silver hair for nuttin'. I even wore it down to hide my hearing aids," she says then winks.

Cherish laughs.

We move to the tented reception side of the yard. The decorations are beautiful. The layout, the flowers, the hanging lights forming their own ceiling – I'm amazed at how quickly the grounds were transformed this way for us.

Before we eat, we get well wishes and congratulatory messages from the family. Siderra and Romulus come by our table with Rayne. I thank them for letting her be our flower girl.

Regal and Felicity follow, then Ramsey and Gianna with their daughter, Rianne. Carson, their butler tags along with them, and I've been watching him eyeing up my mother for most of the reception.

Royal and Gemma tell us we already look like the perfect happy couple, but in my opinion, we're rivaling them for that title.

Magnus holds Shiloh's hand when he comes over. He tells us they'll be leaving shortly since Shiloh is only a couple of days away from her actual due date. They brought along Shiloh's sister, Selah, to assist, but she's busy talking to Major. Or shall I say Major is busy talking to her…

My mother-in-law seems to be hitting it off with Minnie, Isidora and Naomi.

Ms. Kettleworth is drinking champagne and flirting with one of the bartenders.

The people I work with at Hawthorne Innovations who were invited are all sitting and eating, trying to act civilized around the boss like they're afraid they'll lose their jobs if they're caught drinking and twerking. I honestly don't care what they do.

Mason and Bernadette keep to themselves for now. I imagine they're discussing family matters, probably planning our next family event.

I lean close to Cherish and ask, "How do you think everything is going?"

"Hmm, let's see…my husband is looking fly, the weather is gorgeous, everyone is on their best behavior—"

"Everyone except for my mother. She's been over there flirting with that butler dude."

Cherish laughs.

"I'ma have to go break this up."

"No. What you need to do is let your mother live her best life. She's just socializing and having fun. Look at that smile."

I take a hard look at her. She's happy. Brilliant and beautiful. My wife has those same qualities.

We're served food – filet mignon, shrimp and lobster along with a wide variety of sides. I didn't think I'd eat but since I skipped breakfast, lunch and it's now six o'clock in the evening, this food is the best I've ever eaten but I'm sure that's due to the fact that it's my wedding-day food. Cherish makes everything taste good.

I glance at her as she eats lobster. I lean toward her to kiss the butter off her lips. She grimaces like she's embarrassed, especially when the people who witnessed it starts hollering and carrying on. I couldn't care less. She'll get used to it, eventually.

Mother walks over and says, "Eat up newlyweds. The first dance is coming up in twenty minutes."

"I know you're ready since you've been flirting with your dance partner all night," I tell her.

"It's not flirting, son. It's called mingling and socializing."

"That's what I told him, Sylvia," Cherish says.

"You can *socialize* with someone other than the butler,

can't you?"

"Aw, look at you being protective of your mother," Sylvia says. "Isn't that sweet of him, Cherish?"

She sashays away. You'd think she was a bride by the way she's blushing and carrying on.

* * *

It's dusk.

Candles burn on the round tables, decorated with white tablecloths. We dance to *The Point of it All* by Anthony Hamilton. I'm not big on music, but this is now *our* song.

My hands are resting on Cherish's small waist. Her arms are around my neck. She's been staring into my eyes since the song started. Smiling. That beautiful smile. Her cheekbones glow with love. I see my reflection in her eyes. I know what it means to love her as my own body. To *cherish* her. It's at this moment I understand how fragile love is. Her happiness, her life — it all rests in my hands. I won't take that for granted.

"Why are you looking so serious?" she asks me.

"I think the gravity of it all is just hitting me."

"The gravity of being married to me?"

"Yes, because I'm completely responsible for your happiness."

"Then you're already off to a good start, Mr. St. Claire. I'm already happy," she says, rising up to her tiptoes, sweetly pressing her lips to mine.

"Just as a heads up, you know you're going to be up late tonight, right?"

"Yes. I'm aware. I guess I'll have to pack in the morning."

"You don't have to. Naomi was kind enough to pack our suitcases."

"Ah, so she's going to be the woman picking out your clothes from now on?"

"No, that responsibility now falls on my wife," I say

teasing her.

She folds her bottom lip beneath her teeth. "I hope your wife knows your style."

"She does. She knows everything about me," I tell her before capturing her lips as our bodies sway to the music.

Others join us on the floor.

Mason and Bernadette, Siderra and Romulus, Ramsey dances with Gianna while Naomi watches Rianne. Gemma's head rests against Royal's chest while they dance. Major dances with Rayne – looks like he's having a difficult time keeping up. Ms. Kettleworth dances with two glasses of champagne. She's having the time of her life. Belinda is still hanging with Naomi, Isidora and Minnie. Hannah dances with her husband. Magnus and Shiloh make their exit. I'm sure Shiloh needs her rest. My mother is dancing with Carson-the-butler, smiling like the man is whispering sweet nothings in her ear.

A more upbeat song comes on. Cherish is dancing with a nice rhythm. Beautiful curls bounce around her face.

She sees her mother approaching us and her eyes brighten. "Hey, Ma."

"Hey, Cherish. Hey, Montgomery. I wanted to come over and tell you how beautiful everything was."

"Thank you," I tell her.

"Thank you, Ma. Of course, it wouldn't be as glamorous without the people we love here."

She kisses Cherish on the cheek. "I love you, daughter. I know I let you down in the past, but I hope we can move forward."

"You're here. We're already moving forward."

She embraces her mother and I watch, inspired by my wife because I know it takes strength to forgive. I've lived through it. I forgave my foster parents for not adopting me and Major – something that weighed heavily on me until I found out the reason behind their decision – my father especially. He didn't want us to lose the connection to our roots. As I look around and see my blood relatives here, I get it. These people are St. Claires.

My family.

"Oh, and Montgomery, I think I *will* take you up on that offer, too," Belinda tells me. "I would love to move to Concord for a fresh start."

"Great," I tell her. "You and Cherish can go house hunting after we're back from our honeymoon."

"That would be nice," she says.

"Yes, it would," Cherish responds.

She's all smiles, just the way I like her. She has the most adoring look on her face and in her eyes when she looks at me and says, "I never knew love could be this good."

"I never knew I could love someone this much," I tell her and go for her lips again until she whimpers just enough so my tongue can taste hers. "It's pretty crowded on the dance floor. I think we can slip away without anyone noticing."

She laughs. "We can't leave our own wedding reception, Monty. Besides, it'll be time to cut the cake soon."

"I want some cake right now, and I'm not talking about the one over there either."

She grins. "What am I going to do with you?"

"Don't know, but you're stuck with me now, baby."

"I like being stuck with you," she says and nibbles on her lip.

"Okay, that's it…" I take her by the hand as we sneak through the crowd to have our own little private party.

"Monty…" she says. "We can't sneak away."

"Yes, we can. You act like this is the first time we've done this. You don't remember the night we got engaged, girl?"

She giggles.

Soon those giggles will become moans and whimpers. I love this woman. Can't get enough of her. I'm grateful for acknowledging her presence in my life. For my mother to have the foresight to know Cherish Stevens who's now

Cherish St. Claire was my perfect match. I'll love and *cherish* her forever.

* ~ *

Thank you for reading **Monty, A St. Claire Novel**. Please take a moment to leave a review on Amazon. Also, check out other St. Claire books.

More about the St. Claire Series...

Royal (Book 1) is a standalone novel that tells the story of Royal St. Claire and Gemma Jacobsen.

Ramsey (Book 2) is a standalone novel that gives an update on Ramsey St. Claire and Gianna. [To read how these two initially met, check out *The Boardwalk Bakery Romance Series* consisting of Baked With Love, Baked With Love 2 and Baked With Love 3.]

Romulus (Book 3) is a standalone novel that tells the friends-to-lovers story of Romulus St. Claire and Siderra Monroe.

Regal (Book 4) is a standalone novel that tells the story of Regal St. Claire and Felicity James.

Magnus (Book 5) is a standalone novel that tells the story of Magnus St. Claire and Shiloh Winston.

Discover other books by Tina Martin:

St. Claire Series
*All books in this series are standalone novels and are full, complete stories. Read them in any order.

Royal
Ramsey
Romulus
Regal
Magnus
Monty

Seasons of Love Novelettes
Hot Chocolate: A Winter Novelette
Spring Break: A Spring Novelette

The Boardwalk Bakery Romance
*This is a continuation series that must be read in order.

Baked With Love
Baked With Love 2
Baked With Love 3

The Marriage Chronicles
*This is a continuation series that must be read in order.

Life's A Beach
Falling Out
War, Then Love

The Blackstone Family Series
*All books in this series are standalone novels and are full, complete stories. Read them in any order.

Evenings With Bryson
Leaving Barringer
Forever Us: Barringer and Calista Blackstone (A short story follow-up to *Leaving Barringer*. You must read *Leaving Barringer*

before reading this short story)
The Things Everson Lost
Candy's Corporate Crush

A Lennox in Love Series
*All books in this series are standalone novellas and are full, complete stories. Read them in any order.

Claiming You
Making You My Business
Wishing That I Was Yours
Caught in the Storm with a Lennox (A Short Story Prequel to Claiming You)
Before You Say I Do

Mine By Default Mini-Series:
*This is a continuation series that must be read in order.

Been In Love With You, Book 1
When Hearts Cry, Book 2
You Belong To Me, Book 3
When I Call You Mine, Book 4
Who Do You Love?, Book 5
Forever Mine, Book 6

The Champion Brothers Series:
*All books in this series are standalone novels and are full, complete stories. Read them in any order.

His Paradise Wife
When A Champion Wants You
The Best Thing He Never Knew He Needed
Wives And Champions
The Way Champions Love
His By Spring

The Accidental Series:
*This is a continuation series that must be read in order.

Accidental Deception, Book 1
Accidental Heartbreak, Book 2
Accidental Lovers, Book 3
What Donovan Wants, Book 4

Dying To Love Her Series:
*This is a continuation series that must be read in order.

Dying To Love Her
Dying To Love Her 2
Dying To Love Her 3

The Alexander Series:
*Books 1-4 must be read in order. Books 5, 6,7 and can be read in any order as a standalone books.

The Millionaire's Arranged Marriage, Book 1
Watch Me Take Your Girl, Book 2
Her Premarital Ex, Book 3
The Object of His Obsession, Book 4
Dilvan's Redemption, Book 5
His Charity Challenge, Book 6 (Heshan Alexander and Charity Eason)
Different Tastes, Book 7 (An Alexander Spin-off novel. Tamera Alexander's Story)
As Long As We Got Love, Book 8 (Family Novel)

Non-Series Titles:
*Individual standalone books that are not part of a series.
Secrets On Lake Drive
Can't Just Be His Friend
The Baby Daddy Interviews
Might As Well Be Single
Just Like New to the Next Man
Falling Again
Vacation Interrupted
The Crush
Wasn't Supposed To Love Her
What Wifey Wants

Man of Her Dreams
Bae Watch

ABOUT THE AUTHOR

TINA MARTIN is the author of over 60 romance, romantic suspense and women's fiction titles and has been writing full-time since 2013. Readers praise Tina for her strong heroes, sweet heroines and beautifully crafted stories. When she's not writing, Tina enjoys watching movies, traveling, cooking and spending time with her family. She currently resides in Charlotte, North Carolina with her husband and two children.

You can reach Tina by email at tinamartinbooks@gmail.com or visit her website for more information at www.tinamartin.net.

CPSIA information can be obtained
at www.ICGtesting.com
Printed in the USA
LVHW031444260120
644821LV00001B/58

9 781075 158797